THE
CHOIRBOYS

Books by Joseph Wambaugh

Fiction

THE NEW CENTURIONS
THE BLUE KNIGHT
THE CHOIRBOYS

Nonfiction

THE ONION FIELD

THE CHOIRBOYS

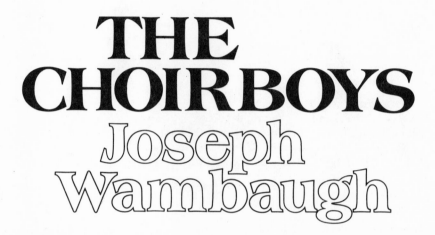

Joseph Wambaugh

DELACORTE PRESS/NEW YORK

ACKNOWLEDGMENT

Lyrics from "Yesterday Once More"
on pages 72, 73, and 74 Copyright 1973,
Almo Music Corp. and Hammer & Nails Music
(ASCAP). All Rights Reserved. Used by permission.
Lyrics by John Bettis. Music by Richard Carpenter.

Manufactured in the United States of America

First printing

Designed by MaryJane DiMassi

Library of Congress
Cataloging in Publication Data

Wambaugh, Joseph.
  The choirboys.

  I. Title.
PZ4.W242Ch [PS3573.A475] 813'.5'4 75–17969
ISBN 0–440–05363–3

For loyal friends
Irving Feffer, attorney at law
Sgt. Richard Kalk, LAPD

and

For the Choirboys
May your songs comfort and cheer

Prologue

The Third Marines were bleeding and dying for three nameless hills north of Khe Sanh in 1967. The North Vietnamese Army divisions were fighting around the DMZ and the marines had found several NVA command posts and crude field hospitals in the cave-pocked hills. The caves ran clear to the Laotian border and patrols were sent out to drop grenades down their air shafts and to flush the NVA out of the ground holes called spider traps.

On a night after the biggest battles were decided a squad of marines was ambushed by NVA and shot to pieces. Just two hours after the sun went down two marines huddled together in a cave that had formerly been an NVA hospital. It was deserted now except for broken beds made from bamboo and fragments of lumber. It was dank and musty and the two marines whispered frantically, trying to decide how to get back to their company. They were bewildered, couldn't comprehend what had happened so suddenly.

The tall marine, a fire team leader, wished desperately that his automatic rifleman had survived, or at least his other rifleman. His companion, a short and frail rifleman, was a new replacement who hadn't the sense to grab the M-14. He crouched trembling like a dog waiting for a command to move.

Then they heard the voices in the darkness. Many voices. The two marines crawled back, back into the cave, pressed against a wall as the NVA killing patrol searched for survivors of the ambush.

Both marines felt their dungarees suck at them as they wiped the sweat from their eyes and clamped their jaws to keep their teeth quiet. The short marine was whimpering.

Then an NVA rifleman said something to a comrade and cautiously entered the cave flashing a light into the cold wet interior.

The marines ground their faces into the slimy soil until they heard some nervous laughter and another soldier walk in as the light was switched off. The tall marine dared to peek from their nest and clearly saw the soldier silhouetted against the mouth of the cave. He was carrying a clump of Chinese stick grenades and a flame thrower. He scuttled toward them.

The soldier stumbled, muttered something and stood looking down a tunnel to his right, fingering the flame thrower while the two marines lay behind him almost at his feet. They could smell his sweat and a powerful odor of fish sauce and raw garlic. Then the soldier turned and walked back toward the cave opening where the voices got louder. Several soldiers propped their weapons against the clattering rocks and sat down for a break.

And as the short marine felt the panic deepen and believed that he could no longer control the sobs he was smothering, the tall marine suddenly started suffocating, or thought he was. He ripped at the collar of his jacket, panting. Only the soldiers' voices outside saved them.

It was the tall stronger one who began to cry. The walls and darkness closed in. He began to hyperventilate and couldn't get enough air. At first he wept almost imperceptibly, but then convulsively, and voices or not, the short marine was sure the NVA could not help but hear him. Desperately, instinctively, there in the darkness he took the tall marine in his arms and patted his shoulder and whispered: "Now now now. Hush now. I'm right here. You're *not* alone."

Gradually the tall marine began to quiet down and breathe regularly and when the patrol moved on five minutes later he was totally in control. He led the short marine back to their battered company. They were nineteen years old. They were children.

1

Territorial Imperative

The man most deserving of credit for keeping the MacArthur Park killing out of the newspapers before it brought discredit to the Los Angeles Police Department was Commander Hector Moss. It was perhaps Commander Moss' finest hour.

The blond commander was so exultant this afternoon he didn't mind that Deputy Chief Adrian Lynch was keeping him waiting the allotted time. Chief Lynch kept all callers waiting precisely three minutes before coming to the phone, unless his secretary told him it was an assistant chief or the chief of police himself or one of the commissioners or a city councilman or anyone at City Hall who reported directly to the mayor.

Moss despised Lynch for having a do-nothing job and a specially ordered oversized desk. Moss knew for a fact that Deputy Chief Lynch had secret plans to increase his personal staff by two: one policewoman and one civilian, both of whom were busty young women. Commander Moss knew this because his adjutant, Lieutenant Dewey Treadwell, had sneaked into Lynch's office and searched his file basket when a janitor left the door open. Of course Lieutenant Treadwell could not receive a specifically worded commendation for his assignment but he did receive an ambiguously worded "attaboy" from Moss.

But there was another assignment which Treadwell had failed to carry out, and Commander Moss' stomach soured as he remembered it. It had to do with Moss' IQ score of 107. Throughout his twenty-one year career his IQ had meant nothing to his rise to the rank of commander. Indeed, he had not even known what his score was. He had been a state college honors student in police science and reasoned that no one with an ordinary IQ could manage this. But with the retirement of a senior deputy chief it had been called to Moss' attention by none other than Deputy Chief Lynch who didn't think the promotion board would consider a man for such a high police post who possessed an IQ of only 107. Lynch's own IQ was 140.

Commander Moss was livid. He took Lieutenant Treadwell to a Chinatown bar one Friday after work and forced the teetotaler to down five cocktails, promising his personal patronage for the rest of Treadwell's career if he could carry off a most delicate assignment. The ever ambitious, thirty year old lieutenant agreed to slip into Personnel Division that night and change Commander Moss' IQ score from 107 to 141.

Commander Moss downed his fourth Singapore sling and said, "Treadwell, I know I can depend on you."

But instantly the lieutenant's ambition gave way to fear. He stammered, "If anything ever . . . well, look, sir, the watch commander of Personnel is a former detective. He might start sniffing around. They have ways in the crime lab to tell if documents have been tampered with!"

"Don't talk crime lab to me, Treadwell," Moss replied. "Have you ever worked the Detective Bureau?"

"No, sir."

"You listen to me, Treadwell. You're an office pogue. You never been anything *but* an office pogue. You don't have the slightest idea what goes on in a working police division. But you keep your mouth shut and do what you're told and I'll see to it that you're a captain someday and you can have your own station to play with. You don't and I'll have you in uniform on the nightwatch in Watts. Understand me, Treadwell?"

"Oh, yes, sir!"

"Now drink your Pink Lady," Commander Moss commanded. (It was Hector Moss who had persuaded the chief of police that the traditional police rank of "inspector" was no longer viable in an era of violence when policemen are called upon to employ counter insurgency tactics. Thanks to Moss all officers formerly of the inspector rank could now call themselves "commander." Moss had "Commander and Mrs. Hector Moss" painted on his home mailbox. Commander Moss had been a PFC in the army.)

Lieutenant Treadwell tried desperately every night for three weeks to sneak into Personnel Division. Each morning he reported a "Sorry, sir, negative" to Commander Moss. Lieutenant Dewey Treadwell lost ten pounds in those three weeks. He slept no more than four hours a night and then only fitfully. He was impotent. On the twenty-first night of his mission he was almost caught by a janitor. Lieutenant Treadwell was defeated and admitted it to Commander Moss on a black Wednesday morning.

The commander listened to his adjutant's excuses for a moment and said, "Did you get a good look at the janitor's face, Lieutenant?"

"Yes, sir. No . . . I don't know, sir. Why?"

"Because that boogie might live in Watts. And you'll need some friends there. BECAUSE THAT'S WHERE I'M SENDING YOU ON THE NEXT TRANSFER, YOU INCOMPETENT FUCKING PANSY!"

Commander Moss did not send Lieutenant Treadwell to Watts. He decided a spineless jellyfish was preferable to a smart aleck like Lieutenant Wirtz who worked for Deputy Chief Lynch. What he *did* was to go into Personnel Division in broad daylight, rip the commendation he wrote for Treadwell out of the file, draw a black *X* through it with a felt tipped pen, seal it in an envelope and leave it in Lieutenant Treadwell's incoming basket without comment.

Lieutenant Treadwell, after his hair started falling out in tufts, earned his way back into Commander Moss' good graces by authoring that portion of the Los Angeles Police Department manual which reads:

SIDEBURNS: Sideburns shall not extend below the bottom of the outer ear opening (the top of the earlobe) and shall end in a clean-shaven horizontal line. The flare (terminal portion of the sideburn) shall not exceed the width of the main portion of the sideburn by more than one-fourth of the unflared width.

MOUSTACHES: A short and neatly trimmed moustache of natural color may be worn. Moustaches shall not extend below the vermilion border of the upper lip or the corners of the mouth and may not extend to the side more than one-quarter inch beyond the corners of the mouth.

It took Lieutenant Treadwell thirteen weeks to compose the regulations. He was toasted and congratulated at a staff meeting. He beamed proudly. The regulations were perfect. No one could understand them.

As Commander Moss cooled his heels on the telephone waiting for Deputy Chief Adrian Lynch, the deputy chief was watching the second hand on his watch sweep past the normal three minute interval he reserved for most callers. Chief Lynch couldn't decide whether to give Moss a four minute wait or have his secretary say he would call back. Of course he couldn't be obviously rude. That bastard Moss had the ear of the chief of police and every other idiot who didn't know him well. Lynch hated those phony golden locks which Moss probably tinted. The asshole was at least forty-five years old and still looked like a Boy Scout. Not a wrinkle on that smirking kisser.

Lynch punched the phone button viciously and chirped, "Good morning, Deputy Chief Lynch speaking. May I help you?"

"It's I, Chief. Hec Moss," said the commander, and Chief Lynch grimaced and thought, It's I. Oh shit!

"Yeah Hec."

"Chief, it's about the MacArthur Park orgy."

"Goddamnit, don't call it that!"

"Sorry sir. I meant the choir practice."

"Don't call it that either. That's all we need for the papers to pick it up."

"Yes sir," Moss said. And then more slyly, "I'm very cognizant of bad press, sir. After all, I squelched the thing and assuaged the victim's family."

Oh shit! thought Lynch. *Assuaged.* "Yes, Hec," said the chief wearily.

"Well sir, I was wondering, just to lock the thing up so to speak, I was wondering if we shouldn't have the chief order quick trial boards for every officer who was at the orgy. Fire them all."

"Don't . . . say . . . *orgy.* And don't . . . say . . . *choir practice!*"

"Sorry sir."

"That's not very good thinking, Hec." The chief tilted back in his chair, lifted his wing tips to the desk top, raised up his rust colored hairpiece and scratched his freckled rubbery scalp. "I don't think we should consider firing them."

"They deserve it, sir."

"They deserve more than that, Hec. The bastards deserve to be in jail as accessories to a killing. I'd personally like to see every one of them in Folsom Prison. *But* they might make a fuss. They might bring in some lawyers to the trial board. They might notify the press if we have a mass dismissal. In short, they might hurl a pail of defecation into the air conditioning."

Chief Lynch waited for a chuckle from Moss, got none and thought again about Moss' low IQ. "Anyway, Hec," he continued, "we have a real good case only against the one who did the shooting and I think we're stuck with that. We'll give the others a trial board and a six month suspension, but we'll take care of it quietly. Maybe we can scare some of them into resigning."

"Some goddamn shrink at General Hospital's saying that killer's nuts."

"What do you expect from General Hospital? What're they good for anyway but treating the lame and lazy on the welfare rolls? What do you plan to do about that dumbass detective who examined the officer the night of the shooting and ordered him taken to the psychiatric ward?"

"Ten days off?"

"Should get twenty."

"Afraid he might complain to the press."

"Guess you're right," Chief Lynch conceded grudgingly.

"Well, hope you're happy with our office, Chief!"

"You did a fine job, Hec," Deputy Chief Lynch said. "But I wish you'd talk to your secretary. I've had reports she didn't say 'good morning' twice last week when my adjutant called."

"Won't happen again, Chief."

"Bye bye, Hec."

Deputy Chief Lynch wouldn't stand for a violation of the Los Angeles Police Department order concerning phone answering. After all, he had written the order. Officers had to answer thus:

"Good morning [afternoon or evening], Wilshire Watch Commander's Office, Officer Fernwood speaking. May I help you?"

If any word was left out of this standard greeting, the officer could be subject to disciplinary action.

It was said that once when a desk officer at Newton Street Station had uttered the entire phrase before giving the caller a chance to speak, the caller, a cardiac victim, fell unconscious before completing the address where the ambulance should be sent and died twenty minutes later.

Deputy Chief Lynch was a man to reckon with because he had thought of the most printable slogan in the history of the department. It was the slogan for a simple plan to spread out the staff officers geographically, giving them line control over everything in a given area. But if the plan were to be newsworthy, it needed a word or words to make it sound sophisticated, military and *dramatic.*

It came to Deputy Chief Lynch in a dream one night after he saw, *Command Decision* on "The Late Show."

"Territorial Imperative!" he screamed in his sleep, terrifying his wife.

"But what's it mean, sir?" his adjutant asked the next day.

"That's the beauty of it, stupid. It means whatever you want it to mean," Chief Lynch answered testily.

"I see! Brilliant, sir!" cried the adjutant.

One often read in the Los Angeles newspapers that the chief of police was shuffling his officers around in the interest of "Territorial Imperative."

2

The Body Count

Deputy Chief Adrian Lynch could sit for hours and stare at stacks of paper and suck on an unlit pipe and look overworked. This alone would not have made him a success however if he had not been the driving force behind Team Policing and the Basic Car Plan which everyone knew were the pet projects of the Big Chief.

"Team Policing" was nothing more than the deployment as often as possible of the same men in a given radio car district, making these men responsible not only for uniform patrol in that district but for helping the detectives with their follow-up investigation. The detectives (now called "investigators") resented the encroachment of younger patrol officers in the investigative work. The patrol officers in turn resented a phase of the Basic Car Plan which in reality was the plan itself. It was the Basic Car Plan Meeting. It was resented by everybody.

This meeting usually took place at a school or auditorium in the district patrolled by the given car. It was more or less a glorified coffee klatch to which doughnuts were added as an enticement. They were picked up free, compliments of a large doughnut chain. Police administrators could swear that crime had dropped because two dozen lonely old ladies had coffee and doughnuts with two charming, well groomed, young uniformed policemen who couldn't wait to get rid of the old ladies so they could get off duty and meet some young ladies.

When Deputy Chief Lynch was still a commander he had had the foresight to transfer to his office an enterprising young policeman who had been a second lieutenant in Vietnam and was an absolute master of the body count. Officer Weishart made sure that all Basic Car meetings in divisions commanded by Lynch would take place in school buildings adjacent to crowded playgrounds. Officer Weishart supplied not only coffee and doughnuts for the pensioners in the neighborhood but cookies and punch for the children. He enticed hundreds of kids from the streets to set foot inside the auditorium wherein they would be duly logged. *Each* time they came and went. If anyone had ever bothered to audit Officer Weishart's statistics he would have discovered that to accommodate the mobs reported, the grammar school auditorium would have had to be the size of the Los Angeles Coliseum.

But Team Policing and the Basic Car Plan had created lots and lots of new jobs for officers of staff rank. Therefore lieutenants made captain, captains made commander and commanders made deputy chief, and everyone had all the time they needed to think up new things for the working cops to do aside from catching crooks, which most of the new captains, commanders and deputy chiefs knew nothing about.

If Deputy Chief Lynch had an Achilles' heel which might someday preclude his elevation to chief of police it was his lubricious lusting after his secretary, Theda Gunther, the wife of Lieutenant Harry Gunther, who every time he turned around found himself transferred farther and farther from his Eagle Rock home, which allowed his wife more and more time with Deputy Chief Lynch who wished there was a police station for Lieutenant Gunther even farther from downtown than West Valley Station.

If the body count at the Basic Car Plan meetings was Chief Lynch's greatest accomplishment as a police officer his most thrilling by far was fornicating with Theda Gunther on top of the desk of that goddamn religious fanatic, Assistant Chief Buster Llewellyn.

They had gotten drunk in Chinatown the night Lynch suggested it, and there had almost been a slight scandal when they staggered into the police building at 2:00 A.M.

It had been a mad coupling for both of them what with the possibility of being caught in such a hallowed spot. Theda Gunther ripped off Deputy Chief Lynch's hairpiece in the throes of orgasm, and he, instinctively grabbing for the three hundred dollar toupee, had a premature withdrawal, leaving evidence all over the irreplaceable hand tooled blotter with Llewellyn's religious slogans engraved on all four corners.

Lynch feared that Llewellyn might immediately recognize the night deposit for what it was. He might send the blotter to the crime lab and seek the assistance of some smartass like his adjutant, a surly former detective. Chief Lynch didn't know *what* a former detective might be able to uncover.

When the case of the MacArthur Park killing came to his attention Deputy Chief Lynch listened to all the details, including the stories of lurid fantastic orgies involving officers and station house groupies. He became angrier than anyone had ever seen him. He wanted to jail the officers. Due to his accident on Llewellyn's desk he had become a nervous wreck. For three weeks Theda Gunther as usual rubbed her hot curvy body all over him when they passed in the office but he was as flaccid as linguini. She eventually got huffy and stopped calling him old donkey dick.

Of course Chief Lynch wasn't the only one affected by the killing. Wilshire Station Captain Stanley Drobeck was fuming because he had to write a thirty page report to the chief of police about the MacArthur Park incident with all available information on the drinking, the degenerates and the dead body. This on top of the Captain Cunkle scandal which itself took ten pages to describe.

Captain Drobeck felt that a station captain truly had the hot seat in the police department. All the big chief did was make speeches and hog headlines. It was the captains who were deluged by paper work, who made the decisions and who were *there*. It certainly wasn't the big chief and it wasn't Deputy Chief Adrian Lynch, who, Drobeck knew, spent the entire day trying to seduce his secretary, Theda Gunther, whose lieutenant husband was not likely ever to get transferred any closer to downtown and had taken to riding a motorbike to save gas.

Captain Drobeck despised libertines like Deputy Chief Lynch and Captain Cunkle of Wilshire Detectives, who had been the cause of his latest and largest internal discipline matter before the MacArthur Park killing.

Cunkle was a loathsome veteran detective who had somehow managed to pass his promotion exams without more than a high school education and had conned his way past the promotion boards. When former Inspector Moss convinced the chief he should change the designation of "inspector" to "commander" it was Cunkle who said that the public associated the title of "inspector" with a police officer and that "commander" was purely a military term and that he wanted to be a cop not a soldier.

It had been Captain Drobeck's recent pleasure to recommend ten days' suspension for a single, male, twenty-five year old policeman who had been found to be living with a single, female, twenty-three year old bank teller. The charge was conduct unbecoming an officer, or CUBO, called "cue-bow" by the policemen. He had recommended twenty days for a policewoman in the same circumstances in that a female officer should be even more above reproach than a male.

When Captain Cunkle was finally caught by a private detective in a motel with Hester Billings, the wife of a prominent attorney, Captain Drobeck made the following recommendation to Deputy Chief Lynch:

> Despite the risk of being accused by the rank-and-file officers of applying a double standard if this confidential investigation leaks, I am recommending that you take no action against Captain Wesley Cunkle, who, as you know, was caught in a compromising position with a female person not his wife. The enclosed photos were taken by a well-known private investigator, himself a former police officer, thoroughly unscrupulous, but reportedly discreet. The negatives will be destroyed if the demand of his employer, the female person's husband, is met.
>
> The demand is: a quick divorce without alimony and with custody of the children for Mr. _____.
>
> There is some complication in that Captain Cunkle is, as you

know, to be elevated to the rank of commander on the next transfer list. If he is not promoted, the field policemen may lose confidence in their leaders and get wind of this scandal despite our efforts to keep it stonewalled.

Respectfully,

Chief Lynch read the correspondence and looked at the photos of Captain Cunkle naked on his knees on the floor of a motel his eyes glazed by martinis and lust. Then the chief looked at Mrs. Billings spread-eagled on the bed unaware of Private Investigator Slim Scully snapping his Nikon for all he was worth.

"What do you think, sir?" asked Captain Drobeck who personally delivered the confidential reports and series of photos to the chief.

"Damn, she's got a hairy box!" Chief Lynch whistled.

At the same moment that Captain Drobeck was making his recommendation to Deputy Chief Lynch concerning the secret matter of Captain Cunkle, an early nightwatch rollcall was being conducted at 77th Street Station. An alcoholic twenty-five year policeman named Aaron Mobley said to the sergeant in charge of the rollcall, "Goddamnit, I don't mind how much pussy Cunkle eats, but why does a working copper get a suspension for the same thing a captain does?"

"Come on," said the florid sergeant. "We been yakking about this for two days. I'd rather *do* it than talk about it. Let's read off the crimes."

Finally, Ruben Wilkie, a twenty-six year cop who was the partner of Aaron Mobley, had the last word: "He gobbles one beaver and gets promoted. I've ate close to three hundred bearded clams in my time and never even got a commendation!"

But perhaps the *very* last word on the subject was uttered by Police Commissioner Howie Morton. The police commissioners were political appointees, titular department heads, who knew little about police work but were generally harmless since the true power rested with the chief. Police Commissioner Morton was a white Anglo. The board always had at least one black, one Mexican-American, one Jew and, of late, one woman. It had never had a Persian, a Filipino or a Navajo and never would until those ethnic groups acquired a political base in Los Angeles.

Police Commissioner Morton was able to learn about the supersecret Captain Cunkle scandal because he had a distant cousin, a garage mechanic at Southwest Station, who overheard the janitors saying they were sick of hearing about it. Commissioner Morton persuaded a sergeant who worked Internal Affairs Division to obtain the photos for him. The last word on the Commander Cunkle scandal was hence uttered by Police Commissioner Morton. He looked at the photos and whistled. "Damn, she's got a hairy box!"

3

Cue-bow

Commander Hector Moss was popular at functions wherein people with causes wanted a member of the police department to beat up verbally.

Commander Moss, the perennial toastmaster, always wore handcuffs on the front of his belt. When he stood before a DAR meeting and had the ladies agog with his wavy blond hair and stories of crime and violence, the coat would be pulled open and the handcuffs would appear. Sometimes the right side of his coat slipped open to show a chrome plated Smith and Wesson Combat Masterpiece tugging down at the alligator belt, custom made to support the weight of the heavy gun. Commander Moss had been in various administrative jobs since being promoted to sergeant sixteen years ago. The gun had never been fired. The ammunition was so old it is doubtful it *could* fire. Commander Moss got the stories of crime and violence from police reports which crossed his desk each day. Commander Moss was an excellent storyteller.

The MacArthur Park killing had in truth been a godsend. Hector Moss thrived on crisis and longed to prove his rapport with the media. Besides, he desperately needed something to relieve the boredom of sitting and poring through the house organ, called *The Beat Magazine,* making sure that as always there was nothing in it more cerebral than who had a baby and who died and that there was at least one picture of some vacationing motor cop in Mexico grinning at a dead fish.

There had never been a controversial article in that magazine to stir up or reflect the opinion of the street cops. He often said that if someone ever organized those ignorant bastards, look out. Commander Moss was like a slaver who lived in fear of native footsteps on the decks in the night.

At this hour, on a hot August afternoon with the officers involved in the killing being sweated in the interrogation rooms of Internal Affairs Division, Commander Moss decided on a technique he believed was essential for dealing with any reporters who might belatedly get onto the story of the dead body in MacArthur Park. He didn't wait to be phoned by the enemies who worked for what he considered a loathsome left wing rag. He phoned his favorite reporter with the other paper, after he made sure the reporter had heard something about the case from a different source.

"I wanted you to know about it as soon as I had the full story," said Commander Moss, smiling at the telephone. "It appears an off-duty officer had an accident with a gun in MacArthur Park at about two A.M. I hope you can soft-pedal it for the sake of the seven thousand fine boys and girls in this department. Yes, it was a tragedy all right. A young man is dead. Yes. One officer's relieved from duty pending an investigation. Yes, yes, there is *some* evidence of drinking. I don't know, could've dropped the gun and it went off. I just don't know yet. Been a policeman almost five years. Vietnam vet. Right. Yes, there's some evidence the officer was with friends. To level with you, Pete, there's a strong possibility some policemen bought a sixpack of beer and stopped in the park on the way home to unwind and talk. Yes, that's Conduct Unbecoming an Officer. We call it cue-bow. Choir practice? No, don't believe I know that term. Choir practice? No, never heard of it."

When the reporter hung up, Commander Moss sat back and put his feet up on his desk, which was actually two square inches larger than Chief Lynch's specially ordered desk, and said to his secretary, "I know that wasn't the first choir practice in that park. I'd love to know about some of the *other* ones."

4

Sergeant Nick Yanov

Actually there were dozens of choir practices in MacArthur Park attended faithfully by ten policemen who worked out of Wilshire Police Station but chose MacArthur Park as the choir practice site because it was in Rampart Station's territory. They believed that one does not shit in one's own nest.

The first choir practice in MacArthur Park took place in the early spring when the nights became warm enough. Most of the choirboys were unencumbered. That was by design of Harold Bloomguard who was really the driving force behind the inception of the MacArthur Park choir practice. Harold always maintained that they shouldn't have married men in the group because they would quite likely have to go home early, and early dropouts were the death of any good choir practice.

"The songs must go on!" was the way Harold always put it.

Of course no one ever really sang at choir practice. Their "songs" were of a different genus but served much the same purpose as rousing choral work. It was called by various names at other police departments. It was merely an off duty meeting, usually in a secluded hideaway, for policemen who, having just finished their tour of duty, were too tense or stimulated or electrified to go to a silent sleeping house and lie down like ordinary people while nerve ends sparked. One hadn't always enough money to go to a policemen's bar. Still one felt the need to uncoil and have a drink and talk with others who had been on the streets that night. To reassure oneself.

Sergeant Nick Yanov could have been a charter member during those five months when the MacArthur Park choir practices were being held. He was invited by Harold Bloomguard one evening after a 3:00 P.M. nightwatch rollcall at which the uniformed policemen had a surprise visit from Captain Stanley Drobeck. The station commander wore a silk suit with a belt in the back, and black and white patent leather shoes. When Captain Drobeck entered the assembly room he caused Lieutenant Alvin Finque, who was conducting the rollcall, to jump unconsciously to attention which embarrassed the blue uniformed patrol officers. Since police service is not nearly as GI as military service, the only time one stands at attention is during inspection or formal ceremonies.

Lieutenant Finque blushed and sat back down. He blinked and said "Hi Skipper" to Captain Drobeck.

"Whoever made the pinch on the burglar in Seven-A-One's area deserves a good smoke!" the captain announced, as he threw four fifteen-cent cigars out into the audience of twenty-eight nightwatch officers and, smiling with self-satisfaction, strode out the door. His hair was freshly rinsed and was blue white that day.

Only three nightwatch officers were old enough to smoke a cigar without looking silly. One was Herbert "Spermwhale" Whalen and he had caught the burglar. He was a MacArthur Park choirboy.

Like all old veterans, Spermwhale sat in the back row and insisted on wearing his hat. Cocked to the side, of course. Spermwhale picked up one of the cigars from the floor, examined the brand, sat on it and loosed an enormous fart which moved out every policeman nearby. Then he tossed the cigar back on the floor. Another choirboy, Spencer Van Moot of 7-A-33, picked it up gingerly with two fingers, stripped off the cellophane and said, "It'll be okay after it dries out."

*   *   *

Lieutenant Finque had just replaced Lieutenant Grimsley whose transfer was mysteriously precipitated by Spermwhale Whalen. Lieutenant Finque was of medium height with straight hair which was parted and combed straight back much as his father had done when his father was still in style in 1939, the year of Lieutenant Finque's birth. The lieutenant was unsure in his new rank but rarely if ever heeded the advice he always asked for from Sergeant Nick Yanov, the hipless chesty field sergeant, who had to shave twice a day to control his whiskers.

Sergeant Yanov was an eleven year officer, and at age thirty-four actually had less supervisory experience than Lieutenant Finque. But he had the distinction of being the only person of supervisory rank ever to be invited to a MacArthur Park choir practice, which he wisely declined.

Sergeant Yanov's only immediate passion in life, like many officers at Wilshire Station, was some night to drag Officer Reba Hadley away from the nightwatch desk and into the basement and rip her tight blue uniform blouse and skirt from her tantalizing young body and literally screw the badge right off her. Which was perhaps symbolically linked with Yanov's avowed belief that superior officers like Lieutenant Finque had been screwing him mercilessly for the past eleven years.

Lieutenant Finque had a different passion. He wanted to be the first watch commander in Wilshire Division history to catch every single member of his watch out of his car with his hat off or drinking free coffee or failing to answer a telephone properly.

When things quieted down from Spermwhale's contribution to rollcall, Lieutenant Finque said, "Fellows, we have some rollcall material to give you on diplomatic immunity in misdemeanor cases. In case you should have the occasion to run into a consul or ambassador in the course of your duties, does everyone know the difference between a consul and an ambassador?"

"An ambassador is a Nash," said Harold Bloomguard of 7-A-29. "Don't see too many these days."

"I heard those consulate cocksuckers just wipe their ass with their parking tickets in New York," offered Roscoe Rules of 7-A-85.

"If you work for the UN you can do no wrong in the first place," said Spencer Van Moot of 7-A-33.

"Well, I hope you all read the material," Lieutenant Finque said jauntily as the drops of acid formed. He was never sure if they were being insubordinate.

"Finque's rollcalls are about as exciting as a parking ticket," whispered Francis Tanaguchi of 7-A-77 to his partner, Calvin Potts.

"And to think I left a sick bed to come to work today," Calvin groaned.

"Your girl wasn't feeling well?" Francis asked.

"On to more important things, men," Lieutenant Finque said, as Sergeant Nick Yanov, who sat on his left on the platform in front of the assembly, looked at the ceiling and drummed nervously on the table with his fingers. "I hope you men have been trying to sell whistles. The nightwatch has been doing pretty badly compared to the daywatch."

This announcement caused Sergeant Yanov to lean back in his chair and start rubbing his eyes with the heels of both hands so that he would not have to see the eye rolling, lip curling, head shaking, feet shuffling, which was utterly lost on Lieutenant Finque who had given birth to the whistle selling campaign.

It had been a master stroke which actually was suggested by an eighty year old spinster who attended every single Basic Car Plan meeting. Since Lieutenant Finque was pretty sure the old woman was senile and would not remember she had thought of it, he adopted the idea as his own and the uniformed patrol force of Wilshire Station found themselves being forced to sell black plastic whistles for fifty cents to women they contacted on their calls. The object was that if a woman were ever accosted on the street by thugs she should pull out her whistle and blow it.

The proceeds from the whistle sales went to the station's Youth Services Fund and quickly earned several thousand dollars. Lieutenant Finque was hoping the idea would earn him a written commendation from Deputy Chief Lynch, which wouldn't look bad in his personnel package.

Spermwhale Whalen had sold the most whistles on the nightwatch, six in fact. But actually he had bought them himself and given them to his favorite streetwalking whores with the instruction that if they ever had a slow evening and felt like giving away a free blowjob to an old pal just to pucker on the whistle when 7-A-1 came cruising by.

There was not a recorded case of a radio car in the vast and crowded district ever hearing a distress whistle, but it was said that the whistle saved the property of one woman on La Cienega Boulevard when a purse snatcher almost fell to the sidewalk in a giggling fit at the sight of a sixty year old matron in a chinchilla coat blowing a little plastic whistle until her face looked like a rotten strawberry.

"One last order of business before we have inspection and hit the streets," the lieutenant said. "The detectives would like the cars in the area to keep an eye on Wilbur's Tavern on Sixth Street. They have reports that the owner is beating up barmaids who're too intimidated to make a report. He apparently only hires girls willing to orally copulate him. And if they start to object after a time, he beats them up and threatens them. Seven-A-Twenty-nine, how about stopping in there once every couple days?"

"Right, Lieutenant," said Harold Bloomguard who looked at his grinning partner, Sam Niles.

Minutes after rollcall, 7-A-29 was speeding to the station call but was beaten by ten other nightwatch policemen swarming all over the tavern checking out the barmaids.

5

7-A-85: Roscoe Rules and Dean Pratt

Probably the most choir practices were called by Harold Bloomguard of 7-A-29. Probably the least choir practices were called by 7-A-85. Roscoe Rules just didn't seem to need them as much.

One choir practice however was hastily called by Dean Pratt of 7-A-85, five months before the choir practice killing. It was on the night Roscoe Rules became a legend in his own time.

Henry Rules was nicknamed "Roscoe" by Harold Bloomguard at another midnight choir practice when Rules, who had just seen an old Bogart movie on television, finished telling the others of a recent arrest: "This black ass, abba dabba motherfucker looked like he was gonna rabbit, so I drew down and zonked him across the gourd with my roscoe."

For a moment drunken Harold Bloomguard looked at his partner Sam Niles in disbelief. Rules had not said "gun" or "piece" or ".38" but had actually said "roscoe."

"Oh, lizard shit!" cried Bloomguard. "Roscoe! Roscoe! Did you hear that?"

"You mean your 'gat,' Rules?" roared Sam Niles, who was also drunk, and he rolled over on his blanket in the grass, spilling half a gallon of wine worth about three dollars.

From then on, to all the choirboys, Henry Rules became known as "Roscoe" Rules. The only one to call him "Henry" occasionally was his partner Dean Pratt who was afraid of him.

Roscoe Rules was a five year policeman. He had long arms and veiny hands. He was tall and hard and strong. And mean. No one who talked as mean as Roscoe Rules could have survived twenty-nine years on this earth without *being* mean. His parents had been struggling farmers in Idaho, then in the San Joaquin Valley of California where they acquired a little property before each died in early middle age.

"Roscoe Rules handed out towels in the showers at Auschwitz," the policemen said.

"Roscoe Rules was a Manson family reject—too nasty."

"Roscoe Rules believes in feeding stray puppies and kittens—to his piranha."

And so forth.

If there was one thing Roscoe Rules wished, after having seen all of the world he cared to see, it was that there was a word as dirty as "nigger" to apply to all mankind. Since he had little imagination he had to settle for "asshole." But he realized that all Los Angeles policemen and most American policemen used that as the best of all possible words.

Calvin Potts, the only black choirboy, agreed wholeheartedly with Roscoe when he drunkenly expressed his dilemma one night at choir practice in the park.

"That's the only thing I like about you, Roscoe," Calvin said. "You don't just hate brothers. You hate *everyone*. Even more than I do. Without prejudice or bias."

"Gimme a word then," Roscoe said. He was reeling and vomitous, looking over his shoulder for Harold Bloomguard who at 150 pounds would fight anyone who was cruel to the MacArthur Park ducks.

"Gimme a word," Roscoe repeated and furtively chucked a large jagged rock at a fuzzy duckling who swam too close, just missing the baby who went squawking to its mother.

Everyone went through the ordinary police repertoire for Roscoe Rules.

"How about fartsuckers?"

"Not rotten enough."

"Slimeballs?"

"That's getting old."

"Scumbags?"

"Naw."

"Cumbuckets?"

"Too long."

"Hemorrhoids?"

"Everybody uses that."

"Scrotums?"

"Not bad, but too long."

"Scrotes, then," said Willie Wright who was now drunk enough to use unwholesome language.

"That's it!" Roscoe Rules shouted. "Scrotes! That's what all people are: ignorant filthy disgusting ugly worthless scrotes. I like that! Scrotes!"

"A man's philosophy expressed in a word," said Baxter Slate of 7-A-1. "Hear! Hear!" He held up his fifth of Sneaky Pete, drained it in three gulps, suddenly felt the special effects of the port and barbiturates he secretly popped, fell over and moaned.

There was however one thing which endeared Roscoe Rules to all the other choirboys: he was, next to Spencer Van Moot of 7-A-33, the greatest promoter any of them had ever seen. Roscoe could, when he cared to, arrange food and drink for the most voluptuous tastes—all of it free—for the other choirboys, who called him an insufferable prick.

At first the only thing Roscoe didn't like about his partner Dean Pratt was his styled red hair. But he soon came to hate his partner for his drunken crying jags at choir practice. There was another thing about Dean Pratt which *all* the choirboys despised and that was that the twenty-five year old bachelor's brain became temporarily but totally destroyed by less than ten ounces of any alcoholic drink. Then it was impossible to make the grinning redhead understand *anything.* Any question, statement, piece of smalltalk would be met by an idiotic frustrating maddening double beseechment:

"I don't get it. I don't get it." Or, "Whaddaya trying to say? Whaddaya trying to say?" Or, most frequently heard, "Whaddaya mean? Whaddaya mean?"

And so, Dean Pratt eventually became known as Whad-dayamean Dean. The first few sessions of the MacArthur Park choirboys found Roscoe Rules, Calvin Potts or Spermwhale Whalen eventually grabbing the lanky redhead by the front of his Bugs Bunny sweatshirt and shaking him in rage with Dean in drunken tears babbling, "I don't get it. I don't get it. Whad-daya mean? Whaddaya *mean?*"

Yet Whaddayamean Dean became the first policeman Roscoe Rules ever took home to meet his family. Roscoe, one of three choirboys who were married, lived on a one acre piece of ground east of Chino, California, some sixty miles from Wil-shire Station. Even the few friends Roscoe had made these past four years would not drive that far to be sociable. Roscoe loved it there and made the daily trek gladly. His children could grow up in a rural setting as he had. Of course they would not have to work nearly as hard. His two boys, eight and nine, only had to hoe and weed and water his corn, onions, carrots, squash and melons. Then after cleaning the animals' stalls, picking the infectious dung and hay from the horse's hooves and treating the swaybacked pony for ringbone, they could have the rest of the day for playing. After they studied for a minimum of one and a half hours on weekdays and two on Saturdays and Sun-days. And after they took turns pitching and catching a base-ball for forty-five minutes on weekends.

Roscoe Rules had convinced both his sons that they would be allstar players their first season in Little League. And they were. And he had convinced them that if they didn't get straight A's through elementary school they would get what the recalcitrant pony got when it misbehaved.

Roscoe's two sons hated riding as much as the pony hated being ridden, but when the pony wouldn't ride, Roscoe would snare the pony's front feet, loop his rope around the corral fence and deftly jerk the animal's legs back toward his hind-quarters, catching the beast when it fell with a straight right between the eyes. He wore his old sap gloves with the lead filled palm and padded knuckles (which a sob sister sergeant had caught him beating up a drunk with and which he had been ordered to get rid of). That jerking rope, that punch and the bone bruising force of crashing to earth never failed to tame the pony who would obey for several weeks until the stupid creature forgot and became stubborn. Then he would require "gentling" again. Roscoe Rules believed that animals and people were basically alike: they were all scrotes.

Roscoe was very proud of the clean healthy life he had provided for his sons away from the city. He counted the years, months and weeks until he could retire with a twenty year service pension to his little ranch east of Chino and live out his days with his wife Clara (a secret drinker), and raise grandchildren in the same American tradition and perhaps buy them ponies and make ballplayers out of them. And give them all the advantages he had provided for his own children.

Roscoe was, like most policemen, conservative politically by virtue of his inescapable police cynicism but more so because of his misanthropy which had its roots in childhood. He had served in Vietnam and had almost made the Army his career until an LAPD recruiting poster had forced him to compare the benefits of police work to military service.

Roscoe was not a religious man. He scowled at American Legion benedictions. He scoffed at his Presbyterian wife and forbade her to make weaklings of their children by taking them to Sunday school. He said that instead of turning the other cheek you should sap the motherfuckers to their knees then choke them out until they were "doing the chicken" on the ground and then step over their twitching, jerking, unconscious bodies and kneedrop them with the full weight of your body down through the spear of the knee into the kidney. And that if Jesus Christ didn't have the balls to treat his enemies like that he was just another faggot Jew. Roscoe Rules wasn't raising his sons to be faggots.

But Roscoe Rules had a sense of humor. He carried in his wallet two photographs from his Army days which were getting cracked and faded despite the plastic envelopes he kept them in. One showed a Vietnamese girl of twelve or thirteen trying gamely to earn five American dollars by copulating an emaciated oxen which Roscoe and several other American cowboys had lassoed and tied thrashing on its back in a bamboo corral.

The second photo, which everyone at Wilshire Station had

seen, was of Roscoe holding the severed head of a Vietcong by the hair as Roscoe leered into the camera, tongue lolling, neck twisted to one side. The photo had "Igor and friend" printed across the bottom. The thought of the photo was to trigger Roscoe's finest hour as a member of the Los Angeles Police Department.

Whaddayamean Dean hated being the partner of someone as mean as Roscoe Rules. He knew his own physical limitations and rarely talked tough on the street unless he was absolutely sure that the other person was terrified of police, in which case he allowed himself the luxury of tossing around a few "assholes," or "scrotes" to please Roscoe.

"Know why niggers survive serious wounds, partner?" Roscoe Rules asked Whaddayamean Dean.

"No, why, Henry?" asked Whaddayamean Dean, using the given name abhorred by the other choirboys.

"They're too dumb to go into shock."

Whaddayamean Dean giggled and snuffled and looked up from his driving at the browless blue eyes of Roscoe Rules, and at his freckled hands which would nervously grab at the crotch, especially when the conversation turned to women. Roscoe was one of those policemen who would sit bored in a radio car in the dark and quiet hours and talk of his incredible sexual encounters in Vietnam or Tijuana and knead and squeeze his genitals until his partners got nauseated.

Working with Roscoe Rules was many things but it was never dull. He was what is known in LAPD jargon as a "Fourfifteen personality," 415 being the California penal code section which defines disturbing the peace. Indeed, Roscoe Rules had turned many bloodless family fights or landlord-tenant disputes into minor riots by his presence. He had been transferred around the department more than any member of his academy class, had been the subject of many complaints of excessive force from citizens and even from a few police supervisors, who generally do not challenge the techniques of policemen like Roscoe Rules. Not if they respond promptly to radio calls, write one moving traffic violation a day and stop at least three people daily for field interrogations.

During their first week as partners, Roscoe started a small

riot. It was in 7-A-77's area, but Calvin Potts and Francis Tanaguchi were handling a call in 7-A-29's area, while Harold Bloomguard and Sam Niles were handling a call in 7-A-1's area, while Spermwhale Whalen and Baxter Slate were parked in an alley near Crenshaw Boulevard, Spermwhale receiving a listless headjob from an aging black prostitute whom he had known from his days at old University Station.

The call had originated as a neighbor dispute, and by the time Roscoe and Whaddayamean Dean arrived, what had been a potentially dangerous situation in an unhappily mixed apartment house on Cloverdale had pretty well petered out to the name calling, face saving phase. There were two tired men involved: a black and a Mexican who did not really want to fight for the honor of their bickering wives or anything else.

"Took a report here one time," Roscoe observed as they climbed the stairway at nine o'clock that night. "Some abba dabba made a report that one a her cubs was missing. Had so fucking many milksuckers running around she forgot the police department summer camp was taking care a the little prick for a week. That's what kind a people we run our kiddie camps for. Didn't know he was gone till she had a head count!"

Whaddayamean Dean shivered as he saw a team of roaches charge on a chunk of slimy red hamburger which lay rotting on the landing.

There was a sign on the manager's door which said: "No loiterers in this building. Due to lady tenants being kidnapped, molested and robbed the LAPD will arrest loiterers."

On the second landing they passed a staggering wine reeking black woman who ignored them. She was barefoot, wore pinned black slacks and an extra large dirty blouse which hung outside. The blouse was hiked in the back because of the lopsided hump which bent her double and reduced a woman who was meant to be of average height to a misshapen dwarf.

Roscoe tapped the hump as he passed, winked mischievously at Whaddayamean Dean and said to the stuporous woman, "I got a *hunch* you're for me, baby!"

Roscoe was still giggling when they found the remnants of the once smoldering neighbor dispute. The rival factions were almost evenly divided. Two sets of neighbors, including husbands, wives, teenage and preteen children, backed the play of each injured party. Mexicans backed Mexicans, blacks backed blacks. There had been twenty-two people screaming and threatening at the height of the dispute. Now there were just the husbands of the aggrieved women. The black man had a trickle of blood running from the corner of his mouth where the Mexican had accidentally bumped him when they were pushing and shoving, preparatory to doing battle.

The black man, a squatty hod carrier with enormous shoulders and a wild full natural hairdo, looked relieved by the presence of the bluesuits and shouted angrily, "You made me bleed, motherfucker! You gonna pay. I'm gonna kick ass for this!"

"Anytime, man, anytime," said the Mexican, a slightly shorter man, a member of the same hod carrier's local, who had been on many jobs with the black man and was almost a friend.

The Mexican, like the black man, was dressed in dirty work pants and was shirtless to unnerve his opponent. He did not have such an intimidating physique in terms of musculature, but his chest, back and rib cage were crisscrossed with many scars: some like coiled rope, some like purple zippers, from old gang wars in East Los Angeles where he had fought his way through the elaborate gang hierarchy to emerge as a seasoned *veterano* covered with battle wounds and glory. But then the Mexican had gotten married, fathered seven children, lost his taste for street war and in truth had not faced a foe for many years.

"What started the beef?" Roscoe Rules asked, deciding to talk to the Mexican.

The Mexican shrugged, touched his hand nervously to the drooping Zapata moustache, lowered his eyes and turned his scarred back to the two policemen.

The black hod carrier's wife spoke first. "The problem is, Officer, that this broad and her daughter always has to hang clothes on the same day that I'm hangin mine. And that ain't no big thang, cept they got no respect and just throws other folks' clothes on the ground like pigs. And I has to put another quarter in the machine and wash my clothes all over agin."

"That's a lie," said the husky Mexican woman, throwing her long sweaty brown hair back over her shoulder. "Her and her daughter are the ones that don't have no respect. Animals, that's what they are."

"Go back to Mexico, bitch," the black woman said.

"I was born here, nigger. Go back to Africa," the Mexican woman said, and Whaddayamean Dean stepped between them as the black woman lunged forward, bumping Whaddayamean Dean into Roscoe, who fell against the black man, who accidentally stepped on Roscoe's plain toed, ripple soled police shoes, which he had spit shined every day for the eight months he owned them.

"Goddamn it!" Roscoe yelled, holding his arms out between the two women, eyeballs white with disgust. "I heard enough!" he thundered, arms still extended, knees slightly bent, face twisted in agony like Samson straining at the pillars.

Then Roscoe dropped his hands to his hips and walked in slow circles. Finally he paused, looked at the people like a sad but patient uncle, nodded and said, "I heard enough!"

"Looky here, Officer," said the black man, "I don't mean no disrespect but I heard enough a you sayin you heard enough. You're makin me nervous."

Roscoe walked over to Whaddayamean Dean, pulled him aside and whispered, "This spade's the troublemaker far as I can see. I think he's got a leaky seabag. Dingaling. Psycho. You can't even talk to him. Look what the motherfucker did to my shoe!"

"I think we can quiet them down," Whaddayamean Dean said as Roscoe stood on one foot like a blue flamingo, rubbing his toe hopelessly on the calf of his left leg.

"Can I talk to you?" Whaddayamean Dean asked the Mexican, walking him to the other end of the hall while Roscoe Rules hustled the silent black thirty feet down the stairway.

"I don't want no more trouble outta you," Roscoe whispered when he got the hod carrier to a private place.

"I ain't gonna give you no trouble, Officer," the black man said, looking up at the mirthless blue eyes of Roscoe Rules which were difficult to see because like most hotdogs he wore his cap tipped forward until the brim almost touched his nose.

"Don't argue with me, man!" Roscoe said. His nostrils splayed as he sensed the fear on the man who stood hangdog before him.

"What's your name?" Roscoe then demanded.

"Charles ar-uh Henderson," the hod carrier answered, and then added impatiently. "Look, I wanna go back inside with my family. I'm tired a all this and I just wanna go to bed. I worked hard . . ."

But Roscoe became enraged at the latent impudence and snarled, "Look here, Charles ar-uh Henderson, don't you be telling me what you're gonna do. I'll tell you when you can go back inside and maybe you won't be going back inside at all. Maybe you're gonna be going to the slam tonight!"

"What for? I ain't done nothin. What right you got . . ."

"Right? Right?" Roscoe snarled, spraying the hod carrier with saliva. "Man, one more word and I'm gonna book your ass! I'll personally lock you in the slammer! I'll set your hair on fire!"

Whaddayamean Dean called down to Roscoe and suggested that they switch hod carriers. As soon as they had, he tried in vain to calm the outraged black man.

A few minutes later he heard Roscoe offer some advice to the Mexican hod carrier: "If that loudmouth bitch was my old lady I'd kick her in the cunt."

Twenty years ago the Mexican had broken a full bottle of beer over the head of a man for merely smiling at his woman. Twenty years ago, when she was a lithe young girl with a smooth sensuous belly, he would have shot to death any man, cop or not, who would dare to refer to her as a bitch.

Roscoe Rules knew nothing of *machismo* and did not even sense the slight almost imperceptible flickering of the left eyelid of the Mexican. Nor did he notice that those burning black eyes were no longer pointed somewhere between the shield and necktie of Roscoe Rules, but were fixed on his face, at the browless blue eyes of the tall policeman.

"Now you two act like men and shake hands so we can leave," Roscoe ordered.

"Huh?" the Mexican said incredulously, and even the black hod carrier looked up in disbelief.

"I said shake hands. Let's be men about this. The fight's over and you'll feel better if you shake hands."

"I'm forty-two years old," the Mexican said softly, the eyelid flickering more noticeably. "Almost old enough to be your father. I ain't shaking hands like no kid on a playground."

"You'll do what I say or sleep in the slammer," Roscoe said, remembering how in school everyone felt better and even drank beer after a good fight.

"What charge?" demanded the Mexican, his breathing erratic now. "What fuckin charge?"

"You both been drinking," Roscoe said, losing confidence in his constituted authority, but infuriated by the insolence which was quickly undermining what he thought was a controlled situation.

Roscoe, like most black-glove cops, believed implicitly that if you ever backed down even for a moment in dealing with assholes and scrotes the entire structure of American law enforcement would crash to the ground in a mushroom cloud of dust.

"We ain't drunk," the Mexican said. "I had a can of beer when I got home from work. One goddamn can!" He spoke in accented Cholo English: staccato, clipped, just as he did when he was a respected gang member.

Then Roscoe Rules pushed him back into an alcove away from the eyes of those down the hall who had made their own peace by now and were preparing to go back into their apartments to fix dinner. Roscoe pulled his baton from the ring and hated this sullen Mexican and the glowering black man and even Whaddayamean Dean whose nervousness enraged Roscoe because if you ever let these scrotes think you were afraid . . .

Then Roscoe looked around, guessing there were a dozen people between them and the radio car, and started to realize that this was not the time or place. But the Mexican made Roscoe Rules forget that it was the wrong time and place when he looked at the tall policeman with the harder crueler larger body and said, "I never let a man talk to me like this. You better book me or you better let me go but don't you talk to me like this anymore or . . . or . . ."

"Or? Or?" Roscoe said, his hairless brows throbbing as he touched the small man on the chest with the tip of his stick. "You Mexicans're all alike. Think you're tough, huh? Bantamweight champ a this garbage dump, huh? I oughtta tear that oily moustache off your face."

Then the flickering eyelid was still and the eyes glazed over. "Go ahead," the Mexican barely whispered.

And Roscoe Rules did. A second later the Mexican was standing there with a one inch piece of his right moustache and the skin surrounding it in Roscoe Rules' left hand. The raw flesh began to spot at once with pinpoints of blood.

Then the Mexican screamed and kicked Roscoe Rules in the balls.

Suddenly Whaddayamean Dean found himself trying to get the Mexican's neck in the crook of his arm, to squeeze off the oxygen to the brain, which would make him lose consciousness and flop convulsively on the ground, thus "doing the chicken."

The Mexican's erstwhile black enemy was experiencing a deep sense of guilt and outrage at the Mexican's plight.

"You honky motherfucker!" the black hod carrier yelled when he finally exploded. He tossed a straight right at Whaddayamean Dean which caught him on the left temple and knocked him free of the Mexican and over the kneeling body of Roscoe Rules who was hoping desperately he wouldn't puke from the kick in the balls.

Roscoe aimed a spunky blow at the black hod carrier's leg with his unauthorized, thirty-four ounce sap which pulled his pants down when he wasn't careful to keep his Sam Browne buckled tightly.

Hit em in the shins. They can't take that, thought Roscoe, swinging the sap weakly, relying on folklore to save him now that he could not stand up.

But the hod carrier did not seem to feel the sap bouncing off his legs as he and the Mexican took turns punching Whaddayamean Dean silly.

The redhead had lost his baton and gun and was bouncing back and forth between the two men. "Partner! Partnerrrr!" Whaddayamean Dean yelled, but Roscoe Rules could only kneel there, look up in hatred and wish he could shoot the nigger, the spick and his puny partner.

Then Roscoe fell over on his back, nursing his rapidly swelling testicles, spitting foam like a mad dog.

It ended abruptly. There had been men, women and children screaming, encouraging, cursing gleefully. There had been bodies thudding off the walls, doors slamming. Then silence.

Roscoe Rules and Whaddayamean Dean Pratt were alone in the hallway. Both on the floor, uniforms half torn off, batons, hats, flashlights, guns and notebooks scattered. Whaddayamean Dean lay moaning, draped across an overturned trash can. Roscoe Rules felt his strength returning as he struggled to his feet, keeping his balls in both hands for fear if he dropped them they'd burst like ripe tomatoes.

Roscoe was finished for the evening. He was content to limp down the stairs to sit in the radio car and wait for the arrival of other units after his partner staggered to the car and put out the "officers need help" call. Roscoe could not return with Whaddayamean Dean when he went back into the building with some sixteen policemen and began breaking down doors in a vain search for the two hod carriers who had escaped and were not arrested for two weeks.

"Give em a few licks for me, partner," Roscoe had whispered to his partner as he shuffled slowly to the ambulance, walking bowlegged, holding the enflamed swollen testicles in both hands as though he had a double handful of heavy bullion or precious gems. Which indeed he did as far as he was concerned. He thought at that moment that he might lose them forever and nothing ever seemed as precious. He refused to release the handful of damaged flesh even to step up into the ambulance, and just stood there, bowlegged, holding himself while two ambulance attendants lifted him up in a seated carry.

Before they closed the ambulance door, he called weakly to his battered partner, "Give em one for me, Dean! One for your partner! And get em in a wristlock! Bend em down! Make em bite their own balls! Then play catch-up with your stick! Then kneedrop them! Puncture their kidneys! Rupture their spleens! Make em do the chicken!"

Five people went to jail that night for various charges ranging from resisting officers to plain drunk. The black man was picked up two weeks later at the Hod Carriers Local. After five court continuances he spent ten days in jail which he was permitted to serve on weekends because of his work and large family. The Mexican hod carrier who also had a large family was given a longer jail term because of his youthful record of violence. All but fifteen days were suspended.

Both men were heroes with their families and neighbors for some time to come, and the Mexican, who had been experiencing a diminished sex drive, discovered after his release from jail that he was like a young stallion. His wife said she never had it so good.

After Roscoe Rules recovered from the beating at the hands of the hod carriers he was anxious to get back to the streets and make the citizenry of Wilshire Division pay for his wounds and humiliation. There was no shame in the injuries themselves. On the contrary, Roscoe wore his scars as proudly as the Mexican wore the mementos of his youthful gang fights. What humiliated Roscoe was that they got punched and stomped two on two. When he told the story to other officers the number of assailants grew in number until even Whaddayamean Dean wasn't sure just how many people had a piece of him. Roscoe never did know. The entire experience was blurred in his mind what with vomiting and painful fearful days in the hospital when he erroneously thought his manhood would be forever compromised. He admitted to his partner that he had no clear recollection of what had happened and even after his total recovery referred to the experience grimly as The Day My Balls Blew Up.

But from then on, Roscoe was more cautious than before. If a suspect even looked as though he might be anxious to cause trouble he would find himself wearing Roscoe's unauthorized sap in his hair. During his one month convalescence Roscoe was unable to raise what Harold Bloomguard called a "diamond cutter" or even a "blue veiner" due to the shooting pains in his groin. His wife told a sympathetic neighbor she never had it so good.

But Roscoe never lost his sense of humor. While he was off duty recuperating he invited Whaddayamean Dean to his ranch east of Chino for a down home pit barbecue.

"Not like that nigger slop you see in all these greasy spoons in town," he promised, but a real barbecue, worthy of the Middle American farmers Roscoe had sprung from.

When Whaddayamean Dean asked Roscoe if he planned to return to the Midwest when he retired from police work, Roscoe said, fuck no, that those redneck maggots like to read their Bibles over you while they screwed you in the ass. Once when waxing philosophical he admitted that he had only truly been happy in Vietnam, and that if he hadn't been dumb enough to knock up his old lady and get married young he'd have loved to have gone to Africa and hired out as a mercenary.

"Imagine getting paid to kill niggers," he mused.

Then he proved that he hadn't lost his sense of humor when his eight year old son Clyde came crying into the yard where Roscoe and Whaddayamean Dean sat drinking beer from the cans and working on a radio controlled airplane which Roscoe Rules had bought for his son's birthday two years ago and not let him play with because he wasn't old enough. Roscoe loved to sit in the yard and terrorize the pony by divebombing it with the roaring little airplane. It was a Messerschmitt with authentic German insignia and an added touch of a swastika on the tail.

"Daddy!" said his son Clyde. "Look at Pookie!"

"What's wrong with him, son?" asked Roscoe solicitously as the boy held the little box turtle in his hands. The creature's head drooped, obviously near death from some reptile malady.

"It's a goner, get rid of it," Roscoe said without touching the turtle.

"No, Daddy!" cried the boy. "He'll be okay! Pookie's gonna be okay!"

"Give him here," Roscoe said, winking at Whaddayamean Dean. "I'll see what I can do."

Then he snatched the little turtle from the child's hand and with the cutting pliers he was using to repair the gas engine of the Messerschmitt, snipped the head of the box turtle off at the base of the shell, the feet kicking frantically in death.

"Now we can use him for a paperweight," Roscoe said.

He told the story all over Wilshire Station the next day,

claiming it proved he was the meanest, baaaaadest motherfucker that ever wore a blue suit in Wilshire Station, while
Whaddayamean Dean unknowingly used exactly the phrase
which had been used by Roscoe's last five partners. He whispered that Roscoe was an insufferable prick.

Roscoe Rules continued pretty much as before despite his
Waterloo at the hands of the hod carriers. He asked to return
to 7-A-85 so he could be in the south end of Wilshire Division
in the thick of the action. And since Roscoe arrested so many
drunk drivers and wrote such an incredible number of traffic
tickets he was still the darling of those police supervisors who
believe that writing one moving traffic violation a day is tangi-
ble proof of good police work.

Roscoe also arrested more drunk drivers than most traffic
cars. Of course, he also went to court more than any traffic car
because he booked the "borderline" drunk drivers. In fact, he
wrote the "borderline" tickets.

"All I see and some I don't see," as Roscoe put it.

On the night that Roscoe Rules was to become a legend he
and Whaddayamean Dean had been trying to catch a drunk
driver by staking out a bar on West Jefferson frequented by
hard drinking blacks who wasted no time with fancy drinks,
but nightly consumed gallons of Scotch, gin and beer. Roscoe
had hoped to find a drunk sleeping in his car in the parking lot
at the rear and wake him gently, telling him that he had better
go home and sleep it off. Then they would wait down the street
in the darkness and arrest the grateful motorist for drunk driving as he passed by.

Some policemen become legends by virtue of accumulated
felony arrests which propel them into the category of instinc-
tive policemen, who doglike smell or sense when something is
wrong: when a suspect is lying, when a turn of the head or
clicking of eyeballs means more than just another case of black
and white fever. When one *knows* which cars to stop, which
pedestrian to talk to, most importantly, which one to *believe,*
since most policemen eventually conclude that in addition to
being hopelessly weak the human race is composed of an incredible collection of liars who will lie even when the truth
would save them, and more often than not haven't the faintest
idea of what the truth really is.

But there are other ways to become police legends, that is, by a single action or reaction which is so outrageous that within twenty-four hours it is the subject of every rollcall in the city. Roscoe Rules was about to become that kind of legend.

That fateful night started pretty much as every other night with Roscoe driving and discussing the merits of fast cars, hotshot chase driving, devastating weapons and ammunition, and even women, since his wounded testicles were once more intact and functioning. As he talked, Roscoe as always, unconsciously squeezed, kneaded and pulled at himself.

The salmon smoggy sun had dropped suddenly that evening. They were driving through their district at dusk, looking for traffic tickets which Roscoe believed in writing at the beginning of the watch. Often, a motorist could blow a red light at eighty miles an hour during the busy late hours and Roscoe would ignore him or not even see him *if* he had already written his ticket for the night.

They passed a construction crew building a new elementary school in a black neighborhood near Washington Boulevard, and Roscoe yelled "Building new cages, huh?" to a white man in a hard hat who grinned and raised a hammer.

"The air's quiet," Roscoe remarked, lighting a Marlboro. "Not too many radio calls in Wilshire, but I got a feeling it's gonna be a busy Thursday night. Animals got their welfare checks today. Should be lots a action."

A battered Texas Chevrolet driven by a grim looking white man with faded eyes pulled up next to them at a red light. The woman passenger, gaunt and weak, had difficulty rolling down the window. She was holding a baby in her arms, and one of the four blond children in the back seat helped her.

"Suh," she said, "kin you tell us where the Gen'ral Hospital is?"

"Sure," Roscoe answered. "Just go straight on this street to the Harbor Freeway and turn right. Keep going ten miles. You can't miss it."

"Thank ye," she smiled, and again battled the window which was jammed in the bent frame.

Whaddayamean Dean looked at his partner quizzically and Roscoe explained, "Fuck this white trash. They're worse'n niggers, coming here and making us pay for their little milksuckers. General Hospital, my ass. Wonder what they'll say when they find themselves looking at the ocean?"

Roscoe then spotted a black man in a business suit walking on Western Avenue with a young white woman in a green tailored jacket and skirt. She was obviously not one of the white prostitutes who worked the area so Roscoe kept his voice low when he drove by, looked in their direction and said, "Price of pork what it is, and a spade can still buy a white pig for ten dollars?"

"You know, I never drove in a pursuit," Whaddayamean Dean observed as he saw an LAPD traffic car zooming past them to overtake a speeder on Olympic Boulevard.

"Remember one thing, babe," Roscoe said, his voice dropping an octave as it always did when he assumed the role of training officer, "don't never try to overtake a fast car on the outside when you're going in a turn. Most cars'll flip on a piece a spit. Hit him on the inner rear fender and he'll eat the windshield. I once saw a freeway car drive a motherfucker right into an abutment by doing that. Sucker's car blew up like a howitzer shell. Took four pricks off the welfare rolls *permanent*. And you gotta know when your engine's gonna flame out. These hogs probably only top out at a hundred ten so you push it very long and you'll probably throw a bearing, drop a rod and blow the engine. That's embarrassing in a good pursuit. Makes you feel stupid.

"In addition to knowing your car you gotta know all your equipment," Roscoe continued, "like that peashooter you're carrying. I wish I could talk you into buying a magnum and carrying some good, gut ripping hollow points in it. I want a gun that'll stop some scrote when I need him stopped. After the prick's dead I'll worry about the ammunition being department approved. I ever tell you about that abba dabba burglar my partner shot when I used to work the Watts car? Ripping off a gas station when he set off the silent alarm. We were carrying those peashooters like you got. That sucker could run the hundred in ten flat till my partner shot him, and then he ran it in nine-nine. So I made a vow to get rid a this worthless ammo and get me some killing stuff. I made a study of velocity and shock."

And then they got their *first* bloody call of the night. "Seven-A-Eighty-five. A possible jumper, Wilshire and Mariposa," said the communications operator. "Handle the call code three."

Roscoe preferred working an extra car, called an "X-car," because instead of saying "Seven-X-Eighty-five" or "Seven-X-ray-Eighty-five," he could improvise by saying, "Seven-Exceptional-Eighty-five," or "Seven-Ex-citing-Eighty-five."

Roscoe was falling in love with the voice of the radio operator on frequency ten whom he had never seen. So Roscoe picked up the mike, pushed the button to send, made three kissing sounds and said, "This is Seven-Ay-ya-Eighty-five. I say Seven-A-for-Atomic-Eighty-five, rrrrrajah on the call."

Then he released the button, turned to Whaddayamean Dean and said, "That'll make her wet her pants."

And the radio operator, who was a fat, fifty-nine year old housewife with six children older than Roscoe Rules, turned to the operator on her left and said, "That guy on Seven-A-Eighty-five sounds like an insufferable prick."

A janitor named Homer Tilden had placed the jumper call when a twenty-two year old receptionist named Melissa Monroe returned to the office some three hours after the building closed and demanded to be let in on the pretext of having left an important document there.

"I never shoulda let her in, it's my fault, all my fault," the plump black janitor later sobbed to detectives.

Then the janitor pictured the pert smiling girl with the jazz age bob, who always yelled "Night, Mr. Tilden!" when she left at night, and he burst into tears like a child.

When Roscoe Rules and Dean Pratt arrived, red lights flashing and siren screaming, there was already a small group of morbid onlookers who had come across from the Ambassador Hotel. Homer Tilden led the two policemen to the elevator and up to the twenty-first floor where the young woman sat on the window ledge of her own office, feet dangling, looking down curiously at the crowd gathering. In the distance the wail of a fire department emergency vehicle trapped by Wilshire Boulevard night traffic three blocks west.

"Don't come near me," the girl said calmly, her hair blowing wispily around her tiny ears as the two policemen ran from the elevator and burst into the office.

"Go downstairs," Roscoe said to Homer Tilden who was holding his chest and panting as though he had run the twenty-one stories instead of taking the elevator.

"Maybe I . . ."

"Go downstairs!" Roscoe repeated. "There's gonna be other people coming."

And as the janitor obeyed, Roscoe Rules began to imagine a picture and write-up in tomorrow's *Los Angeles Times* if he could save the beautiful jumper. She was a fox and would surely rate an inside front page photo, along with her savior.

"Look, miss," Roscoe said and stepped forward. But the girl moved inches closer to her destiny, and Roscoe froze in his tracks.

"Maybe we better back off, partner," Dean whispered, looking for the moment far younger than his twenty-five years, his freckles swimming in streams of sweat.

"We don't back off nothing," Roscoe whispered back. "She's a dingaling, and there's ways to handle them." Then to the girl Roscoe said, "Nothing's as bad as that. Come on in. Let's jaw about it."

He said it fliply with a grin and stepped forward, stopping when the girl moved forward another two inches and now teetered on the very edge, framed against the faded smoggy night sky of the Miracle Mile.

"Oh no!" Dean said. "No, miss! Don't go any closer! Come on, partner, let's go downstairs and give this lady a chance to think!"

But as Roscoe Rules saw a *Times* write-up and perhaps a police department medal of valor slipping through his fingers, he decided to try a different approach. He had seen Charles Laughton or someone do it successfully on an old TV movie. You could shame a jumper into surrendering.

"All right then, goddamnit!" Roscoe shouted to the girl. "You got your audience. It's your life. If it ain't worth a shit to you, it ain't worth a shit to us. Go ahead, girl. We can't stay here all night babying you. We got other things to do. Go ahead, girl! Jump!"

And she did. Without a word or a tear she looked at Roscoe Rules and Dean Pratt and in fact never took her large violet eyes off them as she let herself slip from the ledge and fell at thirty-two feet per second squared, legs first, with a scream that was lost in a woosh of air and rustling skirt which had blown up over her face.

What was left of Melissa Monroe was being covered by a sheet when Dean Pratt stumbled by on his way to the radio car.

"Let me make the reports, partner," Roscoe Rules said, and for the very first time Dean heard Roscoe's voice quiver with uncertainty.

Then Whaddayamean Dean looked at Melissa Monroe and said later it was as though God in Heaven was displeased with dessert and had hauled off and threw it at the Ambassador Hotel but missed and splattered the sidewalk on Wilshire Boulevard. Skull and body had exploded. Organs and brain littered the pavement. She was white and yellow and pink, covered with lumpy red sauce and syrup. Melissa Monroe had been turned into a raspberry sundae.

Dean Pratt was very quiet for the rest of this bloodiest of all nights of his life. He thought they were finished when at the station Roscoe Rules finished writing his 15.7 report: that indispensable police document which handily covers all those police situations which do not conveniently fit into a category such as robbery, burglary or vehicle theft.

"Remember, partner," Roscoe warned as they sat alone in the station coffee room, "as soon as the janitor left, she just jumped. Nothing was said by nobody. She just jumped!"

Dean Pratt nodded and sipped at a soft drink, longing for a water tumbler of straight bourbon as he had never longed for anything in his life. He hoped there might be some downers left in the bottom of his closet at home where his girlfriend left a small cache. He was terrified by barbiturates since drug use was an irrevocable firing offense. But he wanted to get loaded and sleep.

At 11:00 P.M. Roscoe Rules dragged his partner out of the coffee room and said, "Come on, partner, let's go do some police work."

"Huh?"

"Come on, goddamnit, let's hit the bricks." Roscoe grinned. "We ain't through yet. We still got forty-five minutes."

"Jesus Christ," said Dean.

"Come on!" Roscoe commanded, his grin vanishing. He took Whaddayamean Dean very firmly by the arm and walked him out to the radio car.

"Don't go cuntish on me!" Roscoe snarled when he drove away from the station. "As far as I'm concerned we handled that call just right. If that whacko bitch wanted to take gas, fuck it, it ain't our fault."

When Dean didn't answer Roscoe became angrier. His hairless brows puckered and whitened. "Fuck it! Who cares if *all* these rotten motherfuckers take gas. They're all shit sucking, miserable scrotes anyways. What the fuck's a life anyway, less it's yours?"

Still Dean did not answer and Roscoe unconsciously pulled at his crotch and raged on. "You bust a good felony and you tell him to throw up his hands. He don't do it and there's no witnesses, I say put him *down*. Understand? Shoot em down like birds that shit on your roof. Remember that nigger and spick The Night My Balls Blew Up? I'm gonna get them someday. And I'll worship the ground they're laid under. You'd like to blow em down, wouldn't you?"

"I guess so," Dean nodded.

"One nigger plus one spick equals a Mexi-coon!" Roscoe shouted. "That's my hard charging partner! One a these nights we'll get us a couple a scrotes who wanna go the hard way. We'll show some a these so called cops with their withered nuts how a couple a honest to God hard chargers do it! We'll perform a little retroactive birth control and blow the motherfuckers right outta their shoes with my magnum and your little peashooter!"

"I guess so, Roscoe," Dean mumbled.

Roscoe was unconsciously pushing the radio car eighty miles an hour on the Santa Monica Freeway, heading nowhere, feeling the rush of cool wind, stroking himself while Whaddayamean Dean watched the speedometer.

And then they received the last radio call of the night.

"Seven-A-Eighty-five, Seven-Adam-Eighty-five, assist the traffic unit, Venice and Hauser. Code two."

"Seven-A-Eighty-five, roger," Dean responded, banging the mike back in the holder, disgustedly jotting the location on the notebook pad.

"Shit fuck!" said Roscoe Rules, an expression he seldom used anymore since a former partner convinced him that it made him sound like a Central Avenue nigger.

"I've had enough for one night," Dean grumbled. "I was ready for code seven."

"Coulda used some chow myself," said Roscoe. "Don't the scrotes at communications have another car they can pick on? Shit fuck! Give her the handcuffs, partner."

Dean Pratt, as Roscoe Rules had taught him, opened the bracelet of his handcuffs, holding it next to the hand mike, and squeezed the bracelet through five or six times, making a ratchet sound very like a large zipper being ripped open and closed. Roscoe was convinced that the sound would be magnified in the operator's radio headset.

"Sounds like the jolly green giant opening his fly, don't it, partner?"

Whaddayamean Dean nodded, suddenly a bit carsick. He hadn't had a thing to eat for almost twenty-four hours. He had been in court all day and had come straight to work after testifying. And Roscoe Rules sitting there pulling on his dork wasn't doing anything to settle his queasiness.

"I ever tell you about that slopehead we used to gang bang in Nam, partner?" Roscoe asked, in a downright jovial mood since this would be their last call.

Even if it was a quickie he intended to make it an "end-of-watcher," by "milking" the time out and failing to clear when they were finished.

"Don't think you told me that one," Dean sighed, by now deciding that he would rather have four fingers of bourbon than a hamburger.

"This little gook was about fourteen, but retarded. Had the brain of a chicken and nearsighted to boot. We got a translator to tell her that fucking was good for her eyes. She was ugly as a busted blister. Just a little better than jacking off. Best part wasn't the pussy, it was cleaning her up ahead a time. We used to get these fifty cent rice paddy whores like her and throw them in this big wooden tub and eight or ten of us would get hot water and GI brushes and scrub the stink off them. Goddamn, that was fun! We'd lather them up and scrub every inch. Shit, we'd take our clothes off and fall in the water and drink beer and wash those bitches. Seems kinda weird but it was more fun washing them than gang fucking them."

Dean nodded and leaned back while Roscoe drove west on Venice Boulevard and dreamed of thin young yellow bodies in soapy water. He had had many a lay but never had a more exciting sexual experience than scrubbing and lathering the rice paddy whores. Even now he got a blue veiner every time he held a bar of soap.

"Shit fuck!" Dean observed. "There it is!"

And there it was! Traffic was snarled six blocks in every direction. Fifty people were milling around like ghouls, and two frantic traffic officers in white hats were trying to lay down a flare pattern to divert east and westbound traffic. Every eastbound lane was blocked by the wreckage of a spectacular four car collision.

Roscoe pulled on his red lights, crossed the center divider and parked the wrong way on Venice Boulevard.

"Glad you got here," said a heavy middle aged traffic policeman who came running up with a handful of flares and spots of ash on his uniform. "Worst goddamn crash I seen in a long time. Drag race. Two cars laid down sixty feet of skids before they plowed into a northbound station wagon and knocked it clear back into the eastbound lanes.

"What station wagon?" Dean asked, adjusting his hat, getting his flashlight ready as he and Roscoe jogged back toward the wreckage where several souvenir hunters were already starting to prowl.

"Get the hell out of here or you're going to jail!" the traffic officer shouted to the unkempt teenagers.

"Everybody gone to the hospital?" Roscoe asked, waving his flashlight violently at a car which was trying to get past the wreckage to go south on Ridgely Drive.

"Two ambulances been here," the traffic officer said. "You're the only radio car to show up. The fucking fire department hasn't even been here yet and there's two dead bodies jammed inside that station wagon!"

"Will someone tell me where the hell the station wagon is?" Dean asked, holding a handful of flares, preparing to lay a pattern fifty feet south of the corner and divert the horn blowing cars through an east-west alley.

"That's it! That's the station wagon!" the traffic officer said, pointing to a small heap of mangled steel which had knocked down the light standard, plunging the intersection into darkness. "It was cut in half!"

"Blow it out your ass, pizza face!" Roscoe shouted to a sputtering acned man in a white Cadillac who was honking his horn and yelling as though he thought the policemen could magically sweep away ten tons of scrap metal and let him continue about his business which was to get to a west Hollywood bar before it closed and try to pick up a thirty-five dollar prostitute.

By now a dozen of the trapped cars were flashing their high beams in the policemen's faces and blowing their horns while Roscoe violently waved them toward the alley where Dean Pratt was laying flares.

"Terrible wreck," the traffic policeman muttered. "A woman in the station wagon was decapitated. She's one of the ones still inside."

"Yeah?" Roscoe said. He crossed the street, flashed his light at the heaps of debris in his path and stood beside the half of the station wagon, trying to make sense of the pile of mutilated flesh which had been a young couple. The tin cans and "Just Married" sign were still tied to the bumper.

And then Roscoe Rules was reminded of one of the two hilarious photographs he carried in his wallet from his Vietnam days.

"Oh yeah!" said Roscoe Rules excitedly. "Move the flares, partner!" he shouted to Dean, who was angrily waving his flashlight at the string of cars to get them moving through the alley, as at last the fire engines' sirens could be heard.

"What for?"

"I want them to pass by the wreck here across that gas station parking lot."

"What for?"

"I think it'll be easier to divert them down the alley."

"Okay." Dean shrugged, moving the line of flares, and then Roscoe Rules stood quietly on the far side of the station wagon, hoping the fire trucks or another ambulance wouldn't get there too quickly and spoil things.

The first car to pass Roscoe was not suitable. The driver was well dressed, prosperous, just the kind of prick who'd call in and make a complaint, Roscoe thought. Neither was the second car. The traffic was crawling by, most of the drivers gawking hungrily for a glimpse of blood.

The twelfth car in the line was perfect. It was a late model Dodge containing a man and two women. The bulging luggage rack, travel stickers and Ohio license said they were tourists passing through and not likely to take time to stop and complain about a policeman, no matter the outrage.

When the station wagon crawled by, Roscoe, still standing half hidden beside the wreckage, smiled encouragingly at the pudgy woman on the passenger side. Her window was down and she said, "Quite a wreck, eh, officer?"

"Yes, ma'am," Roscoe answered, and he knew this was the one.

"Over here, partner!" he called to Whaddayamean Dean, since every legend needs a Boswell.

The woman shook her head sadly and clucked. As her husband was revving the engine and the creeping traffic was starting, she said to Roscoe, "Anyone hurt bad?"

Then Roscoe Rules came from behind the wreckage and stepped to her window, lifting the dripping, severed head of the young bride, and said, "Yeah, this one got banged up a bit."

The woman from Ohio drowned out the fire engines' sirens with her screams as her husband drove into the flow of traffic.

Dean Pratt told the story to at least thirty policemen before going home that night. Roscoe Rules had achieved a place in police folklore, and was a Legend in His Own Time.

6

7-A-33: Spencer Van Moot
and Father Willie Wright

Willie Wright was also destined to become a police celebrity. It happened four months before the choir practice killing. On the night he met a brother in the basement.

Of course he could not have dreamed of the bizarre turns this tour of duty would take when he sat in the rollcall room late that afternoon and wished he could grow a moustache like the one belonging to Sam Niles of 7-A-29, or Calvin Potts of 7-A-77 who had a heavy one which made the muscular black policeman look even more formidable.

Willie was sure that if he grew one it would look like Francis Tanaguchi's sparse and sad one, which many old women could duplicate.

It was a peaceful, untraumatic rollcall that afternoon. Lieutenant Finque was on a day off and Sergeant Yanov sat before them alone at his table on the platform.

"Got an unusual one last night," Sergeant Yanov said, trying to look through the crimes to find one that might amuse the watch. "Guy tried to shove a Pepsi bottle in his wife's giz after he caught her stepping out on him."

"I took that report," said Sam Niles. "It was nothing. The bottle didn't have the cap on it."

"Reminds me of the guy stuck a screwdriver up his ass to scratch his prostate. Remember that, partner?" Roscoe asked Whaddayamean Dean. "Couldn't get it out and the wife called the police. That was funny!" Rules chuckled as he pulled at his crotch and made Harold Bloomguard sick.

Then Roscoe blushed and got angry when Sergeant Yanov said, "By the way, an unnamed officer turned in a report last night where he wrote a pursesnatcher was l-e-r-k-i-n-g and p-r-a-y-i-n-g on his victims. Check the dictionary if you're not sure. These reports end up in courts of law. Makes us look dumb."

"I told you to check my spelling, goddamnit," Roscoe whispered to Dean Pratt who smiled weakly and said, "Sorry, partner."

"One word of advice," Sergeant Yanov said. "The captain is uptight about the pissy wino they found sleeping in the back of Sergeant Sneed's car. They suspect one of you guys put him there."

"Me? Why me all the time?" Francis Tanaguchi cried when all eyes turned to him.

"Gee, rollcalls are quiet without the lieutenant here," observed Spermwhale Whalen, who then turned to Willie Wright and said, "Hey, kid, how about comin in the bathroom with me? My back's hurt and I ain't supposed to lift nothin heavy."

Spencer Van Moot was happy when rollcall ended early. It gave him more time to shop. Spencer was, at forty, the second oldest choirboy, next to fifty-two year old Spermwhale Whalen, the two of them the only choirboys over thirty. Spencer Van Moot had convinced Harold Bloomguard that he should be accepted as a MacArthur Park choirboy because he was only temporarily married, was hated by his wife Tootie and her three kids and would probably soon be thrice divorced like Spermwhale Whalen.

Harold welcomed the complainer Spencer Van Moot for the same reason he welcomed Roscoe Rules. He invited Spencer Van Moot because he was the most artistic scrounger and promoter at Wilshire Station.

Spencer knew every retail store within a mile of his beat. His "police discounts" had furnished his house princely. He wore the finest Italian imports from the racks of the Miracle Mile clothing stores. He dined superbly in one of three expensive restaurants near Wilshire and Catalina which were actually in Rampart Division. Retailers became convinced that Spencer Van Moot could ward off burglars, shoplifters, fire and vandalism. That somehow this tall blond recruiting poster policeman with the confident jaw and the small foppish moustache could even forestall economic reversal.

Despite his natural morose nature and his self pitying complaints about his unhappy marriage, he was accepted at once by the choirboys. He arrived with a dowry of three cases of cold beer and four bottles of Chivas Regal Scotch. And he brought his partner, Willie Wright.

Willie was one of the smallest choirboys, along with Francis Tanaguchi and Harold Bloomguard, under five feet nine inches tall. Willie in fact had stretched to make five feet eight and was almost disqualified when he took his first police physical. He was a devoutly religious young man, raised as a Baptist, converted to Jehovah's Witnesses when he married Geneva Smythe, his high school sweetheart. Willie was now twenty-four and Geneva twenty-five. She, like Willie, was short and chubby. She took *Watchtower* magazines door to door three times a week. Willie accompanied her on his days off.

Spencer Van Moot loved him as a partner because Willie thought it was crooked to accept gifts or wholesale prices from retail stores, thereby leaving Spencer a double share of everything he could promote. The only concession Willie would make was a nightly free meal in one of Spencer Van Moot's gourmet restaurants.

After being practically dragged to the first choir practice by Spencer, Willie Wright discovered something totally extraordinary: that choir practice was fun, more fun in fact than anything he had ever done in his young life. He was accepted by the other choirboys almost from the start because he entertained them by preaching squeaky sermons. He told them how wrong it was to drink and lust after the two camp followers, Ora Lee Tingle and Carolina Moon, who often turned up at choir practice. But then when drunk he turned into an evil eyed little mustang.

Harold Bloomguard dubbed him official chaplain of the MacArthur Park choirboys. He was thereafter known as The Padre, *Father* Willie Wright.

The night that Father Willie Wright personally called for choir practice was the night he found the brother in the basement. It had begun much like every other night, with Spencer Van Moot driving the radio car madly to all of his various stops before the stores closed. First he had to make three cigarette stops where he picked up two packs of cigarettes for each of them, which Father Willie didn't use. Father Willie suspected quite rightly that Spencer wholesaled the cigarettes to his neighbors.

And then there was the dairy stop where Spencer got his daily allotment of buttermilk and yogurt, one quart for each partner, which Willie likewise refused. Each night at 10:00 P.M. the manager walked swiftly to his car under the protective beam of Spencer's spotlight. Then there were other stops, if he could get them in, at various men's shops on Wilshire Boulevard where Spencer and salesmen tossed around Italian names like Brioni and Valentino and which invariably ended in Spencer's trying on something in a fine cabretta leather jacket over his blue police uniform. Father Willie sat bored in the dressing room holding his partner's Sam Browne, gun and hat while Spencer preened.

Sometimes a new salesman would make the mistake of quoting the retail price to the tall policeman and would find himself cowering before an indignant stare, a twitching toothbrush moustache and a withering piece of advice to "Check with the manager about my police discount."

Father Willie often thought about asking for a new partner but he didn't want to hurt Spencer's feelings. Spencer had tried for years to find a partner like Father Willie, who would not accept his rightful share of free cigarettes, wholesale merchandise and free liquor. It had gotten to be tedious for Spencer breaking in new partners:

"You smoke?"

"No, Spencer."

"Today you do. I'll take both packs if you don't want them."

And inevitably a partner would become greedy. "I'll take a pack today, Spencer."

"What for? You don't smoke."

"I'll give them to my brother. What the hell, three packs a day I'm entitled to."

Spencer got to keep Willie's share of petty booty in every case. And Father Willie never complained when Spencer scrounged up some liquor for choir practices.

"We're having a retirement party for one of our detective lieutenants," Spencer would inevitably lie to a long suffering liquor store proprietor who would take two bottles of Scotch from the shelf behind him.

"We're having a big big party." Spencer would smile benignly until the proprietor would get the message and bring up another two bottles.

But Spencer was considerate about spreading it around and rarely went to the same liquor store more than once a month for anything but cigarettes. The cigarette stop however was a relentless daily ritual. It was said that during the Watts riot of 1965, Spencer drove a half burned black and white with every window shot out ten miles to Beverly Boulevard, his face streaked with soot and sweat, and managed to make all three cigarette stops before the stores closed at 2:00 A.M.

Spencer Van Moot had accepted a thousand packs of cigarettes and as many free meals in his time. And though he had bought enough clothing at wholesale prices to dress a dozen movie stars, he had never even considered taking a five dollar bill nor was one ever offered except once when he stopped a Chicago grocer in Los Angeles on vacation. The police department and its members made an exact distinction between petty gratuities and cash offerings, which were considered money bribes no matter how slight and would result in a merciless dismissal as well as criminal prosecution.

It was not that the citizens and police of Los Angeles were inherently less debased than their Eastern counterparts, it was that the West, being a network of sprawling young towns and cities, did not lend itself to the old intimate teeming ward or ghetto where political patronage and organized crime bedded down together. The numbers racket, for instance, had been a dismal failure in western America. The average citizen of Los Angeles hadn't the faintest idea how it worked. Yet in the Pennsylvania steel town where Spencer Van Moot was born, every living soul had played numbers and consulted dream books for winners and contributed to organized crime's greatest source of revenue in that region. The bookies came door to door. They even accepted children's penny bets. Western criminals had found it impossible to organize a crazy quilt collection of several communities which existed inside the 460 square mile limits of the city, where there was an automobile for every adult. The city had geography and history going for it.

So it was that Spencer Van Moot's supplication provided about half of the beverage consumed at choir practice, the rest provided by Roscoe Rules who bullied the free booze from cowering liquor store owners on his beat.

After making his various stops and depositing his treasures in the back of his camper truck in the station parking lot, Spencer began whining again about his unhappy domestic life.

"I mean how can you understand a woman, Padre?" Spencer complained as the setting sun filtered through the smog and burned Father Willie's sensitive, bulging blue eyes.

"I don't know, Spencer," Father Willie sighed, and wondered how long Spencer would use him as a sounding board tonight. Sometimes when he was lucky the complaining would stop after the first two hours of their tour of duty.

"I'm forty years old, Father Willie," Spencer griped, touching his twenty dollar haircut which he got free in a Wilshire Boulevard styling parlor. "Look at my hair, it's getting gray. Why should I live in such misery."

"I'm twenty-four," Father Willie reminded him, "and you have more hair than I do. Who cares if it's gray."

"She's a bitch, Padre. It's hell, believe me," Spencer whined. "She's worse by far than my first two wives put together. And she's turned her kids against me. They hate me more than she does because she tells them lies about me, that I drink a lot and run around with other women."

"That's not a lie, Spencer," Father Willie reminded him. "You *do* drink a lot and run around with other women."

"It's nothing to tell teenagers, for god's sake!" Spencer answered. "I never shoulda married an older broad with kids. Damn, forty-two years old and her legs're turning green. Green, I tell you! And here I am with only four years to go until

I can pull the pin and retire. And what happens, she gets knocked up!"

"Maybe it'll work out, Spencer," Father Willie offered as his partner drove east on Eighth Street away from the sun's dying harsh rays.

"Work out? Work out? Four years to my pension and she's gonna foal, and then how can I retire with a little rug rat crawling around?"

"Oh well," Father Willie shrugged. "Oh well."

"A man gets drunk and careless and screws himself into another ten years on the job. It ain't fair."

"Oh well," said Father Willie.

"Everything happens to me!" Spencer said.

Spencer Van Moot was interrupted for a moment by catching a glimpse of a seventy year old pensioner who lived in a Seventh Street fleabag called the Restful Arms Motel. He pushed his wheelchair down the sidewalk backward with his *foot* as he held his useless arthritic hands in his lap. The pensioner was trying to get to the mom-and-pop market one block west where he could buy two cans of nutritious dog food for his dinner.

"Things could always be worse, Spencer."

"Oh sure, I'm gonna be unloading shitty diapers at forty years old and . . ."

"You've got a new camper. You can get away with your wife sometimes and go fishing."

"Oh sure. I got a new camper. I'm so thrilled, so happy! I'm in debt again. I was getting insecure not owing money."

"It'll work out."

"Yeah, it will. I'll be dead soon. No one in my family lives very long. I got an uncle that died of old age at forty-five. That's what the doctor said. Every organ in the man's body was old, dissipated. I won't last long. At least then I'll be rid of my old lady. I tell you, Padre, she's got a tongue so sharp it's a wonder she don't cut her mouth to pieces and bleed to death."

"You want to come to church with Geneva and me?" Father Willie offered. "Some of the best Witnesses I know came to God later in life. And what with the early deaths in your family . . ."

"Goddamnit, I ain't dead yet!" Spencer cried, suddenly frightened. "Padre, gimme a chance! I ain't lived yet!"

"Well, I only meant with poor health and all . . ."

"Poor health? Poor health? I'm too young to be thinking about dying. Jesus, partner, you're getting morbid!"

It was almost an hour before Spencer fully recovered from the suggestion of his imminent demise. He had the worst sick record on the nightwatch. He was tall and strong, in the prime of life, and had seen vats of spilled blood and acres of mutilated flesh in his sixteen years of police work, but he became faint when he'd scratch his finger. He could bear any pain but his own.

Just before dark they passed the Mary Sinclair Adams Home for Girls, a funded institution where young women who were pregnant and indigent could be cared for. It was a converted two story home two blocks east of Hancock Park and had once been a palatial residence of an eighty year old virgin who died envying young girls the fun they had growing round bellies.

There was a teenage girl with an eight month stomach standing in front of the house: cigarette dangling, eyebrows plucked to nothing, eyes shadowed to three inch black orbs, talking to three young men on chopper motorcycles.

"The Stork Club," Spencer remarked, shaking his head disgustedly. "They go in there, drop a frog and cut out."

"I hear the county's okayed the installation of interuterine devices in some of these girls they place in foster homes," Father Willie said.

"Someone shoulda plugged my old lady's birdbath and I wouldn't be in this fix," Spencer answered, blowing a cloud of smoke out the window. "Old dried up sponge, I don't know how she ever got knocked up. I'll just have to cut down on expenses, live like a goddamn Trappist monk. I won't be able to eat like a human being anymore, that's all."

"It'll work out all right," Father Willie said. Then, "Spencer, we'll still be able to eat roast duckling with orange sauce, won't we?"

"Oh sure."

"With glazed carrots and shallots?"

"Oh, we'll still eat at our restaurants for free just like we always have," said Spencer, allaying Father Willie's fears. "I meant *at home* I'll have to starve. My wife and kids'll have to go without and maybe wear old clothes with patches."

Father Willie felt like suggesting Spencer could make patches with some of the fourteen Italian suits which hung in his closet, when he spotted a Lincoln blow the red light on Wilshire and Western. The Lincoln pulled over the moment Father Willie tooted his horn.

"You just have to learn to budget," Spencer sighed as they gathered up hats and ticket book and flashlights now that dusk had settled. "Mail your check for the telephone bill to the gas company and theirs to the electric company. By the time they send them back and forth you can balance your checkbook."

Father Willie nodded as they got out of the black and white Matador and walked forward, crisscrossing so that Father Willie, whose turn it was, could approach the driver's side while Spencer went to the other side and shined the light in the window to protect Father Willie's approach.

The driver, a balding fat man about Spencer's age, smiled and said, "What's the problem, boys?" He offered Father Willie his driver's license without being asked.

"You were a full second late on that red light, sir," Father Willie said, his light on the license, checking that it was not expired, noting the Beverly Hills address in Trousdale Estates.

"That doesn't seem possible," the man said, getting out of the car and following the little officer to the police car where Spencer waited in the headlight beam between the two cars.

"Careful, sir," Father Willie warned, as a car sped by very close to the Matador which was stopped behind the Lincoln, three feet farther into the traffic lane to protect the approaching officer from being picked off by a motorist who might be driving HUA which meant: Head Up Ass.

"Officer!" the fat man appealed to Spencer as Father Willie began to write the ticket on the hood of the radio car. "Surely I wasn't late on the red light, and if I was I didn't mean it."

He offered Spencer his business card which said, "Murray Fern's Stereo Emporium."

Spencer Van Moot's eyes brightened with visions of a new stereo system in his barroom at home. At wholesale, of course.

He was about to suggest to his partner that Mr. Fern probably deserved some professional courtesy when he saw that it was too late. The ticket was already started, and since they were numbered it was impossible to cancel one without a report and explanation. So Spencer shrugged sadly and handed the business card back to the man.

"You gonna write me a ticket?" Murray Fern asked Father Willie.

"Yes sir," Father Willie said, never looking up as he wrote.

"Why me? Why me?" Murray Fern demanded, reminding Father Willie of Spencer.

"You ran a red light, sir," Father Willie said, looking up for the first time then continuing with the citation.

"But I can't get another ticket. One more and they'll suspend my license. Christ, gimme a break!"

Father Willie did not answer but continued to write in embarrassed silence.

"Just my luck to get stopped by a couple of pricks," the fat man said as he paced in a tight circle. "A couple of ticket hungry, heartless pricks."

Now Spencer Van Moot no longer cared about a cut rate stereo set and looked around the rear of the car for a taillight violation that Willie could add to the ticket.

"A couple of two bit, ticket happy, stupid fucking pricks!" Murray Fern said as Father Willie continued his writing without comment.

"Sign on the line," Spencer said coldly, speaking for the first time.

"Fuck you," said Murray Fern. "I'm innocent and I'm not signing."

"You're not admitting guilt," Father Willie said quietly. "If you don't sign, thereby promising to appear, we'll have to take you in and book you on the violation."

"Prick!" the fat man said, brushing Father Willie's ballpoint aside, taking a gold plated fountain pen from his inside coat pocket and leaning on the hood to study the ticket.

"It's only a promise . . ."

"I know what the fuck it is!" the man interrupted. "What I'd like to know is why you tinhorns aren't out catching criminals instead of harassing honest citizens, that's what I'd like to know."

The fat man scrawled his name across the ticket and turned his back on the two officers while Father Willie tore off the violator's copy and handed it to him along with his driver's license.

"I'll see you in court!" Murray Fern sputtered as he snatched his copy and license from Father Willie's hand. "I'll have a lawyer. I'll beat you. I'll make you go to court on your day off and I'll make you look like the dumb shit you are!"

He spun around and jammed the ticket, pen and license into his coat pocket. But when he jerked his hand out, a tiny .25 caliber automatic clattered to the pavement.

"Oh shit," said Murray Fern bleakly as Spencer Van Moot quickly pulled and pointed his .38 at the fat man's eyes.

"Who says there's no God?" Father Willie grinned happily.

"I only carry a gun when I make bank deposits," croaked Murray Fern. "I know it's against the law but I'm a business-man! You're not gonna put me in jail for something as petty as this?"

"Who *says* there's no God?" Father Willie repeated as he drew his handcuffs.

By the time the two policemen obtained the booking ap-proval and ran a record check on Murray Fern who had three drunk driving arrests, but no other criminal record, the fat man had threatened every officer at Wilshire Station with a lawsuit. It was 8:30 P.M. when they stood with Murray Fern in front of the booking officer, Elwood Banks, a fifty-year old black man and former partner of Spencer Van Moot.

"How's the retail trade in Los Angeles holdin up?" he asked Spencer when they brought the prisoner inside the lockup.

"Fair to middling, Elwood," Spencer answered. "Booking this guy for CCW."

"Kinda old to be playin with guns, ain't you, Dad?" com-mented Elwood Banks, looking up from his typewriter as he inserted a booking form.

"I'll sue you too, you bastard," Murray Fern warned. "Just one more smart remark and I'll put you on the lawsuit."

Sitting on a bench to the side of the booking cage, waiting

to be fingerprinted, was a tall, once powerful derelict with a bloody wet bandage over one eye. He was forty-eight years old, looked sixty-five, and had fought with the officers who had arrested him for plain drunk. The assault on the officers made him a felon now, but his fourteen page rap sheet included fifty-four arrests for only plain drunk and vagrancy, so now he would be tried and sentenced as a misdemeanant.

Elwood Banks knew the derelict as Timothy "Clickety-clack" Reilly, so called because his ill-fitting false teeth clicked together when he talked. Elwood Banks had booked Clickety-clack three times in the past, had never known him to be violent and rightly guessed that the young arresting officer, Roscoe Rules, had antagonized the derelict. His smashed nose and scarred eyes should have been a tip-off to Roscoe. Clickety-clack had once been a ranked heavyweight.

When Clickety-clack was brought inside the station by Roscoe he had merely said what he said to every arresting officer from Boston to Los Angeles: "I could whip you, Officer. In a fair fight I could whip you from here to East Fifth Street, know that?"

And most arresting officers answered something like: "Yeah, Clickety-clack, I know you could—in a fair fight. But if you try it, it ain't gonna be a fair fight cause my partner and me and half the nightwatch are gonna work out on your gourd with our sticks and do the fandango on your kisser. But in a fair fight you'd kick my ass, that's for sure."

And Clickety-clack would be satisfied. But on this night when he made the same speech to Roscoe Rules, Roscoe replied, "Oh yeah, you're gonna whip me, old man?"

And then in the corridor of Wilshire Station by the front desk in the presence of luscious Officer Reba Hadley whom he was trying to impress, Roscoe Rules took off his hat, slammed it on the desk, stood on the balls of his feet in front of the hulking derelict, put on his black gloves dramatically, both fists on his hips and said, "You think you can whip my ass, you wrinkled wart? You stinking tub a puke. Think you can whip me in a fair fight, huh?"

And Clickety-clack just said, "Yeah." And from a corner of his all but destroyed brain, he found a memory, a rhythm, an instinct and sent a picture left hook whistling through the air. Roscoe Rules woke up three minutes later in the lap of luscious Officer Reba Hadley who said to him, "You dumb shit."

Clickety-clack Reilly was of course buried by five or six blue uniforms and ended up with a badly cut lip and three more stitches in his eyes which made no difference at all to that caved in, monstrous face.

But now he sat, calm and secure and happy in the jail of Elwood Banks who knew exactly how to pacify him, thereby eliminating the possibility of further problems for himself.

"You okay, Mister Reilly?" he asked when Spencer and Father Willie entered the jail with Murray Fern. "Mind if I book this prisoner for these officers so they can get back out on the street?"

"No, Officer, I don't mind," the derelict smiled painfully to the black jailor. He looked as though he would love to hear it again, that word applied to him so seldom in his bitter lonely life.

"Thanks a lot, *Mister* Reilly," Elwood Banks said. "We'll just be a minute."

"Glad to hear you quit eatin in those greasy spoons down on Jefferson," Elwood Banks said to Spencer without even looking at Murray Fern. Then to Father Willie, "Once we was eatin in this soul kitchen and we caught a momma cockroach and three babies crawlin on his plate. Spencer just told them to fry it. It was free."

"My tastes've changed since those days," Spencer remarked.

"I knew you wasn't the soul food type at heart, Spencer," Elwood Banks said. Then he turned to Murray Fern and said, "Name?"

"Go to hell," the arrestee answered.

"Man, your face is red as a bucket a blood," Elwood Banks said. "Calm down, make it easy on yourself."

"I'm including *you* in the lawsuit," said Murray Fern.

"You're sure lucky you got these easygoin officers here," Elwood Banks said. "You was busted by an officer named Roscoe Rules he'd a been up side your head long ago. They'd a needed a sewing machine to put in the stitches."

"I demand an attorney."

"After you're booked you can call one," said Elwood Banks.

"I demand an MD. I'm on medication for a serious allergy."

"Ain't none here," Elwood Banks said. "Boys can take you to the hospital if you want, right now before they book you."

"That'll take too long. I'm bailing out of here at once."

"Then why do you want a doctor?"

"Because I do. I demand an MD be brought here."

"Well there ain't none here."

"Then I demand an RN."

"You keep this shit up and you're gonna get an RIN," the black jailor informed him.

"What's that?" asked Murray Fern.

"A rap in the nuts. Now gimme your full name and address."

"I refuse to answer."

"That does it," Elwood Banks said, his lip curling as he came out from behind the counter. "I usually search *after* booking but I'm gonna make an exception. Strip down."

"What?" Murray Fern asked nervously. "What are you gonna do?"

"Nothin. *If* you do like I say." Elwood Banks wore crisp jail khakis, his LAPD badge was highly polished, his feet were spread as he stood before the fat white man whose courage and insolence were in direct proportion to what was on his body and in his pockets. Or as Elwood Banks often put it, "Strip em down and show em what they are: nothin!"

"You want me to take off *all* my clothes?" Murray Fern asked, looking from one policeman to another as Elwood Banks reached roughly into his pockets, removing his wallet, keys, handkerchief, cigarettes and chewing gum.

"Turn em inside out," Elwood Banks said, and Murray Fern obeyed, trying to beat the jailor to the pockets, fearing he would rip them.

"Satisfied?" Murray Fern asked, when everything including his Patek Philippe wristwatch was on the counter.

"No way, baby," said Elwood Banks. "Get them fancy threads off that chubby body and on the counter. I mean strip and do it now!"

Thirty seconds later, Murray Fern stood before the three policemen wearing only ninety dollar boots of imported Swiss leather, knee length blue silk socks, and silk boxer shorts dotted with tiny hearts.

"Satisfied?" he asked again, but now his authoritative baritone was a tenuous rasp and his eyes darted past the men to the corridor outside.

"I said strip, damnit!" Elwood Banks ordered. "Now get them boots and britches off before I rip em off!"

In a moment Murray Fern stood utterly naked before them, turning his body to one side and another, his composure breaking to pieces before their eyes, the rolls of textured fat shaking as he squirmed and wriggled with nowhere to hide.

"Turn around and bend over and spread your cheeks, Murray," Elwood Banks said, for the first time using the fat man's name.

"Bend over?"

"Bend over and show me that round brown," Elwood Banks said. "I gotta see if you're hiding a machine gun in there."

When Murray Fern timidly did as he was told Elwood Banks said, "Humph, my kid's basset hound got better markins than that. Okay, boy, lift your feet up one at a time and show me the bottoms."

Murray Fern obeyed quickly and quietly.

When he was finished, Elwood Banks said, "Okay, Murray, now turn around and face me and open your mouth and lift up your balls. We don't want you rat-holin twenty bucks in some little crease down there. You can't be no better off than Mr. Reilly when we lock you in the tank together."

As Murray Fern opened his mouth for inspection he unconsciously held his hands over his shriveled penis, which was lost in the hair and layers of overhanging fat.

Elwood Banks then delivered the coup de grace. "Okay, Murray, now take your hands away and skin your wee wee back. I once knew a bookie kept bettin markers hid under his foreskin."

When the search and booking were finished, Murray Fern was docile, tamed by the jailor who knew that this soft wealthy white man could be subdued as easily as a black pimp could be mastered by the threat to book his flash money as evidence. As easily as a fighting derelict could be pacified simply by calling him "sir" and "mister." Elwood Banks had never set foot in a college classroom, but life had made him a psychologist.

"Wanna use the phone now, Murray?" Elwood Banks asked when he finished the fingerprinting and offered Murray Fern a cigarette.

"Yes sir," said Murray Fern, who was ever so grateful to the black jailor for giving him his silk underwear with the little hearts, a cigarette and a dime for a phone call.

After booking Murray Fern, Spencer longed to get up to Wilshire Boulevard and eat liver pâté and poached turbot with sautéed cucumbers. But Father Willie made the mistake of clearing on the radio and they were given a call at once. "Seven-A-Thirty-three, Seven-Adam-Thirty-three, see the woman, Eleventh and Ardmore, possible DB."

"A dead body, at eleven fifteen! Goddamnit, Padre, how many times I told you about picking up that frigging mike and clearing?"

"I know, Spencer, I know," Willie answered.

"You're too goddamn conscientious!"

"I know."

"Wait'll you been on the job awhile. You think the sergeants care we bust our balls? You think that cunt Lieutenant Finque cares?"

"I know, Spencer, I know."

"Christ, I got a headache already. All that jawing from that fat prick, Murray Fern. My head aches and I'm sick to my stomach."

"I know."

"I didn't get my vichyssoise tonight, for chrissake."

"I'm sorry."

"I didn't get my veau à la crème."

"There's nothing I can do . . ."

"And I had my heart set on maybe some Coquilles St. Jacques Parisienne!" Spencer cried.

"Is that the one with scallops, garlic and herbs?"

"No that's Provençale. This is the one with scallops and mushrooms."

"In a white wine sauce?"

"Yeah."

"I like that one."

"And I had my heart set on some artichoke hearts and truffles!" Spencer continued. "Oh God!"

"I'm really awful sorry, Spencer," Father Willie said.

"When you started working with me you thought all menus were printed on the wall. I trained you!" reminded Spencer Van Moot.

"I know, Spencer, I know."

"And this is the thanks I get. All because you're so goddamn gung ho and have to pick up the mike and clear. Now I gotta smell a dead body instead of a soufflé au chocolat! Oh God!"

"I'll make it up to you, Spencer," promised Father Willie, wondering when he was going to learn to act like a veteran.

A wizened crone in a black dress and dirty sweatsocks was drinking beer on the porch of a two story frame house just south of the corner. She waved as Spencer flashed their spotlight around, hoping not to find the caller.

Spencer lagged behind disgustedly as they parked, and gathered up his flashlight and hat slowly. He always put the hat on while looking in the rearview mirror so as not to disturb the hairstyle.

"Yes, ma'am?" Father Willie turned his light on the porch steps as the old woman drained the can without getting out of her rocking chair. She steamed like dank mulching weeds.

"Think my tenant's dead in the basement," the old woman grinned in triumph.

"What makes you think . . . uh, oh," said Spencer as he got to the top step of the porch and smelled the tenant who made them forget the old woman's putrescence.

"When did you discover him?" Father Willie asked, as Spencer sneered, thinking he would have to endure this instead of peach Melba.

"Ain't seen him in about three days. Thought he moved out without paying the rent. Sort of discovered him, you might say, about an hour ago when the wind started stirring things around."

Spencer sighed and nodded and led Father Willie through the musty hallway of the boardinghouse which was partitioned off to accommodate seven single men. They found the basement door slightly ajar.

"Wonder if that witch is drinking beer or bat milk?" Spencer remarked.

"He's down there all right," Father Willie said, almost retching as they tried the stairs.

Then Spencer found the light switch and led Father Willie down the ancient wooden stairway where next to a gravity-heat furnace they found the tenant hanging from the ceiling joists, his knees almost dragging the ground.

"Kee-rist!" Spencer said, forgetting the overpowering smell for a moment.

The neck of the hanging man was almost ten inches long and the dragging legs formed a bridge for a column of ants which trooped up his legs to his face and ears and nose where they nested and fed with a velvety spider. And there were wounds on the man's neck which Father Willie realized were rat bites after he saw the mounds of droppings on the floor beneath the hanging man.

"Wonder how long he's been hanging around here?" Spencer quipped to his little partner who had a handkerchief pressed to his nose.

"He probably reached the end of his rope," Spencer said, but Father Willie didn't hear Spencer's gags.

Willie Wright had not seen that many dead men in his three year police career and he was struck by the youth of this man and by the swollen hands darkened by draining blood and by the gray face which looked as if it belonged in a wax cabinet. And though the elongated neck shocked him, because he did not dream it could happen like this, he was most shocked because for the first time in twenty-four years Father Willie Wright realized something. He looked at that one dull eye open and truly believed that he would join the waxen hanging man. That they were brothers going somewhere. Or nowhere.

It was just a young man consciously coming to a basic truth for the first time. But Father Willie, not knowing the source of his fear, became very frightened by the hunk of fat in his belly and had a hard time keeping Spencer Van Moot from noticing.

This was the night that Father Willie Wright encouraged the others to go to choir practice. It was the first time Father Willie had been the prime mover.

And later that very night, perhaps because of the hanging man, Father Willie Wright was to become a beloved MacArthur Park choirboy for what he did to put that hoity toity bitch, Officer Reba Hadley, in her place.

There were two Officer Hadleys, no relation, in Wilshire Division: Phillip Hadley, a policeman on the daywatch, and Reba Hadley, the policewoman on the nightwatch. So as to know which Hadley one was talking about, the other officers referred to them as Balls Hadley and No-Balls Hadley.

No-Balls Hadley was on the nightwatch desk. She had been in the department two years, had an M.A. in Business Administration from UCLA, and believed that the brass of the department was discriminating against women by not promoting them past the rank of sergeant. And by humiliating women in forcing them to undergo the same police training as the men. She felt it was degrading and ludicrous that women in patrol assignments had to wear short hair and a man's uniform complete to the trousers and hat, obviously an attempt by the brass to discourage those women who had been forced on them. Of course she was right.

She also vociferously proclaimed that it took little or no brains or administrative ability to wrestle a pukey drunk into a radio car, to chase and subdue a burglar in an alley or to drive a high speed chase after some joyriding bubblegummer. She was again right.

No-Balls Hadley, who was sometimes called Dickless Tracy, was also right when she declared fearlessly at a policewomen's meeting attended by chauvinist spies for Commander Moss that he, as well as most high ranking officers of the department, had little or no street experience and had advanced quickly through the ranks because they could pass exams, not because they were street cops.

So No-Balls Hadley was considered a rabble-rouser and troublemaker by those high ranking members of the Los Angeles Police Department who believed that women had *some* value in rape cases, juvenile investigations and public relations. But otherwise should keep their big fat insecure libber mouths shut because they were probably bull dykes at heart and were out to steal men's jobs. No-Balls Hadley knew that the brass was not about to give up those jobs since they had kissed so many asses to get them.

In short, No-Balls Hadley was intelligent, articulate, courageous and correct most of the time. She was utterly feminine, with long shapely legs, tapering fingers, honey colored bobbed hair, naturally jutting young breasts. She was also discriminating in the men she dated, preferring professional men of breeding and affluence, thus dashing the hopes of every policeman on the Wilshire nightwatch. For this reason she was considered an insufferable bitch and it took the person who loved her more than anyone on earth to put her in her place.

It happened after work at 2:00 A.M. on the night Father Willie found the brother in the basement. Father Willie was dozing drunkenly at choir practice in MacArthur Park when Spencer Van Moot grabbed the little man by the jaws.

"Leave me alone, Spencer," Willie squeaked while his partner held him by the chin, saying, "Get up, Padre. Goddamnit, wake up!"

"The hanging man!" Father Willie cried in confusion as the earth heaved. "The hanging man!"

"Never mind the hanging man," Spencer said. "Bloomguard and Niles just showed up. They been at a party at Sergeant Yanov's apartment. We're all going over there."

"No, no," Father Willie moaned, and tried to lie back down on his blanket but Spencer wouldn't have it.

Father Willie was the last choirboy to arise. The others were already gunning their car motors, turning on lights, driving toward the apartment near Fourth and Bronson where the bachelor sergeant resided. Though Yanov wisely declined choir practice invitations, he occasionally threw an impromptu party of his own.

"Come on, Padre," Spencer said, dragging the little man to his feet, careful not to get any of the duck slime from Willie's checkered bermuda shorts on his fifty-five dollar tie dyed jeans with the needlepoint patches which he had bought at a police discount from a men's store on Beverly Boulevard. "Father Willie, listen! No-Balls Hadley's there!"

And Father Willie's swollen eyelids cracked apart. The little man shook his thin wheat-colored hair out of his eyes, shot a hopeful grin at his partner and took his arm as Spencer led him to the car on Parkview Street just south of Wilshire.

"You sobering up?" Spencer asked as he drove them in Father Willie's station wagon, a five year old Dodge with a "God Is Love" bumper sticker on front and back.

"Yes," said Father Willie who was getting drunker with each bump and rumble, catching fire with a consuming passionate gut wrenching love for No-Balls Hadley whom he never discussed while sober.

He had succeeded in driving away his sweet obsessive fantasies except for those infrequent moments when his Jehovah's Witness wife would consent to a five minute straight lay without too much annoying foreplay. At those times it was not the plump little Witness he was mounting, but Officer Reba Hadley, No-Balls Hadley of the splendid breasts, elegant legs and caustic tongue who never so much as glanced at little Father Willie Wright when he passed the desk and screwed up enough courage to say, "Good afternoon" or "Good evening" or "The desk pretty busy tonight?"

She would sometimes mumble a perfunctory reply when not busy with a ringing phone or routine report which she felt beneath her to write in the first place. But once, as she leaned on the counter chatting into the telephone, dressed in the tailored blue long sleeved blouse and fitted skirt of a desk officer, instead of a man's uniform like a female patrol officer, she asked Father Willie if he would mind getting her a soft drink from the machine because she had three crime reports going and couldn't leave the phone.

Father Willie Wright dropped his pocket change all over the floor in his haste to get the coins in the machine and was careful not to spill a single drop as he set it before No-Balls Hadley as reverently as any real priest ever offered a chalice at the altar.

No-Balls Hadley said into the phone, "Look, Madge, we have to have the nerve to walk into the chief's office and say what we think. Of course he hates our guts but he's afraid of us now. We've got the media with us. Damn it, Madge, what've we got to lose? You think I want to spend a career standing at this desk writing bike reports and making inane small talk to a bunch of semiliterate slobs?"

One of the semiliterate slobs of whom she spoke stood shyly across the counter, the large gap in his front teeth bared to No-Balls Hadley who had forgotten he was there until she saw the dime still on the counter in front of her.

"Just a minute, Madge," she said testily into the mouthpiece, then held her hand over it and said, "Officer . . ."

"Wright," Father Willie said. "Willie Wright's my name!"

"Yes, of course," she said impatiently. "You think I don't know every man on the nightwatch? I've only been chained to this desk six months. I ought to know."

"Oh sure," said Father Willie, who was so plain, so small, so unassuming that she could never remember his name.

"Listen, Wright, did you want something?"

"Oh no," Father Willie said to the tall girl while his mad impetuous young heart longed to say, "Oh yes! Oh yes, Reba! Oh yes!"

He had never called her "Reba," never once in the six months she had been in Wilshire Division after being transferred from Parker Center where she tried to stage a policewomen's work slowdown.

"Well, what do you want then, Wright? How about taking your dime and excusing me? I have this important call."

"Sure, Officer Hadley." Father Willie reddened and turned awkwardly.

"Just a minute, Wright. Take your dime for the drink."

"Oh no," Willie mumbled. "It's my pleasure. Honestly, I . . ."

"Take the dime," said No-Balls Hadley, her eyes narrowing as she momentarily forgot the phone she held pressed in her hands.

"Really, it's my . . ."

"Look, buster," No-Balls Hadley said, "I pay my own way just like every officer in this station. I don't need you to buy my Bubble-up. Now you take this dime!"

Father Willie snatched the dime in his sweaty hand, scurried down the steps to the parking lot, got in the radio car and roared out onto Venice Boulevard.

"What's the matter with you?" Spencer had asked, seeing Father Willie's brick red face.

"Nothing. Nothing."

Father Willie had vowed to forget No-Balls Hadley but found to his shame and dismay that she was even more desirable.

When Spencer and Father Willie arrived at the party at Sergeant Yanov's apartment, Willie had not been thinking of his previous unsuccessful encounter with No-Balls Hadley. His gin ravaged brain would not admit those warnings and fears which keep most men from achieving celebrity.

When Father Willie Wright set foot in that raucous smoke filled steamy apartment he was roaring drunk. He squirmed past sweaty bodies which danced wall to wall in the suffocating rooms. The party spilled out onto the balcony and even extended to the pool where at least a dozen clerks from Wilshire and Rampart and Hollywood stations swam bikini clad while goatish policemen swam naked until the apartment house manager threatened to call the police—the ones with clothes on. The men then swam in their underwear or trousers until the manager scurried back inside then stripped again.

Father Willie's protuberant blue eyes were red and raw by the time he bumped his way through the crowd. The smoke was making him slightly sick and defeated when he heard it coming from the bedroom. Her voice!

"Listen, Sheila," she was saying to Officer Sheila Franklin, a personable brunette who worked Juvenile at Central, "I want to leave right this minute and I don't care if you *are* worried about Nick Yanov's feelings. Damn it, he should control these stupid disgusting drunks if he expects people to stay at the party. Of course I got out of the pool! I'm not staying there while these pea brained chest beaters swim around nude! I'm not interested in Sergeant Nick Yanov or any of these creeps and I only came here because you . . ."

And as Father Willie strained to hear the voice of his secret love, Francis Tanaguchi abruptly changed the tape from Elton John to The Carpenters because he had finally managed to get a dance with Ida Keely, a cute communications operator with eyes like a deer. He had a blue veiner even before the song began.

> *Lookin back on how it was in years gone by and the*
> *good times that I had*
> *Makes today seem rather sad*
> *so much has changed.*

Officer Sheila Franklin sighed, stood and made her way out of the cluttered bedroom where most of the living room furniture had been pushed to make room for the dancers. She stopped before opening the door and said, "All right, Reba, I've asked you to be sociable and stay a little while because you know how I feel about Nick Yanov. But if you have to go . . ."

"I can call a cab. You stay."

"Damn it, Reba, I brought you here. I'll take you back to your car. But you know something? It's *not* a rough party. They're just dancing and . . ."

"I was practically mauled in the swimming pool!"

"One drunk grabbed your ass. Come on, Reba, you're a cop too, for God's sake. They're just a little drunk."

"I'll call a cab."

"No, no, no, I'll tell Nick we're leaving. Go ahead and change."

And then as Father Willie ducked into the bathroom the partially opened bedroom door swung open and Sheila Franklin, still wearing her wet bikini under a blue terry cloth robe, crossed the hallway and went out a side door which opened onto a terrace where Sergeant Nick Yanov sat playing nickel and dime poker with five other policemen.

> *It was songs of love that I would sing to them*
> *And I'd memorize each word.*
> *Those old melodies still sound so good to me*
> *As they melt the years away.*

No-Balls Hadley still sat where Sheila Franklin had left her. On a large glass coffee table. In her wet bathing suit. A short robe she had borrowed from Nick Yanov covered her sleek flesh as Father Willie Wright quietly pushed open the door behind her.

The sound of No-Balls Hadley's voice. The heart searing voice of Karen Carpenter. The unbearable nostalgia of his high school days. Twelve ounces of gin fermenting in his young bloodstream. Father Willie Wright had very little to do with what happened next. Seldom has a legend been born more spontaneously.

All my best memories come back clearly to me,
Some can even make me cry—just like before.
It's yesterday once more.

First, Father Willie tried to formulate a perfect sentence: something tender, loving, endearing but he could not. He leaned against the wall, unseen behind No-Balls Hadley. Breathing became labored. Nostrils flared. Bulging eyes rolled back in unbearable ecstasy and passion. Like Byron on the Acropolis.

Ev'ry sha-la-la-la, ev'ry wo-oh-wo-oh still shines
Ev'ry shing-a-ling-ling that they're startin' to sing so fine.

He knew instinctively that this was his moment. His life had led him here. Behind her where she sat perched on the glass table, pissed off at her friend Sheila Franklin and these swinish policemen and men in general. And no man could have stopped what happened next when, still wearing the short robe, she slipped off her bikini bottom and kicked it against the wall in a wet and angry plop.

The coffee table was suddenly cold on the bare buttocks of No-Balls Hadley and she tried to tuck the robe under her as she thought again of that fat hairy ugly pig, Spermwhale Whalen, and how he had tried to dive under the water and grab her by the ass. As she sat fuming on the glass coffee table, Father Willie Wright knew he was not worthy to touch this exquisite golden girl who had filled his young life with torment and guilt.

Ev'ry sha-la-la-la, ev'ry wo-oh-wo-oh still shines
Ev'ry shing-a-ling-ling that they're startin' to sing so fine . . .

Father Willie Wright found himself on his knees crawling across the red carpet. Without willing it he was on his back worming forward under the glass table.

Then No-Balls Hadley thought she heard something. A sound, wet and sticky. But with the noise in the living room she dismissed it and smoldered and waited for her friend, determined not even to go in the other room to get her clothes. She would let Sheila bring them to her. She wouldn't risk an encounter with another drunken cop.

She heard the sound again. Louder. A smacking sound, close but somehow distant. Then she heard it directly beneath her! She uncrossed her legs and spread them and looked down in horror at the white and bloodless nose and lips of Father Willie Wright pressed against the underside of the glass table, smearing the glass directly beneath her bare bottom with wet and loving kisses while his blue eyes crossed and bulged from the meticulous maddening scrutiny of the golden twat of his beloved.

No-Balls Hadley screamed. She shrieked in consummate disgust as Father Willie Wright, unaware that she was gone from the glass, still slurped tenderly and vaguely wondered what someone was yelling about.

No-Balls Hadley screamed. And screamed.

Before the first three policemen had burst through the door Father Willie realized that something was wrong, his face pressed like a fish against the smeary wet glass, eyes popping. Then Father Willie understood that he was discovered.

"God love ya!" Father Willie whispered reverently just before No-Balls Hadley picked up a huge ceramic lamp and smashed it down on the tempered glass while all hell broke loose around the confused and troubled choirboy chaplain.

Then someone pulled him out from under the table to save him while No-Balls Hadley grabbed a three iron from the golf bag of Sergeant Nick Yanov and began breaking chunks from the glass. Father Willie went skidding across the floor, Spencer Van Moot dragging him by the heels.

Someone wrestled the three iron from No-Balls Hadley who yelled, "You filthy disgusting obscene little motherfucker! I'll kill you!"

She tore a picture from the wall and threw it crashing through the bedroom window to the terrace outside where it thudded against the side of the head of a poker player, sending him to the emergency ward for five stitches.

No-Balls Hadley, minus her robe which had been pulled away by a policeman trying to restrain her, clad only in a green bikini top, began beating Father Willie Wright back against the sliding closet door and kicking him in the soft belly.

Then she was sitting on top of Father Willie, pummeling him with both fists as he covered his little face with both arms saying, "But I love you, Officer Hadley. Don't you see?"

Finally, Sergeant Nick Yanov, one of the few sober policemen at the party, overpowered the spitting kicking cursing policewoman and dragged her still naked into the other bedroom where Officer Sheila Franklin got her in a wristlock until she fell exhausted, blurting what Father Willie had done.

As the bleeding bewildered Father Willie Wright was being carried to his car by Spencer Van Moot and Harold Bloomguard, he turned his battered face to Harold Bloomguard and said, "What'd I do wrong, Harold? What'd I do?"

"I'll tell you what you did, Padre! You put that hoity-toity bitch No-Balls Hadley in her place, is all!" Harold Bloomguard cried proudly as they carried Father Willie down the sidewalk. "You just became a Legend in Your Own Time!"

From that day on, in choirboy folklore, the episode of No-Balls Hadley became known as The Night the Padre Tried to Eat Pressed Ham Through the Wrapper.

7

7-A-77: Calvin Potts
and Francis Tanaguchi

A choir practice was certainly in order and was called for by Francis Tanaguchi on The Night the U-Boat Was Decommissioned. It was three months before the killing in MacArthur Park.

The night was bound to be an extraordinary one, beginning as it did with a noisy argument in which the nightwatch ganged up on Lieutenant Finque who was trying to defend the department's disciplinary policies to the rebellious assembly of bluesuited young men who thought he was full of shit.

"Look," the exasperated watch commander argued, "that West Los Angeles officer *deserved* thirty days off for what he did."

"Deserved? Deserved?" Spermwhale Whalen thundered. "His old man and his old man's old man owned that fuckin bar for thirty years. He grew up behind the bar."

"Department policy forbids policemen to engage in off-duty employment in places where alcoholic beverages . . ."

"What would *you* do if your old man was pressed for a bartender for a couple weeks?"

"He *only* got thirty days."

"Only? *Only!* Take thirty days' pay off me and I'd starve to death. So would my ex-wives and my ex-kids and my turtle. Where the fuck else does a guy get fined for somethin he does durin nonworkin hours that don't violate no laws?"

"Professional sports," said Lieutenant Finque.

"They can afford it, we can't," Spermwhale shot back. "All I can say is I'm glad I got my twenty in next January. I'm gonna start speakin my mind then."

"The lieutenant needs that like a dose of clap," said Sergeant Nick Yanov, who winked at Spermwhale.

"Fuckin pussies run this outfit," Spermwhale growled, settling down a little under the placating grin of Sergeant Yanov. "I know why all the brass downtown go up to Chinatown for lunch. They operate this fuckin department from the fortune cookies."

"Well, what say we read the crimes?" Sergeant Yanov asked, much to the relief of Lieutenant Finque who feared gross and ugly and dangerous old cops like Spermwhale Whalen. Lieutenant Finque could never seem to reason with them.

"Here's one on Virginia Road where a housewife invented a do it yourself antiburglary kit," Nick Yanov said, rubbing his bristling chin as he read. "She's an invalid who stays in bed all day with a Colt .38 under her pillow. Blew up a burglar the other day when he opened the kitchen window and tippy-toed in. Her *second.*"

After everyone finished cheering, Sergeant Yanov looked at the clock and said, "Not much time left. Here's a mug shot of that dude the dicks want for shanking his old lady. Cut her long, deep and continuous. Hangs around the poolroom on Adams."

"Hey, Sarge," Spencer Van Moot said, "I'm getting tired of all these station calls to the old broad lives on West Boulevard. Doesn't the desk officer know she's a dingaling? She always wants to know things like where does she buy a crash helmet big enough for her thirty-five year old epileptic son who keeps falling on his head."

"Only takes a minute," Sergeant Yanov said. "Her boy's been dead for five years. Makes the old woman feel good talking to a big good looking blond like you, Spencer. You probably remind her of him."

"Well she's not my type and I got better things to do," Spencer answered, and then he got mad as the assembly room exploded into hoots and laughter because everyone but Lieutenant Finque knew that Spencer's better things to do were bargain hunting on Wilshire Boulevard.

"It's time we hit the streets," Lieutenant Finque repeated, since he believed that a lieutenant should never let a sergeant, especially one as lenient as Nick Yanov, take over the rollcall.

Unquestionably, the biggest pain in the ass on the night-watch at Wilshire Station was Francis Tanaguchi. He was twenty-five years old, a third generation Japanese-American who grew up in the barrio of East Los Angeles and spoke good street Spanish but not a word of Japanese. He adored guacamole, chile relleno, barbacoa, menudo, albondigas soup and tequila with anything. He hated sushi, tempura, teriyaki steak, sake and could not operate a pair of chopsticks to save his life.

As a teenage member of a Chicano youth gang he had spray-painted "Peewee Raiders" on more walls than any other gang member. Still, he was never totally accepted by Mexican boys who lumped all Orientals together by invariably nicknaming them "Chino" or "Chink." Francis fought to be called "Francisco" or at least "Pancho" but settled for "Chink-ano." It stayed with him until he joined the Los Angeles Police Department at the age of twenty-one.

Gradually he found it was advantageous to be Japanese. There were many Mexican-American policemen but there were few Japanese-American policemen, even though Los Angeles has the largest Japanese-American population in California.

Sometimes Francis and his black partner, Calvin Potts, had profound philosophical discussions about their ethnic roots.

"So now if I wanna get somewhere in the department I gotta be a Buddhahead," Francis moaned to his partner.

"You think you got problems?" Calvin remarked. "How about me? How'd you like to be a brother in your paddy world, huh?"

"Who said I'm a paddy for chrissake?" Francis answered. "Goddamnit, I'm a Mexican."

"You're a Nip, Francis," Calvin reminded him.

"So quit calling me a paddy."

"You all look alike."

"It's goddamn hard becoming a Jap when you're my age. I been at it four years now and I still can't take a picture or mow a lawn straight."

"You think you got it rough," Calvin said. "How'd you like to have other policemen put you down when you date a white chick. How'd you like that, Francis?"

"I ain't seen it stop you yet, Calvin."

"That's because I'm drunk when I date a white chick. I get drunk to stop the hurt."

"You get drunk when you date *any* chick. In fact, everybody knows you're an alcoholic, for chrissake."

"I'm only an alcoholic because it dulls the hurtin," said Calvin.

"How'd you like to get sick to your stomach every time you look a fish head in the eye?"

"I *do* get sick to my stomach every time I look a fish head in the eye."

"Yeah, but that asshole Lieutenant Finque ain't trying to duke you into the Oriental community by using you as a part time community relations officer at Japanese luncheons where you force down three raw squid and puke all the way to Daniel Freeman Hospital afterward."

"That's all in your head, that reaction to Nip soul food."

"That's the worst place to be sick—in the head. And that prick Lieutenant Finque is doing it to me."

"We'll talk to the guys at the next choir practice. Roscoe or one a those whackos'll think up some way to fix his ass."

Calvin Potts, at twenty-eight, was three years older than Francis Tanaguchi and had been a policeman two years longer. He was tall, athletic, divorced, the son of a Los Angeles bail bondsman. He had been raised in Baldwin Hills when there were only a few black families on the hill. He had dated girls and women of all colors all his life. In truth he seldom had any trouble with racial slur. It wouldn't have bothered him much if he had. He was an alcoholic because his father was an alcoholic, as was a brother, a sister, two uncles and numerous cousins. He came from a hard drinking family. He had been a Scotch drinker at sixteen. He was also an alcoholic because he was insane about his ex-wife, Martha Twogood Potts, whose father was one of the most successful black trial lawyers in Los Angeles.

Martha Twogood Potts had decided in the second year of their marriage, after several reasonably successful sexual encounters with more marriageable men, that she had been goofy to marry a no-account cop. She scooped Calvin Jr. out of the crib and called her daddy who convinced a Superior Court judge that it would not be unreasonable for Officer Calvin Potts to pay child support and alimony equal to thirty-five percent of his net pay. This left fifteen percent for the car payment, twenty-five percent for food, twenty percent for gas and car repairs, and forty percent for an enormous personal loan he incurred getting started lavishly in married life. Since the total outlay was 135 percent, Calvin remedied the situation by letting the Mercedes be repossessed and buying a second-hand gearless Schwinn bicycle which he rode back and forth to work. He then divided the twenty-five percent food allowance into two equal parts, half for food and half for booze, and discovered that twelve and a half percent of a policeman's net salary would not buy enough booze for even an average alcoholic. So he moved in with a girl known as Lottie LaFarb, a part time telephone operator who made certain calls on company time which earned her up to two hundred dollars a night when she got home.

Calvin Potts had been working with Francis Tanaguchi for six months and they had become inseparable. Calvin could not begin to understand this since he hated people in general and Francis Tanaguchi was by all odds the biggest pain in the ass at Wilshire Station. But there it was. They were always together. Everyone called them The Gook and The Spook.

There were several very good reasons why Francis Tanaguchi was such an enormous pain in the ass. He did annoying things, some of which were cyclical, some more or less permanent. One of the permanent annoying things he was accused of doing was arranging calls to the other choirboys' residences at 4:00 A.M. A mysterious woman with a lasciviously voluptuous voice would begin to talk as the sleepy choirboy was coming awake in the darkness. The listener would be treated to a low crooning lush sexual litany which could transform almost any old three ounce cylinder of flesh, vein and muscle into a diamond cutter. Though it was generally suspected that Francis Tanaguchi was responsible for these bizarre calls, it was never proved and he never admitted it. Drunk and sober, Calvin Potts had begged threatened and bribed him to no avail.

No one had ever seen the Dragon Lady, as they had come to call the owner of the voice. And no one had ever been able to hang up once she was into her routine. All had wet dreams about her. The wife of Spencer Van Moot had left him for the third time when she, on another phone extension, heard the erotic, blood boiling promises.

Perhaps the greatest harm was done to Father Willie Wright one night as his fat dumpling of a wife lay snoring beside him. Father Willie answered the phone and sat galvanized in the darkness while the Dragon Lady promised to use her body and Willie's in a way that any reasonable man should have known was physically impossible. But Father Willie was not reasonable at this moment. He was gulping, dizzy, disoriented. He was speechless and frenzied. The Dragon Lady began making incredibly luxurious, unwholesome, juicy noises. Then she hung up.

Father Willie lay there for a moment then fell on the sleeping Jehovah's Witness who only tolerated sex when she was awake and prepared for it.

The next afternoon before roll call, Father Willie Wright, his left eye blood red from a desperate blow by a chubby little fist in the night, waited at Francis Tanaguchi's locker and challenged him to a fight to the death in the basement of Wilshire Police Station. Calvin Potts and several other officers interceded while Francis professed total innocence. Father Willie was led into the rollcall room swallowing tears of rage, swearing for the very first time in anyone's memory.

"Ya fuck, ya!" yelled Father Willie. "Ya dirty slant-eyed heathen godless little fuck, ya!"

Francis Tanaguchi had other annoying habits, not the least

of which was biting people on the neck. It started when Francis went to a shabby Melrose Boulevard movie house where they were offering a Bela Lugosi Film Festival to a college crowd which hooted and yelled and smoked pot and ate popcorn.

Francis was with a chilly clerk typist named Daphne Simon who worked the morning watch at Wilshire Records and seldom dated policemen because she felt they were too horny. Francis had won her heart by sending a thirty dollar floral arrangement which he had gotten free by stopping at a Japanese nursery near Crenshaw Boulevard and thrilling the immigrant proprietors with his blue clad Oriental body. Francis had only planned to try to get them to bounce for a handful of violets, but when he saw how delighted they were with him, he promoted the soft multicolored carnations.

As he sat in the smoke filled movie house, Daphne Simon roughly pulled his hand out from between her legs every time he let it accidentally fall there. It made him wish he had saved the flowers for Ora Lee Tingle at choir practice. Francis Tanaguchi came to dislike Daphne Simon who was in some exotic way giving him a blue veiner by squeezing his hand saucily before she slammed it down on the wooden armrest between the seats. But if he was starting to dislike Daphne Simon he was falling in love with Bela Lugosi.

"You wanna go where, Francis?" Calvin Potts squinted, when Francis settled into the black and white the next afternoon.

"To that big costume store on Western," Francis repeated.

"You goin to a masquerade?"

"No."

"I know, you're gonna buy a polar bear suit for you and Ora Lee to wear while you flog each other with dead baby ducks at the next choir practice."

"I'm gonna buy some fangs," Francis said simply.

For three weeks, which was about as long as one of Francis' whims lasted, he was called the Nisei Nipper by the policemen at Wilshire Station. He skulked around the station with two blood dripping fangs slipped over his incisors, attacking the throat of everyone below the rank of sergeant.

"It was okay for a while," Spencer Van Moot complained to Calvin Potts one day. "But those frigging teeth hurt. And it starts to get really depressing having Francis draped around your neck all the time."

And even as he spoke Francis leaped from behind a wall and onto Spencer's back, nipping him on the neck with the gory plastic fangs.

Sam Niles finally came to work with a bullet painted silver and let Francis see him putting it in his gun.

Harold Bloomguard hung parsley over his locker and told Francis it was wolfsbane. Then Whaddayamean Dean, and finally everyone else, started carrying crosses to ward off the Oriental vampire who would hiss and snarl when a cross was produced and slink back to his locker until he spotted someone with his back turned.

Spermwhale Whalen finally grabbed Francis by the collar and said, "There's so fuckin many crosses around this locker room it looks like a platoon a nuns' dresses here. Francis, I'm gonna stick those goofy teeth right up your skinny ass if you don't knock it off!"

"Okay. I'm getting sick and tired of tasting all these crummy necks anyway," Francis said, and the vampire returned to earth permanently.

The night that Francis got bloody hands and decommissioned the U-boat was a smoggy evening in late spring. It started as usual with Calvin complaining that he always drove.

"Looky here, Francis, I been on the job longer than you, and I been on this miserable earth longer and I don't know why the fuck I let you jive me around like this."

"Like what?"

"Like drivin you around like a fuckin chauffeur every night."

"I write better English than you so you should drive while I should keep books."

"You what? You write half the time like some ignorant wetback. You didn't learn no English in those Chicano East L.A. schools."

"Well you drive better than me."

"Bullshit. You ever seen a brother drivin at Indianapolis?"

"You ever seen a Buddhahead driving? Every cop knows a Buddhahead is a worse driver even than a brother."

"Tomorrow you drive."

"I can't. I don't want nobody to see me with glasses on. They make me look like an Iwo Jima sniper. It embarrasses me."

"I never seen you with glasses."

"I only wear them when I wanna see."

"And we been partners all this time and you never wanted to see?"

"There's nothing on this job I wanna see, Calvin. The only time I put em on is when other guys take em off. I put em on to get laid. That's all I wanna see anymore."

"Do you put em on at choir practice when you ball Ora Lee Tingle or Carolina Moon?"

"No, that's another thing I don't wanna see."

Then Calvin started getting sullen. It came over him more frequently of late and he was drinking more than ever before. He had been forcing himself lately to stop thinking of that bitch, Martha Twogood Potts and her sleek caramel flesh. But he could not repress his thoughts of Calvin Jr. and how the toddler hardly knew him now and did not even want to be with his father on weekends. And how he truly *didn't* want the boy with him in the apartment of Lottie LaFarb, even though she was a kind-hearted telephone operator and barely a prostitute and lavished him with pussy and what money she had and loved Calvin Jr. unequivocally.

Sometimes he wanted to beat the shit out of Lottie LaFarb and Francis Tanaguchi, the only two people in the world who, he felt, gave a damn whether or not he stuck that Smith K-38 in his mouth and blew the top of his skull all over the tobacco stained plastic headliner in that black and white Matador which at the moment smelled of urine and vomit from the drunk the daywatch had booked near end-of-watch.

Calvin Potts' surging anger was broken when the honey voice the choirboys had come to love said, "Seven-A-Seventy-seven, Seven-A-Seventy-seven, see the woman, family dispute at the bar, Adams and Cloverdale."

"That's us, Calvin," Francis said jauntily, jotting the call on the pad affixed to the hotsheet holder on the dashboard.

"Well, roger it then, goddamnit," Calvin said viciously.

"Seven-A-Seventy-seven, roger," Francis said, looking at his partner whose coffee face was polished by the dipping hazy sunlight as they drove west at dusk. "What're you pissed off at, Calvin?"

"Nothin. I'm just gettin sick and tired a workin this car. Why can't we go back up to the north end next month?"

"We can. I thought you wanted action."

"I'm sick a action. I'm sick a these eastside trashy niggers that've took over this area down here. I'd rather work the Fairfax beat. I could easier put up with all the Hebes in Kosher Canyon chippin their teeth every time you give them a ticket."

"Okay. We'll talk to the boss about working a north end car next month. I know what you need."

"What?"

"A little trim."

"Oh yeah, just what I need," said Calvin looking skyward for a disgusted instant.

"I know Lottie's taking care of your everyday needs but I got a special one just moved in my apartment building. Meant to tell you about her."

"The Dragon Lady?" Calvin said suddenly, and for a moment he felt the depression subside a bit.

"Now, Calvin, you know I don't know any more about the Dragon Lady than you guys," said Francis, with his attempt at an inscrutable mysterious Oriental grin.

"Well, what's she like?"

"Better than that lanky one we met at the party in the Hollywood Hills."

"She better be."

"Too bad you didn't score with that one."

"Yeah, well she woulda came on in if it wasn't for that lawyer throwin his wallet open every two minutes showin all that bread. People just wear me down when they start that bull-shit."

"It's all he has going for him," Francis observed.

"I bet she woulda got up off some pussy if I coulda showed a few fifty dollar bills."

"If you gotta buy it it ain't worth it."

"I *woulda* bought it that night. I was hurtin for certain. She had me by the joint, you know."

"Sure."

"I told you that, didn't I?"

"Another alcoholic fantasy, Calvin. You better come down off that Johnnie Walker bottle you're living in."

"Listen, you slant eyed little fenderhead, I'm tellin you she was lopin my mule under the table."

"Calvin, you were so bombed that night even the Dragon Lady couldn't've given you a blue veiner. I mean a black veiner."

"Now *you're* wearin me down, Francis."

"I just ain't going for it, Calvin."

Calvin Potts was glaring at Francis and almost failed to stand on the brakes in time to keep from broadsiding a dilapidated ten year old Pontiac which had limped onto Adams Boulevard from the driveway of Elmer's Barbeque Kitchen which was one half block from the family dispute call.

"Gud-damn!" Calvin yelled to the driver of the Pontiac who managed a frightened smile and gripped the steering wheel nervously with big dusty work-hard hands, his knuckles like walnuts.

"Whooo-eee!" the driver said and stopped in the traffic lane to wait a command from the black and white which pulled up on his right in the number two lane.

"A gud-damn, Mississippi-transplanted, chittlin eatin nigger," Calvin moaned as he switched on his red light and debated going to the call or writing a ticket first.

Francis settled it for him. "I'm up, Calvin."

"Okay, write him then,"

"I don't wanna write him, Calvin. He doesn't look like he can afford it."

"I'll write him then."

"I'm up. I'm giving up my turn on him. You write the next one."

"Sorry, Officer," the driver said as the black policeman glared at him. "I ain't used to Los Angeles traffic. I'm jist a country boy."

"Drive a tractor then, asshole!" Calvin yelled, switching off the red light and speeding to the call at Adams and Cloverdale where they found two bleary-eyed black women in print housedresses and shower shoes arguing in front of the bar.

"You call?" Francis asked, putting on his hat while Calvin merely shook his head and, cap in hand, followed the two women and Francis inside.

The two policemen found four other combatants all more or less allied against a thirtyish buxom mulatto woman who sat in a corner booth sipping a milkball and tearing at a fat stick of beef jerky.

"There's the bitch that's causin all this ruckus, Officer," said the bigger of the two women who had led them inside.

"Yeah, you hussy," said the other one before the beefeater could speak. "She been livin wif my uncle. My uncle jist up and passed away and she wanna do the funeral, and she think she be gittin the house and the car because this old man wif a brain like pigfeet made some kinda raggedy ass agreement she think is a legal will!"

"She spend all my uncle's bread on wine and beer," said a bony customer at the bar.

"Whadda you spend your old woman's bread on, bastard?" the buxom young woman answered. And then to Francis, "We was livin common law."

"They ain't no common law in this state, bitch," said the smaller of the two women who stepped toward the booth but was stopped by Calvin who walked in front of her.

"Lemme talk to you private," Calvin said and only then did she stop chewing beef jerky and follow the tall black policeman toward the silent jukebox in the corner of the bar.

"What's happenin here, baby?" Calvin asked when they were alone.

"Well see, I was this funky ol man's main momma. I give that man two a the best years he ever had. Ever time I turn aroun he was wantin some face scoldin. Baby, I got calluses on the inside of my mouth from that evil old fool. I woulda went steppin when he died but these people got on my case heavy the first day the ol man was dead. Shoot, I jist decided I was gonna stay and fight for what's mine."

"That all there is?"

"Nothin to it, baby," the woman said and smiled at Calvin for the first time, stepping in close and touching his chest with her swooping breasts.

Just then the man at the bar lurched forward drunkenly saying, "Don't you believe nothin this hussy says about my uncle. It's all a shuck. He was senile and she was usin that ol man."

The man was holding something in his arms pressed tightly against his ribs and in the gloom of the bar room it looked like a rusty bath towel. Then Calvin noticed it was leaking down onto the man's cracked leather wing tips and then to the grimy floor.

"Man, you're bleedin!"

"Yeah," the man said. "I is." And as though embarrassed, he pulled the filthy towel away and a mucous trickle spurted out of the puncture in his chest and ran down his rib cage to the floor. The wound bubbled and gaped a bit larger with every breath he took. "That bitch done it to me."

"Okay, bastard!" said the buxom heiress. "Now I'm gonna show em what you done to me!"

As she spoke she squirmed and wriggled and hiked her tight dress over her wobbly buttocks and displayed a soppy Kotex which had been pressed inside her blue panties to stem the flow of blood from an eight inch knife wound across the hip and stomach which peeled back flesh and fat and bared a sliver of gleaming hipbone.

"What the fuck is goin on?" Calvin exploded, waving Francis over and pointing at both ugly wounds.

"You said you wasn't gonna say nothin if I didn't say nothin, you funky ol devil!" the heiress complained.

"Well, he ast me, bitch. What was I gonna say, that I was holdin a pack a bloody meat in this here towel?"

"Did you get cut in the fracas?" Francis asked, shocked at the slash across her belly.

"No, bout five inches above it," the woman answered.

"So, who cut who?" Calvin demanded, disgusted because now they would have to make crime reports and likely book both antagonists in a "mutual combat" situation so common to ghetto policemen.

"I fell on a ice pick," the man said.

"Who cut *you?*" Francis asked the heiress.

"I fell on a butcher knife," she answered.

"Tell me somethin," the man said as Francis squinted in the bleak dusty light at the chest hole and finally stepped forward to watch the sinister little orifice blow and foam as the man breathed. "If somebody was to attack somebody wif a ice pick, and this here other somebody was to defend hisself wif a butcher knife, would this somebody wif a butcher knife go to jail?"

Before the policemen could answer, the heiress added, "And if this motherfuckin *dawg* of a lyin wino was really the one to attack a *woman* with a butcher knife and she had to defend *herself* with a ice pick, wouldn't this *woman* be a righteous victim of this other evil ol motherfucker? She wouldn't go to jail, would she?"

"Anybody else see this?" Francis asked, but everyone suddenly turned to his beer for some serious drinking.

"The detectives would book em both and let em hassle it out in court," Calvin scowled contemptuously. "And before it got to a court trial there'd be three continuances by the two defendants and in the end they'd both agree not to prosecute each other and it'd be a big motherfuckin waste of *my* time and the taxpayers' money."

"Kin you give me a ride to the hospital?" asked the heiress.

"You wanna make a crime report against him?"

"No."

"Take the bus," Calvin said. "The doctor'll sew you up for free. It's an emergency."

"Don't they send you a bill?" she asked, and finally tamped the Kotex compress back into place and squirmed the dress back down.

"Sure, but jist put it with the rest a your bills inside the hole in your shoe."

"Calvin, we better take *him* anyway," Francis said. "That's a chest puncture. This man's hurt bad."

"You wanna make a crime report against her?" asked Calvin.

"No," the man said and the breath made a rattling bubble on his chest and a soft pop when it burst.

"Groovy," Calvin said, heading for the door. "Jist take two aspirin and stay in bed tomorrow."

"He's hurt bad, Calvin." Francis had to run to catch his long striding partner outside on the sidewalk.

"Hey, jump back, Jack! I made my decision. I ain't fuckin with no more a these people. If they wanna rip each other from the lips to the hips, let em go head on!"

"He could die. His lung could collapse."

"You can't kill these niggers, Francis. I was broke in on the job by a cracker named Dixie Suggs who hated black people like you hate squid. He taught me you gotta practically cut off their heads and shrink em to kill the motherfuckers. Damn, let's work a north end car next month. I can take those big-mouth kikes better than niggers."

"Okay, Calvin, okay." Francis watched his partner for a moment before raising the hand mike to clear from the call.

They cruised, Calvin smoking quietly, until darkness settled. Then Calvin patted the breast pocket of his uniform and said, "Let's stop by Easy's and get some smokes."

Francis, who had been drinking heavily the night before, was dozing in his seat, his head bobbing on his chest every few seconds, his long black hair hanging over his thin face as small as a boy's.

"We get a call?" Francis asked, fumbling for the pencil in his shirt pocket.

"Go back to sleep, Francis. We didn't get no call."

Calvin made a lazy turn onto Venice Boulevard to the liquor store run by Easy Willis, a jolly black man who supplied two packs of cigarettes a day to each of the three cars patrolling the district around the clock. Easy felt that this would promote the reputation that cops came into Easy's at any time, thus discouraging the robbers and potential robbers who lived in the area.

The packs of cigarettes ensured that not only would the officers walk in once on each watch, but they would make it a point to shine the spotlight in the window every time they passed. In truth, a pack of cigarettes did make them drive by a bit more than they would have normally and a policeman's spotlight is most reassuring to liquor store and gas station proprietors in the ghetto. Many of whom have faced a gun and been slugged and attacked more than a squad of policemen and in fact have a far more physically dangerous occupation.

"Say, Calvin, what's shakin?" Easy grinned, as Calvin walked hatless into the store which was stocked wall to wall with beer, hard liquor and cheap wine. The ghetto dwellers were not dilettante drinkers.

"Aw right, aw right, Easy, my man," Calvin said, leaning on the counter while Easy slid three fifths of Scotch into a paper bag for a boozy black woman who had a child in her arms and another hanging from her dress.

Calvin looked around the store at the sagging liquor counters and the display shelves. Like most ghetto establishments the shelves held *no* candy bars or cigarettes because of juvenile shoplifting. Calvin glanced at the rows of skin magazines and then at the elaborate sprinkler system which the white owner of the store had installed in case there was ever another black riot in Los Angeles.

The proprietor, Lolly Herman, had owned a store in Watts which had been looted and fire-bombed in 1965. He feared another black rebellion more than any antebellum plantation owner. The proprietor had all windows barred and a silent robbery alarm button situated in five strategic locations in the store: behind the counter, in the restroom in case a thief would force him in there, in the cold storage locker if that should be where he was forced to go, near the back door of the store which led out into the yard that was enclosed by a ten foot chain link fence with five strands of barbed wire around the top, and finally in the money room which was just to the side of the counter and enclosed by ceiling high sheets of bulletproof glass. The door to the money room was electrically controlled as was the swinging wrought iron gate which protected the front door when the premises were secured at 2:00 A.M.

Perhaps more formidable than the lonely vicious Doberman which prowled the service yard at the rear and lay flea bitten in the blazing sunshine was the carbine that Mr. Herman had displayed on the wall inside the bulletproof money room to dissuade any thief who thought his protection was merely preventative.

Three weeks after he had finished every elaborate antirobbery and antiburglary device, he was sapped by a ninety pound teenager on roller skates when he was getting into his car after closing. Three thousand dollars were stolen from his socks and underwear.

After that, Lolly Herman, with eighteen sutures in his skull, stopped working at the liquor store, retired to his Beverly Hills home and let Easy Willis take over management of the store.

Of course, business was not as good. Easy and the other six employees could not be made to hustle without Lolly Herman watching them. They stole about a thousand a month among them to supplement their incomes, but the liquor store was still a gold mine and Mrs. Herman secretly thanked God that the ninety pound teenager, called Chipmunk Grimes, had coldcocked the old man and driven him into retirement.

"Momma made some souse and head cheese, Calvin," Easy said when the customer left. Then Easy flipped two packs of Camels on the counter without asking.

"Thanks but I don't eat much soul these days." Calvin put both packs in his pockets, glad that Francis didn't smoke.

Of course Easy knew that Francis didn't smoke but went along with the charade since they first came in the store together and Calvin said, "This is my new partner, Easy. His name's Francis and he smokes Camels just like me."

Two packs to a car is what Lolly Herman said to give, and Easy didn't give a damn whether it was to one cop or two. In fact, now that Lolly Herman had retired, Easy often popped for two *extra* packs, and knowing Calvin's drinking problem was reaching an acute stage, bounced for a fifth of Johnnie Walker Black Label once a week.

"Officer!" yelled a young black man in yellow knits as he burst into the store. "Some dude jist stole a radio out of a car there on La Brea!"

"How long ago?"

"Bout twenny minutes."

"How bout jist skatin on out to the car and wakin up my little partner. He'll take a report."

"Ain't you gonna try and catch him?"

"Man, twenty minutes? Sucker's halfway to Compton by now."

"He ain't from Compton. Wasn't no brother. He was a paddy long hair blondey like dude. I think he was one a them cats what works at that place down the street where they talks to you about a job but the oniest ones that's makin any money is the one talkin about the jobs, and they get it from the gov'-ment."

"Yeah, well we'll take a report," Calvin said blandly, "and since that job place is closed tonight the detectives'll check it out tomorrow."

"Oughtta keep the jiveass honkies outta our neighbor-hoods," said Easy. "Most a these young jitterbug social workers don't look like they got all their shit in one bag anyhow. And they be tryin to tell us how to do it. I think most a them is Comminists or some other off brand types."

"Nother thing," the young man said to Calvin. "The brother what owned the radio is bleedin round the eye. This paddy started talkin some crazy shit when the dude owned the car caught him stealin the radio. Then this honky jist fired on the brother and took the box."

"What he look like when he swung?" Easy asked.

"Baaaaad motherfucker. Fast hands. Punched like Ali."

"Wasn't none a them do-gooders then," said Easy. "They all sissies. Musta been a righteous paddy crook jist passin through."

After penciling out the brief theft report, Francis was fully awake and the moment they drove away from Easy's liquor store he said, "How about code seven?"

"Too early to eat."

"How about just stopping for a taco at Bennie's?"

"Aw right." Calvin lit another cigarette, grimacing at the thought of one of Bennie's salty guacamole filled drippy tacos which sent Francis Tanaguchi into fits of joy.

"Driver of the pimpmobile looks hinky," Francis said as they crossed Pico Boulevard on La Brea, slowly passing a red and white Cadillac convertible driven by a lanky black man in an orange wide brimmed hat with matching ascot.

"Let's bring him down. Might have a warrant," Calvin said. "Anything to keep from smellin those greasy tacos."

The driver pretended not to see the red light nor hear the

honking black and white which followed him for a block until Calvin angrily blasted him to the curb with the siren.

"Watch him say 'who me?' " said Calvin as he got out of the car and approached from the driver's side while Francis advanced on the passenger side, shining his light, distracting the driver to protect his vulnerable partner on the street.

"You got a driver's license?" Calvin asked, right hand on his gun, three cell light in his left hand, searching for the right hand of the driver which was hidden from view.

He relaxed when the driver brought his hand up to the steering wheel and said, "Who me?"

"You know, I once shot a player like you," Calvin lied. "Dude laid there with two magnums in his belly and when I said, 'Leroy, you got any last words?' he said, 'Who me?' and fell over dead. Now break out somethin with your name on it since I know you ain't got a driver's license."

"Sure, Officer," the man said, stepping out onto the street without being told after Calvin jerked open the door of the Cadillac.

Calvin shined his light over the alligators and crab apple green knicker suit with silky orange knee length socks while the man fumbled in the kangaroo wallet nervously.

"Here it is, Officer," he smiled, as Calvin admired the five inch hammered medallion on the bare chest of the young man.

Calvin took the slip of paper which was a speeding ticket issued one week earlier by an LAPD motor officer.

"This all you got with your name on it?" Calvin asked.

"That was gave me by one of your PO-licemen. It's official, ain't it?"

"Shit," Calvin said. "Fuckin motor cops only care about writin a ticket. Bet he took your word about who you are. Bet you keep this ticket for ID until it's time to go to warrant and then get another ticket and use that for a while. Bet every fuckin one is in a different name. What's your *real* name?"

"Jist like it say there, James Holiday."

"Why you sweatin, James?" Calvin asked, flashlight in his sap pocket now, both fists on his hips, stretching so that he could be taller than the pimp and look down on him.

"You makin me nervous cause you don't believe me." The man licked his lips when they popped dryly.

"Gimme that wallet," Calvin said suddenly.

"Ain't that illegal search and seizure, Officer?" asked the pimp.

"Gimme that wallet, chump, or it's gonna be a search and *squeez-ure* of your fuckin neck!"

"Okay, okay," the young man said, handing Calvin the wallet. "Looky here, I ain't no crook or nothin. I owns two or three bars in San Diego."

"Two or three," Francis observed.

"Three, probably," said Calvin, pulling a bail receipt out of an inner compartment of the wallet.

"Uh oh," said the man.

"Uh huh," said Calvin.

"What's his real name?" Francis asked, stepping to the open door of the radio car and pulling the hand mike outside to run a make.

"Omar Wellington," Calvin said. "How about savin us a little time, Omar? You got warrants out or what?"

"Uh-huh," said Omar Wellington. "Couple traffic warrants."

"Well that ain't so bad," said Calvin.

"Oh man, I don't wanna go to jail tonight!"

"No big thing," Calvin said, touching his handcuffs. "We don't have to hook you up, do we?"

"Handcuffs? Naw, I ain't gonna give nobody no trouble. I'm nonviolent. How come you stopped me? It's them fuckin license plates, ain't it?"

Calvin looked at the personalized license plate and replied, "Didn't even notice em, Omar."

"Then how'd you tumble? They's lots a players around here in Cadillacs. It was my orange hat, wasn't it? You wouldn't even a saw me if it wasn't for that motherfuckin hat."

"Yeah, it was the hat, Omar," Francis said to pacify the pimp, who like most street people believed superstitiously that there was one explainable reason for being singled out.

"What do your friends call you, Omar?"

"They jist calls me Omar."

"Okay, Omar, get in the black and white. Let's get goin so you can bail out tonight."

"I only got a hundred bucks on me. The motherfuckin warrants are for more than that. And a bailbondsman don't work on traffic cases. And I ain't got no one I can get hold of for four hours. Ain't this some bullshit?"

"Tell me, Omar," Francis said, sliding in beside the pimp in the back seat. "Why don't you just pay the tickets when you get them?"

"Shee-it! You don't give The Man your money till you *has* to!" Omar Wellington looked at Francis as though he were a cretin. "Y'unnerstan?"

After booking the pimp Calvin repeated that he wasn't hungry. Nothing Francis said seemed to help Calvin out of his depression this night and Francis was constrained to try his last resort.

"Calvin, is the periscope still in the trunk?" he asked innocently.

"Now jist a minute, Francis. Jist one fuckin minute!"

"Pull over, Calvin. Lemme just see it."

"Gud-damn you, Francis, you promised."

"Wolfgang's working alone tonight in a report car. He's all alone!" Francis said, trying his inscrutable smile on Calvin Potts.

Wolfgang Werner, a twenty-four year old formidable specimen in tailored blue, had been in America from Stuttgart ten years before joining the police department. Francis and Wolfgang had shared a radio car the month before Calvin Potts and Francis formed their partnership. Francis didn't mind working with Wolfgang. At first he found Wolfgang hilarious. "If you dundt sign zat traffic ticket we must luck you in ze slummer!" He only began to hate Wolfgang when the huge German went to Lieutenant Finque and asked to be assigned to another partner because of a personality conflict.

Francis thought it reprehensible of the German. It was customary on the Los Angeles force for police supervisors to leave unquestioned the ambiguous phrase "personality conflict" which masked a plethora of problems. Often it simply meant that two cops hated each other's guts and would be venting their feelings on the citizens if left together for a protracted period in the incredibly gritty intimate world of the radio car. Francis was furious because too many "personality conflicts" would result in a policeman's receiving a reputation of "not being able to get along."

The department was still controlled by men who wanted subordinates who could "get along" and who firmly believed that "a good follower makes a good leader."

Francis Tanaguchi never believed in following since there was no one to follow when you were making life and death decisions on the street at night. So Francis said that Wolfgang Werner was a schmuck. He said he knew the real reason that Wolfgang had dumped him. It was because he couldn't abide what Harold Bloomguard named them, which was quickly picked up by the other officers. Harold called them The Axis Partners.

One night, after Francis had stopped being an Axis Partner and had become half of the Gook and the Spook team, they were cruising Crenshaw Boulevard on a quiet Wednesday when Francis spotted Wolfgang talking with a red haired motorist whom he had stopped near Rodeo Road ostensibly to write a ticket for a burned out taillight.

"Vell, I dundt sink ve neet to write ze ticket zis time, miss," Wolfgang lisped, standing tall in the street next to the lime Mustang, staring at the driver's license, memorizing the address, eyes hidden under the brim of his hat which was always pulled too far forward à la Roscoe Rules.

"Thank you, Officer," the girl giggled, measuring the massive shoulders and chest of this young Hercules who dripped with Freudian symbolism. There were the phallic objects: the gun, the badge. Not to mention the oversized sap hanging from the sap pocket. And in Wolfgang's case (he was the only nightwatch officer who *never* got out of his car without it) there was the nightstick. The obtuse girl had not the slightest understanding of the siege these accouterments lay to her libido.

When Wolfgang handed her back the license with a practiced Teutonic grin, Francis knew that Wolfgang would now say, "Vut say ve meedt ufter vork for a little chin and tunick?"

"That phony krauthead," Francis complained as he watched the pantomime from his passenger seat in the radio car.

He ordered Calvin to park near the opposite corner, saying, "I'm gonna sink that sausage eating Aryan son of a bitch." Later that night he bought a plastic periscope at a five-and-dime. Francis knew Wolfgang Werner could not abide an assault on his dignity. The U-boat attacks began.

On the evening of the first attack Wolfgang was working solo taking reports. Francis turned his police hat around backward, scooted down in his seat with Calvin Potts driving and brought his new toy slowly up over the window ledge.

"Do you have a mirror in your periscope?" Calvin asked.

"No."

"Then you can't see a fuckin thing?"

"No, you gotta tell me when I'm sighted in on Wolfgang."

"Is that all you're gonna do, sight in on Wolfgang?"

"No, that ain't all. We're gonna sink that *pendejo*," Francis replied, lapsing into Spanish. "Bring her alongside."

Wolfgang was stopped on Wilshire Boulevard between Western and Muirfield. This time his quarry was out of the Mercedes. She was brunette, leggy, bejeweled and pissed off because she rightly suspected that Wolfgang didn't really give a shit about the burned out light over her license plate. It was ten o'clock. A starless night. The traffic was light on Wilshire and Francis was afraid Wolfgang would see them cruising in.

"Turn out your lights," Francis commanded.

Calvin shrugged and did so, bringing the black and white into the curb behind Wolfgang's radio car when Francis suddenly said, "Not behind them, turkey! Pull up *next* to them. And slow."

Then Francis Tanaguchi took a breath and said, "Ssssswwwwwooooooooooooosh," causing Wolfgang to turn and stare at them quizzically.

"A miss!" Francis said suddenly. "Dive! Dive! Dive!"

"What?"

"Get the fuck outta here!" Francis yelled and Calvin pulled away, leaving Wolfgang and the baffled brunette staring after them in wonder.

It took them more than an hour to find Wolfgang Werner the next night they attacked. They finally located him by listening for his calls given by a new radio voice which Calvin suspiciously thought almost as sexy as the Dragon Lady's.

"Seven-X-L-Five, Seven-X-L-Five, see the woman, prowler complaint, Crescent Heights and Colgate."

"He'll drop everything to roll on that one," said Francis. "I know how his mind works. He'll figure it's a peeping tom complaint and that she might be good enough to deserve the peeping. All ahead full!"

Francis turned his hat around backward and brought the periscope out from under the seat as they glided toward Wolfgang's car.

The big German was getting out of the car, flashlight in one hand and report notebook in the other. He didn't see them as they cruised closer, their engine cut by Calvin Potts.

Then Francis yelled, "Achtung! Fire one! Fire two!"

Wolfgang whirled, the flashlight clattered and broke on the asphalt and the German had his clamshell holster open and was halfway into a draw when Francis Tanaguchi said, "Sssssswwwwwwooooosh."

"Francis, did we get him?" Calvin asked as he switched on the engine and lights and dropped a yard and a half of smoking LAPD rubber on the asphalt.

"Banzai! Banzai!" Francis giggled mysteriously.

They didn't see Wolfgang until end-of-watch in the locker room when he came to Francis' locker before changing and said with a tight grin, "Okay, Francis, you sunk me vunce. Vut say ve meg a truce?"

Francis only smiled inscrutably and left with Calvin to choir practice to brag to Harold Bloomguard that he was driving Wolfgang crackers. He called his U-boat the S.S. *Chorizo* after the spicy Mexican sausage.

The very last time Francis' boat went to sea was the night he had blood on his hands, when Wolfgang Werner was standing in front of Wilshire Police Station talking to his newest girlfriend: a big rosy lusty girl named Olga who waited tables at a La Brea drive-in which fed the car in the area for free.

"Let it go, baby," Calvin said as they pulled out of the station parking lot onto Venice Boulevard and Francis Tanaguchi leered at Olga and turned his cap around.

"Go back," Francis said grimly and pulled the periscope from under the seat.

"That dude is gonna kick your little ass and I ain't woofin."

"Go back, Calvin."

"That cat is gonna tear your head off and piss in the hole, Francis."

"You scared of him?"

"You gud-damn right."

"If you take me on one more attack I promise I'll throw away my periscope."

"Okay, but why now?"

"I'm in love with Olga. She's so *big!* Go back and I swear I'll never fire another torpedo."

"You swear?"

"Yes."

"You swear to Buddha?"

"Knock off that Jap stuff, goddamnit. That fuckin Lieutenant Finque made me go to another Nip luncheon today. How'd you like a shirt full of vomity squid, asshole?"

"Okay, I'm goin back. But that storm trooper is gonna burn you down."

"Let's go!" Francis said as Calvin wheeled the radio car around and headed back toward Venice Boulevard.

Wolfgang was turned away from them as they drove in from the west, this time in a fast glide and with lights on because of the westbound traffic.

"This is the last fuckin time I go to sea, Francis," Calvin warned.

"Okay, okay, now you're making me nervous," said the commander, as he sighted in, peeking up over the window ledge because the eyehole of the periscope revealed nothing but a three inch color photograph of a hairy vagina which Calvin had cut from a *Playboy* magazine and glued inside the plastic tube to amuse Francis.

"Steer an evasive course afterward," Francis ordered as Wolfgang turned from Olga who was dressed in the sheerest tightest hiphugging bellbottoms Francis Tanaguchi had ever seen. She was pantyless and her crotch was dark beneath the sheer yellow bells.

Francis leaned out the window, periscope extended, and aimed it not at Wolfgang but at Olga's bulging fluff.

"Sssswwwwwwooooosh," cried Francis Tanaguchi and Calvin Potts sped away, fearfully stealing a glance at the grim face of Wolfgang Werner.

That night in the locker room Wolfgang grabbed Francis by the throat without warning and said, "If you efen tink uf putting your lousy torpedo vere you pudt it tonight, I vill tvist you neg off. You vood be smart to decommission your U-boat, Francis."

Wolfgang made Francis promise by squeezing and encouraging him to bob his head. Then he left Francis gasping in front of the locker while Calvin Potts pretended to need another trip to the urinal, away from Wolfgang Werner.

When Calvin returned he said, "I think we better put the S.S. *Chorizo* in dry dock for good, Francis."

That last dangerous attack on the German came after the call which would awaken Francis sweating in the night with red in the crevices of his knuckles and under his nails.

"Seven-A-Seventy-seven, see the woman, unknown trouble, Pico and Ogden."

"Seven-A-Seventy-seven, roger," Francis muttered and threw the hand mike on the seat. "Damn it, I'm drooling for a guacamole taco!"

"This must be it," Calvin said five minutes later and Francis looked up as Calvin hit the high beam, lighting a man and woman who stood in front of a seedy apartment house which was still located in a predominately white neighborhood, but which was experiencing a high vacancy factor because blacks were getting more numerous.

"Hope this is a quickie," Francis said as they gathered up their flashlights, hats and notebook. The smog hung over the streets and the building like airbrushed, painted smoke.

"I'm the one that called," said a woman in a quilted bathrobe, her orange hair frizzing beneath a hairnet.

A balding man with a sloppy grin sat on the steps beside her. There were six empty beer cans between them.

"What's the problem?" Francis asked, slightly uneasy over an "unknown trouble" call, which can mean anything but sometimes means only that the communications officer who took the call could not think of a convenient category in which to classify it.

"I'm the manager," said the woman, bunching the robe at the bosom as though she were not twenty years past the age when most policemen would look. "I got a tenant up there in number twelve. Name's Mrs. Stafford. She got three little kids and I shouldn't oughtta have rented to her cause we don't want no more than one kid per apartment."

"So what happened?" Calvin asked impatiently, wondering if Francis would object too strongly if he were to stop by McGoon's Saloon and have a little taste. Just maybe one little Johnnie Walker on the rocks . . .

"Well, see don't you think it's unusual? I hear this noise about two hours ago just when it was getting dark. Then I don't hear nothing. They go to bed awful early, her and her kids. I feel so sorry for them I loaned them an old TV. She just got here from Arkansas and ain't eligible for welfare or nothing yet so she's trying to find work as a waitress. But it's hard."

"The noise," Calvin said. "The noise."

"Yeah, so then I thought I heard screaming. Not too loud, but a scream. But kids always holler. And then, then about twenty minutes ago I see a man go out and then nothing. There ain't no lights on in there. Just nothing. I went up and knocked but nothing."

"So?"

"They're home. They didn't go out. I woulda saw them if they went out."

"So they're asleep."

"The TV's on."

"They just forgot . . ."

"Look sir," the woman said, turning to Francis, "it's an old TV but it works good. I can hear the station. It's the same channel as I'm watching. And I peek in through the drapes and I can see the screen and it's all white and sparkly. You can't hardly make out the picture."

"What's that mean?"

"I don't know, sir." The woman turned to Calvin again. "She don't have many friends. Poor little woman stays with her kids all day and all night. Just trying to find work is only time she leaves them and then I keep an eye on them."

"Why don't you use your passkey and go on in?"

"That's the problem, I ain't got one. Last tenant didn't turn his in and I gave her my passkey. Can you just go in and see if everything's all right?"

"Don't suppose you want us to break the door down?" Calvin muttered as the two policemen started up the steps.

"Can't you just slip the lock like all the cops in the movies?"

"No, and I can't open a safe by listenin to the tumblers either," Calvin said as Francis reached the landing first and knocked loudly on the door of number twelve.

"I don't want you to break the door." The landlady stood at the foot of the stairs helplessly.

Francis began fiddling with the sliding window beside the front door and said, "Hold this," to Calvin, giving his tall partner the notebook. Then he pushed hard on the window with the tips of the fingers of one hand while he pried at the frame with a coin from his pocket. There was a metallic snap and the window slid to the left.

"Oughtta be a burglar, Francis," Calvin observed.

"Too respectable. I'd rather be a cop." Francis pushed back the faded draperies and lifted himself up and into the dark room, lit only from the snow filled screen of the TV set whose volume was barely audible.

"Calvin!" Francis suddenly whispered.

"What is it?" His partner instinctively grabbed his gun and stepped to the side of the window.

"Calvin!" Francis repeated, weakly this time, and Calvin Potts dropped the notebook, convinced that his partner was in danger. Calvin crouched, looked for cover, considered the distance to the steps.

"Calvin!" Francis said again, and Calvin Potts drew his gun while the landlady below shrieked and ran to her apartment to escape a gun battle.

The door opened slowly and Calvin flattened himself against the wall, adrenalin jetting. Francis stepped woodenly across the threshold.

"Calvin!" he said as softly as a child.

"What is it? What the fuck *is* it?" Calvin demanded, his gun pointed directly at Francis who did not seem to notice.

"There's some people murdered in there!"

"Gud-damn it, Francis!" Calvin pushed his partner aside and entered the apartment, gun still drawn, flashlight sweeping the room until he found the light switch.

The first one Calvin saw was the woman. She was unbelievably thin and pale with huge eye sockets. She lay on the couch on her back, the nightgown gathered around her hips. Her legs were spread, knees up, head thrown back in agony. The classic pose of a victim raped and murdered.

The TV antenna wire was knotted around her neck and her eyes and mouth were open. The dead eyes, still clear and unclouded, stared at the top of the doorway which led to the two bedrooms. Hanging from the doorway was a blonde baby doll. The doll wore a red party dress trimmed in white. The dress had been washed many times and the painted face of the doll was chipped and worn. The doll was hanging by the neck, dangling from the doorjamb by a bathrobe sash which was taped to the jamb with adhesive tape. The tape roll was on the floor in the doorway to the bathroom.

As Calvin made a mental note to put the tape roll aside for prints, Francis startled him by walking up behind him and saying, "The kitchen!"

Calvin took two steps to his left into a tiny kitchen with a small yellow refrigerator and apartment stove. On the floor by the sink lay a sandy haired boy of seven. The telephone cord was spiraled around his neck and his face rested on a pillow as though the killer wanted him comfortable. The green velvet pillow was wet from the fluids which ran from the child's mouth while he was strangling. His pajama top was pulled up and there were two cigarette burns on his back and another on his neck. His eyes were closed, more tightly than Calvin had ever before seen in death. As though he had died crying hopelessly for his mother, his face pressed into the velvet pillow.

"The bathroom!" Francis said and Calvin nodded mechanically and followed his partner across the little room, pausing to look at the baby doll hanging in the doorway. It turned gently as Francis' hat touched the fat rubber foot when he passed.

Francis looked in the bathroom to verify what he had already seen before he opened the door for his partner. Then he looked at the pink baby doll and back to Calvin.

Calvin Potts knew for certain what he would find in the bathroom and his heart was banging in his ears when Francis switched on the light and stepped aside to let his partner see the child dangling from the bar over the shower stall.

She was the youngest, four, clad in animal cracker pajamas. She was hanging by two pair of panty hose knotted together. The coroner was to say later it probably took her longest to die. Calvin did not want to see if she had been burned. He did not want to touch her. Her eyes were open like her mother's. Her mouth was closed because the head hung forward on her chest. She turned slowly when Francis touched her foot.

"What the fuck you doin?"

"Huh?" Francis said dumbly.

"Keep your hands off them!"

"Huh?" Francis said, not knowing he had reached out and consolingly patted the tiny feet which were strapped together at the ankles with a brown belt and were pointed toes downward like a ballerina's.

"Let's go outside and get the dicks down here right now!"

Calvin wiped his dripping forehead with the back of his hand. "Wait a minute! How many kids she say there was?"

"I'm not sure."

"Three, wasn't it?"

"Yeah, it was three," Francis said, sounding very sick.

"The bedrooms!" Calvin switched on the light in the main bedroom which contained a double bed where the woman slept with the youngest child. He was breathing heavily as he looked in the closet and behind a box of old toys.

"Calvin!" Francis said from the other bedroom where there were twin beds and colorful plastic gimcracks on an old dresser and a painted Formica shelf covered with pictures of daisies, apparently to make the dreary bedroom look as though a child slept there.

Francis was on his knees between the beds, his hat and flashlight on the floor beside him, the beam shining under the bed lighting the body of the five year old boy.

Calvin dropped to his knees, removed his hat and using Francis' flashlight, looked under. The bundle was drenched in blood, the pajamas shredded around the tiny huddled body unrecognizable as a child except for some short blond hair not blood soaked.

"Musta crawled under there to get away from him," Calvin said hoarsely. "The killer musta crawled after him and cut the kid up there under the bed. Just laid there under that bed slashin and slashin. Musta been that way. It's clean all around the outside a the bed. The little thing hidin under the bed and the killer crawlin under after him with the knife. There ain't no God, Francis! I swear there *ain't!*"

Then Francis was on his feet, throwing the bed aside and pulling at the little form, dragging it through the viscous red puddle until Calvin stopped him.

"Don't touch that body!"

"I think I saw him move, Calvin! I think maybe he's still alive!"

"Francis!" Calvin shouted, jerking his partner up as the little body thudded softly to the floor, splashing heavy drops onto the dirty wallpaper. "His insides are all over the fuckin floor! Look!" And he pointed at the ominous red blossoms. "Look at the blood! Look at the face! That child's dead, Francis."

Francis Tanaguchi looked at his partner for a moment, looked at his own bloody hands, then said, "Oh. I can't see too good without my glasses. I guess I should wear my glasses."

"Let's go call the dicks," Calvin said, gently leading his partner out of the apartment which in thirty minutes was swarming with detectives, fingerprint specialists, photographers, deputy coroners and high ranking police administrators who had nothing to do with the investigation but who were always the ones who acted as spokesmen on the television news.

Deputy Chief Lynch was there, his hairpiece a little askew because he had just been in a motel with Theda Gunther.

Commander Moss was there, waving and grinning until he finally persuaded a newsman to take his picture. He pretended that he was examining a lift of a latent fingerprint found on the side of the television set. He held the lift upside down as he scrutinized it. Then he waved with both arms at the newsmen as he was leaving, his blond wavy hair glowing under the lights. One journalist said he acted like a Rose Queen on a flower float.

There were few clues left by the killer. The latent print was found to have belonged to the victim, Mrs. Mary Stafford. An old boyfriend of hers was ultimately arrested for the murders but the evidence was not sufficient for a complaint. Commander Moss' picture never appeared in the newspapers.

It was later that night, with a child's blood still lodged in the creases of his fingers, that Francis Tanaguchi raised a plastic periscope and began that last obsessive U-boat attack on Wolfgang Werner and big Olga. Then he called for a choir practice and drank and worried about the nightmares sure to come.

8

7-A-1: Spermwhale Whalen
and Baxter Slate

At first, Spermwhale Whalen was uncommonly quiet at rollcall on a smoggy June afternoon, just two months before the choir practice killing. Spermwhale was not over the death of a son who claimed to despise him as much as he loved the son. Actually, they hardly knew each other.

Baxter Slate, his partner, was never a boisterous young man so it was not unusual that he said very little while half the nightwatch hooted and jeered at Roscoe Rules and Lieutenant Finque.

"Damn it, Lieutenant, I resent the investigators showing my picture all the time to rape victims," Roscoe Rules complained. "I didn't know they were doing it till last month."

"Apparently they just noticed that your picture mixes well with white sex suspects," Lieutenant Finque replied, getting a migraine as he always did at rollcall these days.

"Yeah, well I shoulda got suspicious when that pussy kiddy cop caught me in civvies and asked to let her snap a Polaroid a me to test out the new camera."

"No harm, Roscoe," Sergeant Yanov grinned.

"No? That cunt's been using my picture in a mug shot showup every fucking time a paddy rapes somebody around here!"

"She can't help it you look like such a deviate," Spermwhale said, as his partner Baxter Slate grinned. "I think she'll stop, Roscoe, by the time two or three victims pick *you* out of the lineup."

"They'd probably have the right guy," said Harold Bloomguard.

"Naw, he can't even get a blue veiner, let alone a diamond cutter," said Calvin Potts. "We ever get a limp dick bandit around here he'll be a prime suspect."

"Very funny, Potts, very fucking funny," Roscoe Rules said murderously as he unconsciously pulled on his limp dick.

"Well, I'll see what I can do, Rules," the lieutenant said. "Now onto the next subject of our supervisors' meeting. That is: excessive force complaints. The captain says he had an awful lot of paper work to do because an officer on the morning watch broke a suspect's arm with a wristlock. Just be careful in the future. Remember, a wristlock is very hard to put on if a man resists, so don't get carried away."

"Question, Lieutenant," Baxter Slate said.

"Yes?"

"If a man *didn't* resist, why would you ever put it on in the first place?"

Sergeant Yanov saved his superior officer by taking control of the rollcall and saying, "How about my reading the crimes. Here's a sex story. Might perk up your evening."

And as Sergeant Yanov rescued his lieutenant from further embarrassing faux pas, Lieutenant Finque smoldered. Yanov related so easily with the men, was so obviously well liked, that Finque knew he had to be a rotten supervisor. This belief was bolstered in that Yanov had been working for him three months and had never yet been capable of catching a policeman with his hat off or smoking in public view. Lieutenant Finque made a note to mention to Captain Drobeck that Yanov, at thirty-four, just a few months younger than Lieutenant Finque, was probably too young and inexperienced to be an effective field sergeant and should be encouraged to go into the detective bureau.

Captain Drobeck would be the first to agree with such a proposal because he had hated Yanov ever since the sergeant openly disagreed with the captain at a meeting of all the Wilshire Division supervisors. Yanov refuted an "administrative suggestion" from the captain and argued that he would willingly fool the chief of police and lie to the mayor, and to his own wife if he still had one, but never to his men. Because he never asked his chief, mayor or wife to fight for him or save his ass.

Captain Drobeck wrote on Sergeant Yanov's rating report: "Is yet too young and immature to grasp the fundamentals of supervision."

To get even with the troops Lieutenant Finque interrupted Sergeant Yanov's reading of the noteworthy crimes. Lieutenant Finque decided to inform them of what he had just heard prior to rollcall: that a Superior Court jury had acquitted a man charged with the murder of a Los Angeles police officer.

"Acquitted?" thundered Spermwhale Whalen when the lieutenant announced it, but even Spermwhale's bellow was lost in the deafening clamor which went up in that room.

The accused was thought to be a narcotic dealer. He went to a hotel with an undercover officer who posed as a buyer, and a third man, a police informant. The officer was prepared to make a large buy but as it turned out the accused had no drugs. He *did* have a small caliber pistol with which he shot and killed the officer who returned fire ineffectively before his death. The accused stole the suitcase full of money and ran out the door but was arrested immediately by other officers hiding outside.

The police called the shooting a straight ripoff operation in which the plan was to steal the money. The informant testified that the defendant grabbed the suitcase and fired without warning. The defendant's testimony was that the slain officer unaccountably drew his gun and the defendant, thinking *he* was to be ripped off, fired first to protect himself. The investigating officers scoffed. They said it was a "dead bang" case. A cinch. The evidence was overwhelming. There was an eyewitness. The defendant's story was desperate and ludicrous. He was acquitted.

The judge, upon hearing the verdict, proclaimed that he was shocked. But he was not nearly as shocked as the twenty-eight men in Lieutenant Finque's rollcall who would never become accustomed to shocking jury verdicts. It took five minutes to quiet them down and get several questions answered. But they weren't questions. They were statements of indignation and disbelief. Outcries. Then threats. Then a violent obscene damning of the jury system.

Baxter Slate, perhaps the most articulate choirboy, said grimly that this bulwark of democracy was actually a crap game in which twelve telephone operators, mailmen, public utilities employees, pensioners and middle aged housewives, with no knowledge of the law and less of the sociopath, make irrevocable decisions based upon their exposure to movies like *Twelve Angry Men* and television shows like *Perry Mason.*

Lieutenant Finque let them rail until he was sure their stomachs were as sour as his always was because of them. He beamed contentedly. He wasn't even afraid of them at the moment.

Their outrage was so complete that they quickly talked themselves out. One moment shrill trembling voices. Questions unanswered and unanswerable. Then silence. Defeat. Depression. And smoldering fury.

Lieutenant Finque sent them out to do police work with one further blandishment: "You men take with you the captain's last warning from the supervisors' meeting. Any wetfoot hotdogs who like to put a shoe in the carburetor better stand by. The next preventable traffic accident is going to mean the commander comes down on the captain, who's going to come down hard on me and I'm going to have to come down hard on you!"

Finally Spermwhale Whalen spoke. He said, "I know shit rolls downhill. But why am I *always* livin in the valley?"

Herbert "Spermwhale" Whalen despised the new station Wilshire Division had moved to in early 1974. Daily he would drive by the dilapidated, inadequate old building on Pico Boulevard which, by God, *looked* like a police station. He longed for the old days.

Spermwhale, at 260 pounds with the pig eyes of a whale, was aptly named. He was of Irish Catholic stock, divorced three times, considering himself thus excommunicated. "It's just too bad I ain't rich enough to've got a fancy annulment approved by the Pope like all these rich cunts and cocksuckers you read about. Then I coulda stayed in the church."

It was a refrain often heard at MacArthur Park choir practice when Spermwhale was almost in the tank, a fifth of bourbon or Scotch in the huge red hand. "Now I gotta go to hell cause I'm excommunicated!"

And if Father Willie Wright was drunk enough and suffering from his frequent attacks of overwhelming guilt for having just dismounted Ora Lee Tingle or Carolina Moon, claiming his plump little wife would only ball him dispassionately twice a month, he would say softly, "I'll be with you, Spermwhale. I'm afraid I'll be with you!"

Baxter Slate was a good partner for Spermwhale Whalen because he didn't talk too much and give Spermwhale a headache. Also he had almost five years on the job, having been sworn in on his twenty-second birthday. Spermwhale, a nineteen year veteran, considered anyone with less time a fuzz nutted rookie and couldn't stand to work with rookie partners.

Also Baxter didn't complain when Spermwhale would occasionally pick up a streetwalking prostitute whom Spermwhale knew from his old days on the vice squad, saying, "It's time for a little skull." Were he to be caught it would mean their jobs, and Spermwhale Whalen was just months away from a pension. It was a calculated risk and Spermwhale sweated it out each time because the LAPD brass definitely did not approve of uniformed officers in black and whites getting a little skull.

It was surprising that Spermwhale would take such a risk. He often said that a sergeant who caught him doing something for which he could be fired would never get back to the station alive, because he, Spermwhale Whalen, would kill any cocksucker who tried to keep him from making his twenty years and getting that irretrievable pension. Anyone Spermwhale didn't like was either a "cunt," a "gelding," a "eunuch," or a "cocksucker," and that included almost all civilians, certainly all police brass and station supervisors (except Sergeant Nick Yanov) and all employees of the Civil Service Department who had designed nitpicking promotional exams which had frustrated him all these years and kept him from advancing past the basic policeman rank.

It was especially galling in that Spermwhale Whalen was a major in the Air Force Reserve and often ran into LAPD lieutenants and captains, also military reservists, who, during summer military exercises, had to salute him.

Spermwhale was proof positive that polish was not necessary to achieve staff rank in the United States Air Force Reserve, just as Commander Moss was proof positive that common sense was not needed to achieve staff rank in the Los Angeles Police Department.

But Spermwhale Whalen was just possibly one of the coolest most competent transport pilots in the 452nd Wing. He had flown in World War II and later in Korea until he left the Air Force and joined the police department. He was the only Los Angeles police officer in history to engage in one of his country's wars while still an active member of the department. His remarkable feat was accomplished by flying C-124 Globemasters on three and four day missions from March Air Force Base to Danang in 1966 and 1967, almost being shot down twice by Communist surface to air missiles. Spermwhale was, for this reason, a minor legend in the department. In those years it had been fun for the Wilshire policemen to play straight man for Spermwhale among police officers from other stations, saying things like:

"Oh, Marvin, where'd you go on your days off?"

"Disneyland with my sister's kids, how about you?"

"Fishing with Simon and his girlfriend up to Big Bear Lake, and how about *you*, Spermwhale?"

"Danang. Wasn't much happenin. Few rocket attacks is all."

Spermwhale seldom took two days off a week in those years. Like many policemen, he preferred to work nine and ten days straight to string his days off together. But his were for combat missions for which he was paid a bonus by the government of the United States to give to his three wives, each of whom had borne him a child before the divorce. When Spermwhale was off flying and the nightwatch sat bored in the assembly room, someone would always say when a low-flying aircraft roared over making an approach to LA International:

"Well, sounds like Spermwhale's late for rollcall again."

Spermwhale bore a Z-shaped scar which began in the fur of one black tufted eyebrow, crossed the flattened bridge of his nose, swooped under his right eye and came back onto the nose showing white in the swatch of red veins. Once at choir practice Carolina Moon asked him how he had gotten that scar.

"Landin in the rain with half my tail shot away."

"Where, Spermy? Where'd it happen?"

An extraordinary thing happened: Spermwhale could not remember. Not for almost a full minute. The alcohol had temporarily debilitated his brain but it was more than that. He had flown so many missions for his government in which he had been asked to kill or cause the deaths of Oriental people that they had started to run together: Japanese, Korean, Vietnamese. He truly couldn't answer. Not immediately.

"Oh yeah," he said finally. "Korea. Jesus Christ! Korea. Jesus Christ! I couldn't remember which war!"

After the Vietnam War ended, Spermwhale still flew but of course lost a good deal of his military pay and had a difficult time paying off the three wives and keeping enough to drink and take out a broad when he got lucky. It was for economic reasons more than anything else that he became a faithful choirboy and put up with the younger policemen who gave him such a headache. At choir practice there was always free booze supplied by Roscoe Rules and Spencer Van Moot. And there was sometimes Carolina Moon whom Spermwhale fell in love with at every single choir practice. The fat girl and the fat policeman would go off hand in hand for a stagger around the duck pond, sucking at a bottle of Scotch and cooing like doves. The other choirboys called them the campus couple.

Both Spermwhale Whalen and Baxter Slate were in a foul mood after rollcall. What had them generally pissed off was that they were both just now feeling the loss of pay from a four days' suspension.

The suspension had resulted from Lieutenant Elliott "Hardass" Grimsley's deciding to celebrate his fortieth birthday by going out in the field for the evening and showing the station commander, Captain Drobeck, that he could be as big a prick as Captain Drobeck any old day, and that even though he had only been a lieutenant eight months, his nine years as a field sergeant had given him plenty of experience at being a prick.

Captain Drobeck on the other hand had recently tried to demonstrate he was not a prick but a prince, during a formal inspection conducted by Deputy Chief Lynch himself. Every patrol officer in Wilshire Station wore lintless blue, and polished black leather for that inspection. They were formed into three sweating platoons.

Captain Drobeck, with his plumy white mane freshly done, was resplendent in his blues, wearing all the campaign ribbons he earned in Patton's Third Army. The Wilshire policemen knew that he had only been a clerk typist in that army and not a tank commander as he hinted and they often whispered that Captain Drobeck never retreated but backspaced lots of times.

Deputy Chief Lynch always showed up for ceremonies after a twenty minute wait, just as he answered the phone after a three minute wait. Captain Drobeck fussed nervously with his trouser creases and hoped his shoes were spit shined well enough by his adjutant, Sergeant Sneed, who learned such things while a trombone player in the U.S. Army band. The captain waved to Ardella Grimsley, the wife of Lieutenant Elliott "Hardass" Grimsley. She stood on the sidewalk by the parking lot where a dozen other spectators waited with cameras.

During one of the anxious moments, Lieutenant Grimsley nodded and winked at his wife of twenty years who wore a hat, gloves and, incredibly enough, a corsage for the occasion. Ardella Grimsley beamed and blew her husband a sweeping kiss which was answered by a horrendous fart in the rear ranks and a voice saying, "And here's a kiss for *you!*"

"WHO DID THAT?" Lieutenant Grimsley screamed, almost literally scaring the crap out of the already nervous Captain Drobeck.

"What the hell's going on, Grimsley?" demanded the captain.

"Somebody farted!"

"Is that so terrible?"

"At my wife!"

"I don't understand you, Grimsley."

Just then, Sergeant Sneed, called Suckass Sneed by the men,

came running forward from his place at the rear of the first platoon.

"I think it was a colored voice, sir," he whispered breathlessly to the captain. "I mean a black voice."

"If I may," said Officer Baxter Slate, who stood in the front rank, "a voice may have timbre, resonance, even pitch but it is singularly without color." He said it with a wide easy grin at Captain Drobeck which Lieutenant Grimsley knew was phony but which was so well done it was impossible to accuse him of insubordination.

Captain Drobeck, sure of the affection of his men, smiled benevolently and said, "Please, gentlemen, let's calm ourselves. This is perfectly silly."

"It's *not* silly, Captain. Somebody insulted *my* wife," Lieutenant Grimsley answered.

"Please, Lieutenant, please!" Captain Drobeck whispered. "The deputy chief is going to be here any minute and you're acting like a child. My god, I can't believe this."

"It was personal, sir. It was vicious!"

"All right, all right, will you settle for an apology? It was undoubtedly some young policeman's idea of a joke. Christ, most of these men here are closer to twenty than thirty. They're kids! I'll have the boy apologize and we can forget it." Captain Drobeck turned to the platoon of men and showed his toothy paternal grin and said, "Okay, fellas. Let's fess up. Who farted?"

And he laughed uproariously with the men as he waited for the culprit to reply so he could show the men how silly Hardass Grimsley was and how magnanimously he could forgive the insult to Ardella Grimsley who was one of those garrulous bitches Captain Drobeck couldn't stand in the first place.

But a funny thing happened: nobody fessed up.

"Come on now, boys," Captain Drobeck laughed, but the laughter was a little strained. "Just cop out whoever you are. Tell Lieutenant Grimsley it was an accident and it's all forgotten."

And the laughter continued but was not joined in this time by Captain Drobeck who smiled patiently and waited for the guilty party to show Lieutenant Grimsley how he, Captain Drobeck, could relate with his men.

Still, nobody fessed up.

"I just can't understand this," Captain Drobeck said. "I've given you every opportunity to show some maturity here and I think Lieutenant Grimsley deserves it. Now, by God, I'd like the young man to just apologize to the lieutenant and it'll all be forgotten. But we can't wait all day and I expect it to be done immediately."

But nobody copped out.

Captain Drobeck was suddenly not laughing nor was he smiling. He was fidgeting with the crease in his uniform pants and nodding angrily. "All right, that's the way it's going to be, huh? By god, you wanna act like kids I can treat you like kids. You want the field sergeants to start coming down on you, huh? Well that can be arranged, I assure you. Now this is your last chance. If the man that farted isn't man enough to admit it I want the man next to him to do it."

And the man next to him obediently did it. His fart was louder than the first.

"ATTEN-HUT!" screamed Captain Drobeck and the platoon snapped to attention. The captain began pacing the rear ranks like a lion, muttering viciously as he looked each man in the eye and tried to apply some detective techniques he had learned from reading books on investigation when he studied for the captain's exam. He looked for nervous twitches, telltale blinking. The trouble was he was so nervous waiting for Deputy Chief Lynch and now so angry himself that his own eyes were winking like semaphores.

After he paced the entire platoon he strode angrily to the front and whispered to Suckass Sneed, "You find out who did it, hear me?"

"Yes sir. The first or the second fart?"

"I *want* that man! The *first* one!"

"It was a colored voice, I mean a black voice, I'm sure of it," said Sneed. "That narrows it down to six."

Just then Deputy Chief Lynch's car arrived. The incident was set aside temporarily. The inspection was conducted and it was a great success. Captain Drobeck thanked the chief for his gracious compliments and assured him the credit was due to the loyalty of the men.

Thirty minutes after the inspection, Captain Drobeck was in

a cubicle in the restroom relieving his rumbling bowels from the tension of the day. He had the morning paper there and was grunting happily and smoking his pipe. Suddenly the door to the restroom burst open and someone released a terrible, vengeful fart. Before the footsteps ran back out a voice said, "Take that, you jive turkey!"

Captain Drobeck never solved the mystery. But one thing was certain: it was a colored voice.

On one of his weekly evenings out on the streets, Lieutenant Grimsley caught eight officers with their hats off, one smoking in public and three others drinking coffee which proved to have been gratuitously received. Just before calling it a night, he added to his score by bagging Spermwhale Whalen and Baxter Slate staked out on a stop sign at 11:00 P.M. on a residential street where a car didn't pass more often than once every half hour. Both officers were slumped in their seats, heads resting against the windows. But like any veteran policemen, they could rely on years of experience to trigger signals in deep slumber when 7-A-1 was mentioned among the ceaseless garbled almost unintelligible radio messages.

Legally speaking, Lieutenant Hardass Grimsley was a strict constructionist. He could not prove his suspicions that Spermwhale and Baxter were asleep, so their suspension papers said:

> Officers failed to remain alert in that officers assumed a position of repose in a parked police vehicle with eyelids pressed together, breathing heavily and regularly. Four days.

In addition, through diligent police work, Lieutenant Grimsley found a bag of avocados in the trunk of the black and white, which he traced to Francis Tanaguchi, who, it turned out, accepted them gratuitously from a Japanese produce market wherein the owner was proud of Francis' being a Japanese policeman, not knowing that Francis was Mexican at heart and would use the avocados in making guacamole which he would ladle into his tacos. Spermwhale and Baxter were given an additional punishment of a divisional admonishment which read:

I hereby admonish you in that you accepted some avocados from another officer who received them from a private party who was not, in fact, morally correct in giving the avocados without recompense. Moreover, the other officer was guilty of moral turpitude for accepting the free avocados. The acceptance of gratuities is against Department regulations and you were aware of this regulation at the time you imprudently accepted the avocados from the officer who was also aware when he imprudently accepted the avocados from the man who should have been more prudent.

Francis Tanaguchi was not given an admonishment or any other penalty because the community relations officer, Lieutenant Gay, was trying to make public relations inroads with the Oriental community by putting Officer Tanaguchi up as a model policeman. He persuaded Captain Drobeck not to let Lieutenant Grimsley reprimand Francis officially. Lieutenant Grimsley acceded to the decision since it came from the station captain but he was frustrated because there wasn't something he could get on the old Japanese who gave Francis the avocados. He asked the vice squad to keep an eye on the market in case the old man should sell beer to minors. And he certainly put Lieutenant Gay and Francis on his list.

But if Lieutenant Gay, Francis Tanaguchi and the old Japanese were on Lieutenant Grimsley's list, Lieutenant Grimsley was certainly on Spermwhale Whalen's list.

"His dance card's all filled up," Spermwhale vowed at choir practice when the whole night had been spent on plotting revenge.

"I get the first waltz," said Francis Tanaguchi, who sat in the dark on a blanket under a tree.

The choirboys began various subtle attacks on Lieutenant Grimsley which ultimately ended up in his transfer from Wilshire Station because according to the station captain he was getting too chummy with certain officers.

The officers he was apparently getting so chummy with were two of the MacArthur Park choirboys, namely Spermwhale Whalen and Baxter Slate, who when they were finished with him could actually walk into Lieutenant Grimsley's office and muss up his lint covered, thinning hair and say things like, "How about a day off tomorrow, Hardass?" When no one else under the rank of lieutenant ever dared to address him even by his first name, Elliott.

This remarkable familiarity was accomplished by some groundwork supplied by Francis Tanaguchi which included shimming the door of the lieutenant's private car and putting three MacArthur ducks in the back seat.

It was entertaining for the choirboys to stake out the police parking lot after end-of-watch and see Lieutenant Grimsley trudge through the dark, sleepy after a hard night of paper work, and get into his car only to come flying out five seconds later and fall on his ass from the duck excrement on his shoes. It was said that his wife nagged him for months about the green slime she would find stubbornly clinging to the creases of the leather upholstery.

The choirboys also put a particularly fierce black gander in Lieutenant Grimsley's locker at the station which resulted in an investigation by officers of Internal Affairs Division which lasted a week.

Harold Bloomguard, the protector of ducks and all animals, in each case volunteered to take the hissing, squawking birds and get rid of them after the duck shit hit the fan. This should have made him a logical suspect since he mysteriously showed up after each duck attack but Lieutenant Grimsley was too outraged to put two and two together. Besides, it was extremely hard to add two and two when your personal belongings were dripping and foul smelling and an enraged loathsome creature had been banging on your head with its bill.

There were minor attacks wherein the siren on the Lieutenant's police car was fixed so that it wailed and could not be shut off when he started the engine. And his baton, which he kept in the door holder, was removed, carefully sawed in half and replaced.

But the coup which utterly demolished Lieutenant Grimsley and made him a slave to Spermwhale Whalen and precipitated his transfer occurred when Spermwhale bribed a black whore named Fanny Forbes, who was tall and curvy and slender despite her years, to entertain Lieutenant Grimsley. Spermwhale Whalen told her in which restaurant the lieutenant ate on Thursday nights when he could break away from his duties which consisted of signing routine reports and trying to catch policemen loafing in the station when they should be handling their calls.

It took Fanny Forbes, who posed as a tourist from Philadelphia, exactly twenty-five minutes to talk Lieutenant Grimsley into driving her and her bogus suitcase, containing the dirty laundry of Spermwhale Whalen, to a motel on La Brea. He parked his black and white on a side street and insisted on carrying her bag up the back stairs while she registered alone.

Eight minutes after she registered, and while Lieutenant Grimsley, naked except for his black police socks, was hotly kissing the well worn source of her income and whispering endearments like, "Oh baby, you don't seem like a Negro. You look like a Samoan!" Spermwhale Whalen and Baxter Slate crept up the same back stairway and opened the door which the whore had left unlocked.

The two choirboys waited a few minutes more, their ears to the door, and heard Lieutenant Grimsley panting so loudly they were afraid they'd miss the prearranged signal from Fanny Forbes.

"She's really got him sucking wind."

"Yeah!" Spermwhale whispered, his hat in hand, ear pressed to the door, waiting, waiting.

And then they heard it, the signal: "Oh honey!" cried the whore. "You got balls like a elephant and a whang like a ox!"

Just as Spermwhale burst through the door Lieutenant Grimsley was in the throes of blissful agony. When he withdrew and jumped from the bed his face was like a dead man's.

"Okay, who called the pol . . . Lieutenant Grimsley!" cried Spermwhale Whalen.

"What're you men doing here?" cried Lieutenant Grimsley.

"We got a call a woman was being raped in this room! We had no idea!" cried Baxter Slate.

"Musta been some cop hating neighbor saw you come in with the young lady!" cried Spermwhale Whalen.

"How humiliatin!" cried the whore.

"Let's keep our voices down," whispered Lieutenant Grimsley, still motionless and pale.

"Sir, there's some dew on the lily," offered Spermwhale Whalen.

"Oh," said Lieutenant Grimsley, coming to his senses and wiping his whang with his jockey shorts while Fanny Forbes lay nude on the bed and winked at Spermwhale Whalen who was possibly enjoying the sweetest moment of his life.

"Well, we better be goin . . . Hardass," Spermwhale grinned, as Lieutenant Grimsley toppled clumsily over on the bed trying to get his pants on two legs at a time.

"Yes, well, meet me at Pop's coffee shop, will you, fellas? I'd like to buy you a cup of coffee and talk over a few things before we go back in."

"Sure . . . Hardass," Spermwhale grinned, playfully mussing up Lieutenant Grimsley's hair.

Lieutenant Grimsley was actually glad when, three weeks later, Captain Drobeck suggested that he was getting too chummy with certain officers and perhaps should think about a transfer. Lieutenant Grimsley was glad because he was sick and tired of Spermwhale Whalen sitting on his desk and winking and mussing up his hair every time he came in to have a report approved.

Fanny Forbes complained when Spermwhale only slipped her a ten dollar bill, but when he reminded her that it was ten bucks more than she had gotten for similar activity with himself, she shrugged and accepted the stipend.

But on the night they caught the Regretful Rapist, both Spermwhale and Baxter were still mightily pissed off from receiving the four days' suspension for sleeping with the avocados. Lieutenant Grimsley had by then been transferred to Internal Affairs Division where he could catch lots of errant policemen.

The arrest of the Regretful Rapist was possibly the best pinch Baxter Slate had ever made. The rapist had sexually attacked more than thirty women at knifepoint on the streets of Los Angeles and got his name from apologizing profusely after each act and sometimes giving the women cab fare when the attack was finished. The rapist had been fortunate in that not one of his victims had violently resisted and it was unknown how far he would have gone with his eight inch dagger if he had met a real fighter. Nevertheless, he was rightly considered an extremely dangerous man, not only to the female citizens he preyed upon, but to any potential arresting officer.

The night they caught the rapist had been a fairly uneventful night. The first call of the evening was to warn a resident of a twenty-three room house in Hancock Park that he should not go outside to swat flies in the afternoon, particularly when he had to climb a ladder to get them, and especially when his next door neighbor's daughter, a nineteen year old blonde, just happened to be washing her Mercedes 450 SL and couldn't help seeing that he was stark naked beneath his bathrobe, which kept flapping open.

The second call of the evening had been to take a burglary report at an air conditioning manufacturer's whose company had been closed for three days. They heard the burglary victim's opinion which Spermwhale had heard perhaps a thousand times in his police career:

"It must've been kids who did it," said the victim, since burglary victims of both residential and commercial burglaries hate to consider the prospect of a grown man viciously and dangerously violating the sanctity of their premises by his presence. If there is nothing taken, or if property of any value whatsoever is left behind, the victims invariably allay their fear of prowling deadly men with the refrain, "It must've been kids."

Spermwhale just nodded and said, "Yeah, kids," and noted that the burglar went through the file cabinet by opening the drawers bottom to top so that he would not have to push the drawers shut thus taking a chance of leaving a fingerprint. That he had carefully ransacked all file boxes, drawers and logical places where money is hidden. That he had pocketed only easy to carry items. That he had stolen fifteen rolls of postage stamps which could be sold for eighty cents on the dollar and had left, closing the self-latching door behind him so that any doorshaking watchman would find nothing amiss during the evening rounds.

"All the good stuff he didn't even touch," the vice president of the company said. "The typewriter, the calculator. Anyone but kids would've taken something besides stamps, wouldn't he, Officer?"

"Oh sure. Had to've been kids," Spermwhale agreed as the

vice president managed a relieved smile. Spermwhale wrote "Stamp and money burglar" in the MO box of his report.

Spermwhale had lapsed into a very bad mood when they took the burglary report to the station that night. He had just been turned down by Lieutenant Finque on his request to hang a picture of his old friend Knuckles Garrity in the coffee room. Garrity had been a Central beat cop for fifteen years and finished out his twenty-five year career at Wilshire Station where he and Spermwhale were radio car partners. Just before Garrity was to have retired on a service pension he became involved in his third divorce and was found shot to death in his car in the station parking lot.

The car was locked from the inside with the keys in the ignition and his service revolver was on the seat beside him. Yet, despite all logic, Spermwhale refused to believe that his partner had not been murdered. He had to be given three special days off to get his thoughts together. Finally he accepted Knuckles Garrity's obvious suicide and became the partner of Baxter Slate and eventually a MacArthur Park choirboy.

Spermwhale Whalen had been broken in on a Central beat by Knuckles Garrity who told his rookie partners that a policeman only needed three things to succeed: common sense, a sense of humor and compassion. That none of these could be taught in a college classroom and that most men could succeed without one of the three, but a policeman never could. Spermwhale shivered for an instant, wondering how Knuckles had lost his sense of humor.

Spermwhale obtained the last picture ever taken of Knuckles in his police uniform and had it enlarged and framed with a brass plate on the bottom of the picture which said simply:

Thomas "Knuckles" Garrity
E.O.W. 4–29–74

It was on a lovely April afternoon with arrows of sunlight darting through the smog that Knuckles Garrity went End-of-Watch forever in the old police station parking lot on Pico Boulevard.

But the lieutenant said the picture would have to come down from the coffee room wall and that Spermwhale Whalen should take it home because Knuckles Garrity was not killed on duty like the other dead officers in the pictures which hung in the station.

"He was!" Spermwhale growled to the lieutenant who handed him the picture and turned away from the burning little eyes of the fat policeman.

"Listen, Whalen," Lieutenant Finque explained. "It's the captain's decision. Garrity shot himself, for God's sake."

Spermwhale Whalen very quietly said, "Knuckles Garrity died as a direct result of his police duties. As sure as any cop who was ever blown up in a shootout. Knuckles Garrity was the best fuckin cop we ever had in this station and that cunt of a captain should be *proud* to have his picture on the wall."

"I'm sorry," the lieutenant said, turning and walking back to his office, leaving Spermwhale with the picture in his enormous red hands.

"I could shoot somebody," said Spermwhale Whalen when he got back in the radio car after the incident.

Baxter Slate fired up the engine and turned on the lights as darkness settled in.

"Anybody in particular?"

"The captain. The lieutenant maybe. Anybody," Spermwhale said, not knowing that in exactly two hours he *would* shoot somebody and that it would give him almost as much pleasure as if it had been the captain or the lieutenant.

But before Spermwhale had that pleasure he and Baxter received a call in 7-A-85's area because Roscoe Rules and Whaddayamean Dean were handling a call in 7-A-33's area because Spencer Van Moot and Father Willie had received a fateful call which almost made them the only team in LAPD history to get beaten up by a man three feet tall:

"Seven-A-Thirty-three, Seven-A-Thirty-three, see the woman, three-eleven suspect, First and Harvard."

"Seven-A-Thirty-three, roger on the call," Father Willie automatically answered and then turned suddenly to Spencer. "She say First and Harvard?"

"Yeah," Spencer replied absently.

"A wienie wagger at First and Harvard!" said Father Willie. Spencer was puzzled for a moment and then said, "Oh."

"Filthy Herman!" they both cried at once and then a noisy string of obscenities from the black and white startled a woman pedestrian waiting for the light to change on Beverly Boulevard.

"Niles and Bloomguard are out fucking off again!" Spencer whined. "Why aren't they handling the call? It's their area!"

"Darn it!" Father Willie said. "No, wait a minute, I saw them in the station penciling out an arrest report."

"Filthy Herman!" Spencer groaned as the black and white came to a stop in some heavy evening traffic near the Wilshire Country Club, which further angered the policeman.

"Just put your mind in neutral with the car, partner," Father Willie advised. "We aren't going anywhere in this traffic for a while."

"Goddamnit!" snapped Spencer, yelling to any motorist within earshot. "If you're gonna camp here, pitch a fucking tent!"

The reason that Spencer Van Moot was so angry and Father Willie so apprehensive was Filthy Herman. He was a legless wienie wagger who lived in a boardinghouse near First and Harvard owned by his daughter Rosie Muldoon who struck it rich by marrying an extremely successful anesthesiologist and now could afford to keep her father, Filthy Herman, in a piece of rental property across town from her.

It was ordinarily a good arrangement. The house was large and Herman often had it filled with other alcoholics who congregated in the Eighth Street bars, a half mile from Herman's home. Filthy Herman was somewhat of a celebrity on Eighth Street, partly because of his grotesque physical presence. He was a torso in a wheelchair. Both legs had been amputated at the buttocks when he was thirty-seven years old, a powerful ironworker until a steel beam crushed him. He was also a celebrity because, with the monthly allowance from the daughter who visited him once a year on Christmas, Herman would buy drinks for every man who could not afford to buy his own. This meant that Filthy Herman had a group of some thirty to forty admirers and hangers-on among his Eighth

Street entourage. What he didn't spend on drinks for the house he gambled away in gin rummy games or with the many bookies who frequented the area.

About twice a year, for no apparent reason, Filthy Herman would live up to his name and his normal alcoholic binge would end with his standing on two inch stumps on the wooden porch of his home, naked except for a Dodger baseball cap, screaming, "My cock's dragging the ground, how about yours?" Which indeed it was, what with the absence of legs.

Then the unfortunate radio car officers who got the call would be subjected to a barrage of incredible obscenities, empty bottles, beer cans, spitting, bites on the leg and surprisingly painful punches from the gnarled fists of Filthy Herman, who at fifty was not devoid of the strength acquired while an ironworker.

Any officer who had worked the division long enough had seen the legless torso of Filthy Herman bouncing across the asphalt as he was dragged cursing into the station by two disheveled policemen. Because of his physical impairment he was a pathetic sight when cleaned up and no judge had ever given him more than sixty days in the county jail for battery on a police officer.

The outraged victim of Filthy Herman was standing with her husband on the northwest corner of First and Harvard when the policemen arrived. Spencer sighed, parked on the east side of Harvard, slowly set the brake and turned off the headlights. He grabbed his flashlight and baton and followed Father Willie across the street.

"You call?" Father Willie asked the fortyish mousy woman who held a white toy poodle to her face and deferred to her tight lipped husband, a big man in a loose golf sweater and checkered pants.

"My wife was walking the dog," the man sputtered. "Just out walking our dog and she passed a house up there on Harvard and this filthy little *animal*, this *creature*, exposed himself to her!"

"Where'd it happen?" Father Willie asked, opening his report book and leaning against a car at the curb, his hat tipped back as he wrote.

"Back up the street," the man said. "The third or fourth house."

"You see it, sir?" Father Willie asked.

"No, my wife ran home and got me, and I came back here with her and she pointed out the house, but there was nobody on the porch. I was going to kill him." And the man put his arm around the skinny woman who clutched the toy poodle more tightly, lip quivering.

"What'd he do, ma'am?" asked Willie as he filled in the blanks for type of crime and location.

"He exposed himself! I told you!" said the man.

"Have to hear it from the witness," Spencer said.

"He yelled something horrible to me as I walked by," the woman answered brokenly. "And he showed himself. Oh, he was a horrible creature!"

"What'd he look like" asked Father Willie, writing a cursory narrative.

"He . . . he had no legs!" cried the woman. "He was a horrible ugly little creature with, oh, I don't know, grayish hair and a horribly twisted body. And he had no legs! And he was naked! Except for a blue baseball cap!"

"I see," said Father Willie and then, unable to resist, "Did you notice anything *unusual* about him?"

And the woman answered, "Well, he had a tattoo on his chest, a woman or something. His porch light was on and I could see him very well."

"What'd he say to you when you passed?"

"Oh, God!" the woman said and the poodle yapped when she squeezed it to her face.

"Do we have to?" the man asked. "I'd like to go back and kick that little freak clear off the porch."

"You could," shrugged Spencer, "but he's a wiry little guy. Probably bite you in the knee and give you lockjaw."

"He said . . . he said . . . God!" the woman sobbed.

"Yeah," Spencer encouraged her.

"He said, 'I ain't got no left knee and no right knee, but look at my wienie!' Oh, God!"

"Yeah, that's our man all right," said Father Willie grimly. "Filthy Herman!"

After taking the complaining party's name, address and other routine information, the two policemen told them to go home and let the law deal with the little criminal. And they knew they stood a good chance of being punched in the balls or bitten on the thigh if they weren't careful. In that Filthy Herman was a legless man, not one team of policemen had ever had the good sense to call for assistance when arresting him. It was a matter of pride that two policemen with four legs between them should not have to call brother officers to help with this recurring problem.

"I'd like to punt the little prick sixty yards," Spencer said nervously as they climbed the steps to the darkened house of Filthy Herman.

"Wish we had a gunnysack to put him in. I hear he bites like a crocodile," said Father Willie, leading the way with his flashlight beam trained on the doorway.

The officers banged on the door and rang the bell several times until Spencer finally said, "Let's cut out. We tried. He's probably in there hiding. Let the dicks get a warrant and go down on Eighth Street during the day and pluck him off the bar at one of those gin mills where he plays the horses."

"Fine by me," Father Willie breathed, starting to imagine he heard a ghostly dragging chain above him in the dark old house. He looked up and saw dust falling from the porch roof which was sagging and full of holes and patched in several places with plywood and canvas.

Then they heard canvas tear and shingles fell on their heads as Filthy Herman sprung his surprise which put Spencer in Central Receiving Hospital for observation.

Spencer Van Moot was jolted forward almost out of his shoes, leaving his hat and flashlight behind as he flew crashing through Filthy Herman's front door while Father Willie stared in shock.

Father Willie slowly and incredulously realized what had happened when Filthy Herman came swinging back out the door, suspended by a heavy chain, and spit as he passed. Then he swung back in toward the doorway screaming, "C'mon and fight, you big sissy!" and spit again.

Detectives who filed felony charges against Filthy Herman

for the violent assault against Spencer Van Moot were to piece together the story the next day. The self-confessed attacker said he had become tired of being dragged off to jail every time he got a little bit drunk and flogged his dummy on the porch. Filthy Herman had decided to frustrate the next arrest by chaining himself to an ancient steel and porcelain freestanding bathtub in the second story bathroom of his home. He had acquired a fifty foot piece of chain from a fellow horse player on Eighth Street who worked at a wrecking yard, and with a tempered steel lock supplied by the same friend, had criss-crossed his torso, using the chain like the bandolier of a Mexican bandit. Then he encircled his waist and locked it in the front.

After his crime against the woman with the poodle, Filthy Herman had been in the bathroom on the second floor when he saw the officers arrive. He had planned to fight it out there in the bathroom but suddenly the swashbuckling plan burst forth. He crawled out on the porch roof, dragging his chain, until he was just over the unsuspecting officers at the front door beneath him. And without anticipating the consequences, he yelled "Geronimo!" and pitched forward through a hole in the porch roof, swinging down and in, striking Spencer Van Moot behind the neck with 150 pounds of beefy torso and propelling the policeman through the front door, splitting it in two and knocking the doorjamb ten feet across the room. Then he was swinging back and forth, screaming obscenities, spitting, snapping and challenging the bewildered Father Willie.

When Father Willie eventually came to his senses with Filthy Herman swaying dizzily in front of his eyes, the choirboy began yelling, "You *dirty* little bugger!" and swinging the nightstick wildly until he broke it on Filthy Herman's head.

Then by the time the neighbors, who were sick and tired of the crashing and screaming, called for additional police, Father Willie had Filthy Herman punched silly.

It took an hour and a half to get Filthy Herman dragged back up on the roof by his chain, pulled into the bathroom and covered with a bathrobe until an officer from Central Property could arrive with bolt cutters large enough to handle the heavy links.

Spencer Van Moot was in the hospital for three days with neck and back spasms. Father Willie was on light duty for a week with two broken bones in his right hand. Filthy Herman had one tooth knocked loose, two black eyes and a broken nose.

Both Filthy Herman and his daughter wept in each other's arms in court three weeks later and Herman was eventually put on probation for one year with the stipulation that he drink no alcoholic beverage. One week after the sentence Filthy Herman got drunk again, masturbated from the step of a fire truck and threw a fire extinguisher at an amazed fireman. Filthy Herman got six months in jail for that one, which proved what all policemen already knew: it's more risky to beat up firemen because they're popular.

So, while Spencer was meeting his Waterloo at the hands of Filthy Herman, Spermwhale Whalen and Baxter Slate had to meander south into the ghetto of Wilshire Division, which would probably not be called a ghetto in any other large city in the world, to answer a call that ended up being just another attempt by Clyde Percy to get into Camarillo State Hospital.

Clyde Percy was a seventy year old black man who lived in the vicinity of the Baldwin Hills reservoir. Because in the great flood of 1963 he had plunged into the raging water and rescued a drowning woman who was trapped in her overturned car, Clyde Percy was presented with a commendation by the City of Los Angeles, the first official praise he had ever been given in his entire life. Now he simply couldn't wander too far from the scene of his triumph and was the object of numerous radio calls. People would find Clyde Percy asleep in their unlocked cars or in the storage sheds of small businesses, and once, in a pièce de résistance, he slept all night on a posture perfect mattress in the window of a department store in the Crenshaw shopping district. The next morning he was discovered by passing shoppers still in the store window, fully clothed, muddy shoes and all. He was snoring peacefully, slobbering out the side of his toothless mouth, dreaming of some woman far far back in his memory, holding onto an erection which only came in sleep. Clyde got ninety days that time.

"Wonder why Spencer Van Moot and Father Willie weren't

assigned the call," Spermwhale grumbled to Baxter Slate. "I'll bet they're off in some fuckin clothin store buyin some Lord Fauntleroy bow tie for Spencer or some tooty fruity boots. Man's forty years old and he dresses like an interior decorator or somethin."

The radio call which Spermwhale and Baxter Slate received concerned an open door a tremulous security guard had found while making his rounds at a furniture store on the east side of Crenshaw. The security officer had heard ghostly sounds coming from within the store and though the sun had not yet set, it was dim and shadow filled inside. The guard was seventy-five years old and didn't really want to be a security guard but if he relied on Social Security to support him and his seventy-three year old wife they'd have to eat dog food five days a week instead of two.

"Go on about your rounds," Spermwhale told the old man. "We'll check it out."

"I'll be right over there across the street by my car if you need me," the guard promised. "I'll be close to my radio in case you need help."

"Sure," Spermwhale said, "stay there in case we need you."

And he patted the guard on the shoulder and pointed him toward his car which was not across the street as he thought but in the parking lot back of the building. The old man lost his car at least once a night.

When they were alone and dusk was deepening, Baxter said, "We're calling for another car, aren't we?"

"Nope," said Spermwhale, "it's just old Clyde Percy."

"Who?"

"Clyde the lifeguard. The old dingaling that pulled the broad outta the sewer back in the flood. Ain't you heard a him? He's always gettin busted for somethin or other."

"How do you know it's him?"

"His MO. He breaks into places right after they close and he eats up whatever's around and goes to sleep. I know it's him because a the noises the doorshaker said he made. Like a ghost. They always say that, people who call in."

"What's the noise?"

"He cries. Sits in there and cries. He sounds like a mournful moose. I tell you it's Clyde Percy in there."

But just in case, Baxter Slate unlocked the Ithaca shotgun from the rack and jacked one in the chamber when they walked single file into the darkened store looking for the mournful moose.

It was a small furniture store which advertised entire living room sets for six hundred dollars. Clyde Percy would have none of the cheap furniture. They found him in the rear on the second floor by the manager's office sprawled out on a nine hundred dollar tufted Chesterfield, eating a half empty bag of potato chips and a banana, which one of the clerks had left behind. He wore his regular attire, which was two dirty undershirts and three outer shirts with a ragged colorless turtleneck sweater over all, a pair of stout flannel pants over longjohn underwear, run over combat boots and a World War II flier's hat without the goggles.

"H'lo, Clyde," Spermwhale said as Baxter lowered the riot gun and ejected the live round from the chamber.

"Aw right, Officer, aw right," said Clyde Percy, grinning happily and standing at attention, his purple lips smeared with banana, his skin blue-black in the shadows. "Y'all caught me fair an square. Don't need no handcuffs. I'm gonna come peaceable. Course if you wanna use handcuffs it's okay too."

"Ain't seen you around for a while, Clyde," Spermwhale said as they walked the old man down the stairs, each policeman holding an elbow because he reeked of wine and staggered on the landing.

"Got locked up last November. Jist in time for Thanksgivin. Ain't missed a Thanksgivin at Central Jail in twenny-eight years."

"You've been in jail since November?" Baxter asked as he navigated down the steep stairs gingerly, holding Clyde and the shotgun and now needing a flashlight in the gloom.

"No suh," Clyde Percy said. "This time a wunnuful thing happened to ol Clyde. I was sent to Camarilla State Hospital. The public defender say ol Clyde's crazy. An first I din't wanna go cause I likes your jail. I likes the sheriff's jail even better, no offense to you officers. He tell me, Clyde, we gonna get you sent to this crazy hospital and you gonna like it even better'n jail. So I say okay, and off I go up to Camarilla, and know what? They gives me a job up there teachin."

"Teaching?" Baxter said and stumbled with Clyde at the bottom of the stairs, dropping his riot gun and flashlight, kicking the light under a counter in the dark.

While the two policemen got down on their knees to look for the lost flashlight, Clyde Percy picked up the riot gun helpfully and was holding it cradled in his arms like a baby when Sergeant Nick Yanov came through the front door.

"Holy shit!" yelled Nick Yanov, drawing, crouching, throwing his flashlight beam on Clyde Percy who had lifted the gun to his shoulder upside down and started eating potato chips over the prone bodies of the two policemen.

"Drop the fucking gun or I'll blow you away!" Nick Yanov screamed.

The next few minutes involved several panic stricken shouts after which Spermwhale sat the sergeant down on a display couch, gave him a cigarette and convinced him they were alive, that Baxter had unloaded the magazine when he ejected the live round, that Clyde Percy was a harmless old acquaintance of Spermwhale Whalen's and that Sergeant Yanov should remain on the couch until his legs steadied.

"Sure glad it was you, Sarge," Spermwhale Whalen said to the chesty, bristle jawed sergeant. "If it was one a them other cunt supervisors he'd a probably cut old Clyde in half and we'd a ended up with another suspension for lettin Clyde get wasted."

"Why do you do things like this to me," Nick Yanov said, drawing heavily on the cigarette as some color returned to his face.

Then the two policemen and Clyde Percy helped the weak kneed Sergeant Yanov out of the store and to his car, Clyde Percy apologizing profusely for scaring him to death.

"Where's the nearest gas station?" Sergeant Yanov asked as he got back in his black and white and threw his hat and light on the seat, running both hands through his heavy black hair.

"Why, you gotta take a crap?" Spermwhale grinned.

"No, I just did! I gotta clean up!" said Nick Yanov as he fired up the radio car and roared away.

"Good fuckin sergeant," Spermwhale Whalen mused in an extremely rare moment, and then reverted to his old self. "Not like that eunuch lieutenant and that gelding captain and all the other cocksuckin sergeants on the nightwatch."

"So what's with the teaching you say you did at Camarillo?" Baxter asked when they got Clyde safely in the radio car and were on their way to jail to book him for drunk.

"I tell you, Officer," said Clyde Percy, munching tooth-lessly on potato chips, "it was *such* a fine place. They was all these kids, retarded, you know? Ain't nobody come to visit em most a the time. They gives em jobs to keep em busy, like makin these little balloon toys. You puts the balloons on the little blow-up stems like. So they gives me the job a helpin watch over all the kids. So I does things like make sure they kin attach balloons right and that they don't fight too much and don't fall on their heads and bite their tongues and so forth like that. And then one day I made a invention. I drills holes in this board to put the stems in and then the kids kin attach three balloons at once and makes it easier to hold em. One a the bosses there says to me, 'Clyde, you jist about the best we ever have workin here.' So I tells him bout the time I save the lady in the flood and he say, 'Clyde, you kin stay here if you wants to.'"

"Why're you out then?" asked Spermwhale, driving the black and white west on Venice Boulevard.

"They say one day they jist ain't no more room, jist room for real crazy people and I ain't that crazy. So that night I start sayin I'm the President and mayor, and like that. But they say it ain't no good, Clyde, we know you ain't really crazy like some folks, leastways you ain't so crazy you gonna hurt some-body. And then I thought bout hurtin one a the technicians, punchin em or somethin, but they all so nice to me I couldn't. So they put me out and here I is, back home agin."

"That's a goddamn shame," Spermwhale said angrily, turn-ing in his seat toward Baxter. "I seen fifty dollar a trick whores, and dopers and pimps, and thieves and assholes for three gen-erations all on welfare and we can't even afford a fuckin bed and three squares at a state hospital for Clyde. That pisses me off!"

"Think you kin do somethin to git me back there?" asked the old man, his blue lips flaked with potato chips, the left earflap of his flier's cap turned up from the scuffle with Sergeant Yanov.

"By God, if there's any justice in this miserable world, which there ain't, somebody oughtta help you. Tell you what, you plead not guilty at your arraignment tomorrow. Then I'll be in court on trial day. I'll talk to the city attorney and tell him that you're always walkin around the street threatenin everybody and sayin you're the Easter Bunny and wavin your dong at housewives and stuffin dog shit in mailboxes and settin trash fires and in general bein a bigger pain in the ass than Francis Tanaguchi."

"Francis who?"

"Oh, never mind," Spermwhale said as they parked in the station parking lot and got out of the car. "Anyways, I'm gonna tell him you're the Wilshire Division whacko and a horrible asshole and you shouldn't be put away for ninety days for drunk like you usually are because you're a dingaling. And then I'll say I think you should get a sanity hearin and shipped off to Camarillo again."

"Oh, Officer," said Clyde, and the tears welled in the old man's eyes and he even stopped eating potato chips. "Oh, I'll be crazier than you say I is, I kin stand on my head . . ."

"No, don't go too far," Spermwhale said. "Just stare off in space and say somethin goofy every time somebody asks you somethin."

"I'll shoo skeeters that ain't there," said Clyde as they shuffled toward the steps of the station.

"Yeah, like that," Spermwhale said as they half lifted the old man up the steps.

"I'll punch a policeman right in the mouf," said Clyde.

"No, don't do that," said Spermwhale.

"A public defender?" Baxter Slate suggested.

"No, no," Spermwhale said as they opened the side door and took Clyde inside.

"A judge? How about a judge?" Baxter offered.

"No," Spermwhale said, "let's not overdo it. Just swat invisible mosquitoes or beat off at the jury or somethin."

Then Clyde Percy came to a limping halt in front of the barred jail doors and looked up at Spermwhale, and Clyde's face, dust covered, but charcoal black in places, was streaked and wet.

"I appreciates it, Officer," he said to the fat policeman. "I wants to go back to the chirruns, back to Camarilla. I appreciates what you doin for me." And then he took Spermwhale's big hand in his and wept.

"Jesus, Clyde! Okay! Okay!" Spermwhale said, pulling his hand away and looking around to see if other policemen were looking. "It's okay. You don't have to . . . it's gonna be all right. I don't mind bein there in court. I ain't got nothin to do anyways. Jesus, it's okay. Quit cryin, will ya?"

Spermwhale Whalen *did* go to the court trial of Clyde Percy, and *did* succeed in getting a sanity hearing for the old man. But Clyde Percy was deemed not to be a hazard to himself or others and sane enough to be released. He *was* released, after which he walked one mile downtown, shoplifted a short dog of wine, poured it over his head and lay down in the middle of the intersection at First and Los Angeles streets, having to wait only ninety seconds until a police car heading into the police building was forced to stop, pick up the Baldwin Hills lifeguard and book him into Central Jail on a plain drunk charge. He was given ninety days in the county jail, which was better than nothing but a far cry from Camarillo State Hospital where he invented the device to help retarded children blow up balloons.

When Whaddayamean Dean broke into one of his numerous drunken crying jags at choir practice after hearing of the ultimate fate of Clyde Percy, Roscoe Rules called him a nigger lover and said the old cocksucker probably wanted to go back to Camarillo in the first place just to molest the little dummies.

Spermwhale Whalen was in a foul mood after they booked Clyde Percy. The mail drop had arrived at Wilshire Station and contained an eight by ten glossy photo sent to Spermwhale by his classmate, Sergeant Harry Bragg of the police department photo lab. The picture was a mug shot of Spermwhale Whalen's eldest son, Patrick, who had died thirteen months earlier of a drug overdose. It was the only picture the boy had taken in the last two years of his life, this one when he was arrested for car theft in Van Nuys.

Spermwhale, the veteran of three failed marriages, had not seen much of the boy after adolescence, and he studied the photo carefully, appreciating the skill of Sergeant Harry Bragg who had removed the booking number and profile shot, and blown up the full face part of the double mug shot until probably only a policeman would suspect from whence it had come.

Technically it was a successful picture, artistically a dismal failure. He could detect none of the boy's considerable intelligence in the arrogant eyes and narrow mouth. The shoulder length hair was totally unfamiliar, as was a small fresh scar over the right eye. It was not the son he wanted to remember, not if he wished to keep the guilt from overtaking him.

Spermwhale was scowling and chewing a cigar to shreds when he and Baxter went back to the radio car. The night had become exceptionally black.

"What's wrong with you?" Baxter asked.

"Nothin."

"Look a little mad."

"I ain't mad. Why should I be mad? I make seventeen grand a year, don't I? Course after income tax and pension contribution and Police Relief and Police Protective League and the credit union and three wives and rent, I have about a dollar thirty cents to eat on between paydays. And I just come off a four day suspension so I gotta stop eatin for about two weeks. So what've I got to be pissed off about?"

"That it? Money?"

"Money, who needs money? Just because I been cuffed around a little bit by the heavy hand a justice? Just because I lost four days' pay? Shit, that ain't nothin. I only got three ex-wives to support, and three ex-kids . . . no, *two* ex-kids to feed. And an ex-dog and my turtle. Course the turtle's sometimes in hibernation so he don't eat too much. It's only fair that I got four days' suspension for keepin those avocados Francis gave me. But the thing bothers me. I wonder if Lieutenant Grimsley and all them IAD headhunters get a finder's fee when they nail a cop? Maybe they get a percentage of what the city saves off our paycheck when we get suspended. Ever think a that?"

"I could loan you twenty bucks till payday."

"Fuck it, I don't need money. Old Clyde Percy gets along without it, don't he?"

"It's pretty decent what you're going to do for him," Baxter Slate said. "The way you're going to bat to get the old man back in the laughing academy."

"Listen, partner," Spermwhale said, and now the cigar was almost eaten and he was spitting black leafy tobacco out the window of the radio car, "just because I *seem* to care about people once in a while, don't make no mistakes about me. Nineteen plus years a workin these streets has taught me that people are shit. They're scum. Only reason I don't treat em like Roscoe Rules or some a those black glove hotdogs is what's that do for you? Gets you fired for brutality or an ulcer or somethin. For what? The human race is no fuckin good but workin with these rotten bastards is all we got, right? It's the only game in town so you gotta play like you're still *in* the game. If you don't, if you drop out, you take your fuckin six inch Colt and see can you pull the trigger twice while you're eatin it. I just don't wanna off myself like so many cops do. So once in a while I do somethin that might look to you like I give a fuck about some a these scumbags. But there's nothin more rotten than people."

And the very next call of the night did nothing to change Spermwhale's mind.

"Think I'll go see my ex-wife tomorrow," Spermwhale said to Baxter who had just suggested taking code seven at the half price restaurant north of Wilshire on Western.

"Which one?" asked Baxter.

"The second ex-wife," Spermwhale said. "I like her best in some ways. She had the most balls. Took every dime I had. I like to see her once in a while and visit my ex-dog and my ex-car."

"She still give you a little?"

"Wouldn't want it. Her ass is so big she has to sit down in shifts. And she's as old as runnin water. I like them young animals like Carolina Moon. Her fat's all smooth and bouncy. I like em with enough strength to fight!"

"Gonna have to call a choir practice one of these nights," said Baxter Slate, as the Regretful Rapist was pulling a black woman out of her Ford sedan just two blocks ahead and trying to drag her off behind a large trash dumpster in the darkness.

She screamed at two men passing by who just kept walking, observing the golden rule of city dwellers: Do unto others if you want to risk getting your fucking head blown off.

"I'm getting awfully hungry," Baxter Slate said as the Regretful Rapist was discovering that the black woman was almost as strong as he and was not going to submit, knife or no knife. The rapist was furiously trying to find the dagger she had knocked from his hand to plunge it into her throat.

"You know, there's somethin about Nick Yanov reminds me a my youngest kid," Spermwhale said as he lit a fresh cigar and Baxter glided slowly around the traffic consisting of diners looking for parking off La Cienega's Restaurant Row, to avoid tipping valet parking lot attendants.

"Your kid isn't that old," Baxter said.

"No," said Spermwhale, "but he just looks somethin like Yanov. You know, I'm afraid he's gonna get in trouble like the others. Last time he came to see me he wouldn't even accept some clothes I bought him. Only wants to hang around Venice Beach with the hippies. Don't even want some clean underwear. You see, he can't stand ownin *anything.* He only wants the clothes on his back. Can't even stand the responsibility of changin his skivvies. I'm afraid if he ever went to jail and had someone make all his decisions for him, he might like it."

Baxter Slate tried to think of something to change the subject because he didn't want Spermwhale to start thinking of the oldest boy.

And the Regretful Rapist, not a bit regretful at the moment, grabbed the black woman by the throat and almost choked the life out of her before she succeeded in burying her teeth in his bicep and squirming free just long enough to manage a chilling scream which was nearly her very last.

"Jesus Christ, what was that?" Spermwhale jerked upright in his seat and grabbed the flashlight as Baxter wheeled the car around and screeched into the darkened parking lot, catching the screaming woman and the raging rapist full in the headlight beams as they fought on the ground.

Then Spermwhale, moving like a younger slimmer man, was out of the car before it stopped, chasing the fleeing rapist across the parking lot shouting, "Stop, you motherfucker, or you're maggot meat!"

Baxter Slate, finally getting his flashlight to work by banging it on his hip as he ran, caught up with Spermwhale who was standing motionless and aiming two handed at a running shadow eighty feet away. Then there were three explosions in Baxter's ear and the Regretful Rapist dropped to the asphalt shrieking in terror from a slight wound which entered his lower back, broke two ribs, ricocheted around the rib cage, following the path of least resistance, and exited in the front, causing, aside from the broken ribs, little more than a flesh wound. And this caused Roscoe Rules at the next afternoon's rollcall to scream loudly for the hundredth time that they should be permitted to carry dumdums and high velocity ammo.

When the two policemen got to the wounded suspect and stood over him, he shook his mop of sweaty hair out of his face and yelled in panic and shock, "You shot me in the back, you chickenshit!"

Spermwhale, panting heavily from excitement and exhaustion, yelled back, "There ain't no rules out here, you cocksucker! The Marquis of Queensberry's just some fag over on Eighth Street!"

And the Regretful Rapist was caught. Spermwhale Whalen and Baxter Slate each received a Class A commendation which was worth exactly nothing in terms of promotion, prestige or economic remuneration. They both offered to trade it for the four days' pay which had been taken away for accepting the imprudent avocados, but the watch commander told them he didn't think that was very funny.

Perhaps Spermwhale Whalen's greatest contribution was the rapport he established with the rapist in the five hours they were together at the emergency hospital, the detective bureau and finally the General Hospital jail ward where they booked him.

It started when Spermwhale bought two candy bars for himself and his starving partner and discovered that he had punched the wrong button and got one full of caramel which he never ate because it stuck to his partial plate.

"Here, want some candy?" he asked the rapist as the young man was sitting handcuffed to a chair in the emergency ward.

"Thanks," the rapist said, and Spermwhale noticed that his eyes were glassy and shining from tears, and though he had refused to speak to detectives, the fat policeman said, "Pretty good candy, ain't it? You like candy?"

"It's okay," the rapist said, his large blue eyes moving around the room.

Then Spermwhale said, "I did you a favor by shootin you."

The rapist turned, wiped his face on the shoulder of his torn jacket and said, "How's that?"

"You woulda been booked in an LAPD jail. We wake our prisoners up at five A.M. and serve them meals of red death, Gainesburgers and donkey dicks. This way you're gonna be in the hospital jail ward and then in the county jail when you heal up. Chow's a hundred percent better. Same with the bed and cell. I did you a favor."

"Thanks."

"You know, I don't blame you for what you done. I get the urge sometimes myself. Ugly guy like me and all the pussy around just teasin a guy with this no bra stuff and tight pants. Shit, they ask for it."

"You think so?"

"Sure. We all got our bad habits. Hell, I can't quit smokin and drinkin, how can I criticize you?"

The Regretful Rapist smiled at the fat policeman and eventually accepted two more candy bars with caramel and almonds and confessed to more than thirty rapes, including twelve which had never been reported to the police but were verified through a detective follow-up.

Spermwhale Whalen was given his usual subpar score the very next time he went before a board on a promotional exam. He had for years been wasting his off-duty time flying 200,000 pounds of mechanized and human cargo for his country instead of taking police science classes at night school.

As Captain Drobeck said at a private staff meeting, who in the hell wants supervisors and executives who were only good for flying airplanes and catching dangerous crooks like the Regretful Rapist? Besides, Spermwhale Whalen was unpolished and fat and had ridiculous feet. He wore a wide triple E shoe but his feet were an abnormally short size 7 1/2. It looked like he was walking on waffles.

9

Tommy Rivers

"Kudos to Roscoe Rules!" Sergeant Nick Yanov announced at rollcall on the night Baxter Slate shot the ordinary guy. "Roscoe just had his annual physical, and the medical report here says his *Phthirius pubis* count is very low this year. I looked that up and it means body crabs."

After the nightwatch stopped applauding the scowling Roscoe Rules, Lieutenant Finque tried to get everyone in really good spirits by showing them photos he had borrowed from homicide detectives of the monstrously bloody corpse of Nathan Zelinski, a seventy-two year old janitor who had been stomped to death by two sixteen year old boys during a burglary at a junior high school three years earlier.

"Drove his nose bones right down his throat," Lieutenant Finque said. "Old man actually drowned on his own blood. Took him almost forty-five minutes to die. According to their confessions they kept coming over and looking at him every once in a while."

"They have a fascination for such things," Baxter Slate whispered to no one in particular.

"Who?" Spermwhale asked.

"Kids."

"Reason I showed you," the lieutenant continued, "is that

the second boy was just released from camp and is back in our division. The first got out four months ago."

And while the nightwatch passed the pictures around and cursed the courts and penal authorities and their lot in general, Sergeant Nick Yanov asked under his breath, "Lieutenant, did you have to do this?"

"Of course," the lieutenant answered. "I want them to know what kind of idiots we have to fight within the system."

"Don't you think they know? Why keep reminding them they're shoveling shit against the tide? Why?"

"We'll talk about it later," Lieutenant Finque said.

But they never did. On Nick Yanov's next rating report Lieutenant Finque wrote, "Sergeant Yanov needs a lot of seasoning before he can hope to be a top supervisor. Lacks maturity."

And to continue to show Sergeant Yanov who was boss, Lieutenant Finque said to the assembly, "Oh, and by the way, did you hear about the other young kids the Youth Opportunity folks placed at General Hospital for summer employment. They had *lengthy* drug records so they put them in the *pharmacy* washing bottles. You can guess the rest. And a couple of things we discussed at the supervisors' meeting," the lieutenant went on, now that he was getting warmed up. "We have some local businessmen who make frequent burglary and theft reports and don't want uniformed officers coming in the front door to take reports. Gives the place a bad name."

The lieutenant smiled smugly when he heard the roar this tidbit aroused. "Of course the captain gave them what for. You would've been proud of him."

"I always knew he was behind us," said Spermwhale Whalen. "I felt him there many times."

The lieutenant didn't know how to interpret Spermwhale's observation so he continued with the good news. "And you can all just quit grousing about how long you have to wait in court until your case is called. I've talked it over with the captain and he talked it over with the commander and he talked it over with the deputy chief . . ."

"And he talked it over with Dear Abby who's runnin this fuckin department," said Spermwhale Whalen.

"And he talked it over with his counterpart at the courts,"

said Lieutenant Finque ignoring the laughter. "Private counsel simply has priority at court trials over defendants with public defenders."

"Yeah," Spermwhale said, "most a the people we bust have public defenders who don't have to get out quick to make a few more bucks from some other client, so us cops and our civilian witnesses and victims have to cool our heels while these black-robed pussies take care a their fuckin fraternity brothers. If they ain't got a monopoly I don't know who does. Who worries about cops?"

"Who worries about victims?" Baxter Slate observed.

"Them too," Spermwhale nodded.

"Well, it's good to get these things off our chests at roll-call," Lieutenant Finque said jauntily now that he had turned twenty-eight cheerful men into seething blue avengers. Then Lieutenant Finque said, "Sergeant Yanov's going to hold a gun inspection while I keep an appointment with the captain. There've been some dirty guns in recent inspections and the captain says he's going to start coming down hard on you men. You may not appreciate it but you work a damned good division. Even the people we serve are the best. Our citizens show a great interest in the Basic Car Plan meetings and they purchase lots of whistles."

"Hey, Lieutenant," Spermwhale said. "Is it true the station buys those whistles for seven cents?"

"I don't know the details," said Lieutenant Finque.

"That's a forty-three cent profit on each whistle," said Spermwhale.

"I don't know the details."

"Jesus, we musta made thousands a bucks with this caper," Spermwhale observed.

"I don't know, but it's for our Youth Services Fund so it's a worthy cause."

"Is is true there's some civilian whistle maker flyin all over the goddamn country tryin to sell the idea to other departments?"

"I'm not familiar."

"What a scam. You gotta hand it to some a the eunuchs in this department. Once in a while they come up with an idea.

Why didn't I think a that? I coulda made enough in one year to pay off all my ex-wives!"

"Enough on whistles," Lieutenant Finque smiled nervously, since he was the eunuch who thought of it or at least who stole the idea from the senile old lady who thought crime could be stamped out if there were thousands of other old ladies running around blowing whistles at bad guys.

"Maybe I could get in on the action, Lieutenant," Spermwhale persisted. "I got this idea for sellin one to every broad in the city. See, we design a whistle shaped like a cock and the part you hold is shaped like a pair a balls with two LAPD badges pinned to them. Our sales motto could be 'Blow for your local policeman.' "

"It might work, Lieutenant!" cried Francis Tanaguchi.

"That's a swell idea, Spermwhale!" cried Spencer Van Moot.

"I know a guy could design the whistles!" cried Harold Bloomguard.

Lieutenant Finque felt like crying. It always happened like this. He'd discuss a serious subject with the men and they'd end up making fun of him. Supervisor or not, he would have given anything to punch Spermwhale Whalen right in his big, red, scarred up nose. And he'd have done it too if he weren't petrified of the fat policeman and if he weren't absolutely sure Spermwhale would break his back.

"I think you better hurry if you're going to make your appointment," Sergeant Yanov suggested, to save his superior officer from further trauma.

But before Lieutenant Finque walked out the door he said, "I'll tell you men one thing. Because of our whistles we've developed excellent rapport with the people we serve. If you should get in a fight with a suspect out there on these streets you don't have to worry. Our good people won't stand by and let you get kicked in the head!"

"No, they'll cut it off and shrink it," Roscoe Rules said dryly as Lieutenant Finque exited trembling.

Sergeant Yanov tried to make the gun inspection palatable by taking Harold Bloomguard's gun, looking down the barrel and saying, "Kee-rist, Harold, when was the last time you

cleaned this thing? There's a spider been down there so long
he has three hash marks on his sleeve."

Baxter Slate was one of three college graduates among the
choirboys, the others being Sam Niles and Harold Bloomguard,
both of whom obtained degrees while police officers. Two of
the others were upperclassmen in part time studies, and all but
Spermwhale Whalen had some college units. Baxter Slate not
only had his baccalaureate in the classics, but had been a
graduate student and honors candidate when he dropped out
of college in disgust and impulsively joined the Los Angeles
Police Department five years earlier. He was an unusually
handsome young man, almost twenty-seven years old. He lived
alone in a one bedroom apartment. He had no plans for marrying and no ambition to advance in rank. He said he liked
working uniform patrol, that it gave him a chance to live more
intensely, that sometimes he seemed to live a week or a month
in a single night.

Whereas Calvin Potts read every new book in the police
library which he thought might help him pass the coming
sergeant's examination, Baxter Slate read no books in the police library since they invariably dealt with law, crime and
police. Though Baxter Slate enjoyed doing police work he
hated reading about it. And though Baxter Slate firmly believed that his extensive education in the classics had been the
most colossal waste of money his mother had ever squandered
and that his degree would never at any time in his life be worth
more than the surprisingly cheap paper it was printed on, he
nevertheless could not break old habits. He would occasionally, for the fun of it, struggle with Virgil and Pliny the Elder
to see if he could apply their admonitions to the sensual, self-
contained, alcoholic microcosm of choir practice which to Baxter Slate made more sense than the larger world outside.

Most of the choirboys had worked with Baxter as a partner
at one time or another. He had been in the division three years
and had worked Juvenile for nine months until he discovered
he was a lousy Juvenile officer. Baxter thought he was also a
lousy patrol officer. No one else said that Baxter was a lousy
anything, except Roscoe Rules, who disliked Baxter for having

ideas which confused Roscoe. At choir practice Roscoe often drunkenly accused Baxter of using ten dollar words just to show off in front of Ora Lee Tingle who was so bombed out on gin and vodka she wouldn't have known the difference if Baxter had spoken Latin. And as a matter of fact, Baxter *could* tell dirty jokes in Latin which amused the choirboys except for Roscoe.

"You and your faggy big words," Roscoe shouted one night as he soaked his feet in the MacArthur Park duck pond, watching warily that the ducks did not swim by and attack his toes.

"Baxter don't use big words," Spermwhale Whalen said, looking as though he would like to pulverize Roscoe Rules, who feared and hated Spermwhale even more than he feared and hated the little ducks.

"Well I think he does, goddamnit," Roscoe said but was careful to smile at Spermwhale when he said it.

Baxter was some forty feet away in the darkness, lying on a blanket and shaking his head in wonder that even here in the idyllic tranquilized and totally artificial world of choir practice, it was not entirely possible to escape hostility and violence.

"I think it's faggy and uppity to talk like that," Roscoe Rules said, while the other choirboys drank and teased Ora Lee Tingle or played mumbletypeg in the grass with confiscated and illegal ten inch stilettos or, like Spermwhale Whalen, tossed little stones on the water to watch the ripples, and to neck with Carolina Moon.

Finally Baxter uncoiled his lean body, brushed back his heavy umber hair, longer than anyone's but Spencer Van Moot's, who was constantly under fire from the watch commander to get a haircut, and said, "Roscoe, I sincerely try not to use any big words."

"There! See, you did it again!" Roscoe pointed, banging on the arm of his partner Whaddayamean Dean Pratt who was dozing on his blanket. "See, you said 'sincerely.' Shit. Faggy word. Faggy is what it is."

"I simply asked the fellows if . . ."

"See! You did it again!" shouted the mean and drunken Roscoe Rules as he punched on Dean to arouse him, but his partner only whimpered drunkenly. " 'Fellows.' How many cops you ever hear say 'fellows'? Cops say 'guys' or 'dudes' or 'studs' or 'cats,' but *no* cop in the history of LAPD ever said 'fellows.' Nobody but you, Baxter Slate."

"He didn't say nothin faggy I heard," Calvin Potts said, and the tall black policeman was suddenly standing behind Roscoe Rules who was thinking that the only thing worse than a fag is a nigger and how much fun it would be to kneedrop Calvin Potts and puncture his kidney and smash his spleen like a rotten peach.

"For chrissake, Baxter, tell Roscoe what you said so I can relax," said Francis Tanaguchi who was lost in the expansive bosom of Ora Lee Tingle, trying to persuade her to pull the train for a few of the choirboys. She was now wearing only Spermwhale's T-shirt and her own skintight black flares as she held Francis Tanaguchi in her arms saying how fucking cute Nips are.

"Roscoe," Baxter said patiently, "I only said that policemen see the worst of people and people at their worst. I was simply trying to explain to you and me and all of us our premature cynicism. That's all I said and I wish I'd keep my big mouth shut."

"So do I," muttered Roscoe. "Fucking ten dollar words. A policeman only needs about a hundred words in his whole vocabulary."

"The only big words I use were taught me in the police academy, Roscoe," said Baxter. "Words like hemorrhage and defecation." Baxter took a drink of cold vodka and said, "You know, Roscoe, even you use euphemisms, police euphemisms, like calling your nightstick a baton because the LAPD says to call it that. I refuse to call it that. A baton is a plaything for young girls. There's no phallic connotation whatsoever. If I'm going to carry something to beat people over the head with I insist it have Freudian implications. I learned that in graduate school. Everything must have Freudian implications."

"You making fun a me, Slate?" Roscoe demanded, trying to stagger to his feet.

"You know, a graduate student would love to use a big faggy word like 'emasculated' on you, Roscoe. That's a favorite word of all graduate students. And they would say of your baton that

the true symbol of your sexual identity is the wooden append-
age you store at the station. In other words, your cock's in your
locker."

"Oh, I don't like you, Slate, I never liked you," said Roscoe
Rules who really didn't like Baxter Slate any less than he liked
Harold Bloomguard, Francis Tanaguchi, Calvin Potts and
Spermwhale Whalen, not necessarily in that order. He only
just tolerated his partner, Dean Pratt, who was starting to get
on his nerves, and Father Willie Wright who seemed to be
afraid of him.

"Let's talk economics instead of philosophy, Roscoe," Baxter
Slate said, deciding to test the meanest choirboy. "I think that
the inflationary period follows the prediction of the deficit
meanders of corollary Harry, that Roscoes cannot breed in
captivity and that Chandu the Magician is a cousin of the
condor at Santa Barbara."

"I don't buy that faggy idea any more than the last one,"
Roscoe Rules said, passing the test.

"Whaddaya mean, Baxter? Whaddaya mean?" asked Whaddayamean Dean who had crawled across the grass into the
conversation area.

"What do I mean, Dean, my friend?" said Baxter Slate. "I
mean that I was a lousy Juvenile officer, that's what I mean. I
mean that a battered child has a marvelous capacity to adjust
to his torture and will ceaselessly love his battering parents. I
mean that the mother of a sexually molested child will not
leave nor truly protect the child from the father as long as the
man has a good job or otherwise preserves that mother from
an economic life which is more horrifying to her than the
molestation of her child. I mean that the weakness of the human race is stupefying and that it's not the capacity for evil
which astounds young policemen like you and me, Dean.
Rather it's the mind boggling worthlessness of human beings.
There's not enough dignity in mankind for evil and *that's* the
most terrifying thing a policeman learns."

"Whaddaya trying to say, Baxter? Whaddaya trying to say?"
pleaded Whaddayamean Dean drunkenly.

"I mean that twelve good men and true are a gaggle of
nonprofessional neophytes conditioned by the heroics of

cinema juries which inevitably free the defendant who is inevitably innocent. I mean that they can never really believe that a natural father could do such an unnatural thing to his child."

"I don't get it! I don't get it!" cried Whaddayamean Dean.

"I mean that doctors and professional men are the most arrogant and incompetent witnesses at any criminal proceedings and that they'll screw up your case for sure.

"I mean that the weak and inept parents will always refuse to surrender their neglected children to the authorities because they want to atone for failures with older children and the cycle inevitably repeats itself.

"I mean that perhaps economics, not morality, is our last consideration, and that the judge has a point when you plead with him to put a man away to save that man's family and the judge says, 'Swell, but who do you want me to let out?' "

"What's he mean? What's he mean?" yelled Whaddayamean Dean to the drunken choirboys. Dean was boozy enough for a crying jag now, the tears welling as he bobbed and weaved and almost fell over backward.

"And I mean that when policemen have to deal with small inflexible men in their own ranks, perhaps it becomes too much. And perhaps part of the reason that Roscoe Rules is small and inflexible and insensitive is because traditional police administrators—men like Captain Drobeck, and Commander Moss and Chief Lynch—are small and inflexible and insensitive and . . ."

"I heard that faggy remark, Slate, you scrote!" said Roscoe Rules, still unable to stand.

"I mean that cops chase society's devils as well as their own, which becomes unbearably terrifying since the devil is at last only the mirror image of a creature utterly without worth or dignity. And that the physical dangers of police work are grossly overrated but the emotional dangers make it the most hazardous job on earth."

"Oh, Baxter, oh, Baxter," moaned the bewildered Whaddayamean Dean who was starting to get sick.

"I mean that I carry only two memories from my childhood in Dominican boarding schools where I was placed by my beautiful, well traveled mother: if you touch the communion wafer with your teeth it's not so good and should be avoided. And the only unforgivable sin is to murder yourself because there is absolutely no possibility of absolution and redemption, and . . ."

"What the fuck're you babblin about, Baxter?" asked Sperm-whale Whalen who was suddenly behind Baxter, having slept long enough to be more or less capable of driving home before dawn.

"Spermwhale! Thought you were stacking those Z's." Baxter Slate offered his partner a quick wide grin and a drink of vodka.

"Baxter, you sound like a silly pseudointellectual horse's ass. You're gettin embarrassin. C'mon, I'll drive you to your pad." Spermwhale felt a stab of pain across the front of his skull when he lifted his young partner to his feet and helped steady him.

Actually, Baxter Slate was rarely such a silly pseudointellec-tual horse's ass, but he had been undergoing a prolonged pe-riod of despondency brought about partly because he thought he had been such an unsuccessful Juvenile officer.

The murder of Tommy Rivers was the final blow to his ca-reer as a Juvenile officer because Baxter Slate had foreseen the imminent demise of Tommy Rivers and had been powerless, or rationalized that he was powerless, to prevent it.

It was three months to the day after Tommy Rivers' death and almost two months before the choir practice shooting that Baxter Slate became the only one of the ten choirboys to kill a man on duty.

Contrary to film and fiction, policemen rarely fire their guns in combat, and even Spermwhale Whalen with nineteen and a half years service and Spencer Van Moot with sixteen years had never killed a man on duty. The flesh wound to the Regret-ful Rapist was the only time Spermwhale had ever fired his revolver outside of monthly qualification shooting, even in-cluding the Watts Riot. So it naturally became a topic of con-versation during choir practice when Baxter Slate killed a man.

The night Baxter Slate killed a man started out a busy one. Ten minutes after they hit the bricks and cleared at 3:45 in the afternoon, Roscoe Rules and Dean Pratt put out an "officers need assistance" call on Chesapeake Avenue in the vicinity of Dorsey High School.

A call for either help or assistance demands all-out coverage, and every car on the nightwatch made a squealing turn and headed south through the heavy afternoon traffic, figuring that Roscoe Rules had probably caused a riot at the school.

As it turned out the call was indeed put out by Roscoe Rules. He and Dean had been driving by the campus so Roscoe could show off by parading his tailored blue body and gleaming badge in front of the high school girls, when they spotted a young black car stripper struggling with the bucket seats of a Porsche which was parked in the faculty parking lot.

Whaddayamean Dean had dropped his baton getting out of the radio car and the clatter of wood on asphalt caused the sweating car stripper to look back and see the "Mickey Mouse ears" on the roof of the police car, which is what students call the siren lights. The car stripper was off in a 9.5 hundred yard dash which left Dean far behind and Roscoe radioing for assistance.

During the chase, the car stripper ran right into the arms of a pretty, twenty-five year old, white history teacher named Pamela Brockington who saw the exhausted policeman hotfooting after the boy. She pushed the boy into the gymnasium and was standing in front of the door when the lanky redhead came panting up to her.

"That boy go in there?" Dean gasped.

"I know that boy, Officer," Pamela Brockington said. "Whatever happened we can settle it without your running through the school grounds and starting a problem."

"Out . . . out of the way, lady," Dean puffed.

"Listen, you're on Board of Education property," the teacher said, planting her feet and spreading her legs, which wasn't easy, her blue jersey skirt being so tightly fitted.

"You know him, okay, it's no problem," Dean said, catching his breath. "Just give us his name and we'll pick him up at home."

"Well, what did he do?" For the first time the teacher looked unsure of herself.

"Tried to rip off the bucket seats from a white Porsche in the parking lot. What's the kid's name?"

"Oh," the teacher said in a small voice.

"Your car?"

"No, Mr. Krump's car. Oh."

"What's his name?"

"Well, I don't actually know his name but he's always around." Pamela Brockington moved aside to let Dean into the gym. But it was far too late and the car stripper had gone out the other door.

"He goes to school here, doesn't he? You can pick his picture out of your school mug shots," Dean said, removing his hat and wiping the sweat from his freckled brow.

"Well, I don't think he actually goes to school here, but . . ." and the young woman started to wither under the outraged scowl Dean was working up to. "He's . . . he's always hanging around the streets after school and I'm sure you could find him again tomorrow or the next day."

When Dean returned to the radio car without the car stripper and with the tale of Pamela Brockington, Roscoe Rules smiled ironically and in a very soft voice said, "Now ain't that typical, partner? I mean that's just so typical of some bleeding heart, left wing social science teacher, now ain't it?"

"I don't know if she teaches social science," Dean offered as Roscoe's voice rose an octave.

"Yes, well it certainly is typical and now our little mother-fucking car stripper is halfway to Watts or wherever the hell."

"You broadcast a description?" Dean asked as he saw the familiar mad glint working its way into Roscoe's blue eyes as his hairless brows knitted and unknitted, making Dean terribly nervous because he didn't know if Roscoe would suddenly turn on him. Which he did.

"And *you* . . . partner," Roscoe said, his voice getting louder still as he revved the black and white, ready to leave half a tire on the pavement. "*You*, partner, let this little pinko, scum eating, shit sucking cunt keep you from hot pursuit? It's hard to believe!"

"Well . . . partner," Dean gulped. "We'll get him some other time. Maybe."

"And now you're sounding just like what this nigger loving split tail must've sounded like, partner. If I'd a been there I'd a grabbed that come licking, do-gooder little cunt and CHOKED

HER OUT AND MADE HER DO THE FUCKING CHICKEN! YOU HEAR ME?"

It was quite an ordinary Roscoe Rules incident, interesting later to Baxter because the car stripper ran across Exposition Boulevard and up Palmgrove Avenue where he made the almost fatal error of crossing through the fenced yard of Yolanda Gutierrez, aged sixty-two, and her niece, Rosario Apodaca, aged fifty-one, who, unlike Pamela Brockington, spoke no English but understood immediately what it meant when this young boy leaped their fence and crouched behind a hibiscus as a black and white cruised by with the officers craning their necks.

Yolanda Gutierrez calmly opened a trunk belonging to her son who had been killed in Korea twenty-three years earlier, removed his Colt .45 automatic and drew down on the boy.

The young car stripper laughed like hell at the old woman holding the heavy gun until Yolanda Gutierrez fired one for effect and blew out the window of the car parked in front of the house. The car stripper fell shrieking to the ground, not knowing the old lady had lost the bucking gun and her glasses and was crawling around the porch trying to find both when two black and whites attracted by the explosion came roaring down the street and arrested the car stripper.

"Something to be learned here," Baxter Slate remarked later to Spermwhale. "How two social classes perceive reality. The educated schoolteacher and the simple old woman."

"Who gives a fuck about reality anyways?" Spermwhale mumbled.

"Not me," Baxter grinned cheerfully. "I prefer choir practice to reality any old day."

Then Baxter's wide grin vanished as he watched a yellow gangrenous dog being dragged down the street by a larger bitch who had him locked inside her, his passion having turned to agony and howling terror. A gang of black kindergarteners, as guileless as a bunch of plums, laughed and pelted both muddy animals with rocks and tin cans.

"Maybe I'll fly another raid with some a the guys my next day off," Spermwhale suddenly said. "Need some excitement around here."

"Don't start that nonsense again," Baxter said, putting on his sunglasses and driving back toward their beat.

Spermwhale began to think about the mission he had flown three weeks earlier. It had started innocently enough with some alcoholic conversation at choir practice about how the white men of Palm Springs had cheated the Indians out of their birthright by stealing the desert spa from the Indians. Roscoe Rules had corrected them by pointing out that Jews and not white men had done it and that he wished the tribe would rise up and massacre every one of those kike bastards and cut off their scalps and kneedrop them.

Then, at precisely fifteen minutes before dawn, Francis Tanaguchi slapped Spermwhale Whalen awake where he slept entwined in the chubby arms of Carolina Moon.

"I'd love to see those two in a lewd movie," Francis Tanaguchi remarked as they threw dirty pond water in Spermwhale's face until he gagged and choked for air.

"Why bother?" Calvin said. "You can see them in real life anytime you want just by sneakin behind the bushes where they usually mate."

"Yeah, but it'd be different in a movie," Francis answered. "You know, a red sexy room with a red silky bedspread and Carolina and Spermwhale all fat and white and oiled and sliding around!"

"You'd need a cinemascope lens," Baxter Slate offered. "A wide wide angle to take in all that flesh."

"Wall to Wall Meat! What a title! Outta sight!" cried Francis Tanaguchi.

An hour later, Francis, Calvin, Dean and Spermwhale, who were all off duty the next night, were in Spermwhale's rented orange and white Cessna 172 at Burbank Airport where Spermwhale often flew if he could get someone to pay for the rental and gasoline. Spermwhale had taken off without a flight plan, but with three hungover choirboys, two fifths of Scotch and one of gin, on a mission to recapture Palm Springs by way of Ontario Airport where Spermwhale reluctantly agreed to land because Whaddayamean Dean wanted some potato chips. They were reprimanded at Ontario by a man in the tower for landing without using the radio, but Spermwhale told him to fuck off and decided to hire a taxi to the Ontario Motor Speedway to watch some motorcycles qualifying for a race.

It was a long hot day at the racetrack spent sleeping shirtless in the bleachers, drinking the two fifths of Scotch and a case of beer and eating all the potato chips Whaddayamean Dean could hold.

Nothing eventful happened at the speedway until late in the afternoon when the choirboys wandered down to the track and a bearded racer told Spermwhale to get his fat ass off his bike. Spermwhale replied that he could fix it so the bearded racer could equal Evel Knievel's record for broken bones on a motor track.

The racer then called for track security officers and after being threatened with arrest the four choirboys put on their tank tops and basketball jerseys and scuttled off, moaning about never being able to find a cop when you want one. Whaddayamean Dean was so drunk he had to be helped into his filthy yellow sweatshirt and they got it on backward with the picture of Bugs Bunny on the back and "What's Up, Doc?" on the front.

The choirboys discovered something extraordinary during the flight from Ontario to Palm Springs: that flying with a blood alcohol reading of .20 was actually invigorating. They celebrated by breaking open the fifth of gin almost immediately after takeoff and cruising at a carefree five thousand feet.

"I hate gin," Spermwhale said, tipping the bottle and drinking a quarter of a pint without taking it from his lips, flying the airplane as steady as a rock.

"It's what the brothers drink when they can't get Scotch," remarked Calvin Potts, who rode behind the self styled navigator, Francis Tanaguchi, who had never flown in any aircraft except once in the Army on the way to Fort Ord.

"But you people can drink airplane fuel," Francis said, grimacing from the burning gin.

"Yeah, and you Chicanos are models of sobriety," said Calvin.

"He's not a Chicano, you fuckin idiot. He's a Jap." Spermwhale said.

"That's right," said Calvin Potts, shaking his head. "Guddamn. I better start layin off the booze. I'm gettin simple!"

"It's confusin workin with a madman like Francis, is all," said Spermwhale, belching wetly.

"Gin! Gin!" cried Whaddayamean Dean, taking the bottle from Calvin and after three long swallows dropping into complete obliterating drunkenness.

Twenty minutes from the Palm Springs Airport, Spermwhale discovered he was well off the course through Banning Pass and was coming in dangerously low over the San Jacinto Mountains. "Aw shit!" he said and took the plane up to seven thousand feet.

"Dynamite!" chuckled Calvin Potts as they climbed.

"My ears hurt! My ears hurt!" Whaddayamean Dean moaned.

"Far out!" Francis exclaimed as they soared through a cloud and came in like a Ping-Pong ball in the turbulence over the mountains.

"Hey, I can see that guy's eyeballs down there!" Calvin Potts said.

"What guy?" Spermwhale asked.

"The guy in the brown uniform. Looks like a forest ranger or somethin. The guy that jumped off the rock and fell on his ass when we buzzed him."

"We didn't buzz nobody," Spermwhale said. "Not on purpose."

"Well, ain't we flyin a little low to the mountaintop?" asked Calvin.

"Whaddaya mean? Whaddaya mean?" asked Whaddayamean Dean.

"You know, there's somethin wrong. Somethin's fucked up," Spermwhale said. "We ain't comin in on the airport. We're comin in on somethin else looks a little different. I think maybe I'm a little more off course than I thought."

Then Calvin Potts was suddenly draped around Spermwhale's neck screaming, "Are we gonna crash?"

"Whaddaya mean? Whaddaya mean?" yelled Whaddayamean Dean.

"Get off my fuckin neck, Calvin, goddamnit!" Spermwhale ordered, prying Calvin's fingers loose. "Damn! You remind me a that vampire partner of yours. Jumpin around people's necks!"

"We are most certainly *not* going to crash," said Francis Tanaguchi, who was giggling idiotically as the airplane swooped down and up again. "As long as I am navigator we shall not crash!"

"Crash? Crash?" said Whaddayamean Dean.

"Give Dean another drink and take one yourself, Calvin," Spermwhale said as they dropped down toward the business district of Palm Springs and the airplane's engine started to attract attention below.

Then they were buzzing the Canyon Country Club. Calvin Potts, his red tank top soaked and plastered to him, cinnamon shoulders gleaming, said, "That's a *green* motherfuckin airport, Spermwhale. That's a . . . GUD-DAMN! THAT'S A GOLF COURSE!"

And Spermwhale jerked the wheel and the airplane pulled out and up, throwing them all back against their seats.

"We're gonna be all right," Spermwhale assured everybody. "I'm just a little lost is all."

"Lost? Lost?" cried Whaddayamean Dean. "What's he mean, Calvin? What's he mean, Calvin?"

"Here," said Francis Tanaguchi and Whaddayamean Dean accepted the bottle and was happy again.

As often happened when the choirboys would get drunk with the simpering redhead, they would find themselves unconsciously talking rapid fire and double action after hearing Whaddayamean Dean for a time.

Spermwhale was next to do it when he said, "I could use a drink. I could use a drink."

"Here. Here. Drink. Drink," said Francis.

"You had enough. You had enough," said Calvin Potts.

"What're you trying to say? What're you trying to say?" said Whaddayamean Dean.

Francis played with the gauge and pretended he was a real pilot while Spermwhale turned around for a second pass over what he thought had to be the airport but was another golf course.

"Motherfucker's shootin at us!" screamed Calvin Potts as Spermwhale Whalen swooped down over the fifteenth fairway and then up toward the mountaintop.

"Who is?" demanded Spermwhale Whalen, deliberately turning the roaring little airplane around and diving belligerently toward the golf course.

"It was nothing," said Francis disgustedly. "Some guy pointing a golf club is all it was. He jumped into the sand trap that time down."

Then Spermwhale circled downtown Palm Springs for another few minutes as the police department sent two cars to sight and identify the aircraft.

Francis suddenly turned surly to the chagrin of Calvin Potts who had stopped drinking fifteen minutes ago.

"Rotten paleface assholes!" screamed Francis. "Steal the Indians' land! I wish Roscoe Rules was here, you lousy scrotes. Roscoe'd fix you. He'd make you do the fucking chicken!"

"Whaddayamean, Francis? Whaddayamean, Francis?" asked Whaddayamean Dean.

"They stole the land!" said Francis, and the sadness in his voice was all that Whaddayamean Dean understood but it was enough to make him cry and wail, "They stole the land! They stole the land!"

"Shut up, Dean, goddamnit!" growled Spermwhale. "That's all we need now, for you to start bawlin."

"Have a drink, Dean," Calvin Potts said, shakily handing Whaddayamean Dean the bottle as Spermwhale circled the town and Francis raged against all white men.

"Thank you, Calvin. Thank you, Calvin," Whaddayamean Dean said, smiling bravely. Then he wiped his moist eyes on his sleeve and sat back sucking up the gin, wondering what everything meant.

"Dive! Dive! Dive!" commanded the angry navigator, but Calvin Potts said, "Don't you motherfuckers be talkin that crazy shit now! You sound like when we sunk ol Wolfgang. But this ain't no play submarine. THIS IS A REAL MOTHERFUCKIN AIRPLANE!"

"Dive! Dive! Dive!" Francis repeated, staring saucer eyed at the reeling pilot who said, "I want gin!" causing Calvin Potts' heart to stop and making him want to weep with Whaddayamean Dean, who actually wasn't weeping but was giggling at Calvin as he held the almost empty gin bottle in front of his face, playing peekaboo, enjoying Calvin's hilariously distorted black moustache through the glass.

"Where should I dive to?" Spermwhale asked finally and Francis said, "That fucking golf course. We're landing and claiming this whole town for the tribe. If you don't you're chickenshit!"

"Me, chickenshit? Me, chickenshit?" Spermwhale yelled, and as Calvin screamed the airplane dove in a gut-erupting 190 mph dive which threatened the design limitations of the little aircraft, and Whaddayamean Dean shouted, "I just wanna know: What's it all mean? What's it all mean?" which Calvin Potts decided was the most intelligent remark he had heard lately, as the airplane leveled out and climbed with Whaddayamean Dean throwing up all over everybody.

"Goddamn you, Dean!" Spermwhale yelled.

"That does it!" Francis raged. "I hate *all* thieving white men, even the ones in this airplane. I feel like crashing just to kill all you pukey pricks!"

"How about me? How about me?" Calvin Potts pleaded. "I ain't a white man. Why kill *me?*"

"You're all alike," Francis said.

"Whaddayamean Dean puked. I didn't puke," Calvin pleaded, and then Calvin realized that Whaddayamean Dean was vomiting in Calvin's lap so Calvin did too, in his own lap.

"See, you're all alike," said Francis disgustedly. "All a bunch of pukey white men. I wish Roscoe Rules was here to rupture your spleens!"

"I swear I'm not a white man," said Calvin Potts as he upchucked a second time.

"Okay, I dived. What the fuck else can I do?" Spermwhale Whalen challenged. "Want some aerobatics? Might as well spread all this vomit around."

"Buzz that golf course one more time," the exultant navigator commanded, while both Whaddayamean Dean and Calvin moaned and rolled their heads and craved sweet cool air.

"Where is it?" asked Spermwhale.

"Jesus Christ, Spermwhale, it's green, ain't it? Just go straight ahead only down lower. We can't miss something that big!"

But they could. They just missed the mountains, barely.

Spermwhale obeyed the navigator and dived down toward the golf course again, though he was starting to come to his senses from the concentrated effort of flying. He was beginning to realize that someone might not like Francis' little prank of landing on a golf course, claiming it for the Cahuilla Tribe. He was flying so low he made Calvin Potts scream in terror when he got over the golf course and Francis flapped the windows open and threw the empty gin bottle which shattered on the patio of the clubhouse, ending the attack on Palm Springs Indian land.

Ten minutes later, Spermwhale Whalen was heading in the general direction of Los Angeles, starting to think of mundane things like whether or not they would be arrested upon landing at Burbank. But within an hour he had stopped worrying about being arrested at Burbank. Night had fallen and brought with it dense fog, and he was glancing at his fuel gauge and wondering why he could not see the Burbank Airport. For the first time that day he made the concession of turning on his radio and he said to the other choirboys, "You guys see anything through all this soup? I mean in the last five minutes or so?"

"I saw somethin about fifteen minutes ago," Calvin Potts said, the only one of the passengers sober enough and frightened enough to be completely awake. "I saw a string a lights."

"Whaddaya mean lights? Whaddaya mean?" asked Spermwhale. "Jesus, I'm startin to sound like Dean."

"Well, it looked like a ribbon a lights. Coulda been street lights or headlights."

"Headlights?" murmured Spermwhale, straining his eyes but seeing nothing below them. Nothing but fog and darkness. "Hold on, I'm goin down."

"Down, you're goin down?" yelled Calvin Potts.

"Who's going down?" Francis asked, waking with a smile. "Ora Lee?"

"You sober now?" Calvin asked. "You're gettin sober, ain't you, Spermwhale?"

"Yeah, I'm gettin . . . Oh, mother! Oh, mother! I think I know where we are!"

"I see somethin. I see somethin," said Calvin Potts when they were at a hundred feet.

"What is it? What the fuck is it?" Francis demanded, awake and sober enough to share Calvin's sweaty terror.

"The ocean!" yelled the horrified choirboy. "That's the fuckin ocean down there! Oh, Lord!"

"The ocean!" screamed Francis.

"The ocean! The ocean! Which ocean?" yelled Whaddayamean Dean, waking from his deep alcoholic sleep.

"Keep the fuck off my back, Calvin," shouted Spermwhale, shoving Calvin back and making the black policeman jump on Francis' back instead.

"We gonna go down, Spermwhale? We gonna go down?" Francis croaked, unaware that Calvin was choking him.

"We ain't goin nowhere but back to Burbank. Now shut the fuck up!" Spermwhale yelled.

But he looked at his fuel gauge and believed deep in his heart that this was his last flight. He hoped that somehow he could get in close to the coast when he was forced to put her down in the water, probably killing them all on impact. But he still flew as calmly as he had flown into Ontario Airport that morning.

"I see it! I see it!" shouted Calvin suddenly. "The ribbon a light!"

"Okay, that's the coast highway," Spermwhale said, sighing imperceptibly. "Santa Monica Airport's probably really socked in." He turned on his Burbank VOR, watched the dial and said, "Come on needle, come on needle."

Then he took the plane up over the Santa Monica mountains, and ten minutes later with less than two gallons of gasoline in each tank the choirboys landed at Burbank Airport, dragged Whaddayamean Dean out of the plane and drove home together.

"That old bastard ain't got a nerve in his body. He ain't afraid a nothin," Calvin said to Francis Tanaguchi the next night on patrol.

"Nobody got our airplane numbers?"

"Guess not. Nothin's happened," said Calvin.

"Outta sight!" cried Francis Tanaguchi, shaking his black

hair off his thin little face, as he started making airplane noises behind the wheel of the radio car, pretending he was Spermwhale Whalen flying a fearless mission into downtown Palm Springs. *"Too* much!" Francis exclaimed, now that he had a real hero. "I just *gotta* see Spermwhale and Carolina Moon in a lewd movie if I have to produce it myself!"

And at the next choir practice, Francis tried to convince her that she should star with Spermwhale Whalen in the dirty movie he was going to produce. Spermwhale said okay, but next year after he had his twenty years' service and a pension locked up. Carolina Moon said she wasn't that kind of a girl.

Spermwhale was joking when he mentioned another mission like the Palm Springs raid to Baxter Slate on the night Baxter killed the ordinary guy, but Baxter Slate, not knowing the full extent of their terror that night over the dark lonely water, wondered if he meant it. Baxter was about to ask him if he was serious when they received a radio call to meet the officers at Ninth Street and Hudson.

Baxter drove easily to the location since there was no code on the call and met Sergeant Nick Yanov and 7-A-33. Spencer Van Moot was laughing while Father Willie stood glumly, hands in the pockets of his uniform pants, pushing out his gun on one side and baton on the other, making him look shorter and chubbier than he was.

When they got out of the car Spencer said to Baxter, "Ever hear of somebody lipping off to you?" And he held up a clean mayonnaise jar which contained a ragged pink object something like a sliver of veal.

"It's a piece of a woman's lip." Father Willie grimaced while Spencer Van Moot laughed uproariously.

"There was a fight here half an hour ago," Sergeant Yanov explained. "Two neighborhood women got in a hassle over the husband of one of them. There was kicking and gouging and biting and one broad ran home with her eyeball half torn out. When she recovered from the shock fifteen minutes later she found her neighbor's lip in her mouth. She must've bit off half of it. At least it looks like a lip."

Baxter Slate examined the raw meat in the jar and said, "It's a lip."

"The lipless lady, Mrs. Dooley, was taken to the hospital by a friend," Nick Yanov said. "So we're gonna take the biter on down to the hospital for an MT too. After that, we'll bring them both to the dick's bureau. Meantime, how about taking the lip in and seeing if they have to book it in any special way to preserve it. I really don't know. I never had a lip to take care of before."

So Baxter and Spermwhale drove part of Mrs. Dooley to the detective bureau in Wilshire Station while Spencer and Father Willie located the rest of her at Daniel Freeman Hospital. The detective just smiled when Baxter showed him the lip and said it would require no special handling because undoubtedly both ladies would make up before the case ever went to trial and it would be dismissed in the interest of justice after four court continuances.

When Spencer Van Moot and Father Willie found the rest of Mrs. Dooley at the emergency ward and arrested her for mayhem, she objected and they had a row with her. She had to be handcuffed and Spencer received a handcuff cut on the finger, a common injury for policemen who wrestle with slippery arms and sharp steel ratchets. The cut was not deep enough to require sutures and Spencer sat on a stool in the same emergency ward, no longer weak from laughing at the lip in the jar but from seeing his blood running down his hand.

He was white and dizzy when the crusty old nurse applied disinfectant and a butterfly bandage to the one inch wound. Father Willie helped support him on the right side while Spencer stood shakily. He was too nauseated to get mad when the nurse said, "Why don't you bite a bullet?"

When Baxter Slate and Spermwhale left Wilshire Station without Mrs. Dooley's lip, Baxter turned south on La Brea, causing Spermwhale to ask, "Where we goin, kid? Our area's east."

"Just felt like driving around the ghetto for a while," Baxter smiled. The slim policeman had an extraordinarily wide mouth which made his smile infectious and convincing even when he didn't mean it. And he didn't mean it now.

"Suit yourself," Spermwhale shrugged. "I just wanna take it easy tonight."

Suddenly Baxter said: "You know what I think is the best a cop can hope for?"

"Tell me, professor."

"The very best, most optimistic hope we can cling to is that we're tic birds who ride the rhino's back and eat the parasites out of the flesh and keep the beast from disease and hope we're not parasites too. In the end we suspect it's all vanity and delusion. Parasites, all of us."

"Yeah," Spermwhale said, trying to think of where they could get a free or half price meal tonight now that greedy Roscoe Rules had burned up their eating spot at Sam's by not only demanding free food for himself and Dean, but wanting four hamburgers to go after they finished. Roscoe Rules could fuck up a wet dream, Spermwhale said.

"Do you know how sad it would be to live in a place where a woman couldn't walk on the street after certain hours because she would either be robbed, raped or taken for a prostitute?"

"I don't think about it," Spermwhale answered.

"See that pedestrian underpass? When I worked Juvenile I met with some black mothers who said that six children were hit by cars at this intersection in one school year and yet the underpass had to be fenced off and locked up because juvenile muggers made it dangerous to use. The city couldn't keep lights in the tunnel. They were broken twice a day. So it's locked up and the children get hit by cars."

"What can we do about that kind a bullshit? It's not our problem."

"It's somebody's problem. I caught two of the muggers down there one day waiting to rip off the smaller kids for their lunch money. They were loaded from sniffing paint and had felony records from when they were ten years old. At the hearing the judge went along with the defense contention that I should've had the paint analyzed in the lab to determine if the kids really were under the influence of paint. I told them we were talking about the health of these boys. They were staggering when I busted them. But the case got kicked and . . ."

"Look, the whole juvenile justice system is a fuckin joke. Everybody knows that, so what's new?"

"It's just that it used to be an equity proceeding. It was supposedly for the good of the child. Now every kid has the public defender representing him and it's just as adversary as adult court. Kids are taught early on to get a mouthpiece and keep their mouths shut."

"That's the way it should be, you want my opinion. Give every five year old a shyster. Then send em to the joint if you convict em."

"But at sentencing it reverts to an equity court or a burlesque on one, and a kid who should be taken away from his miserable home is left on the streets after the fifth serious felony. It's crazy. Juvenile court is a revolving door, and then suddenly the kid turns eighteen, goes out and commits a strong arm robbery just like always but ends up in *adult* jail for six months. Then he's crying for his mother and saying, 'But you always sent me home before. You always gave me another chance.' And he can't understand it and why should he?"

"Baxter, I'm startin to worry about where your head is. I mean if you're gonna start frettin about injustice in the system . . ."

"I just hated being a kiddy cop. I'm glad I'm out. Today's street warriors were yesterday's hoodlums but now they're government funded. Do you have any idea how many ineffectual parents with whiskey voices and unconcerned delinquent kids I've counseled? Hundreds. Thousands, maybe."

As Baxter talked, a black child about five years old stood at the corner and waited for the police car to drive off from the stop sign.

"Go ahead, kid," Spermwhale said, waving at the boy to cross.

But the child walked up to the car on the driver's side and grinned and said, "Who you lookin for?"

"I'm looking for a little guy in a blue shirt with two teeth missing in front," Baxter said. "Seen him around?"

The boy giggled toothlessly and said, "You really be lookin for Ladybug, ain't you?"

"Maybe, what's she doing wrong?" Baxter asked.

"She round behind the house right now wif her head in a glue bag," said the child.

"Well, we'd sure like to bust her, sonny," Spermwhale said. "But we got this big murder case to work on. Now you tell Ladybug to get her dumb head outta that glue bag, okay?"

"Okay, Mr. PO-lice."

The boy waved as Baxter drove away saying, "Bet Ladybug's mother runs off and leaves her in a county foster home. And I'll bet the county just places her right back with her when she comes off her little spree because the taxpayers can't afford to *keep* Ladybug in a foster home. And what the hell, if we supported every little black kid that's neglected . . ."

"I am *really* startin to worry about you, Baxter," Spermwhale said. "You are *really* startin to worry me with all this crybaby social worker bullshit. Man, you never shoulda left patrol and went to Juvenile. I don't know what happened to you workin with those kiddy cops but whatever it was you better get your mind together. Shine it on, baby."

"Okay," Baxter grinned, pushing his umber hair back from his forehead. "I'm just going to shine it on."

But Baxter Slate wasn't sure what in his life he should shine on, unless it was Foxy Farrell. And anyone with an ounce of sense should know that. But the more despondent he had become lately, the more he wanted Foxy Farrell. The five foot two inch, ninety-eight pound, copper haired nude dancer somehow scratched deep and bewildering itches in Baxter's soul.

And no other girl would do though there were many possibilities. Baxter Slate's imposing figure, penetrating green eyes, heavy lashes and wide boyish grin made him quite popular with the clerk typists around the station as well as with the single girls in his apartment building. He tried to enjoy other women and made it a point to stay away from Foxy for days at a time. But he would always go back and despise her as she laughed and talked obscenely about what she didn't do to other men in his absence, while she did it to him. And afterward she would chatter about a flashy boyfriend of one of the dancer's and talk of how cute and sexy he was and why didn't Baxter dress in a white jump suit with a fur collar instead of a stupid woolly herringbone sport coat and a dumb striped necktie like a fucking schoolteacher.

Spermwhale had persuaded Baxter to take him to the Sunset Strip once after work to meet Foxy and the two policemen were taken backstage by a burly assistant manager. Foxy was standing nude in her dressing room combing her pubic hair and pushing the vaginal lips back inside before the second show.

"Flops out once in a while," she smiled, upon seeing the two men standing there. "Hi, you must be Spermwhale. I'm Foxy."

"Yes, you are! You are!" cried Spermwhale Whalen. Spermwhale found that Foxy Farrell made him itch all over—to throw her down and bury his face in the burnished thatch of pubic hair which had been shaved to the shape of a heart, and dyed by squatting in a dish of hair color twice a month and brushing it carefully.

"Jesus, Foxy," Baxter said, "can't you occasionally act like a . . . oh what's the use?"

"He's a prude," Foxy laughed, throwing her coppery hair over her shoulder and slipping into a sheer peignoir. "Baxter's such a prude. That's why we love each other."

And she stepped over to the disgusted young policeman and rubbed her naked body against him and pulled his face down to hers, holding him by the ears.

Spermwhale watched and swallowed twice and developed a diamond cutter which delighted Foxy Farrell.

Baxter Slate despised Foxy Farrell. Which was why he wanted to be with her every moment he was off duty and even dared to drive the black and white up to the Sunset Strip in full uniform and leave Spermwhale in the car while he sneaked in the back door of the nightclub and listened at the door, catching Foxy Farrell blowing some fat cat in the dressing room.

Baxter had actually done this twice and each time he had the presence of mind to leave without being seen and wait to deal with Foxy Farrell when he was off duty. The way he dealt with her the last time was to accuse and rage and finally slap her, which she didn't mind as long as he didn't raise lumps or make her so black and blue that it would show on the stage.

When his anger was spent and he fell in her arms she smiled. Peppermint breath. Perfumed. Overripe. "Baxter, sweetie, it's okay, it's okay. Mama *understands* her baby. Honest, honey, I didn't do nothing to that guy. Only fooled around with him a little. I wasn't Frenching him. It sounded like that because you were all upset and playing vice cop and your imagination ran away with you."

Baxter smiled grimly and said, "You disgusting bitch. You're worthless, you know that? Irredeemably worthless. Without honor. Without humanity. And someday somebody'll kill you. But really, what good would that do?"

Foxy smiled slant eyed and licked Baxter on the cheek. "Honest, honey," she purred, "I wouldn't go down there and kiss that rich man's cock and suck his balls like I'm gonna do to you right now. You know I wouldn't do that to no other man, don't you, honey?"

And while she did it, Baxter Slate clenched his teeth and whispered, "You worthless slut. You worthless slut. I hate you."

He whispered it again and again. She gave him the most sensual and agonizing moments of his entire life and this time even *she* enjoyed it and laughed excitedly all the way, her cheek throbbing where he had struck her.

Baxter seldom talked to Foxy Farrell cruelly. Usually he treated her like a perfect lady which she hated. And took her to intimate French restaurants which bored her. And brought her bottles of Bordeaux wines he really couldn't afford, which she served to other friends over icecubes. In fact she rather disliked everything about Baxter except that he was unquestionably good looking, and being a cop could get her out of minor scrapes with the law or at least might help if she were ever picked up by vice cops for going too far during her nude dancing routine. She sometimes did go too far and once was taken from the stage by a vice officer for pulling a customer's face into her bumping groin. A phone call to Baxter Slate saved Foxy from going to jail because the vice cop was an academy classmate of Baxter's and liked him very much, as did all other policemen with the exception of Roscoe Rules.

Eventually, Foxy Farrell found Baxter Slate a terrible bore and was starting to hate him as much as Spermwhale found Foxy Farrell exciting and was starting to love her. But she found a twenty-five year old pimp named Goldie Grant irresistible. He saw her whenever she could ditch Baxter and eventually he became her real old man instead of her play old man and moved in with her and let her support him and go down on lots of fat cats and high rollers for lots of money and beat her up maybe twice a month whether she needed it or not. They were very happy together and everyone said made a handsome couple.

When Baxter did not appear unhappy enough one night Foxy told a story of how a cute and sexy player had taken her out for a drink after work and tried to give her a hundred dollars just to let him push her face in his lap and only stopped when she told him how her boyfriend was a cop. And what a hard on the player had!

Then Foxy feigned hurt and shock when Baxter grinned crookedly and said, "What a cheap stupid little animal you are."

She pouted and said, "Honest, Baxter, I didn't do *this* to him." And she began the little charade which would end in his passionate moaning and her excited laughter.

But no matter how much she despised Baxter Slate, Foxy Farrell could not have begun to fathom how much he was starting to despise the same young man.

The relationship with Foxy Farrell had begun after Baxter's tour of duty at Wilshire Juvenile where he felt he failed miserably as a kiddy cop and had not prevented the demise of Tommy Rivers, age six and a half.

Of course no one guessed that Baxter Slate somehow felt responsible for the fate of Tommy Rivers.

What made Baxter think he could have prevented Tommy Rivers' death was that he had, before transferring to Juvenile, received the very first radio call to the home of Lena Rivers shortly after she was reunited with her then five year old son Tommy who in his blue sailor suit looked like little Shirley Temple with a haircut.

Lena Rivers had three children by the husband who preceded Tommy's father who was a petty officer in the U.S. Navy. Lena had farmed the boy out to her mother six months after his birth when the sailor shipped out for good and never returned. Lena Rivers had undergone shock treatments after that and had hated the sailor relentlessly and never wanted the child he spawned. Now, five years later, with Lena's mother ill, Lena had been forced to drive to the Greyhound Depot in downtown Los Angeles and pick up the little sailor who had traveled several hundred miles alone without a whimper, the darling of the bus.

The first thing Lena Rivers did, according to later statements from her other children, was to take Tommy home and tear the sailor suit from his body. Some weeks later Baxter Slate received a radio call to the Rivers house from a neighbor who reported that several older neighborhood children had begun hanging around the Rivers home and that some behaved as though they had been drinking. And that the new arrival, Tommy, seldom came outside and looked very sick when he did.

Baxter Slate, working alone on the daywatch at that time, had gone to the Rivers house and met Lena Rivers. She was drunk and dirty and her house was a mess. He had asked to see her youngest child and held his ground when she protested that he was taking a nap.

Finally, Lena Rivers did admit Baxter Slate to the child's room and he did in fact find the child: unwashed, fully clothed, in a crib too small for him. When Baxter later became a Juvenile officer and saw many neglected children he was to remember that Tommy Rivers' pants looked almost as though they were pressed flat on the bed but he did not realize at the time that starving children can often be distinguished from very thin children by the absence of buttocks.

But at that time Baxter Slate knew very little about starving children, never having been in war like some of the other choirboys. So he had retreated when Mrs. Rivers ordered him out of her house. Baxter had often retreated, especially when working alone, if he felt he was on shaky constitutional grounds. Baxter Slate had always believed implicitly in limited police power, due process, the jury system. And even now though his years on the street had eroded his beliefs he still insisted on not overstepping his authority. This caused many partners to say, "Baxter's a good partner to work with, goes along with most anything you want to do, but he's so naïve I think he was brought up in a bottle."

The Wilburn Military Academy was not exactly a bottle, but it was a hothouse for upper middle class children, which Baxter was until his mother foolishly lost her fat alimony check by impetuously marrying an alarm clock manufacturer who lost most of his money by diversifying into offshore oil drilling. Then the years at the authoritarian Dominican boarding school taught the boy what pansies the teachers at Wilburn were as they *played* at being soldiers. God's army had much more dedicated generals. It was surprising that a boy who had been cuffed around and dealt with so strictly and splendidly educated in the traditional sense—virtually without parents unless one counted holidays and summers with Mom—would be the kind of policeman who would worry about human rights and due process. After all, they had always been denied him. But he *did* worry about such things. Fiercely. Even after he concluded that he had been a fool to entertain such notions.

Once, Baxter Slate, working alone in the West Adams district, saw a car driving by with two young white children waving frantically from the rear window and then dropping out of sight on the seat. The driver was a black man in a stingy brim hat. Baxter followed the car two miles for another glimpse of the white children, asking himself if he would be doing this had the driver been white, wondering if it were just a children's prank. Finally, Baxter turned on his red lights and stopped the car. The white children were crouched down on the seat in the rear, giggling. The man, a boyfriend of the children's mother, asked angrily, "Would you have stopped me if those kids had been black?" And Baxter Slate lied and said he would, but he never forgot.

Two weeks before Tommy Rivers died Baxter Slate received the second radio call to the Rivers home. This one from a neighbor on the other side of the street who reported that there was definitely something wrong. Tommy had come to live with his mother nine months before but had been seen only occasionally as he sat with a brother or sister in the front yard.

"I believe he's a sick boy," the woman had said to Baxter Slate when he responded to the radio call.

And this time Baxter Slate did overstep his authority a bit in demanding to see Tommy Rivers and scaring Lena Rivers with an implied threat to call in Juvenile officers if she refused.

Lena Rivers finally consented, and the gaunt young woman with bright darting eyes went to the bedroom and returned with a dirty but obviously fat and healthy child of seven who smiled at the policeman and asked to touch his gun.

"Satisfied?" Lena Rivers said. "Meddling neighbors oughtta mind their own business."

Baxter Slate looked at Lena Rivers, at her scraggly colorless ponytail and dark rimmed blinking eyes, at the face already starting to bloat from alcohol despite her skinny build and relative youthfulness.

"That little boy looks different from when I saw him last," said Baxter.

"When did you see him?" the woman slurred as Baxter smelled the booze.

"I was called here once before," Baxter said, still standing in the doorway. "I was the one you let into the bedroom to look at Tommy, remember?"

"Oh yeah. You're gonna spend your career hassling me, is that it?"

"No, I guess not," Baxter said.

Every skill he had picked up during his four years as a policeman told him that this woman was lying. As with most policemen the hardest thing to learn was what consummate liars people are, and it was even more difficult for Baxter because he had been brought up to believe there is such a thing as unvarnished truth and that most people speak it.

"Is that the same boy I saw before?" Baxter asked and he believed it was a lie when she said, "Of course it is!"

"What's your name, son?" Baxter asked, stooping and smiling at the child.

"Tommy Rivers," the boy said and looked up at his mother.

"I don't believe that's the same child I saw. He was thin, very very thin."

"So he's gained a few pounds. He was sick. Did my nosy neighbor tell you he was sick?"

And Baxter Slate nodded because the neighbor *had* said that, and yet . . .

"Look," Baxter said, trying his broad winning smile on Lena Rivers, "this is my second call here. Tell you what, I'll just come in for a look around and then everybody'll be satisfied and you won't see me again. Okay?"

And then the woman stepped out on the porch in the sunlight and Baxter was no longer looking at her through the screen door and could see the yellow pouches around her sparkling demented eyes.

"You been cooperated with all you're gonna be. You got no right here and I want you outta my face and off my property. So I don't keep a spic and span house, so what? My kids're cared for and here's the one you're so goddamn worried about. Now tell that bitch she got any more complaints I'll go over there and kick her ass all over the neighborhood!"

Lena Rivers went inside and slammed the door, leaving Baxter Slate standing indecisively on the front porch.

For months after that Baxter wondered how much of his hesitancy would be attributed to his boarding school politeness and whether perhaps the more obtrusive working class produced the best cops after all, that perhaps police departments were foolish to recruit from any other social group.

But no matter how many times he postulated a hypothetical situation to other policemen, never daring to admit to them he had contact with Tommy Rivers, he had to come to the inescapable conclusion that very few would have stood on that porch. As tentative as Hamlet. Only to wipe sweat from his hat brim and drive away to another call.

The answers to his hypothetical question varied slightly:

"I think I'd have called for a backup unit and maybe a supervisor or Juvenile officer and gone on in. I mean if I really suspected she had switched kids on me." That from Father Willie Wright.

"I'da walked over the cunt and looked for the little whelp." That from Roscoe Rules.

Not one of the choirboys, and he asked each privately, had suggested that he would consider that there was not enough probable cause to enter the woman's home or cause her further discomfiture. Most agreed with Francis Tanaguchi who shrugged and said, "I don't worry about it when a little kid's safety's at stake. If the court wants to kick the case out, groovy, but I'll see that the kid's okay."

They thought it absurd even to consider constitutional questions which get in the way of police work. "We'll worry about the United States Supreme Court when we're writing our arrest reports," as Spencer Van Moot succinctly put it.

And Baxter Slate believed that was the general attitude of all policemen, not just the choirboys. It was absurdly easy for any high school graduate with a year's police experience to skirt the most sophisticated and intricate edict arrived at by nine aging men who could never guard against the fact that restrictive rules of law simply produced facile liars among policemen. There wasn't a choirboy who had not lied in probable cause situations to ensure a prosecution of a guilty defendant.

Not a choirboy except Baxter Slate who had heard too much about Truth and Honor and Sin in Dominican schools. Even Father Willie Wright lied but when he did it from the witness stand he always held his hands under his legs, fingers crossed.

And in the case of Tommy Rivers Baxter Slate need not have lied. He simply had to open the unlocked door and enter Lena Rivers' home and walk through her house ignoring her drunken threats and search for the real Tommy Rivers. But since he had only a suspicion, since he was not sure, since he could never be convinced that people lied so outrageously, since it was too bizarre to suspect foul play when Mrs. Rivers had several other healthy children, since he was Baxter Slate and not Roscoe Rules, he threw in his hand and lost to a bluff. And Lena Rivers was free to continue with her gradual murder of Tommy Rivers.

When Baxter Slate read Bruce Simpson's arrest report the first time, his heart was banging so loud he actually believed the man next to him could hear it, and he foolishly cleared his throat and shuffled his feet on the asphalt tile in the squadroom. The second time through the report he believed his heart had stopped, so shallow was his breathing. The third time through he didn't think about his heart at all.

Bruce Simpson's arrest report was a minor classic in kiddy cop circles because he did not write like most policemen in the bald vernacular: "Person reporting stated . . ."

Arresting officer Simpson composed a horror story which included every tiny fragment of gruesome detail—when it was necessary and when it was not. Simpson did it because there was a policewoman named Doris Guber, whose pants Simpson was trying to penetrate, who loved to work the sex detail and always asked teenage runaways about their illicit sex lives and included in her reports exactly how many times an illicit penis was inserted and withdrawn from an illicit vagina. Which wasn't all that important to the prosecution of delinquent youngsters.

Doris always loved to find out about the orgasm, whether it occurred, and if so how big it was and of what duration. She'd get Simpson hot just talking about it so he started doing his reports the same way.

"Did you have an orgasm with the girl?" Doris once asked a surly eighteen year old black boy she wanted to prosecute for banging his neighbor.

"Did I have a what?"

"Did you come?" asked Doris Guber, eyes shining.

"Oh yeah. Like a hound dog."

Bruce Simpson's inimitably colorful prose left nothing out. The pages reeked of agony and death. He described how Lena Rivers had shredded the little sailor suit from Tommy Rivers the first day. He hypothesized how Tommy had resembled the long gone, fair haired sailor who had shattered the romantic dreams of Lena Rivers by taking his discharge from the Navy and heading for parts unknown. Bruce Simpson delineated in the sharpest detail how Tommy Rivers entered hell that day and was not released from torment until he died ten months later.

Lena Rivers had begun by subjecting Tommy to a sustained barrage of verbal abuse which was unrelenting up to and including the period when daily beatings gave way to starvation and torture. But as cruel as Lena Rivers was to Tommy she was kinder than ever before to her other three children who ranged in age from seven to ten. And she was exceptionally kind to the older children of the neighborhood and frequently entertained the teenage boys by supplying beer and gambling money from her bimonthly checks from the Bureau of Public Assistance and finally by deflowering three of them after a game of strip poker.

It became gossip among the adolescents of the block that Lena Rivers was awfully tough on the new arrival, her six year old son Tommy. Then later it was positively established that at least two of the lads, who were learning more than poker from

Lena Rivers, had seen acts amounting to felony crimes committed on Tommy Rivers. Lena had been observed on two occasions thrusting the boy's hand into the flame of the gas stove for bedwetting. On another occasion she had ordered the child to copulate orally one of her poker playing sixteen year old lovers but the older boy claimed he declined, during his testimony at Lena's trial. Finally, no less than three teenage boys who were ordinary products of the ordinary neighborhood saw Lena Rivers carrying the naked, screaming, twenty-eight pound child through the house by a pair of pliers clamped to his penis.

Lena Rivers had less exotic punishment for Tommy Rivers during that ten month siege of terror, such as locking him in a kitchen broom closet every time he cried for his grandmother whom he would never see again. The broom closet eventually became a refuge for Tommy, and Lena Rivers would often forget he was there and leave him alone in the peaceful darkness for hours at a time. His older siblings sometimes brought food to him beyond his daily ration but never enough to sustain him in health, and eventually the broom closet became his permanent bedroom. He built himself a nest of rags and newspapers next to a water heater which was warm in the night.

Baxter Slate was always to rationalize that even if he had been less indecisive that day he might never have found the little figure cowering in the corner of the broom closet, might never have verified his suspicions that Lena Rivers had shown him the wrong son.

Baxter was to question more experienced Juvenile officers at a later time and consult texts on abnormal psychology and ask again and again: "But *how* could the other children, especially the older neighborhood children, have failed to report it to the police? They *knew* what was going on. Even the little ones knew how wrong it was!"

But the most frequent explanation was: "Kids are awfully curious and have a morbid fascination for the bizarre. She was supplying booze and sex for the older ones and her own could see by Tommy what could happen to them if Mama stopped loving them, so . . ."

Later as a kiddy cop Baxter encountered case after case of witnesses who ignored flagrant acts of brutality, not just youngsters, but adults: neighbors and family. Then Baxter Slate, former Roman Catholic, age twenty-six, learned how tenuous is the life of the soul. And realized that his soul, if he truly had one, was starting to die.

Baxter asked for and received a transfer back to patrol for "personal reasons" and decided to quit police work. But he made inquiries and discovered how valueless was his education in the classics. He had an offer to teach elementary school but that job was conditional since Baxter did not have a teaching credential and had not the ambition to get one. And actually, policemen received a better wage.

So he became satisfied with working uniform patrol again and did not aspire to a more exalted position. He never again tried to borrow money from his mother who was now divorced for the fourth time, and most of all he was very cautious never to let anyone know he was intelligent and educated since it could offend people like Roscoe Rules who assumed that Baxter had studied police science in college.

Baxter always made it a point to throw a few "don'ts" in place of "doesn'ts" in his conversation with other policemen and unless he was drunk at choir practice he never used adverbs in the presence of Roscoe Rules who became infuriated because it sounded so faggy.

Tommy Rivers, reduced to a shroud of flesh on a little skeleton, eventually died from the blow of a hammer that a healthy child could probably have survived. Lena Rivers was arrested, giving Bruce Simpson the opportunity to titillate Doris Guber with his purple prose. And Baxter Slate quit being a Juvenile officer because he thought he was the worst one in history and intensified his relationship with Foxy Farrell. He only broke it off when during their mating she bit into his chest so savagely she tore the skin and kissed him with a bloody mouth crooning, "You liked it, Baxter! You *liked* it, you bastard! Admit it, you pig motherfucker! Want me to do it again? Or do you want me to tell you what I did to Goldie last night after I left you? Goldie's cock is so . . ."

And then Baxter was weeping for shame and fury and was

backhanding Foxy Farrell and more blood was on her mouth mixing with his blood. Then her eyes glassed over and she held his wrists and the words dripped like blood from thin dark lips: "That's enough. I know what you like, honey. It's okay. Mama knows. Mama *knows.*"

So after he stopped being a kiddy cop and after he stopped thinking so much about the things Foxy Farrell had taught him about himself which he never should have learned and after he started dating other women and trying to enjoy a more ordinary sex life, Baxter Slate became the only choirboy to kill a man in the line of duty. He killed the ordinary guy.

Baxter and Spermwhale liked to meet for coffee with the other north end cars, particularly 7-A-29, manned by Sam Niles and Harold Bloomguard. They would meet at about 7:00 P.M. on week nights at the drive-in on Olympic Boulevard when the air wasn't too busy.

Policemen always asked, "How's the air?" or "The air busy?" referring to the radio airwaves which directed their working lives. "Quiet air" was what the policemen longed for so that they could be free to cruise and look for real crooks instead of being twenty-five year old marriage counselors to fifty-five year old unhappily married couples.

To Baxter Slate quiet air meant only a prolonged coffee break at the drive-in, where they might meet one or two other radio cars and hope an angry citizen didn't call the station and report them for bunching up and wasting taxpayers' money by swilling coffee instead of catching burglars and thieves.

It was usually the same outraged citizen who, when getting a traffic ticket by a policeman who was *not* drinking coffee, would demand to know why he was writing tickets instead of catching burglars and thieves. The same question about burglars and thieves was asked of narcotics officers by dopers and of vice cops by whores, tricks and gamblers. And of motor cops by drunk drivers.

Burglars and thieves sometimes complained that they only committed crimes against property, not like muggers and rapists. Muggers and rapists never faulted policemen at all, which caused the choirboys to comment that as a rule muggers and rapists were the most appreciative people they contacted.

But Baxter just wanted to drink coffee on the night he killed the ordinary guy. He was content to sit at the drive-in with Spermwhale and joke with the carhops.

While Baxter and Spermwhale drank their coffee a Porsche pulled in beside them and Spermwhale remarked to the lone driver that her blonde hair was complemented by the canary yellow Porsche.

The girl laughed and said, "How many girls do you stop for tickets because their hair coordinates with their paint job?"

"None that I ever wrote a ticket to," Spermwhale leered as Baxter automatically put his hand on his gun because a man shuffled over to the left side of the car with his hand inside a topcoat.

It was seventy-five degrees that night but the man wore his tan trench coat turned up. He also wore a black hat with a wide brim that had been out of style for twenty years but was now coming back. His face was round and cleft like putty smashed by a fist.

He reached inside his coat, and while Spermwhale talked to the girl with canary hair, he flipped out toy handcuffs and a plastic wallet with a dime store badge pinned inside. He said, "I'm working this neighborhood. Any tips for me? Anybody you're after? Be glad to help out."

Baxter relaxed his gun hand and still sitting behind the wheel of the radio car, looked up at the man, at the vacant blue eyes peering out from under the hat brim, with a hint of a mongoloid fault in those eyes. Baxter guessed the man's mental age to be about ten.

Spermwhale just shook his head and said, "Partner, you're a born blood donor," because Baxter Slate dug through their notebook and found some old mug shots of suspects long since in jail and gave them to the retardee who could hardly believe his good fortune.

"Gosh, thanks!" said the play detective. "I'll get right on the case! I'll find these guys! I'll help you make the pinch!"

"Okay, just give us a call when you find them," Baxter smiled as the young man shuffled away, beaming at the mug shots.

After being unable to entice a telephone number from the laughing girl in the yellow Porsche, Spermwhale looked at her license number and ran a DMV check over the radio, writing down her name and address. Then he leaned out the window of the police car and said, "You know, you remind me of a girl used to live up in Hollywood on Fountain, next to where I used to live."

The girl looked stunned and said, "You lived on Fountain?"

"Yeah," Spermwhale said convincingly. "There was this girl, lived in the six thousand block. I used to see her coming out her apartment. I fell in love with her but I never met her. Once I asked the manager of her building what her name was and he said, Norma. You sure look like her."

"I look . . . but that's me! My name's Norma!"

And then she saw Baxter grinning and she reddened and said, "Okay, how'd you know? Oh yeah, my license plate. Your radio. Oh yeah."

"But it coulda happened like that," Spermwhale said, his scarred furry eyebrows pulled down contritely.

"Well, since you have my name and address, I might as well give you my phone number," said the girl with the canary hair who was impressed with the powers of the law and by Baxter's good looks.

While Spermwhale flirted, Baxter sipped coffee and thought of how the smog had been at twilight. How blue it was and even purple in the deep shadows. Poison can be lovely, thought Baxter Slate.

Then another radio car pulled into the drive-in and parked in the last stall near the darkened alley and Baxter decided he'd leave Spermwhale to romance the blonde. Baxter left his hat and flashlight but took his coffee and strolled over to talk with the other choirboys.

And at that moment the rear door window on the passenger side of 7-A-77's car shattered before his eyes! Then the front fender went THUNK!

Calvin Potts screamed, "SOMEBODY'S SHOOTIN AT US!"

Baxter Slate dove to the pavement as the doors to the black and white burst open. Calvin and Francis were down with him crawling on their bellies and no one else, not even Spermwhale who had a blue veiner, even noticed.

Then Spermwhale turned down the police radio which had

begun to get noisy and looked across the parking lot at the three choirboys on their bellies just as his windshield shattered and he went flying out the passenger door even faster than Lieutenant Grimsley when they put the angry ducks in his car.

"Did you see the flash?" yelled Baxter, who was on his knees scrambling for the protection of his black and white as business went on around them as usual. Car radios blared cacophonously. Dishes clattered. Trays clanged. People slurped creamy milkshakes. Chewed blissfully on fat hamburgers. Gossiped. No one perceived a threat. No one noticed four blue suited men crawling on their bellies. Finally, a miniskirted carhop stopped and said to Baxter, "Lose your contact lens or something, honey?"

Then all four policemen were on their feet running for a fence which separated the parking lot from the alley where the shots had to have come from.

Baxter got his wits about him and yelled, "Spermwhale, go call for help!"

Then gingerly shining his light through the darkness, Francis Tanaguchi shouted, "There's a rifle in the alley!"

Calvin Potts crawled forward out of sight for a few minutes, then, crouching, ran back out of the alley carrying a modified .22 caliber rifle with a tommy gun grip and an infrared scope lovingly mounted on the stock. The gun could fire hollow points almost as fast as you could pull the trigger, and what possibly saved the policemen was that the sniper had jammed the gun in his excitement.

Baxter Slate was the first to suggest driving around to the street on the west, and while Francis and Calvin quickly cleared glass from the seat, Baxter was squealing out, knocking coffee cups all over the parking lot as the siren of the nearest help car could already be heard in the distance.

Spermwhale asked to be dropped near the mouth of the alley on the next residential block west while Baxter circled one block farther on the theory that a man could run very far and fast after just having tried to ambush some policemen.

On St. Andrew's Place, Baxter Slate saw a dark running shadow. He jammed down the accelerator and the next sixty seconds became a fragmented impression as he screeched to a stop beside the running figure and jumped out in the darkness, gun drawn. He was met by a fanatical screaming charge by what turned out to be a weaponless man, and for once Baxter Slate did not intellectualize. He simply obeyed his instinct and training and emptied his gun at point blank range, hitting the man three times out of six, one bullet cracking through the left frontal lobe killing him almost at once. He discovered that unlike choreographed slow motion movie violence the real thing is swift and oblique and incoherent.

After an intensive interrogation by the Robbery-Homicide Division shooting team and after his own reports were written, a pale and tense Baxter Slate met the other nine choirboys at MacArthur Park and tried to fill them in as best he could on the details. The trouble was there weren't any.

The young man's name was Brian Greene, and luckily for Baxter his fingerprints *were* found on the rifle. He was twenty-two years old. He was white. He had no arrest record. He had no history of mental illness. The Vietnam War was long over and he was not a veteran. He was not a student. He cared nothing about politics. He was a garage mechanic. He had a wife and baby.

Francis was beside himself that night at choir practice, not so much in fear but rage. And finally despair.

"So quit talkin about it," Calvin said. "I'm sick a hearin about it. The asshole tried to shoot us and it's over and that's it."

"But Calvin, don't you see? He didn't even *know* us. We're just . . . just . . . blue symbols!"

"Okay, so we're blue," Calvin reminded him. "You only see black and blue around the ghetto when the sun goes down."

"But we were on Olympic Boulevard. That's not a ghetto. He was white. Why'd he shoot? Who *was* he? Doesn't he know we're more than bluecoats and badges? It's weird. I don't know where these people are coming from. I dunno."

"I dunno where *you're* comin from," Calvin said angrily.

"I dunno where I'm coming from either," Francis said. "I don't know where my head is."

"What fuckin Establishment did we represent to him?" Spermwhale demanded to know. "I'm tired a bein a symbol! I'm not a symbol to my ex-wives and ex-kids. Why does an ordinary guy wanna shoot me?"

And all the choirboys looked at each other in the moonlight but there were no answers forthcoming.

"I didn't want to kill him," Baxter Slate said quietly. "I never wanted to kill anybody."

It was suddenly cold in the park. They were ecstatic when Ora Lee Tingle showed up and hinted she might pull that train.

10

7-A-29: Sam Niles and Harold Bloomguard

Lieutenant Finque had a splitting migraine at rollcall on the night Sam Niles and Harold Bloomguard met the Moaning Man and called for choir practice.

The migraine was brought about by his defense of the Police Protective League, the bargaining agent manned by Los Angeles police officers for the department.

"How the fuck can the Protective League do anything for us?" Spermwhale demanded. "As long as brass're members of the league. Don't you see, the league gotta be more like a real union. It's management against labor. You people are management. Only the policeman rank and maybe sergeants should be in the league. The rest of the brass are the *enemy,* for chrissake!"

"That's not true!" Lieutenant Finque said. "The commanders and the deputy chiefs are just as much police officers as . . ."

"My ass, Lieutenant!" Spermwhale roared. "When did you last hear of a deputy chief gettin TB or a hernia or whiplash or pneumonia or shot or beat up or stabbed? Only cop's disease they ever get is heart trouble and that's not cause they have to jump outta radio cars and run down or fight some fuckin animal who wants to make garbage outta them, it's cause they eat and drink so much at all those sex orgies where they think up ways to fuck and rape the troops!"

"How many deputy chiefs or commanders ever get suicidal?" Baxter Slate asked suddenly, and for a moment the room was quiet as each man thought of that most dangerous of policemen's diseases.

"Yeah, it's usually the workin cop who eats his gun," Spermwhale said as he unconsciously thought of at least ten men he had served with who had done it.

"I'd hate to be a member of this department if we ever go from the Protective League to a labor union," Lieutenant Finque solemnly announced with the consuming hatred and distrust of labor unions that was prevalent in those police officers who had sprung from the middle class and whose only collective bargaining experiences had been as Establishment representatives facing angry sign wavers on picket lines.

"Protective League my ass!" Spermwhale Whalen said. "They take our dues and wine and dine politicians while I eat okra and gumbo at Fat Ass Charlie's Soul Kitchen."

"I thought you liked eatin like a home boy, Spermwhale," Calvin Potts grinned.

"We gotta sue the fuckin city for nearly every raise we get," Spermwhale continued. "I'm sick a payin dues to the Protective League. I get more protection from a two year old box a rubbers!"

"Anyone for changing the subject?" Sergeant Nick Yanov suggested, as the lieutenant held his throbbing head and vowed to check Spermwhale Whalen's personnel package to see how many more months he had to go before retirement. And to ask the captain if there weren't a place they could transfer him until then. Like West Valley Station which was twenty-five miles away.

Lieutenant Finque's eyes were starting to get as red and glassy as Roscoe Rules' always were. Of late the lieutenant always had drops of grainy white saliva glued to the corners of his mouth from his incessant sucking of antacid tablets.

"I'm going to change the subject, change the subject," Lieutenant Finque announced strangely. "The captain inspected the shotgun locker and found a gun with cigars stuffed down the barrel! If that happens again somebody's going to pay!"

No one had to turn toward Spermwhale who was the only cigar smoker on the watch. "Young coppers they hire these days'll rip you off for anything," said Spermwhale. "Gotta hide your goods, Lieutenant."

Lieutenant Finque had begun losing weight of late what with his migraines and acid stomach and inability to relate with Captain Drobeck who had turned down three dinner invitations this month despite the fact that Lieutenant Finque had done everything he could think of to woo the captain, including joining his American Legion Police Post. The lieutenant knew he should be clear headed what with the ordeal of studying for the captain's exam three hours a day when his wife and children would leave him alone. And here at the job he had to deal with recalcitrant uglies like Spermwhale Whalen.

"Let's read some crimes," the watch commander said, picking up a sheaf of papers. "There was an ADW on a teacher at the high school. Says here a thirty-four year old schoolteacher had just started her third period when . . ."

"Kind of late in life, ain't it?" Francis Tanaguchi giggled and Lieutenant Finque jerked spasmodically and tore the report.

Lieutenant Finque blinked several times and simply could not regain the thread. "This report's terrible. It's sloppy. Who did it?" And his eyes were so watery he couldn't read the name.

"Just a few pencigraphical errors, sir," said the culprit, Harold Bloomguard.

"Uh . . . Intelligence has a rumor," Lieutenant Finque said, forgetting the crimes and going on disjointedly to a note in the rotating folder. "We may have a riot in the vicinity of Dorsey High School between four and four thirty this afternoon. Some militant . . ."

"A half hour riot?" said Calvin Potts and Lieutenant Finque's thread came totally unraveled. He began talking to Sergeant Yanov on his right as though they were alone in the room.

"You know, Yanov, there's a rumor that these young Vietnam vets they're hiring these days are smoking pot. You see how hard it is to make them keep their hair off their collars and their moustaches trimmed? And there's a rumor about *fragging!* Someone heard some policemen talking about bombing a watch commander!"

"I'll read the crimes," Sergeant Yanov said abruptly, putting a steadying hand on Lieutenant Finque's arm while the assembly of policemen looked at one another in growing realization. "Let's see, here's one to perk up your evening. A rapist stuck his automatic down in his belt while he made the victim blow him and he got so excited he shot his balls off right in the middle of the headjob!"

The explosion of cheers startled the shit out of Lieutenant Finque who thought he was being fragged. He only kept from jumping up because Sergent Yanov's strong left hand held his arm pressed to the table top as the sergeant regained control of the rollcall.

"Keep an eyeball out for Melvin Barnes," Sergeant Yanov continued. "His picture's on the board. Local boy and he's running from his parole officer. He'll be around Western Avenue. He likes to run because he's a celebrity on the avenue when the cops're looking for him. But he'll be around because he doesn't mind getting busted. He's an institutional man. There're thousands like him."

"Amen," Spermwhale Whalen said. "Ask me, I think half the fuckin population craves some kind a institution or other. They can't get it, they'll get taken care of some other way. If we just made our jails comfortable, gave the boys some pussy and all, shit, we couldn't blast em out on the streets. Be a lot cheaper makin em happy and keepin em inside the rest a their lives than runnin them through the fuckin system over and over again while a few people get hurt along the way."

"You got lots of ideas, Spermwhale," said Harold Bloomguard. "Ever consider getting perverted to sergeant?"

As Sergeant Yanov got everyone in a better frame of mind to go out into the streets, Lieutenant Finque sat going through some envelopes which came to him through department mail. The voice of Yanov and the others seemed far away. He never noticed Francis Tanaguchi grin at his partner Calvin Potts when the lieutenant tore open the last envelope. It was a crime lab photo of a ninety year old black woman who had been dead for three weeks when her body was found and the picture taken. Her white hair was electric. Her silver eyes were open and her blackened tongue protruded. The note attached to the photo said, "Dear Lieutenant Finque, how come you don't come to see me no more now that you transferred to the westside? You cute little blue eyed devil!"

The lieutenant blinked and twitched and hoped he could get out of the station this night alive without being either framed or fragged. He stood up suddenly and said something unintelligible to Sergeant Yanov before walking out the door.

That night someone put a taped roll of freeway flares attached to a cheap alarm clock under the watch commander's desk when Lieutenant Finque was out having coffee. At 10:00 P.M. the bomb squad was at Wilshire Station assuring the captain by telephone that it was not dynamite but only a prank evidently played by some member of the nightwatch. At 11:00 P.M. Lieutenant Finque left Daniel Freeman Hospital severely tranquilized. He was off sick for seven days with something not unlike combat fatigue. Due to his splendid record as a whistle salesman he was taken downtown and made the adjutant of Chief Lynch. He was definitely an up-and-comer.

At six feet two inches and 185 pounds Sam Niles was not a particularly big man but next to Harold Bloomguard he felt like Gulliver. Harold Bloomguard was, at 149 pounds on a delicate frame, the smallest choirboy of them all. He had gorged himself with a banana-soybean mixture for three days to pass his original police department physical.

The choirboys always said that what Harold lacked in physical stature he made up for in physical weakness. Both Ora Lee Tingle and Caroline Moon had beaten him in arm wrestling on the same night at choir practice, and Harold, who usually loved fun and frolic, waded off in his underwear and sulked with the ducks on Duck Island. He wouldn't come back until all of the choirboys had either gotten drunk or gone home.

"What's it all about, Harold? What's it all about, Harold?" cried Whaddayamean Dean to the lonely white figure huddled in the darkness of Duck Island which was a thirty by thirty mound of dirt and shrubbery in the middle of the large duck pond they called MacArthur Lake.

"What'd he say, Dean?" asked Harold Bloomguard's partner, Sam Niles, as Whaddayamean Dean rejoined the choirboys who were trying to persuade Carolina Moon to pull that train even if she *was* tired from being on her feet all night hustling drinks at the Peppermint Club in Hollywood.

"What'd who say?"

"Harold! Who the hell were you just off yelling at, for chrissake!"

"I don't know," said Whaddayamean Dean, his brow screwed in confusion.

"Harold Bloomguard, goddamnit!" said Spermwhale, who got more pissed off at Whaddayamean Dean than anyone since Spermwhale more or less looked after him when he was drunk like this.

"You were yelling at Harold over on Duck Island, weren't you?" asked Ora Lee Tingle patiently as Francis Tanaguchi crawled around behind her on the grass in his LAPD baseball shirt with number 69 on the back and pinched her ample buttocks and yelled when she punched him in the shoulder and knocked him over the cushiony Carolina Moon who grabbed him and smothered him in her enormous breasts and chubby arms and said, "Ya cute little fuckin Nip, ya!"

"I admit I was yelling but I don't remember at who," said Whaddayamean Dean, wishing everyone would stop picking on him and just let him drink and lie down on top of Ora Lee Tingle and rest his brain for a while. "I think I heard someone answer."

"Well, you simple asshole, what'd he say?" demanded Spermwhale.

"I think he said, 'Quack quack.' "

As all the choirboys moaned and fell over and rolled their eyes disgustedly, Spermwhale grabbed Whaddayamean Dean by the back of the Bugs Bunny sweatshirt and said, "That was a fuckin duck! Ducks say quack quack. Harold don't say quack quack. You was talkin to a duck!"

"At least he didn't yell at me," Whaddayamean Dean sniffled

and a large salty globular tear rolled out his left eye. "I don't know what you mean. What're you trying to say? Why is everybody picking on me? Huh? Huh?"

And so they gave up and left Whaddayamean Dean to finish his vodka and within three minutes he forgot that everyone had been picking on him and that Harold Bloomguard was almost naked and alone with the ducks on Duck Island. As a matter of fact, everyone forgot Harold Bloomguard but Sam Niles, and he would like to have forgotten.

At 5:00 A.M., when only the two girls and three of the choirboys were left sprawled on their blankets, Sam Niles stripped down and waded through the sludge to Duck Island, knocked the sleeping ducklings off Harold Bloomguard's shivering body, shook him awake and dragged him through the cold dirty water to his blanket and clothes. But Sam decided that Harold was too covered with filth to put him in Sam's Ferrari so he broke the lock on the park gardening shed with a rock and found a hose with a strong nozzle. Then he forced the protesting Harold Bloomguard to stand shivering on the grass and be sprayed down from head to foot before drying in the blankets and dressing.

"I'd never do this to you, Sam!" Harold screamed as the merciless jet of water stung and pounded him and shriveled his balls to acorns.

"You're not getting in my Ferrari covered with that green slimy duck shit," said Sam Niles who had a thundering headache.

"I loaned you part of the down payment!" reminded Harold and shrieked as the spray hit him in the acorns, waking up Roscoe Rules who saw two nearly nude men by the gardening shack and figured it was a pair of park fairies.

Roscoe belched and shouted, "All you faggy bastards in this park better keep the noise down or I'll make you do the chicken!" And then he went back to sleep.

When Harold was relatively clean Sam Niles vowed that somehow, someday, he would rid himself of Harold Bloomguard who was by his own admission a borderline mental case.

Sometimes Sam Niles felt that he had always been burdened with Harold Bloomguard, that there had never been a time in his life when there was not a little figure beside him, blinking his large hazel eyes, cracking his knuckles, scratching an ever-present pimply rash on the back of his neck with a penknife and worst of all unconsciously rolling his tongue in a tube and blowing spit bubbles through the channel into the air.

"It's sickening!" Sam Niles had informed Harold Bloomguard a thousand times in the seven years he had known him. "Sickening!"

And Harold would agree and swear never to do it again, and whenever he would get nervous or bewildered or frightened by one of the several hundred neurotic fears he lived with, he would sit and worry and his tongue would fold in two and little shiny spit bubbles would drop from his little pink mouth.

Sam Niles realized that at twenty-six, just four months older than Harold Bloomguard, he was a father figure. It had been that way since Vietnam where Harold Bloomguard more or less attempted to attach himself to Sam Niles for life, taking his discharge two months later than Sam and following him into the Los Angeles Police Department after returning to his family home in Pomona, California, where Harold's father practiced law and his mother was confined in a mental hospital.

It was always the same, with Harold begging Sam to sit quietly and help him interpret his latest dream full of intricate symbols, Sam always protesting that if Harold were really worried about joining his mother in the funny place, he should see a psychiatrist. The problem was that Harold Bloomguard always believed that it was her weekly session with a shrink that put his mother in the hospital in the first place, and until she went into psychotherapy when Harold was overseas, she was more or less an ordinary neurotic. So Sam Niles became the only psychiatrist Harold Bloomguard ever had and it had been this way since Sam took pity on the skinny weak little marine.

"Sam, I gotta tell you about the dream I had last night," Harold said as they left Wilshire Station at change of watch and drove into the gritty personal night world of police partners, most intimate perhaps because they might have to depend upon each other for their very lives.

"Yes, Harold, yes," Sam sighed and pushed his fashionable,

heavy, steel rimmed goggles up on his nose and promised himself to get his eyes examined because he was becoming more nearsighted than ever.

He cruised steadily through the traffic as Harold said, "There was this black cat that crossed my path and I was very afraid and couldn't understand it and I reached in my pocket and pulled out an eight inch switchblade to defend myself from I don't know what as I walked down this dark street with apartments on both sides. God, it was awful!"

"So what happened then?"

"I can't remember. I think I woke up."

"That's it?"

"Sure. It's horrible! Makes my hands sweat to think about it."

"What's so horrible?"

"Don't you see? The knife is phallic. The cat is a pussy. It's black. Black pussy. I'm unconsciously wanting to rape a black woman! Just before I crack up like my mother that's what I'll probably do, rape a black woman. Watch me very carefully around black women, Sam. As a friend I want you to watch me."

"Harold, I've watched you around black women and white women. You're perfectly normal with women. For God's sake, Harold . . ."

"I know, I know, Sam. You think it's my imagination, these deep stirrings in my twisted psyche. I know. But remember my mother. My mother is mad, Sam. The poor woman is mad!"

And Sam Niles would push up his slipping glasses, finger his brown moustache, light a cigarette and search for something else for Harold to worry about, which was generally the way to shut him up when any particular obsession was getting too obsessive.

"Harold, you know you're losing some hair lately? You noticed that?"

"Of course I've noticed," Harold sighed, touching his ginger colored sideburns. He admired Sam Niles' deep brown hair and his several premature gray ones in the front. Harold admired everything about Sam Niles, always had from the days when Sam was his fire team leader at the spider holes, and though they were in the same police academy recruit class,

Harold always treated him with the deference due a senior partner and let him be the boss of the radio car. Harold even admired Sam's steel rimmed goggles and wished he was nearsighted so he could wear them.

Sam Niles admired almost nothing about Harold Bloomguard and especially did not admire his annoying habit of amusing himself with doubletalk.

Harold would tell about a traffic accident that befell 7-A-77 the night before which resulted in a "collusion at the interjection" of Venice and La Brea. Or when Sam asked where he would like to take their code seven lunch break Harold might say, "It's invenereal to me."

Or in court Harold would ask the DA if he had any "exterminating evidence." And then ask if the DA wanted him to "draw a diaphragm." On and on it went and became almost as unbearable as the plinking spit bubbles.

But none of that was as bad as Harold Bloomguard's relentlessly sore teeth. He claimed he was a sufferer of bruxism and that he ground his teeth mercilessly in his sleep. If the nightmares were memorable the night before Harold would eat soup and soppy crackers during code seven.

But as with Harold's other maladies, Sam Niles suspected it was imaginary. He had once demanded to see Harold Bloomguard's teeth at choir practice and Ora Lee held Harold's head in her comfy lap while Father Willie struck matches for all the choirboys to examine Harold's molars which were not flat and worn down but were as sharp and serviceable as anyone's.

"They *are* worn down, I tell you," Harold said that night in the park. And he opened his mouth wider as Sam struck matches and everyone looked at his teeth.

"Let's see yours to compare, Roscoe," said Father Willie who was already very drunk.

Roscoe Rules only agreed because he wanted to take Harold's place on Ora Lee's lap and cop a feel. But while they were comparing, Father Willie accidentally dropped a match down Roscoe's throat.

Then everyone started yelling frantically with Roscoe who got up and began jumping around.

"Gimme a drink!" Roscoe shrieked.

"Give him some bourbon!" shouted Spermwhale.

"No, it'll start a fire in his tummy!" yelled Ora Lee Tingle.

"Give him the fuckin bourbon then!" yelled Spermwhale.

But Roscoe had panicked and run for the duck pond and was on his belly drinking pond water.

"He'll get typhoid!" shouted Ora Lee Tingle.

"He might at that!" yelled Spermwhale hopefully.

"Stop, Roscoe, you'll get typhoid!" Carolina Moon yelled.

"Do what feels best, Roscoe!" shouted Spencer Van Moot.

A few minutes later, Roscoe walked back to the blankets very calmly and frightened everybody because, though he had a blister on his tonsils, he was actually smiling.

"Gee, I'm sorry, Roscoe!" said the terrified Father Willie as he sat down next to Roscoe and punched Roscoe's arm playfully. "You're not mad at me, are ya?"

And Roscoe still smiled as he said, "Heavens, no, Padre! Let's have a drink."

"Sure!" said the choirboy chaplain. "Here, have a shot of vodka."

"No," Roscoe smiled, pointing at his throat. "No thank you. Think I'd prefer beer."

"Oh sure, Roscoe," Father Willie said eagerly. "I'll get it."

Roscoe said quietly, "I think there's a full six-pack down by the water."

"There is? I'll get it for you," Father Willie said.

"I'll help you," Roscoe said, putting his arm around Father Willie's shoulder and strolling with him toward the duck pond.

Thirty seconds later the other choirboys were running headlong toward the pond to rescue the screaming padre whose neck was in the arm of Roscoe Rules who was trying his best to make Father Willie do the chicken. It took four choirboys to overpower Roscoe and pin him until he promised not to choke or kneedrop the chaplain. He only relented when Ora Lee Tingle promised him she'd let him be engineer the next time she pulled the choo choo.

Ironically it was Harold Bloomguard who got Sam Niles the temporary duty assignment to the vice squad which he had been hoping for. When asked by the vice lieutenant to work the squad for two weeks because they needed some new faces

to use on the street whores, Harold had surprised the lieutenant by saying, "I know I don't look like a cop, I'm so little and
all, but why don't you take my partner, Sam Niles, too? He
doesn't look like a cop either."

"You kidding?" Lieutenant Handy said. "He's the dark
haired kid with a moustache, isn't he?"

"Yeah."

"Got cop written all over him."

"He wears glasses," offered Harold. "Not too many policemen wear glasses, sir."

"No way. The girls'd make him for a cop in a minute. You're
the one I want. We'll dress you up in a Brooks Brothers suit and
they'll swarm all over you."

"Well sir," Harold said shyly. "I sure do appreciate it. You're
the first one in the four and a half years I've been on the job
who offered to put me in plainclothes. And I really do appreciate it. But . . ."

"Yeah?"

"You see, Sam and I were in the same outfit in Nam. And
we've been radio car partners here at Wilshire for . . ."

"Okay. Look, I can bring in two more of you bluesuits for the
two weeks. I'd already decided on Baxter Slate because he
seems like a heads-up guy, and I'd decided on some morning
watch kid. But if you just gotta have Niles, okay. I'll bring him
along instead of the morning watch rookie."

"That's great, Lieutenant," Harold said. "You won't be sorry.
Sam's the greatest cop I've ever worked with. And the greatest
guy."

"Yeah, yeah, okay. We'll use you till the middle of August.
Gonna have a little crusade against the whores. Let you know
more about it later."

Sam Niles never knew about Harold's meeting with the vice
squad lieutenant and was a little nonplussed when he heard
that Harold Bloomguard was also being brought in.

"I've been trying for thirteen months to get a crack at vice,"
Sam Niles said to his partner on the night he was told. "What
made them ask you, I wonder?"

"I dunno, Sam," Harold said. "Tagging along on your coat-
tails, I guess."

But before they took their temporary vice assignment, Sam Niles and Harold Bloomguard were to have an experience which prompted Sam Niles to call for choir practice. It was before they worked vice, and before the August killing in MacArthur Park. Sam and Harold were to meet the Moaning Man.

They made a pretty good pinch, or almost did, five minutes out of the station that evening. It was four o'clock in the afternoon. Without question, the skinny hype in a long sleeved dress shirt at the corner of Fourth and Ardmore had to be suffering. And he had to be a hype, standing there on the sidewalk so weak and sick he didn't see the black and white gliding down the street against the late afternoon sun with Sam Niles behind the wheel and Harold Bloomguard writing in the log.

The hype was a Mexican: tall, emaciated, eyes like muddy water. He had recently recovered from hepatitis gotten from a piece of community artillery passed from junkie to junkie in an East Los Angeles shooting gallery.

"There's one that's hurtin for certain," Sam Niles said as he pulled the black and white into the curb, going the wrong way on the street.

Harold jumped out the door before the addict saw them. The addict spun and tried to walk away from Harold but Sam trotted up, grabbed him by the shirt and spun him easily into Harold's arms.

"Just freeze and let my partner pat you down," Sam Niles said and the hype responded with the inevitable, "Who me?"

"Oh shit," said Sam Niles.

As Harold finished the pat down on the front, neck to knee, and moved his hands around to the back, the hype made what he thought was a quick move for his belt but was grabbed in a wristlock by Sam Niles who lifted him up, up on his tippy toes and made him forget the other hurts plaguing him.

"Easy, goddamnit, easy!" yelped the hype.

"I told you not to make any sudden moves, baby." Sam crooked his arm around the hype's throat and applied just enough of a vise to the carotid artery to show him that the colorless odorless gas he breathed could be even more sweet and precious than the white crystalline chemical he had for twenty years buried in his arms and hands and legs and neck and penis.

"I got it, Sam." Harold stripped a paper bindle from the inside of the hype's belt where it had been taped.

"Pretty makeshift bindle, man," Sam Niles said, removing the pressure from the neck but keeping a wristlock which made the Mexican stand tall, sweating in the sunlight.

"Okay, okay, you got it," the hype said and Sam released the pressure.

"You sick?" Harold Bloomguard asked.

"Lightweight, lightweight," the hype said, wiping his eyes and nose on his shoulder while Sam Niles handcuffed his hands behind his back. "Listen, man, you don't wanna book me for that little bit a junk. I shoulda fixed. That'll teach me."

"Sick as you are, how come you *didn't* shoot it up?" Sam Niles asked when the hype was safely cuffed.

"This broad. Fucking broad. She was gonna pick me up here. Take me home. I was supposed to score and she was supposed to meet me here. She had the outfit and she digs on me. Oh Christ . . ." And he looked lovingly at the bindle in Harold's hand and said, "Look, I'll work for you. Gimme a break and I'll tell you where you can bring down a guy that deals in ounces. Just gimme a chance. I don't want no money, just a break. I'll be your main man for free. You can leave a little geez for me hidden away sometimes when you rip off a doper's pad. Just stash a dime bag or two in a corner and after you're gone with the guys I roll over on, I'll skate on in and pick it up. We can work like partners. You guys'll make more busts than the narcs! How about it?"

"Let's go," Sam Niles said, shoving the hype toward the police car but Harold's eyes widened as he envisioned the sick addict having international dope connections.

He said, "Sam, let's hear him out."

"Harold, for God's sake, this junkie'd say anything . . ."

"And burglars, Christ, I know a million of them!" the hype said, still handcuffed, talking desperately to Harold as Sam Niles tried to aim him toward the open door of the police car. "Mostly daytime burglars. All dopers. Lazy broads lay around in bed so long these days it's pretty hard to rip off the pads in the morning like we used to, but I still know lots and lots of burglars. Want a burglar, Officer . . . ?"

"Bloomguard."

"Officer Bloomguard, yeah. Want a burglar, Mr. Bloomguard?"

"Why not listen to him, Sam?" Harold asked as Sam Niles tried to push the addict down into the back seat of the police car.

"And tricks. Man, I can teach you a few tricks. You could learn something from me, Mr. Bloomguard. I been around this world over forty years. Been shooting dope since I was fifteen and I'm still alive. Listen, you know how to tell a hype even if he's healthy? Look for burn holes in his clothes and blisters on his fingers. When he's geezing and on the nod, he'll burn himself half to death when he's smoking cigarettes. That ain't a bad tip, is it?"

"Not bad," said Harold Bloomguard. "Sam, lemme just talk to him for a minute."

Sam Niles dropped his hands in disgust, threw his hat in the radio car, sat on the front fender of the black and white while the hype told Harold Bloomguard of his miserable life and his jealous rage at a girlfriend who had been cheating on him.

". . . and I got me some plans for that bitch, Mr. Bloomguard. I'm gonna wait down the hall in her apartment house and when her new boy comes sneaking in, I'm gonna creep up behind him, see? I'm gonna hit him over the gourd with a wrench then I'm gonna drag him into the broom closet and pull down his pants and fuck him! Yeah! And then I'm gonna drag his beat-up, fucked over ass to my old lady's door and ring the bell and say, "Here, bitch! Here's your girlfriend!"

"This guy's got style!" Harold Bloomguard said to Sam Niles who replied, "Oh yes. Real panache. Let's invite him to choir practice, Harold."

"And listen, Officer, because you been nice enough to listen to me I'm gonna save you from embarrassment. Guess what? You want the real truth? I ain't even sure you can get me booked. Know why?"

"Why?" asked Harold Bloomguard while Sam Niles was ready to throw the hype *and* Harold into the car.

"Because I think I mighta got burned on this score. This

rotten motherfucker I bought the dope from sometimes tries to sell you pure milk sugar and hope you don't catch him for a few days. He's so strung out he'll do anything to make a little bread."

"You think this is milk sugar?" Harold asked and took the bindle out of the pocket of his uniform shirt as Sam Niles got off the car, stepped on his cigarette, adjusted his steel rimmed glasses and said, "Harold, let's go."

"I think it's probably milk sugar," the hype nodded, "and you're gonna have to let me go soon as you run one of those funny little tests at the station. Taste it. I think it's pure sugar."

"Harold!" Sam Niles said as Harold opened the bindle curiously, making sure that the hype's hands were securely cuffed behind him.

"Harold!" Sam Niles said, stepping forward just as Harold licked his finger to touch the sugar and just as the hype made good his promise to teach Harold a few tricks.

The addict blew the gram of heroin out of the bindle into the air and Sam Niles watched the powder fall to the Bermuda grass at his feet and disappear.

"Oh God," said Harold Bloomguard, dropping to his knees, pulling up grass, looking for the evidence the hype had just blown away.

The addict held his breath for a moment as Sam Niles stepped forward towering over him, gray eyes smoldering. But then Sam Niles wordlessly unlocked the addict's handcuffs, put them in his handcuff case, returned the key to his key ring, took the car keys from the belt of his Sam Browne and got behind the steering wheel while Harold Bloomguard crawled around the grass searching for a few granules of powder.

"I don't think you could even pick it up with a vacuum," the hype said sympathetically. "It's very powdery. And there was only a gram."

"Guess you're right," said Harold Bloomguard, getting in the police car beside the silent Sam Niles just in time to keep from losing a leg as Sam squealed from the curb heading for the drive-in for a badly needed cup of coffee.

"Sorry, Sam," Harold smiled weakly, not looking at his grim partner.

The junkie waved bye-bye and decided that Harold was a very nice boy. The addict hoped that all five of the sons he had fathered to various welfare mothers would turn out that nice.

It was almost ten minutes before Harold Bloomguard spoke to Sam Niles which was probably a record for Harold Bloomguard who sat and tried to think of something conciliatory to say.

Unable to think of something he decided to entertain Sam.

"It was consti-pa-tion, I know," sang Harold Bloomguard to the melody of "Fascination," watching Sam Niles who did not smile, which forced Harold to sing, "I'll be loving you, maternally. With a love that's true . . ."

Getting only a languid sigh from Sam Niles he switched to a livelier melody and sang, "Gee, but it's great after eating my date, walking my baby back home."

Finally Sam Niles spoke. He said, "Harold, I don't mind your dumb songs but if you don't stop stratching those pimples on your neck with that penknife, I'm gonna stick it up your ass."

And then Harold tried to forget about losing the heroin by remembering a disturbing dream he had last Thursday and had not yet discussed with his partner. And as he concentrated he folded his tongue into a long pink tube and blew little spit bubbles which plinked wetly on the dashboard and made Sam Niles grind his teeth.

"Sam, there's something I'd like your advice about."

"Yes, yes, yes. What the hell is it this time?"

"I think I'm getting impotent."

"Uh huh."

"I haven't awakened one morning in the past week with a diamond cutter. Or even a blue veiner."

"You're not impotent."

"How do you know that, Sam? I mean how do you know it's not happening to me? I was reading about impotency recently and . . ."

"Stop reading, Harold. That's part of your problem. You read about these diseases and then you've got the symptoms."

"You think it's hypochondria but . . ."

"You're going to choir practice too often. Cool it for a while. Too much booze makes a limp noodle. Also you're getting old.

Twenty-six. You're over the hill. At your age you should drink Vano starch instead of booze."

"It's not funny, Sam. It's serious."

"Really scares you, huh, Harold?"

"Indeed," said Harold and Sam Niles gritted his teeth again. He had come to hate the word "indeed" because it was one of Harold's favorite expressions.

"Well, I'll tell you, Harold. Being impotent wouldn't be too bad for you because Carolina Moon and Ora Lee Tingle are just about the only broads you ever ball lately and I think you only do that to be a respectable member of an unrespectable group that gets drunk once a week and gangbangs two fat cocktail waitresses."

"That's not fair of you to say that, Sam. You know some of us don't approve of more than one guy mounting the same girl the same night. You and Baxter and Dean never do it. You know *I* don't."

"You did it last week!"

"I didn't!"

"Then what the hell were you and Ora Lee doing off in the bushes?"

"Only fooling around. I just can't board the train like horny old Spencer or that pig Roscoe Rules."

"Did you have a blue veiner?"

"A diamond cutter as a matter of fact."

"Then what makes you think you're impotent?"

"Because I haven't woke up for a week with anything but a limp noodle!"

"So you'll be low man on the scrotum pole at the next choir practice," said Sam Niles, turning a Bloomguardism against him.

"God, that's cruel, Sam."

"Harold, you're not impotent. Take my word. And you're not going to end up in a rubber room like your mother. But *I* might end up there if you keep using *me* for your shrink. Now if you only wanna wake up with a hard on, then ask the captain to put you on the morning watch. When you're out there at about sunrise, waking up in a radio car, after trying to sleep with an upset stomach from the crazy hours and the greasy eggs you ate at two A.M., and the nervous sleep in some alley where you're worrying about a sergeant catching you and you're longing for all the normal things people do at that hour like being flaked out in a warm bed with a warm friendly body, you know what? You'll wake up with the hardest diamond cutter you ever had. Try it if you don't believe me."

"Morning watch, huh? Don't think I'd mind that. How about it, will you go with me?"

"No, I think you'd be better off going it alone with a new partner. Who knows? Maybe you'll catch one with an MS in abnormal psych."

Harold Bloomguard thought it over for five seconds and said, "I think I'll stick with you, Sam. We'll just have to come up with another solution for my impotency."

Then they received a routine radio call to the south end where a black man had thrown a pot of hot soup on his teenage daughter and beaten the mother over the head with the pot lid. But since he was gone and the girl had already been removed to the hospital by ambulance there wasn't much to do but take the report from the mother and phone the hospital for the treatment information on the child.

After dark they received another routine call, this time on the north end to a small house inhabited by a disheveled white woman, who was barefoot in a torn dress, with three small children literally hanging on her clothing. She lurched from dragging the weight but also from the pint of bourbon she had consumed that afternoon.

Sam Niles let Harold Bloomguard handle it since somehow Harold always did anyway, excitedly jumping into a conversation with a distraught married couple or the victim of a burglary with every sort of advice, wanted or otherwise. Harold's notebook bulged with the addresses of referral agencies that ostensibly provided a remedy for any malaise Los Angeles had to offer.

The tired eyed woman had called them to report that her teenage daughter had threatened to run off with a forty-nine year old piano tuner who lived next door. Harold Bloomguard promised to arrange an appointment with juvenile officers at Wilshire Station the next morning, then he advised the mother to try to help police ascertain if she had been taken advantage of by the older man.

"If she been what?" the woman asked as Sam Niles turned on his flashlight and prepared to descend the porch steps.

"Taken advantage of," Harold said as Sam was halfway down the walk heading for the radio car.

The woman nodded dumbly and Harold said, "Well, I'm very glad we could be of service. I certainly hope we can help the young lady get back on the track tomorrow, ma'am, and if there's any way we can expedite matters prior to your appointment, you just call us back and we'll be here at once."

"Ex-pee-dite?" mumbled the woman as the lassitudinous Sam Niles, hands in his pockets, hoped the little bubblegummer's keys had been well pounded by the piano tuner so she could get out of this house, even to go to the home for unwed mothers.

"So long, ma'am," Harold said cheerfully as he took off his hat and opened the door of the radio car, turning back to wave at the stooped woman who now had no less than seven children flocked around her on the sagging wooden porch in the dim light of a naked bulb. "By the way, wherever did all these children come from?"

"From fuckin," yelled the woman, wondering how the little policeman could be so stupid as not to know that.

"Now you know where they came from, Harold," Sam said as he drove away.

It was always like this with Harold Bloomguard and always had been. Yet for reasons impossible to explain Sam could not rid himself of the clinging little man any more than the weary woman could rid herself of the clinging children.

But I didn't fuck to *get* him, thought Sam Niles. I just *got* fucked the day I accepted him into my fire team in Nam. And then Sam Niles felt the fear sweep over him as he thought of Vietnam and for a second he actually hated Harold Bloomguard. It always came this way: first fear at the memory and then a split second of incredible hatred which he assumed was for Harold Bloomguard who knew the secret of the cave. And relief for Harold's never having revealed the secret to anyone, for never having mentioned the secret even to Sam Niles.

If he'd just bring it up once, thought Sam Niles, but he never did. And that was perhaps the reason he could never rid himself of Harold Bloomguard.

"You know, Sam, I think it's time I got married," Harold suddenly announced, interrupting Sam's fearful reverie.

"Anybody I know? Ora Lee maybe? Or Carolina?"

"Don't be silly, Sam."

"If it's Ora Lee be sure to rent her out to us once a week for choir practice."

"I'm serious, Sam," Harold said as Sam Niles winked his headlights at an oncoming car and cruised west on Beverly Boulevard, glancing in store windows, most of which were darkened by now.

"So who're you going to marry?" Sam asked, not truly interested.

"I dunno. I haven't met her yet. I wonder what she'll be like?"

"Just like the girl that married dear old dad," said Sam Niles, thinking it would be rather difficult to find one like the mother Harold described to him, who up until the day he went overseas had twisted the tops off the catsup bottles and pried the lids from the cottage cheese containers, replacing them gently so that Harold would not strain himself when getting something to eat.

But she was never there to care for him again, after a certain summer afternoon when Harold was in Vietnam and her psychiatrist was on vacation in Martinique and Mrs. Bloomguard decided she was Ann Miller and did a naked tap dance in front of the Pomona courthouse and had to be taken to the screw factory to get rethreaded.

As they patrolled the nighttime streets and Harold complained that perhaps he should never get married because his mother's insanity might be congenital, Sam Niles was reminded of his own fifteen month marriage which had just been finally dissolved last year.

His ex-wife, Kimberly Cutler Niles, was a tall athletic student he had met in a college night class. She was a blonde tawny cat of a girl with daring amber eyes that looked inquisitively and boldly at you. She was bright, articulate, personable.

She said Harold Bloomguard was a doll and asked Sam to invite him home to dinner often. And incredibly enough she could cook. Not like a twenty-two year old student wife can cook but like a cook can cook. She was tidy and their little apartment was always immaculate. Harold Bloomguard loved her like a sister. He was ecstatically happy for his best friend, Sam Niles. Kimberly was darling. Sam Niles hated her guts.

But he didn't hate her at first, that came later. They were probably married three weeks before he started to hate her. But he didn't *know* that he hated her after three weeks, he just knew that she made him terribly uncomfortable. She was as terrific in the sack as he knew she would be the first night they met in class. She had introduced herself by shaking hands smoothly and firmly and saying, "I knew you were a Taurus. I just love bulls."

And moments later she was chatting glibly about tennis which interested Sam, saying, "You're a pretty good sized boy, but I'll bet you could get into size thirty-three tennis shorts. My brother left some at my place when he went away to school. Want them?"

"Sure, I'd like to play with you," Sam said with a hint of a smile so he could withdraw gracefully but she delighted him by saying, "You could probably get into much smaller tennis shorts given the opportunity, couldn't you, Sam?"

And Sam Niles had a blue veiner going on a diamond cutter and was impulsively married within four months, wondering, as did Kimberly Cutler, how the hell it all happened.

The first thing Sam Niles didn't like about being married to Kimberly Cutler was having to sleep in the same bed with another human being. It wasn't that Kimberly wasn't carnal and syrupy, she certainly was. But prior to marriage he had seldom had to spend a whole night in a bed with anybody. And early on, Kimberly's doubts were heightened by Sam's saying that he'd like to trade their king size bed for twins.

"That's unnatural," Kimberly told him as they lay in their king size bed unable to sleep.

"What's unnatural about it?"

"Newlyweds should sleep in the same bed, for God's sake."

"Where does it say that?"

"Sam, don't you enjoy me in bed?"

"That's dumb. Do I act like I enjoy you?"

"As a matter of fact you act like a man who does a pretty good act of making love. Oh, I don't mean fucking. You like *that* all right. I mean *loving*. You don't really give yourself. You hold lots and lots back from me. It's purely physical, your lovemaking."

"All this because I want twin beds. Kim, it's just that my old man and old lady were drunks and we were so goddamn poor I grew up on the floor. Or when we could rent a pad with a bed I always had to share it with two brothers. And I'm talking about a *little* bed, an army surplus cot. Christ, I felt like a married man at seven years old, always crowded into bed with one or both brothers. I just can't bear it anymore to be . . ."

"Close?"

"Yeah, close."

"You never want to get close to anybody."

"What're you talking about?"

"I'm saying that you won't let yourself get close to anyone. I can't understand how you could be friends with Harold so long. He's a sweet little guy but he's like glue. How do you stand it?"

"Whaddaya mean?" Sam asked, then added, "Jesus, I'm starting to sound like Dean."

"There's something about Harold. You've yelled his name in your sleep."

"So maybe I'm fruit for Harold."

"You don't like people, Sam. You've had a mean rough life with weak parents and you hate them even though they're dead. You won't even see your brothers and sisters unless you have to. It's very sad. You don't really want to be close to anyone. Not even me."

"There oughtta be a law against people taking Psych 1b," Sam Niles said.

"But *why* do you stay friends with Harold, Sam? You're so different. You've both been in war and police work, yet he still sees honey where you see slime. He's always enthusiastic, you're always bored. Why do you let *him* crowd you? There's something, something in the marines. In Vietnam . . ."

"My mother always told us it cost a nickel a minute to burn a light," Sam Niles said as he switched off the lamp, leaving Kimberly Cutler Niles to wonder in the darkness. "Of course it doesn't cost a nickel but I'm a creature of habit. It was just another thing that lousy drunken bitch lied about."

And Sam rolled over, wishing the king sized bed was a twin, and went to sleep, yelling in the night about a spider hole and a cave, which Kimberly Cutler knew would never be explained, not to her.

From then on the marriage deteriorated very quickly, especially after Sam Niles began to attend various choir practices with various groups of choirboys, much to the disapproval of Harold Bloomguard who tried to hint that he should go home to Kimberly.

Three months later two bitter young people lay side by side in their twin beds, both doing poorly in their college classes because of their miserable relationship. They seethed over an argument they had about one watching television when the other was trying to study.

"So I'll just quit school in my senior year," Sam said. "Why's a cop need an education anyway? No more than a trash collector. That's all we do, clean up garbage."

"The garbage is in your mind, Sam."

"Fine, I'll just feed on it. That's what pigs do, isn't it?"

And then bitter silence until Kimberly made a gambit. "Sam, do you wanna come over here and make love to me?"

"No, I'd rather have a wet dream."

"Well then go up on Hollywood Boulevard and pick yourself up a queer if I can't turn you on, you cocksucker!"

"Just like a woman. Never tell a man to go out and get some pussy. Too vain to think another woman might be able to do what you can't. It's go get a fag, never a broad."

"Fuck you!"

"Tennis, anyone?" said Sam Niles, and that was the last word spoken that night.

Two nights later, after they had not seen each other except as she came and went to class and he to the police station, Sam came in after getting off the nightwatch. He found Kimberly sleeping soundly, but as he looked at her long tan body, the blue veiner he brought with him became a diamond cutter. He quickly stripped and got in her bed, nudging her.

"Hi, Kim," he whispered.

"Oh Christ, what time is it?"

"Two thirty, maybe. I wake you up?"

"Oh no, Sam, I've been lying here worrying about you getting shot like those idiotic cops' wives on television. Where were you? Out drinking with the boys again?"

Then Sam was up close, breathing in her ear, touching her with a diamond cutter, saying, "This'll keep you awake."

"Only if you stick it in my eye," replied Kimberly and she didn't mind at all when Sam slammed out the door, half dressed.

The next night was perhaps the worst since they were both thinking about sex, hoping they could bring some of the drama back into their lives, neither wanting to make the move across the two feet of carpet to the other's bed.

"You wanna come to my bed?" Kimberly finally asked pugnaciously.

"What do you have in mind, a prizefight?"

"Goddamnit, do you or don't you?"

"Aren't you too tired tonight?"

"I'm too tired every night after I've been studying for four hours and you come tripping in at some godawful time."

"Well I'm a policeman and I work godawful hours!"

"You wanna get in bed with me?"

"Sure, but I'm tired too. Just for once, why don't you come to my bed?"

"If we had one bed we wouldn't have to be walking a beat across the goddamn carpet."

"All right, I'll come to your bed."

"Not if it's too much trouble."

"You want me to or not?"

"All right, all right."

Sam Niles pulled himself up and walked two steps and lay down beside Kimberly Cutler Niles, and after three minutes of silence wherein neither of the stubborn young people stirred, Sam finally said, "Shall we *both* put it in and toss a coin to see who has to move?"

Five minutes later it was Kimberly who was half dressed and slamming out the door.

The honeymoon was definitely over, but like so many people, Sam and Kimberly needed a dramatic moment to convince them of what they should have known. Six days later they got it.

It started with Sam Niles deciding to drive Kimberly bananas much as Celeste Holm tried to drive Ronald Colman bananas on a movie Sam had seen on "The Late Show." He felt a little silly that night as he lay in his twin bed, knowing that he had made enough noise coming home from work to wake up the landlady downstairs. He knew that Kimberly could not possibly sleep through his drawer banging, toilet flushing, door slamming, shoe dropping, and would have to respond as Sam lay in the darkness with his back to her and forced out a muffled hilarious laugh guaranteed to drive her wild.

After the third stream of laughter he heard Kimberly stir in her bed and say, "Sam, are you drunk or what?"

"No."

"Then what's so damn funny at three A.M.?"

"Nothing."

"Then please let me sleep."

"Okay."

And moments later Sam Niles was giggling more hilariously than before, because, by God, it worked! He knew she would soon be beside herself with jealousy, curiosity and debilitating rage. Then Sam began chuckling in earnest, his body and bed shaking.

Finally Kimberly spoke again. "Sam, honey."

"Yes?"

"No offense, but any guy who won't screw his wife and giggles a lot really should try to get himself together on Hollywood Boulevard. Why don't you put on my yellow miniskirt and go out trolling. You might get lucky."

So Sam Niles angrily decided that what worked for Celeste Holm would not work on Kimberly Cutler Niles. He was not yet convinced that Oscar Wilde was right and Aristotle was wrong: that life imitates art. So he went back to television for an answer to his domestic misery. And he found it on "The Late, Late Show."

It was John Wayne telling Maureen O'Hara that there'd be no locked doors in their marriage as he broke down a three inch oak door and threw the stunning redhead onto their four-poster, breaking it to the ground.

Like so many policemen, Sam Niles was a John Wayne fan, though he had never fallen prey to the malaise the Los Angeles police psychologist called the "John Wayne Syndrome," wherein a young hotdog responds with independence, assurance and violence to all of life's problems and comes to believe his four inch oval shield is as large as Gawain's ever was. Roscoe Rules, who swaggered and talked police work every waking moment and wore black gloves and figuratively shot from the hip and literally from the lip, was surely suffering from the syndrome. But though Sam Niles had never been a hotdog or black glove cop, he admired the direct, forceful, simplistic approach to life found in a John Wayne film. And he was given the chance to be the Duke that very week.

It started over Sam's bitching about Kimberly's cooking which like everything else in their marriage had deteriorated to the point that even she could hardly eat it. It ended with her in angry tears, which was not unusual, and running into the bathroom and locking the door, which was extremely unusual.

"Goddamn women," Sam Niles muttered in consummate frustration, hurling his half-eaten plate of food against the wall, his stomach afire from the poisons he was manufacturing.

Sam found himself standing in front of the bathroom door, making a fist and shouting, "There'll be no locked doors in our marriage, Kimberly Cutler Niles!"

And when there was no answer he John Wayned the door, kicking it right next to the lock and sending it crashing across the bathroom to smash into the wall and crack the porcelain toilet.

The door exploded. It made a loud boom. But nothing like the boom his Smith and Wesson .38 made in the hands of Kimberly Cutler Niles as she stood inside that bathroom, half out of her mind, watching the door sailing past.

Then Sam Niles was lying flat on his stomach from his feet trying to run backward. Then he was kneeling on his broken glasses pleading, "Please, Kimberly! Please don't kill me! Oh God!" And then there was another explosion and a third, and

Sam Niles was up and crashing through the aluminum screen door and running down the walk and across the street to a vacant lot where he lay trembling in the knee-high weeds, watching the front of the apartment building, waiting for a wrathful figure to emerge from the darkness. Ready to run like a turpentined cat as far as his legs could carry him from the maniacal Kimberly Cutler Niles.

The police were called by three neighbors that night, but the walls and concrete walks of the apartment building had played tricks with the sound of gunfire and no one knew the shots had come from the Niles' apartment. It was finally thought that someone had driven by and shot up the place. Two detectives worked for three weeks on the theory that an unknown assailant had a grudge against the apartment house manager who sweated off ten pounds during the investigation. Kimberly bought a new door and toilet and had the interior bullet holes patched before she moved out and filed for her divorce.

When he was sure Kimberly was in class Sam Niles came back and got his clothes, ready to bolt out the door any second. He found his belongings on the living room floor. There was a note beside his gun which read, "Who's got the biggest balls now, hero?"

Sam Niles never fully appreciated a John Wayne film after that night.

But he wasn't thinking too much about Kimberly Cutler or John Wayne the night the hype blew their case away and they arrested the man who painted himself red.

Both Sam Niles and Harold Bloomguard had heard of the man who painted himself red. But prior to the contact with him he was known only as the man who painted his *car* red. His name was Oscar Mobley and he was fifty-eight years old, white, unmarried, lived alone, was unemployed and liked to paint his car red. It would never have been called to the attention of the Los Angeles Police Department if it weren't for the fact that Oscar Mobley did it with a paintbrush and bucket and did it perhaps once a month. The policemen who knew him said that his fifteen year old Ford outweighed a Cadillac limousine, so thick were the coats of peeling red enamel.

And yet Oscar Mobley would probably never have become the subject of rollcall gossip if it weren't that he would occasionally paint his headlights red and drive along Wilshire Boulevard at night, making cars pull over. Oscar Mobley had many warnings and traffic tickets over painting his headlights red, but just as it appeared that he would give up painting his headlights red, Oscar Mobley suddenly for no apparent reason painted all the windows of his car red, and unable to see through a red opaque windshield, got himself into a traffic accident on Washington Boulevard. He was ordered by a traffic court judge never ever to paint his headlights or windshield red again.

Oscar Mobley had not been heard from for several months, apparently content to have a car with a red body, red bumpers, red tires, red hubcaps and red grille, but with unpainted windows and headlights. Then something happened on the night Sam and Harold met Oscar Mobley.

"Seven-A-Twenty-nine, see the woman, male mental case, Eleventh and Irolo, code two."

"Seven-Adam-Twenty-nine, roger," Harold responded as Sam picked up speed a little and drove through the nighttime traffic to the residential neighborhood of Oscar Mobley.

"It's about time you got here," said the caller, Mrs. Jasper, the next door neighbor of Oscar Mobley. Her hair was wet with red paint and a blue cotton dress she held in her hands was covered with the stuff. "I just asked that crazy nut Oscar why he was painting his headlights and windshield red, that's all I did . . ."

"Wait a minute," Sam Niles said as he and Harold stood in the street with Mrs. Jasper, her husband, her brother and eight other neighborhood men and women who had almost decided to lynch the frail Oscar Mobley until someone had the presence of mind to call the police.

"Oscar started to paint his car again tonight," said Mr. Jasper, a man with receding hair and a parrot's face, who was even more frail than Oscar Mobley and who had no stomach for fighting for Mrs. Jasper who could have licked Oscar Mobley and Mr. Jasper at the same time on her worst day.

"Yeah, we know about Oscar," Sam Niles said.

"Well he started to paint again," Mr. Jasper continued. "He

ain't done that for three, four months now. He won't ever tell anyone on the street why he paints his car red and we asked him a thousand times, maybe a million. He just smiles and keeps painting and won't answer you. Well tonight he done what the judge told him *not* to do, he started painting the headlights and the windows red, and my wife just came out on the front porch and asked him why."

"That's all I done and that crazy little . . ."

"Please, ma'am, one at a time," Harold said.

"Well, my little woman just comes out and sees him there under the streetlight, painting everything red and she asks him why he's doing it and he says something she can't hear and she thinks at last maybe she's gonna learn the secret of why Oscar Mobley paints his car red and she just walks over . . ."

"Out of curiosity," added Mrs. Jasper.

"Out of curiosity," said Mr. Jasper, "and when she gets close she says, 'Oscar, why do you paint your car red?' And he don't say a word. Then he done it."

"Done . . . did what?" asked Harold.

"Painted *me* red!" Mrs. Jasper shouted. "The little son of a bitch started painting *me*. I got the paintbrush in my mouth and I couldn't breathe. He was painting my hair and neck and arms. If he hadn't a surprised me I'd a knocked the little bastard down the sewer, but pretty soon I couldn't even see for the paint in my eyes. And I turn and run for the house and he chases me painting my . . ."

"Her ass," said Mr. Jasper.

"Yes, the dirty beggar even did that to me and I've been scrubbing with paint thinner till my skin's almost wore off. Look at me!"

Harold shined the flashlight past Mrs. Jasper's face so as not to hit her eyes with the beam and it was true, her face and neck were a splotched and faded red like a pomegranate.

"Well, it's time someone did something about Oscar," Sam Niles sighed and he and Harold got their batons and put them in the rings on their Sam Brownes and went to find Oscar Mobley and let Mrs. Jasper make a citizen's arrest on him for painting her red.

As Sam expected, Oscar Mobley did not open the door when he pounded and rang the bell.

"It's unlocked, Sam," Harold said when he turned the knob of the front door of the little three room house where Oscar lived with two cats and a goldfish.

Sam shrugged and readied his revolver and Harold Bloomguard also fingered his gun, ready to touch the spring on the clamshell holster. Both men entered the darkened kitchen and tiptoed toward the narrow hallway to the tiny bedroom where a lamp burned.

Sam went in first, his gun out in front and he said quietly, "Mr. Mobley, if you're in here I want you to come out. We're police officers and we want to talk to you. We won't hurt you. Come out."

There was no answer and Sam entered the room, seeing nothing but an unmade bed, a box of cat litter, a broken down nightstand with an old radio on it, a pile of dirty clothing on the floor and a napless overstuffed chair.

Sam was about to check under the bed when he and Harold were scared half out of their wits by the naked Oscar Mobley who suddenly leaped out from behind the overstuffed chair, painted red from head to foot, arms outstretched.

"Up popped the devil!" yelled Oscar Mobley cheerfully.

It was miraculous that neither officer shot him. Both were exerting at least a pound of trigger pull on their guns which like all department issued guns had been altered to fire only double action. They stood, shoulders pressed together, backs to the wall, gaping at Oscar Mobley who posed, arms extended, grinning proudly, the paint hardly dry on his small naked body.

Everything had been painted: the palms of his hands, the soles of his feet, his hair, face, body, genitals. He had managed with a roller to get the center of his back. He had neglected his teeth only because he forgot them. He had not painted his eyeballs only because he started to and it hurt.

As Sam Niles later stood in Oscar Mobley's kitchen and smoked to steady his nerves, the equally shaken Harold Bloomguard patiently persuaded Oscar Mobley that despite the beautiful paint job he should wear a bathrobe to go where they were going because it was a nippy evening and he might catch cold.

After agreeing that Elwood Banks, the jailor at Wilshire Station, might object to their bringing in a man who painted himself red since it would be messy to try to roll fingerprints over the coat of red enamel, Sam and Harold took Oscar Mobley where he belonged: Unit Three, Psychiatric Admitting, of the Los Angeles County General Hospital. The hospital now had a grander name: Los Angeles County, University of Southern California Medical Center. But it would forever be General Hospital to the indigent people it served.

Oscar Mobley was admitted, later had a sanity hearing wherein he steadfastly refused to tell anyone why he painted his car, himself and Mrs. Jasper red, and went to a state hospital for six months where he refused to tell anyone else his secret.

After his release he moved to a new neighborhood, took a job delivering throwaway circulars, did it beautifully for eight days, then painted his boss and his boss' wife red and was recommitted to the state hospital. But all this happened long after Sam Niles and Harold Bloomguard took him to Unit Three, in time to miss code seven though they were starving, and just in time to meet the Moaning Man.

The call came just after 11:00 P.M. "Seven-Adam-Twenty-nine, shot fired vicinity of Ninth and New Hampshire."

"Rampart Division," Sam Niles said to Harold Bloomguard who nodded, picked up the mike and said, "Seven-A-Twenty-nine reporting that the call is in Rampart Division."

"Seven-Adam-Twenty-nine, stand by," said the radio operator as she checked with one of the policemen who supervise the girls and assign the call tickets.

"Goddamn Rampart cars've been pulling this shit too often lately," Sam said to Harold who didn't mind handling the call in someone else's division because Sam had been exceedingly quiet and Harold was getting as bored as Sam always was.

"If we have to handle this one, next time a Rampart car gets a call in our area we'll just let the bastards handle it," Sam said.

"Seven-Adam-Twenty-nine, handle the call in Rampart Division," said the radio operator. "No Rampart units available."

"Seven-Adam-Twenty-nine, roger on the call," Harold Bloomguard said as Sam Niles pushed up his drooping steel rimmed glasses and threw a cigarette out the window saying,

"They're probably all over on Alvarado eating hamburgers, the lazy pricks."

Sam drove slowly on the seedy residential streets, mostly a white Anglo district, but with some black and Latin residents. He shined the spotlights on the front of homes and apartments, hoping not to find anyone who may have phoned about shots being fired. Sam Niles wanted to go to an east Hollywood drive-in and eat cherry pie and drink coffee and try to score with a waitress he knew.

"There it is," Harold said as Sam's spotlight beam lighted a chinless withered man in a bathrobe who waited in front of a two story stucco apartment house. The door glass had been broken so many times the panes were replaced by plywood and cardboard.

Sam took his time parking, and Harold was already across the narrow street by the time Sam gathered up his flashlight and put his cigarette pack in his pocket and locked the car door so someone didn't have fun slashing the upholstery or stealing the shotgun from the rack.

"Heard a shot," the old man said. His eyes were a quiet brown like a dog's.

"You live here?"

"Yep."

"You the manager?"

"Nope, but I got a passkey. I help out Charlie Bates. He's the manager."

"Why do we need a key?" Harold asked.

"Shot came from up there."

And the man in the bathrobe pointed a yellow bony finger up to the front window on the second floor where a gray muslin drape flapped rhythmically as the gusts of wind blew and sucked through the black hole of an open window on what had become a chilled and cloudy night.

"Give us the passkey, we'll have a look," Sam Niles said and later he wondered if he felt something then.

It seemed he did. He was to recall distinctly wishing that a Rampart unit would feel guilty that Wilshire was handling their calls and perhaps come driving down Ninth Street to relieve them.

The stairs creaked as they climbed and the whole building reeked, dank and sour from urine and moldy wool carpet on the stairs. They stood one on each side of the door and Sam knocked.

The dying tree outside, the last on the block, rattled in the wind which rushed through the narrow hallway upstairs. The building was surprisingly quiet for one housing eighty-five souls. Sam reached up and unscrewed the only bulb at their end of the hall, and said, "We better be in the dark."

"Might be some drunk sitting in there playing with a gun," Harold nodded and both policemen drew their service revolvers.

Sam knocked again and the sound echoed through the empty hall which had no floor carpet, only old wooden floors caked with grime which could never be removed short of sanding the wood a quarter of an inch down. A mustard colored cat, displaying the indifference Sam Niles usually feigned, watched from the windowsill.

The wind blew and it was a cold wind, yet Sam was to remember later that he was sweating. He tasted the salt running through his moustache into the dimple of his upper lip. Then they heard it.

At first Sam Niles thought it was the wind. Then he saw the look on Harold Bloomguard's face in the dark hallway when he moved into a patch of moonlight. He knew that Harold heard it and that it wasn't the wind.

Then they heard it again. The Moaning Man was saying:

"Mmmmmm. Mmmmmm. Mmmmmuuuuuuuhhhhhhhh."

Then Sam was sweating in earnest and Harold's pale little face was glistening in the swatch of moonlight as he pressed himself against the wall, gun in his left hand. Sam Niles turned the key slowly and then kicked the door open with his toe and jumped back against the wall.

"Mmmmm," said the Moaning Man. "Uuuuhhhhh. Mmmmmuuuuuhhhhh."

"Jesus Christ motherfucker son of a bitch!" Sam Niles, like many men, swore incoherently when he was frightened.

The moans sounded like cattle lowing. They came from inside. Inside in the darkness.

Finally Sam Niles moved. He dropped to his knees and with his flashlight in his left hand and gun in the right, crawled into the tiny apartment ready to switch on the flashlight and ready to shoot. He crept toward the bedroom which was just behind the cluttered kitchen.

Sam Niles smelled blood. And he felt the flesh wriggling on his rib cage and on his back and up the sides of his dripping neck into his temple when the Moaning Man said it again. But it was loud this time and plaintive:

"Mmmmm. Uuuuuhhhhh. Mmmmmuuuuuhhhhh!"

Then Harold Bloomguard, tiptoeing through the kitchen behind Sam who was on his knees, accidentally dropped his flashlight and the beam switched on when it hit the floor and Sam Niles cursed and jumped to his feet and leaped to the doorway, his gun following the beam from his own flashlight in the darkness. And he met the Moaning Man.

He was sitting up in bed, his back pressed to the wall. He was naked except for undershorts. Every few seconds the wind would snap the dirty ragged drapes and the moonlight would wash his chalky body which otherwise lay in the slash of light. He held a 9 mm. Luger in his left hand and had used it for the first and last time by placing it under his chin, gouging the soft flesh between the throat and the jawbone and pulling the trigger.

The top of the head of the Moaning Man was on the bed and on the floor beside the bed. The wall he leaned against was spotted with sticky bits of brain and drops of blood. Most of his face was intact, except it was crisscrossed with rivulets of blood in the moonlight, filling his eyes with blood. The most incredible thing of all was not that the Moaning Man was able to make sounds, it was that the gun he had killed himself with was clenched tightly in a fist across his body at port arms. He moved it back and forth in rhythm with the moans.

"Oh my God oh my God oh my God," Sam Niles said as Harold Bloomguard gaped slackjawed at the Moaning Man whose gun hand was swaying, swaying, back and forth with the snapping of the drapes in the wind as he said:

"Mmmmmm. Uuuuuhhhhh. Mmmmmuuuuuhhhhh."

And Sam Niles knew that he *never* would have done what

the terrified Harold Bloomguard did next, which was to walk slowly across that room, watching the Luger swaying in the hand of the Moaning Man, the pieces of skull crackling under his leather soles, crackling with each step, until he stood beside the bed.

Sam Niles would forever smell the blood and hear the wind and the snapping drapes and Harold's shoes crackling on the fragments of bone and Harold's teeth clicking together frightfully as he moved a trembling hand toward the Luger which the Moaning Man held in front, swaying to and fro as he said:

"Mmmmm. Uuuuuhhhh. Mmmmmuuuuuuhhhtherr!"

And then Harold Bloomguard spoke to the Moaning Man. He said, "Now now now. Hush now. I'm right here. You're not alone."

Harold Bloomguard gripped the wrist and hand of the Moaning Man and the moaning stopped instantly. The fist relaxed, dropping the pistol on the bed. The bloody eyes slid shut and overflowed. The Moaning Man died without a sound.

Both policemen remained motionless for a long moment before Harold Bloomguard controlled his shaking and said, "He was calling his mother, is all. Why do so many call their mother?"

"He was dead!" Sam Niles said. "He was dead before we saw him!"

"He only needed the touch of a human being," said Harold Bloomguard. "I was so scared. *So* scared!"

Sam Niles turned and left Harold in the darkness with the Moaning Man and called for a detective to take the death report and he did not speak to Harold for the remainder of the watch and demanded a choir practice when they changed into civilian clothes later that night. It was a bitter night for choir practice and only half the choirboys showed up. But Carolina Moon was there so it wasn't too bad.

11

Sergeant Dominic Scuzzi

With a galloping heartbeat Harold Bloomguard entered the opened door of the vice squad office on the first night of his vice assignment. Harold was twenty-five minutes early. He wore a conservative gray suit, white button-down shirt, a paisley tie and traditional wing tip brogues.

The office was open but empty when Harold arrived. It looked different from the detective squad room. It was much smaller. And more cluttered. Covering one wall were three large street maps dotted with multicolored pins. Certain streets were covered with green pins signifying prostitution activity. Other streets were sporadically dotted with pins marking suspected bookmaking locations: cashrooms in the southerly black neighborhoods, phone spots in the northerly white neighborhoods. Cocktail lounges were marked where handbooks and agents operated.

There was a painted motto over the door. It said: "What you say here, What you see here, What you hear here, Let it stay here, When you leave here."

Harold Bloomguard read that motto with shining eyes. He shook back his thin, ginger-colored hair and smiled enchantedly. For a dreamy moment he sipped from a frothy goblet in

Bombay, Macao, Port Said: white linen suits, narrow teeming passages, mingled aromas of spice, rich dried fruit, dusky succulent women, clawing danger. The mystique of the secret agent enveloped this room.

Just then a swarthy unshaven overweight man of fifty in a dirty short sleeved dress shirt shuffled through the door in run over sneakers. He looked Harold up and down and said, "You don't look big enough to fight, fuck or run a footrace. You one a the new kids on the block?"

"I'm . . . I'm . . . are *you* a policeman?"

"I'm a sergeant. I run the nightwatch." The man shambled to a desk, rummaged through piles of papers until he found a cigar, belched three times before he offered his hand and said, "Name's Dom Scuzzi. You can call me Scuz. You Slate, Niles or Bloomguard?"

"Bloomguard . . . Sergeant."

"I said call me Scuz. Ain't no formality in the vice squad. Not since I got rid a that prick, Lieutenant Cotton-Balls Klingham. I'll never understand how he got on the squad. Cotton-Balls. One hundred percent sterile like they say on the box. Everything about him was sterile, especially his conversation."

Sergeant Scuzzi paused long enough to puff on the cigar and belch once or twice before continuing. "Anyways, we got rid a him. Can't tell you how I did it. But I'll always be beholding to one a your nightwatch bluesuits, name a Spermwhale Whalen, for giving me the idea. How long you been at Wilshire?"

"Almost two years. You know, Sarge . . . Scuz, I've seen you around but . . ."

"That's Scuz. Don't rhyme with fuzz. Rhymes with loose. That's Scooose. As in scuse a me."

"Scooose."

"That's it! I ain't been here at this station too long."

"Yeah, I've seen you around, but I always thought you were . . ."

"A janitor?"

"Yeah, I guess so."

"I don't mind. My old man's a janitor. Supported nine kids pushing a broom. Never talked a word a English, hardly. I don't mind looking like a janitor. The other two loaners look good as you?"

"What do you mean?"

"You look good. I mean *good*. How tall're you?"

"Five eight."

"Weigh about a hundred fifty?"

"Just about."

"How the hell you get on the department?"

"I stretched and ate bananas and stuff."

"You look *good*. Here." Scuz pulled open the drawer of his desk, propped his tennis shoes up in front of him, leaned back, puffed his cigar and said, "Try em on."

Harold picked up the horn rimmed glasses, held them to his eyes and said, "They're clear glass."

"Sure. Makes you look even less like a cop if that's possible. You're gonna be a real whore operator, my boy. Glad you wore a suit tonight. You're definitely the suit and tie type. Tell em you're an accountant. Here."

And Scuz reached back in the drawer, rummaged through it for a few seconds and found a packet of business cards which said, "Krump, Krump and Leekly, Certified Public Accountants."

"Any broads get cute with you trying to guess if you're a cop, just lay a card on her. Tell her it's your private business phone and she can call you during business hours. That's our straight-in line here. We got a girl works here on the daywatch who's good at conning callers. If a whore won't go for you tonight she'll go for you tomorrow night after she checks you out with our girl."

"I don't know anything about vice, Scuz," Harold said, relaxing in the chair in front of the unshaven sergeant who reached inside his shirt and scratched his belly which was almost as big as Spermwhale's, and puffed the cigar blissfully with his eyes closed.

"Now don't go worrying . . . what's your first name?"

"Harold."

"Harold, don't worry about nothing. I never let my coppers get hurt, specially not a loanee like you who I gotta return to the patrol lieutenant in a couple weeks in as good a shape as

I borrowed him. There ain't nothing to working whores. They offer you a sex act for money. Got it? Sex, money. You in the service?"

"Marines."

"Overseas?"

"Vietnam."

"All right," Scuz nodded, chewing his cigar, leaning back in the chair, hands behind his head. "Overseas the broads got it made. Fucky sucky, five bucks. See, they say what every whore said in war or peace for five thousand years. Sex, money. Now, these whores today know that there's a thing called entrapment, which means you can't plant an evil idea in their heads, as if that was possible. So in effect they're gonna wanna say sucky fucky and let *you* say the price. Or they're gonna say the price and let *you* say sucky fucky. Get it?"

"I think so."

"It's just a game but I don't wanna see you perjure yourself for a shitty little whore pinch so you play it straight. Figure out a way to make her say the whole thing: Sucky fucky, five bucks. But of course it ain't five bucks, it's twenty on the street. And she ain't gonna say sucky fucky usually. She's gonna say French or half and half or party, and all these words been construed by the black robed pussies that sit on the bench to be words with sexual connotations. So soon as she says one a these words and she mentions money, Boom! Bring her down. Hook her up. You got a legal pinch. Got it?"

"God, I hope so," said Harold.

"Well, just don't entrap them. Course you're gonna run into guys who say, bullshit, she says sucky fucky and gets cute about the price, I pull out the iron and zoom her. I say no. Nice and legal."

"Sucky fucky, five bucks," said Harold.

"You got it, kid, I knew you was smart!" Scuz said, moving the cigar from the right side of his mouth to the left. "Course she might throw you a curve."

"Like how?"

"She might say, 'I think you look like a cop. If you ain't a cop, take out a twenty dollar bill and wrap it around your cock and wave it at me.' One did that to me once."

"What'd you do?"

"I only had a ten," said Scuz, closing his eyes, enveloping himself in a shroud of cigar smoke which was starting to choke Harold Bloomguard. "But don't worry about these brain teasers. Don't happen too much. Most girls're just gonna say . . ."

"Sucky fucky, five bucks."

"I like you, kid," said Scuz. "Wanna cigar?"

"No thanks, Scuz," Harold said, thinking about inviting the vice sergeant to choir practice, just as Sam Niles and Baxter Slate came through the door.

Scuz opened his eyes, peeked through the cloud of smoke which hung over him and shook his head disapprovingly at the two strapping six footers, at their hair styled just over the ears, but not long enough to offend the station captain totally. Baxter wore tie dyed jeans, a denim jacket and a red velvet shirt. Sam Niles wore a buckskin shirt over a tank top, brushed denims and Wallabees. His neat brown moustache did not drop down around the lip far enough to anger the same station captain and his sideburns did not quite flare out into muttonchops. The steel rimmed goggles did not help mitigate the whole picture.

"Shit!" Scuz said, fanning the smoke away from his face. "You look just like two healthy, clean cut, twenty-six year old studs, which is what you are. You look like young *cops*. Why can't you look sick and puny like him?" And Scuz pointed to Harold Bloomguard who decided not to invite him to choir practice.

"This is a sergeant," said Harold Bloomguard to Sam and Baxter in case they wouldn't believe it.

"Just call me Scuz," said Scuz.

"Anything wrong with the way we look?" Sam Niles asked.

"No, you can't help it," Scuz said. "It wouldn't even help if I made you funky. You just got copper written all over you. It's okay, you guys can work in the trap."

"Trap?" said Baxter Slate.

"Fruits," Scuz said, dropping his feet to the floor and remembering they had not shaken hands, offering his hairy paw to both policemen. "What's your first names?"

"Sam, Sam Niles."

"Baxter Slate."

"Okay, guys, glad to have you. Hope you enjoy the two weeks here. Anyways, you can work fruits with the regular team tonight and maybe tomorrow, then you can have some fun on the weekend working a Wilshire Boulevard bar. We got a complaint there's a big game going on in the back room a this cocktail lounge after closing time. Gotta check it out. Give you some front money maybe. See how you operate. Call it Secret Service money. The department is cheap. Cheapest fucking outfit you ever saw. The money's just for flash. You spend as little as you have to and bring the rest back. You lose it or somebody burns you for it, I gotta shoot myself like a Jap general. You don't wanna see old Scuz fall on his sword, do you, Sam?"

"No, Sergeant."

"Scuz."

"Scuz."

"You, Baxter?"

"No, Scuz."

"Okay, boys, then when your partners get here and start your teaching, pay attention to what they tell you. They'll tell you better than me. Just remember a couple things. One is that we work a misdemeanor detail and I don't want any man hurt for a shitty little misdemeanor. *Don't get hurt.* Got it, boys?"

And as Harold Bloomguard gulped nervously all three young men nodded at Scuz. "And another thing, I'm sorry I gotta give you some a the shitty jobs but we get a vice complaint we gotta investigate it. I wish I could just let you work fun things like gambling and call girls and bookmaking back offices and fancy bars with good drinks, but that usually ain't what we gotta do. So try to have fun but don't get hurt. That's the only rule I got. You let yourself get hurt and I'll break your arm!"

For the next fifteen minutes six regular vice officers straggled into the squad room and said hello to Scuz who continued to befoul the entire room with the cheap cigar. The vice cops introduced themselves all around and worked in their logbooks and vice complaints.

The regular vice cops looked like Hollywood's version of

Tripoli buccaneers, Turkish brigands or Viking warriors. One, a black, looked like a Sudanese caravan raider. All were young men, fiercely moustachioed and bearded with enough hair to stuff a mattress. They wore stylishly funky clothes like most young people. Yet beneath it all they were carefully washed and sprayed and powdered. They were so baroque and theatrical they *had* to be cops. Only Dominic Scuzzi could fool the street people.

"This one here's Harold Bloomguard," Scuz said to his troops. "Look at him. This is what I been trying to tell you guys about how you should look. Ain't nobody gonna make him for the heat, right?"

"Right," answered the Viking.

"Then why don't you guys try to look like him? Why do you wanna look like you walk a beat for Attila the Hun?"

"Scuz, I ain't looked like Harold since I was twelve years old," said a Turkish brigand while Harold blushed at the laughter.

The three loanees were given a further briefing and within an hour they were heading for their vice cars.

"One more thing I almost forgot," Sergeant Scuzzi said, stopping the squad of men in the doorway. He sat back down, lit a new cigar and said, "You new kids listen. If you go sneaking and peeking and prowling around backyards, you gotta *always* pay attention to the *size* a the dog shit. Got me?"

Then Scuz put his tennis shoes up on the desk and leaned back and puffed while a persistent fly who wanted desperately to light on the vice sergeant's pungent flesh decided to fly from the choking polluted clouds. Fleeing for his very life.

The three new kids on the block found themselves standing in the parking lot just before dark, each with a tiny flashlight the other vice cops lent them since their three and five cell lights were unwieldy on the vice detail. They waited for each of the three teams to pick one of them and were totally bewildered when no one did.

As Pete Zoony, a loose limbed vice cop with a woolly dust-colored hairdo and a Fu Manchu moustache, got in his car he turned to the three loanees and said, "We're not being unfriendly, it's just that Scuz is gonna come slipping and sliding out the door in a couple seconds. He can't relax when there's new guys around. Thinks you'll get killed if he don't break you in personally. Tomorrow night you'll work with us and we'll get better acquainted. Oh, oh. Here he comes."

And the three choirboys turned to see Scuz shuffling through the door, stepping on the frayed ends of his shoelaces and scratching his balls, which was easy to do given the shiny baggy gabardine pants ready to wear through. Then he banged his little flashlight on the heel of his hairy hand, puffed a cloud of smoke into the summer breeze and scuttled across the parking lot, just stepping back in time to keep a black and white from running over him.

The officer driving, who was Roscoe Rules, said to Whaddayamean Dean, "Fucking janitors they hire these days look like goat shit! Oughtta make that prick clean up or fire him!"

As Scuz reached the three choirboys and his teams of regular vice cops who sat grinning in their cars, he said to Pete Zoony, "Don't mind if I take the new kids out, do you, Pete? Just for tonight. I ain't got nothing to do anyways except the progress report for our psycho captain. Can't seem to think a any good lies to put in there tonight."

"No, we don't mind, Scuz," Pete Zoony said. "Just tell us where you're gonna take em so we don't bunch up in the same place."

"Well, we got that three-eighteen about the shithouse up there in the department store."

"Yeah."

"And I might try this wimpy little kid here out on the whores on Western. Don't he look terrific?" And Scuz threw a heavy arm around the wimpy little kid and hugged him.

Five minutes later, Sergeant Scuzzi was driving north on La Brea in a four door, five year old Plymouth which looked every bit like a detective car and disappointed the choirboys.

Sam Niles sat in the back seat with Baxter Slate and Harold sat in front, nervously blowing spit bubbles off his tongue which plinked on the dashboard as he scratched the strawberry rash on the back of his neck with a little penknife. Sam Niles decided then that Harold and Scuz would make perfect partners.

"This ain't much of an undercover car, is it, boys?" Scuz remarked as they bumped and pounded over dips in the asphalt.

"Not much," Baxter Slate said. He looked at Scuz in disbelief but not without affection from time to time.

"Cheap outfit, boys. I mean we work for a cheap outfit. Be amazed how little Secret Service money I get. End up spending my own bread more often than not. Think we can go in the bar and nurse one drink for three hours? Shit, they *know* we're cops when they see how fucking stingy we are."

"Where we going first, Scuz?" Harold asked, perspiring because the sun had not yet set and it was muggy for Los Angeles. And because he was very nervous.

"Boys, I gotta take you to a trap first off tonight. And I gotta apologize which I don't like to do cause I always feel a cop shouldn't have to apologize for doing his job. But the truth is —and don't tell your lieutenant old Scuz told you this when you go back to patrol—but the truth is that most of a vice cop's job is just public relations. See, we can say we're protecting the city's morals and point to statistics to prove it, but fact is we ain't doing much a anything. So you might say, Scuz, what the hell we doing it for? And I say, boys, it's part a the game. Every business has its PR department where they manufacture bullshit, right? General Motors got it. U.S. Steel got it. AT&T got it. For sure the White House got it and City Hall. We can tell all the folks who pay our salary that we're guarding the morals a the citizens from the degenerates that wanna pay money to suck, fuck or gamble with someone they ain't married to outta the privacy a their own bedroom. You only work this vice detail for eighteen months and then you're out. I say it's a little break from routine for me so I work it but I ain't got no illusions about cleaning up maggots. In the first place how do I know I ain't just a maggot myself, you stand back and look at the whole picture in general?"

The choirboys glanced at one another and gave Scuz no argument.

"So anyways that's my philosophy about vice work. And you kids're gonna work for me for a couple weeks. And since you're doing a job that ain't gonna help nobody anyways, I just don't

want you to get hurt, see? So let's say you run into some six foot
six fruit with nineteen inch arms who's a foot fetishist. And he
buys a pair a black satin shoes from the shoe department a this
store I'm taking you to, and takes the shoes into the shitter
where he pulls out a can a whipped cream which he shoots all
over the shoes. And then he stands there and licks the whipped
cream off. Whadda you do about it, seeing as how you're gonna
be behind a wall looking through a screen into the john and
protecting the public morals?"

"Huh?" said Harold Bloomguard.

"I asked, whaddaya gonna do about this weird guy?"

"Well, I dunno, Scuz," Harold said, blowing a spit bubble
while Sam Niles toyed with his moustache and shook his head
disgustedly, as Baxter Slate's wide smile grew wider with affection for Scuz.

"Harold, my boy," Scuz said. "First place, I gave you a hint.
I said the weirdo has nineteen inch arms!"

"Oh, I see!" said Harold. "Shine him on. Pass him by."

"You got it!" Scuz said, driving only fifteen miles per hour
which was driving Sam Niles to distraction. "Course there ain't
no misdemeanor here in the first place. So happens that some
guys like to eat whipped cream off black satin shoes. Just wish
they'd do it home and we wouldn't get no calls about it but
thing is they like to do it in public. Anyways there ain't no law
against it I know, so you just hope he gets full a whipped cream
in a hurry and gets the hell out before someone calls the station
and the station turns the problem over to the vice squad.
Ready for another hypothetical?"

"Sure, Scuz," grinned Baxter Slate, accepting a cigarette
from the lethargic Sam Niles who was wondering how it was
he had wanted to work vice.

"Okay, you're in the trap, peeking through the screen and
some dude walks in the john and he pulls down his jeans and
there inside the underwear he carries a toothbrush and a
feather. And his dick's all wrapped in rubber bands and rags
to make it bulge outta his tight pants. And he sits down on the
pot and reaches down in the toilet water and after he unwraps
it he starts splashing cold water up on his dong. And he brushes
it off with the toothbrush. Then he pulls out the feather and

tickles his balls and when all this is done he's able to take a leak, which he does sitting down, and then he leaves. Any violation there?"

"None," Baxter Slate said.

"Okay, what if there ain't no door on any a the toilets, which there ain't because the manager a this department store is trying to discourage the fruits who like to meet here and poke their cocks through glory holes and all that. Now there he is, no door, just side walls around the toilet and everybody walks in can see him, including little kids."

"Well . . ." Baxter hesitated.

"And just to mix you boys up a little, let's say that our vice complaint which brought us here in the first place is from some lady lives near here and her kids always come use this rest room on the way home from school, and she says they got propositioned by some grown up fruits and don't her kids got no rights?"

"Well . . ." Baxter Slate hesitated.

"Sure, if the fruits didn't get a naughty kick outta doing it in public johns because it's guilt and sin and fun and anal obsession and everything all mixed up and it ain't the same in a private room, well then we wouldn't have to come here at all. But that ain't the case and it's pretty hard to tell the lady her kids just have to put up with some dude propositioning them or blowing some other dude in front a them in the shithouse, ain't it, Harold?"

"I guess so, Scuz."

"Agree, Baxter?"

"I guess. Seems as though there should be some other solution."

"Seems like," Scuz said, "but there ain't. Not for us. We got the problem and the complaint. We gotta do something and that something is to make at least one arrest so when the lady calls back cause some other fruit tried to grope her kid, we can show her that we took action on her last complaint. See, boys, there's just a million problems in this world that there ain't no solutions to and cops get most a those kind."

"So how would you handle the guy who doesn't bother any children and just does his number with the toothbrush and feather?" asked Sam Niles whose pose was always boredom whether or not he was bored.

"I shoot him," Scuz answered.

"You what?" Harold exclaimed.

"I shoot him. With this," Scuz said, pulling a pink plastic water pistol from the pocket of his baggy gabardines. "I just shoot him through the screen where I'm peeking. First it confuses him, then it scares him soon's he realizes where it's coming from. See, I don't add to his thrill by bracing him and threatening him or any a that shit. Just makes him wanna come back some more. Remember, guilt and punishment and stuff from his kiddy days is partly the reason he has to do all this in a public place. So I just shoot him with my gun. Pretty soon he don't know who or what's behind that wall. Sometimes he yells, 'Who're you? You store security? You a cop? Who's shooting me?' "

"What do you say?" asked Harold.

"Nothing. I just shoot him again. It's humiliating. It degrades him in a way he can't stand. See, he might wanna degrade himself with the stuff he does in a public shitter but he can't take the kind a humiliation I give him. I'm saying to him with my water gun that his little act ain't worth no more than a few squirts a water. *That* he can't stand. I've seen em go out in tears and never come back. At least not to *that* rest room and that's all I can worry about at the moment. Make any sense?"

"Maybe it does at that," Baxter Slate said as Scuz lit another cigar and turned on Wilshire Boulevard.

"See, I don't wanna get in a big fight with these guys. I don't wanna hurt them but I sure don't wanna have them hurt me or my boys. So I spend most a my time figuring out how I can satisfy the citizens that make the vice complaints and keep my boys from getting hurt at the same time. I know most vice supervisors wouldn't agree with me but I don't think it's too bad a way to run a vice squad."

"Not bad at all, Scuz," grinned Baxter Slate, rolling down the window to let out some of the smoke.

"Reason we gotta work this department store tonight is they stay open till nine, and some fruit picks up some cat in the rest room couple weeks ago and offers him ten bucks to let him give the guy a headjob which is okay except he don't have no money after he does it. And to keep from getting his skull caved in he agrees to let the guy buy ten dollars worth a merchandise on his credit card. And the butch guy goes out and buys a hundred dollar suit and tells the fruit if he don't sign for it he'll do a fandango on his gourd with his boots. So then the fruit comes and complains about the cowboy. So I say to the guys in the dicks' bureau, you got an extortion, maybe a credit card hustle, you ain't got no vice squad case. But our captain says, 'I think you better take a three-eighteen, Sergeant, and let your vice boys make an arrest there.' See, he always calls me 'Sergeant' when he's on the rag which is most a the time. So anyways we gotta work the trap in the john and I hope we make a pinch tonight so I can put this vice complaint to bed. I don't like to make my guys sit around smelling shit."

A few minutes later the battered vice car bumped into the parking lot at the rear of the large Wilshire Boulevard department store where shoppers were carrying bundles and fighting each other for parking places and stealing packages out of each other's cars, as smoggy summer darkness finally fell on Los Angeles.

As Scuz led the three choirboys into the building and to the storage room which was attached to the rest room on the second floor, Baxter Slate spotted a man sitting on the floor of the corridor leading from the rest room. A stack of ten newspapers was on the floor beside him. His legs were folded under him like hinged sticks. His right hand was a claw, his left was worse. He scratched at the wall like a mutilated insect, unable to gain his feet. He was a forty year old newspaper vendor and several times a day he had to leave his newsstand to use the rest room in the department store. He had cerebral palsy but could usually get to the rest room and back to his chair quite easily, often selling a paper or two along the way. Tonight he was suffering from a summer cold which weakened him like an attack of pneumonia would disable a healthy man.

Scuz turned around and saw two of the choirboys looking down the hallway at the man. Sam Niles wanted to help the man stand up but hated to attract attention to himself and make the other policemen think he was a do-gooder. Baxter

Slate wanted to help the man stand up but was afraid the man would interpret his gesture as patronizing and snarl him away with righteous indignation. So both Sam and Baxter pretended not to see the man lolling on the floor and averted their eyes self-consciously. And felt guilt because they were unable to help.

Just then Harold Bloomguard saw the man. He didn't think much of anything. He just said, "Oh," walked down the corridor, took the palsied newspaper vendor by the arm and started to raise him up.

Then Scuz, who wondered why his parade had slowed, turned and saw Harold Bloomguard. He didn't intellectualize either. He walked past Sam and Baxter and joined Harold who almost had the man to his feet.

"Stumbled, huh?" Scuz said, bending over and picking up the fallen man with one arm as easily as a doll, while he gathered up the stack of newspapers with the other. "Slippery goddamn floors in this store. Someone always going on their ass."

He half carried the man to a bench near the rear door and seated him there with the stack of papers beside him as the man perspired and panted, unable to speak.

"Got the late edition?" Scuz asked, taking a coin from his pocket and putting it in the lap of the man as he took a paper from the stack and folded it into the back pocket of his gabardines. "Feel okay, partner? Want me to take you anywheres?"

The man managed a twisted smile and shook his head, and Scuz nodded, saying, "See you around, partner." Then he shuffled off down the hall with Harold Bloomguard at his side and the other choirboys trailing.

As Scuz passed an old man people-watching on a bench by the elevator, he said, "Here you go, Dad," dropping the paper beside the threadbare pensioner. "It's a late edition. I ain't got time to read it."

"Well, thanks," said the old man as Scuz opened the door of the storage room and led the three choirboys to the platform.

Two men could stand and look through a heavily screened one by two foot opening into the lighted rest room where shoplifters hid merchandise under their clothing and where men publicly masturbated and buggered each other, forcing Sergeant Dominic Scuzzi to force the choirboys to peek and smell shit.

They weren't in the trap ten minutes before a man in a candy striped shirt and double breasted blue blazer walked in, looked nervously in each toilet stall and, finding himself alone, withdrew his penis and wrote a lazy S on the rest room floor from wall to wall.

"That deserves a shot," whispered Scuz from the platform in the darkened room. "See if I remembered to load it. Yeah, I did." And he put his pink plastic water pistol up to the screen and gave the man two bursts.

The man looked up at the ceiling for leaky pipes, saw none and tried to write some more. Scuz gave him two more bursts which caused him to cry out and walk around the rest room for another puzzled look into each toilet stall. Then Scuz gave him another burst and the man screamed and ran outside.

"He was easy," Scuz said, stepping down from the platform to let Sam Niles have a look. "Reason I ran him off is I suspect he's one a these pissy pork pullers. Takes a leak and beats off and cuts out. Guy can do most anything legally long as he's alone. Gotta catch one that does his number with somebody else. Then we can make a pinch and close the vice complaint and get the fuck outta here and say we protected the people's morality. Until somebody else makes another vice complaint. Some fun, hey, boys?"

"Yeah," muttered Baxter Slate as Sam Niles grimaced disgustedly and longed for a cigarette because he couldn't have one in the close dark room.

"Tell you what," Scuz said. "I'm gonna leave you two guys here and take Harold with me for a pass down Western Avenue. See if we can catch ourselves a whore. Now I don't like leaving two new guys here like this so I'll be sending a team to come and sit with you. You two guys just hang loose and wait here and don't go busting nobody unless a murder is being committed before your eyes, got me?"

"Uh huh," Sam Niles said.

Scuz opened the door to the outside corridor and let Harold out into the light. Then Scuz turned and said, "You get bored you might amuse yourselves by betting quarters whether the next guy in will be a helmet or a anteater."

"What's that mean?" Baxter Slate asked.

"Circumcised or uncircumcised," said Scuz as he shoved another cigar between his teeth. Then he threw his pink water pistol to Sam Niles saying, "Careful, it's loaded."

The first man into the rest room stepped up to the urinal and emptied his bladder. The two choirboys looked at each other and wondered how they had gotten here. He was an anteater.

The second man was also an anteater. However, the third, fourth and fifth were helmets. The sixth was an anteater and cost Baxter Slate twenty-five cents. The seventh was a helmet and Baxter won the money back. Neither man cared what the eighth one was. The ninth was an anteater but he soon turned into a helmet because he sat down on the toilet and began playing with himself after looking at a picture of Raquel Welch in a movie magazine. But then he looked at a picture of Warren Beatty and seemed just as excited.

Sam Niles gave him four bursts with the pistol and he ran out cursing, wiping the wet pages of the magazine on his shirt.

Baxter Slate said, "I can't take two weeks of this."

Sam Niles offered Baxter a cigarette, opened the door for ventilation and nodded.

Meanwhile Sergeant Dominic Scuzzi was sitting in the parking lot of a food market near Pico and Western briefing an exceedingly nervous Harold Bloomguard.

"So I'm gonna be right here in the parking lot," Scuz said as Harold nodded and compulsively blew spit bubbles and cleaned the bogus horn rimmed glasses for the third time and made ready to get in his own car, a three year old Dodge Charger which they had picked up at the station parking lot after leaving Sam and Baxter.

"I don't want you roaming too far, Harold, got me? Just go a block or so down Western and no more than a couple blocks east on Pico. You get a broad in the car, you get your offer like I told you, then badge her and bring her back here quick. She wants to jump out, let the bitch do it. You drive here to me and we'll just cruise on back and scrape her off the street. You don't go roaming more than a couple blocks from me, right?"

"Right," said Harold.

"You nervous, Harold?"

"No. Not too much," he lied.

"Got a comb?"

"Yeah."

"Comb your hair back off your forehead. You goddamn kids all gotta look like rock singers. Comb it back. Show your high forehead. Makes you look even more square than you already look."

Scuz turned the rearview mirror for Harold who parted his ginger hair and combed it back.

"Help if you had some greasy kid stuff," said Scuz, who put the glasses on Harold when he was finished.

"I look okay?"

"Shit, ain't nobody gonna make you, Harold. Nobody."

"Guess I'm ready then."

"Okay, try going east on Pico there, circle south on Oxford, maybe, then back to Western. I want you close to me."

As Harold fired up the Charger, Scuz fired up a fresh cigar and swatted at a swarm of gnats which had discovered him.

Meanwhile, as Harold Bloomguard began his maiden voyage into the land of vice, things were happening in the store where two revolted choirboys sat smelling human defecation in a dark and stuffy room.

First, Pete Zoony, the veteran vice cop with the woolly hair and the Fu Manchu strolled into the rest room, grinned up at the screened hole on the wall and said, "Don't bother making a bet. I'm a Jew."

"How long we have to stay in here?" asked Sam Niles, whose voice boomed through the vent hole and echoed off the tile of the rest room.

"Scuz called us on the radio," Pete Zoony said, examining his teeth in the mirror. "Told my partner to drop me here to sit with you. Said to give it an hour, no more. We wanna close this complaint bad. Wish we had a drunk wagon like Central. I'd have them carry two sleeping winos inside and leave them in the same toilet stall, then call the store manager to witness the orgy we discovered. After that we could close the complaint."

"Well, nothing's happened since we've been here," Baxter said. "Maybe the fruits stopped coming here."

"Maybe so. Think I'll mosey outside and see there's any new

broads I haven't met. When you come out for a break take a
look at the set of tits works the perfume counter right across
from junior miss clothes. I hear a policeman from North Hollywood's balling her. Dynamite! Catch you later."

And Pete Zoony was out the door looking for willing young
clerks when he spotted two uniformed policemen entering the
office of store security. Out of curiosity he sauntered across the
floor and caught one of the three night security officers coming
out.

"What's happening?" Pete Zoony asked the plainclothes
security officer who knew all the vice cops from the rest room
watch.

"Shoplifter. No big thing. Second time we caught her.
Gonna put her in the slammer this time to see if it discourages
her. Make her steal from Sears instead of us."

Pete Zoony nodded and decided to go leer at the girl who
balled the North Hollywood policeman but had been coyly
resisting Zoony's persistent advances.

Then one of the uniformed policemen came out of the
security office and headed straight for the rest room. Pete
Zoony, who generally worked daywatch vice, was not known
by many bluesuits on the nightwatch. He made a regrettable
error in judgment by deciding to have a little fun and entertain
the two new kids on the block. He followed the uniformed cop
into the rest room.

"Roscoe Rules!" whispered Sam and Baxter simultaneously
when the door to the rest room opened.

Then it was a matter of trying to suppress giggles as Roscoe,
a helmet, relieved himself at the urinal and afterward stepped
to the sink singing some Stevie Wonder.

He took off his cap carefully and teased his mousy hair,
making it fall over the ears as much as possible without offend-
ing the lieutenant. Then he squeezed a watery pimple on his
nose, straightened his tie and smiled with satisfaction while
Baxter and Sam leaned on each other, smothering back the
laughter. Their fellow choirboy stepped from the mirror, put
the hat squarely on his head, held both fists against his hips and
stood spraddle legged and broad shouldered, admiring the
whole picture. And Sam Niles almost fell off the platform in

muffled hysterics just as the rest room door flew open again and Pete Zoony came swishing in.

"Sam! Sam!" Baxter whispered, pulling his friend back to the screen as Pete minced past Roscoe Rules singing, "I Got a Crush on You, Sweetie Pie!"

He stepped to the urinal, peeked coyly over his shoulder at the unbelieving policeman and pretended to be taking a leak while he batted his eyelashes at the choirboy.

"Well I'll be a motherfucker!" said the outraged Roscoe Rules.

"Oh, I hope you're not!" Pete Zoony squealed as he zipped up his pants and swished across the room to the washbasin where he put a few drops of water on his fingers and patted his cheeks.

He dabbed daintily with a paper towel, singing, "Couldja coo, couldja care . . ."

"You got a lot a guts, you know that?" Roscoe Rules said as Pete Zoony peeked at him from time to time and giggled.

"Why whatever do you mean, Officer?" Pete lisped.

"You . . . you, you come in here and act like . . . like I'm a civilian!"

"Well I don't care what you are. You're just cute as can be, is all you are," said Pete Zoony, primping in the mirror as the choirboys behind the wall desperately tried to see through their tears.

"Goddamn you! How dare you talk to a police officer like this! Gimme some identification!" Roscoe sputtered.

"Gosh, don't get so upset," Pete Zoony lisped. "I mean just because a person pays you a compliment."

"You break out some ID right now," Roscoe demanded and Pete Zoony was preparing to pull his police badge from his back pocket when he erred, not knowing Roscoe Rules.

"Now, I'm gonna show you my driver's license, see, but I want you to promise you won't ask for my phone number cause I don't know you that well yet."

"You fag! You insolent fucking sissy!" screamed Roscoe Rules.

"Well!" said Pete Zoony huffily, so carried away with his role that he underestimated the light in Roscoe's close set eyes.

"You wouldn't make fun of a person because he's crippled, wouldja? Huh?"

"You bastard!" Roscoe shrieked.

Pete Zoony pursed his lips and smacked a little kiss and said, "Oh, you're so cute when you're all mad! You blue meanie!"

Then Roscoe Rules reared back and slapped Pete Zoony across the moustache with the heel of his hand, catching him flush on the jaw and the vice cop was skidding across the slippery floor and banging against the metal trash can.

The two choirboys in the trap yelled, "No, Roscoe!" and jumped down from the platform and out the door, running down the corridor to the rest room.

They entered in time to intercept Pete Zoony who was growling and cursing and sliding on the floor attempting to get his feet under him as the bewildered Roscoe Rules looked up at the walls and ceiling, certain that he had heard ghostly voices shout his name.

"Niles! Slate!" Roscoe exclaimed as his fellow choirboys jumped on Pete Zoony to keep something terrible from happening which could get them all in trouble.

"You cocksucker!" shouted the outraged Pete Zoony, desperate to play catchup with Roscoe.

"*Me*, cocksucker? *Me*, cocksucker? You got a lotta guts, ya fag!" said Roscoe Rules.

It took a full five minutes to get Pete Zoony calmed down and Roscoe filled in on the prank that backfired. Finally the glassy eyed Pete Zoony smiled tightly and said, "No hard feelings, Rules," and swung a roundhouse left which caught Roscoe on the right cheekbone and dumped him into a toilet stall, wherein both choirboys switched their attack to the cursing, raging Roscoe Rules who might have shot Pete Zoony to death were it not for Sam Niles keeping a wristlock on his gun hand.

The toilet stakeout was called off for the night then and there. Sam Niles would not release his wristlock on Roscoe until Baxter Slate had taken Pete Zoony out of the rest room to the parking lot in the rear. They found a pay phone and had Pete's partner pick them all up to rendezvous with Scuz and Harold Bloomguard.

When Spermwhale Whalen heard about the incident later that night at choir practice, he shook his head and said, "Someone's always punchin Roscoe Rules. Kid, you oughtta wear a catcher's mask."

"Greetings and hallucinations!" cried frightened Harold Bloomguard to the first street whore he spotted after cruising the streets for twenty minutes.

"Say what?" the tawny black girl said as she stopped on the sidewalk and cautiously approached the Charger which was parked under the streetlight in the red zone at Pico and Western.

She wore mint green pants, skin tight to the ankles where they flared out over patent green clogs. Her stomach was bare and she wore a green halter top which tied at the neck. Harold was sure he had seen her several times before but Scuz had assured him that the girls have a difficult time recognizing uniform cops when they see them in plainclothes. To whores, as to most people, the patrol cop is a badge and blue suit and little more.

"Hello hello!" said Harold Bloomguard, turning off his headlights and bravado as the girl approached the car, walking with the traffic so that customers could pull to the curb without making an illegal U-turn that might draw a police car.

"Well, hi there, baby," smiled the whore when she saw how "good" Harold looked.

But just then a set of headlights behind them flashed a high beam and a black-and-white pulled up beside him, preparing to write a parking ticket, thus doing its bit to combat prostitution. It was Spencer Van Moot and Father Willie.

"Okay, sir," Spencer said as the radio car double parked. "Let's . . ."

And then Spencer found himself looking into the tense, bespectacled face of his fellow choirboy, Harold Bloomguard, whom he knew was on temporary vice loan.

"Yes, Officer?" Harold Bloomguard winked.

Father Willie, thinking faster than his partner, said loud enough for the whore to hear, "Partner! We just got a hot call!" and he dropped the car into low.

"You're in a red zone, buster!" yelled Spencer Van Moot as Father Willie pulled out. "Don't be here when I come back!"

"Now don't be scared, honey," said the girl as the radio car sped away. "They jist love to scare off our tricks. Got nothin else to do, jist hassle people."

"And they're never around when you need them," Harold added.

"Tha's right."

Then the girl looked up as a white Lincoln pulled in behind Harold and a big suntanned man waved to the girl. She looked him over but opened Harold's door and got inside.

"Motherfucker looks like a cop to me," she said. "They borry these big shiny cars and try to fool us sometimes."

"Cop?" cried Harold Bloomguard, trying his hand at acting now that the attractive, sweet smelling whore was sitting next to him, looking much less exotic and threatening.

"Now, you jist calm down, honey. Ain't no cause to git scared."

"Cop?" repeated Harold Bloomguard, speaking in dry monosyllables, trying to remember the good opening lines Scuz had fed him as he drove east on Pico.

The whore pretended to be fixing her lipstick in the rearview mirror but was actually watching for a vice car.

"Now jist calm right down. Ain't no worry about cops. Those two told you bout the parkin ticket? I got a friend pays them off. Fact he pays off all the black and whites and all the vice in this district for me. So see, we kin jist have us a nice party and don't have to worry bout nothin."

"Party?" Harold wanted a more explicit word for a better case. His hands were sweating and slipping on the steering wheel.

"Party. You know? Love. Half and half. French. Whatever you wants."

"Oh yeah, I want!" Harold turned south on Oxford, hoping she would hurry and mention the money, too nervous to appreciate her billowy breasts as she dabbed at her lipstick and making sure there was no vice car slipping behind them with lights out.

"You got twenny-five dollars, sweetie?"

"Sure."

"That's the tariff. And it's cheap for all you get."

Then Harold turned west on Fourteenth Street and the girl said to turn left on Western but Harold turned right.

"Hey!" she said suspiciously but Harold pressed the accelerator to the floor, sped north for half a block, screeched across the southbound traffic lanes and skidded into the market parking lot while the whore yelled, "Gud-damn!" and bounced around in the car. Then Harold saw Scuz in the vice car sitting in the dark at the rear of the market. Only then did he feel heady and elated.

He pulled off his glasses, the triumphant unmasking of an undercover man, and said, "You're under arrest!"

"Oh shit," she replied.

Then for effect Harold put the glasses back on, skidded to a stop beside Scuz, pulled them off again and said, "You're under arrest, young lady!"

"You already said that. I got ears, stupid," said the whore.

Scuz shuffled around the car and opened the door for the whore as Harold decided he should show her his badge.

"Don't bother, Harold. She knows who you are—now. I'll baby-sit Bonnie here. We're old pals. You go out and see you can get another one."

The girl stalked gloomily to the back door of the vice car and said, "Sergeant, where'd you get this little devil? He don't look nothin like a cop."

"See? See, Harold?" grinned Scuz, puffing happily on his cigar, delighted with the professional accolade.

"You're so young," Harold said to the girl as she slid across the seat of Scuz's car. Harold noticed her smooth brown legs for the first time and her pretty mouth and shapely natural hairdo.

"She's even younger than you, kid," Scuz said, closing the door and getting in the front seat where he could blow cigar smoke out the window and not suffocate the whore. "See you can get us another one that easy, Harold."

"You're so young and pretty," said the saddened choirboy. "How'd you get started in this business?"

"Oh no!" the whore cried, slumping back in the seat, appealing to Scuz.

"Harold, just go on back out, see you can get another one," Scuz said. "Let Bonnie here rest her sore feet."

Harold Bloomguard emptied his gas tank driving and made himself dizzy circling around and around the block looking for another whore so Sergeant Dominic Scuzzi could write a good progress report for that psycho of a captain, while a sullen young whore named Bonnie Benson got sick from the air befouled by Dominic Scuzzi's ten cent cigar.

While this was happening Sam Niles and Baxter Slate were sitting in a cozy dark cocktail lounge much farther north on Western Avenue where there was obviously little chance for a vice arrest but lots of chances for free drinks which the management gladly supplied Pete Zoony and his fellow vice cops.

Pete sat in the booth with Baxter and Sam and sipped a Scotch on the rocks, using the ice to rub on the bruise which Roscoe Rules had put on his jawbone before he put a much larger one on Roscoe.

Finally Pete said, "Mind if my partner and me disappear for a while? We gotta check out an answering service supposed to be taking call girl action. More than one or two guys'd look suspicious. Be back in an hour. We'll raise Scuz on the radio and tell him where you are, so either he'll pick you up or we will. Meantime, drink all you want and get a beef dip, they're pretty good. It's all on the house."

"Sure, Pete," Baxter said.

After the vice cop left, Sam said, "Wonder how big her tits are? Wish she had a couple friends."

Baxter Slate downed his bourbon and ordered a double. "Just as well drink like a vice cop," he grinned as they sat on tufted seats and felt fortunate to be out of the toilet. "Guess you might say we had a fruitless night."

"That sounds like something Harold would say," Sam yawned, starting to look bored. "Just like everything else. It'll start to be a drag."

"What?"

"Vice work. Jesus, what a way to make a living."

"Did you feel embarrassed, like we were peeping toms or something?"

"Christ, yes. You see enough shit on the streets without going to rest rooms to look for more."

And then Baxter, who was getting a glow from the bourbon, said, "There're worse jobs than vice."

"What for instance?"

"Juvenile."

"Oh yeah. I always wondered what made you leave so soon."

"Just didn't like it," Baxter said, draining his glass and signaling to the waitress.

She looked even more bored than Sam Niles as she padded across the carpet in a silly tight costume which was supposed to push her breasts up and out and make her look like a sexy tavern wench instead of what she was: a blousy divorcée with three young children who were running wild because she worked nights and wasn't supervising them.

"Don't think I'd like Juvenile either," Sam Niles said, ordering a double Scotch. "Bad enough working with adults without taking crap from bubblegummers."

"You handle some dangerous little criminals over and over again and you can't get them off the streets because of their tender age. Despite the fact that they're more predatory and lack an adult's inhibitions. But I could live with that. It was the other things that bothered me. The children as victims."

"Can't let it bother you," Sam Niles said as he drained his glass. "Must water their drinks here. Oh well, the price is right." And he was ready to signal for another round.

"You know, you expect certain dreadful cases," Baxter continued, "like the child molester who loved to see little girls tied up and screaming. Or, the four year old I saw on my first day in court when her mother's boyfriend was brought in and she started crying and a policewoman said to me, 'He stuck it in one day and gave her gonorrhea.' "

Sam Niles wished a couple of unattached girls would come in and end Baxter's stories.

"What I wasn't prepared for were the other things." Baxter's speech was beginning to slur as he stared at the glass, for the first time failing to smile and thank the waitress who put a fresh one in front of him. "You should see what the generic term 'unfit home' can mean. The broken toilet so full of human excrement that it's slopping over the top. And a kitten running through the crap and then up onto the table and across the dirty dishes. Brown footprints on the dishes which won't even be washed."

"Can't we change the subject? I've literally smelled enough shit for one night."

"And a boy who's a man at nine years of age. And wants to bathe his filthy little brothers and sisters and tries to, except that he accidentally scalds the infant to death."

"Baxter . . ."

"And a simple thing like a bike theft," Baxter Slate continued, looking Sam Niles in the eyes now. "Do you know how *sad* a bike theft can be when there's only one broken down bike in a family of eight children?"

"That kind of thing doesn't phase me, Baxter, you know that?" Sam Niles said angrily, and *his* speech was thick and boozy. "I have only two words of advice for guys like you and Harold Bloomguard. *Change jobs.* If you can't face the fact that the world is a garbage dump, you'll jump off the City Hall Tower. Christ, when I was a kid we never had *any* bikes, broken or not. My brother and I made a tether ball out of a bag of rags and I tied it to a street sign. That's the only toy I remember. Baxter, you can't save the world."

"But you see, Sam, I thought I could!" Baxter said, spilling some bourbon on his velvet shirt as he drank excitedly. "I thought it *was* possible to save the world—the world of the one specific child I was dealing with. Sometimes I would work as hard as I could to get a kid out of his environment and into a foster home. And he would run back to his degradation. Once I handled a case of child abuse at a county licensed foster home where I'd placed a little child. She'd been beaten up by the foster mother and I had the job of arresting the foster mother and taking the child out of the very home I had placed her in."

"So what?"

"The child had marks on her stomach. Strange cuts, almost healed. She was only three years old, Sam, and she wouldn't talk to me. She got hysterical around policewomen too. Finally I was the one to find out what the marks were. They were letters: L.D.B., which turned out to be the initials of an old boyfriend of the foster mother. *She* put them on the little girl with a paring knife. I'd placed the kid in that foster home to save the world of that one specific child. I was the worst Juvenile officer the department's ever had!"

"Hey, miss," yelled Sam and held up two fingers and sighed languorously as the waitress brought another round while Baxter Slate held his empty drink in both hands and stared at rings on the table.

"Listen, Baxter," Sam said. "We have crime in direct proportion to freedom. Lots of freedom, lots of crime. All I know for sure is something I've believed all my life. And it was verified for me in Vietnam and certified in the four and a half years I've been a cop. It's that people are never more pathetic than when they're asking themselves that absurd, ridiculous, laughable question, 'Who am I?' "

And then it was Sam's turn to spill several drops as he tipped his glass. He paused, wiped off his moustache, pressed the nosepiece of his glasses and said, "If most people ever let themselves find the answer to *that* question they'd go into the toilet and slash their wrists. Because they're nothing! The sooner you understand that, the sooner you can do police work without torturing yourself."

"I wouldn't be telling you this, Sam, if it weren't for this," Baxter Slate apologized, holding up the glass. "Sometimes I try to tell my partner but Spermwhale's only interested in paying off his ex-wives." And Baxter tried a broad Baxter Slate smile which did not work because there was fear in his bourbon-clouded green eyes. "After I left Juvenile I started experiencing strange flashes in the middle of the night. I could almost see glimpses of what it is *not* to be, to have life go on without you. It happens in a half sleep. It's happened a lot since I killed that man. Have you ever experienced it?"

And then Sam Niles touched his moustache and said, "No." And Baxter Slate, who always believed his friends, did not know that Sam Niles was lying. "I wish some broads'd come in. I wish the drinks weren't so watered down," Sam Niles said.

"Sam, I know you're right about people being nothing. All my life, all my religious training in Dominican schools was built on an explicit belief in evil. But there is none. Man hasn't the dignity for evil. And if there's no evil there's very likely no goodness! There're only accidents!"

"Please, Baxter," Sam Niles said, "I'm just a cop. I don't . . . I'm not . . ."

"Sorry, Sam," said Baxter Slate, draining the bourbon and turning green watery eyes to his friend. "I don't always go on like this. I'm not usually such a silly pseudointellectual horse's ass. Ask Spermwhale."

And then he managed a real Baxter Slate grin, candid, disarming, and tried to make light of it. "It's that I know you just got your degree in political science. I love to talk to someone who won't get mad at me for using an adverb or two."

Then Sam Niles managed an embarrassed chuckle because it was over. "Okay, Baxter, it *is* nice not having to move your lips when you read so as not to offend a Philistine like Roscoe Rules."

Sam Niles was starting to like his friend Baxter Slate so much he never wanted to see him again.

And while Baxter and Sam were getting drunk and being horses' asses, and while Baxter secretly thought of the ordinary guy he killed and the tortured child he let die, Harold Bloomguard finally found another whore.

The Cadillac Eldorado had not been there on his last pass, Harold was sure of it. Then he saw the white girl saunter out of the bar and head for the car. Harold tried to get over to the number two lane but the car behind him began hitting his headlight dimmer switch and blowing his horn. Harold drove two blocks east of Western Avenue, turned his Dodge around and came back. The white girl was gone. But in her place was a black girl who opened the door of the silver Eldorado, had an afterthought, turned and went into the bar.

Harold started to head for the vice car to ask Scuz if he could go in the bar. But he thought about it a moment and knew what the answer would be. Then he thought about getting a two-banger on his first night as a vice cop and he parked the car on Western Avenue, put his gun, handcuffs and badge under the seat, locked the car, wiped his moist hands on his handkerchief and entered.

The tavern was not a white man's cocktail lounge. It poured an extraordinary amount of hard liquor and the bartender didn't like to be troubled with fancy drinks. There was a juke-box playing Tina Turner, the volume turned five decibels higher than Harold could bear. There was a pool table on the side crowded with men playing nine ball at a dollar a ball and filling the room with blue tobacco smoke. There was a back room where nightly crap games attracted dozens of customers and occasional vice cops. As with most black men's crap games there was always a set of crooked dice in use and sometimes two sets, with one crooked gambler using shaved cubes against another.

But there was a vitality in the bar and Harold was excited as well as frightened when he saw that aside from the white girl, he was the only paddy in the place. Then he got a good look at the brassy blonde in the open red satin coat who sat on a bar stool holding an eight month pregnancy against the vinyl-covered cushioned railing.

It was ambition and curiosity, but mostly youth, which drove Harold Bloomguard to one of the empty stools on the near side of the bar as several black men at the pool table stopped the game and slipped any money from the table into their pockets until they were satisfied that Harold was a trick and not a cop.

The black girl who had almost gotten into the Eldorado was sitting next to the white girl and she, like the bartender, looked Harold over carefully and became satisfied that he could not possibly be The Man.

Then she smiled and said, "Why don't you sit over here?" And she moved to the right and gave Harold the bar stool between the two of them.

"Why not? It's invenereal to me where I sit," said Harold, using a Bloomguardism they didn't seem to understand or appreciate.

"What'll you have, chief?" asked the bartender, a graying black man with a bass voice that could drown out Tina Turner any old day.

"A Bombay martini straight up, very dry, with a twist, please."

The bartender just leaned on the bar and stared at Harold

while the two girls edged closer. Then the bartender said, "I been workin hard all night, chief. Can't you make it easy on me?"

"Give him what the fuck he wants," said the black girl, who was taller than Harold and outweighed him but who was solidly proportioned, buxom and attractive.

"Look, I ain't trickin with him," the bartender said. "Besides, I ain't got no more Bombay."

"J&B and water?" offered Harold Bloomguard, rightly assuming from the number of black bandits who asked for J&B Scotch before sticking up a liquor store that the bartender would have no problem filling that order.

"Comin up," the bartender said. "You buyin for the ladies?"

"Indeed," said Harold Bloomguard, and he immediately thought of Roscoe Rules who disapproved of Harold's saying "indeed" because it made him sound like a fag.

After the three of them had their drink, the blonde with the eight month pregnancy put her hand on Harold's thigh and said, "Got a match?"

Harold picked up the match pack from the bar and found that he couldn't get it working. He was crestfallen when the blonde took the pack from his hand and lit her own cigarette. The choirboy feared that his nerves might give him away, but it had the opposite effect in that most inexperienced tricks were every bit as frightened as Harold Bloomguard.

"My name's Sabrina," said the big black girl who had a sensual glistening mouth.

"My name's Tammy," the pregnant blonde said. She had terrible teeth she was going to have pulled as soon as she dropped her frog and adopted it out and could hustle enough money to see a dentist, which she was having trouble doing what with her grotesque shape.

"My name's Harold Leekly. I'm a certified public accountant."

"Nobody asked you what you did," said Sabrina. "Why'd you say that? Maybe you're a cop."

"A cop!" cried Harold. "Ha ha! A cop!"

The bartender put the three drinks in front of them and said, "If this sucker's a cop, I'm a astronaut."

Then the blonde put her hand on Harold's thigh again and moved it up his leg. The leg began to tremble as Harold realized that Sabrina had her hand around his waist and both girls were smiling and making incoherent small talk and patting him down caressingly, expertly, just to reassure themselves. Then Sabrina put her hand on his right leg, the quiet one. It began to shake worse than the other.

"You shakin like a paint mixer," Sabrina said. "But we gettin outta here in a minute. We goin somewheres to quiet you down."

"Where we going?" Harold asked, thinking that if he swallowed the Scotch it might help relax him.

"Maybe to our pad, baby," Tammy smiled, showing her decaying fangs.

"That'll be eight dollars, chief," the bartender said as the girls gathered up their cigarettes and purses.

"For three little drinks?" Harold said. The bartender straightened up and glared down at him and Harold added, "Oh yes indeed, very good drinks, too, I must say!"

Harold tipped the bartender fifty cents which drew a sneer and a grumble and he followed the girls outside, remembering that Scuz had warned him that under no circumstance was he to go into a room with a whore because of the danger involved. He was hoping the girls would have given the offer before now and since they hadn't he decided to push it.

"By the way, what am I gonna get when we get where we're going?"

"Don't be in such a hurry, you cute little blue eyed jitterbug," Sabrina smiled as she fished the Cadillac keys out of a red leather handbag.

"Am I going with you?" Harold asked, thinking frantically for an excuse not to.

Sabrina answered, "No, you follow us in your car."

"Okay," Harold said, much relieved. "But I wanna know what's gonna happen. How do I know I'm gonna like it?"

"Oh, you gonna like it," Sabrina said, and she stepped over to him, there on the corner of Pico and Western, under the streetlights in full view of passing cars, and gave his genitals a squeeze.

"Woooo," said Harold Bloomguard, pulling back in embarrassment. "Woooo."

"I was just gonna tell you what you're getting," Sabrina said, as Harold stood off a few steps and blushed and swung his arms around, wondering if anyone had seen that.

He knew that he had just been "honked," as the vice cops called it, in a public place and that Scuz had said something about honking being a misdemeanor. But he couldn't remember if it applied only to fruit cases or whores as well. And he couldn't remember if the honking precluded the need for a money offer.

And as he stood there considering the next move, Tammy bounced over to him, grabbed his arm and said, "Let's go, cutie," and she gave him two more toots with a thumb and forefinger.

"Wooooo," said Harold Bloomguard, honked again.

"Gud-damn, man!" Sabrina said testily. "We ain't got time to stand around here all night and listen to you woo woo. Follow us down the street there where it's dark. We gonna talk about money."

"Money," said Harold Bloomguard, grateful to Sabrina for solving his problem.

He ran across Pico to his car, made a U-turn in a gas station and pulled back onto Pico facing east, following the slow moving Cadillac which turned right onto Oxford where it was residential. And very dark. The Cadillac pulled into the first available parking space on the right. Harold pushed his borrowed glasses up on his nose like his partner Sam Niles and found a parking space fifty feet farther south.

Then Harold carefully reached down, found his two inch off-duty gun, which he had decided to carry working undercover, and his badge and handcuffs. He shoved the gun and cuffs inside his belt in the back, put the badge in his back pocket and affected a jauntiness he did not feel as he quickly walked back to the Cadillac, to the whores waiting in the darkness.

Harold stepped up on the sidewalk, leaned in the passenger window, looked at Tammy's pathetic teeth and said, "Well, girls, let's bring this pimple to a head. Get down to business. How . . ."

"Git in," said Sabrina.

"Well before . . ."

"Get in," Tammy said, pushing the Cadillac's door open.

"Shouldn't we . . ."

"We gonna talk business *after* you inside," Sabrina said. Then she purred, "We want you here between us where we can feel your hot little body so maybe we kin git you to give us another dollar or two for our work."

"Slide over me, honey," Tammy said as Sabrina pushed the electric switches which took the white leather seats back and down.

As he was gingerly lifting himself across Tammy's enormous belly, he worried that she might feel the gun, but she didn't. And he thought how sad it was that a pregnant girl should be doing this kind of work, and while he was feeling sad she reached up between his legs and squeezed, making him say, "Woo woo," and sit down on her hand.

"Ouch!" she cried, pulling her hand out. "You fucking near broke my wrist!"

"Sorry," said Harold.

Then he began to wonder if he was doing the right thing by getting in the car. But he knew he was very close to bringing in a two-banger and he just couldn't stop now.

"You got fifty dollars, sweetie?" Sabrina asked abruptly.

"Sure."

"Well let's see it."

"Later, after we get where we're going."

"Ain't goin nowhere. We gonna do it right here."

"We are?"

Then it occurred to Harold that he had been honked and he had been solicited for money, but no one had specifically mentioned a sex act and he wondered if the arrest would be legal without it and just then Tammy honked him again and he grabbed her hand.

"Wait a minute, wait a minute," Harold said, desperately trying to remember the phrases Scuz had told him which would not be construed as entrapment.

"Why you just sittin there blowin bubbles off your tongue?" Sabrina asked.

The air was close in the darkness of the Cadillac with both

big women pressing him. Then Harold remembered a word: "I'm looking for *excitement!*" he cried.

"Well, no shit!" said Tammy, and she honked him again but harder this time because she was getting sick and tired of dicking around with the little creep.

"What the fuck's wrong with you?" Sabrina demanded and she leaned back against the driver's door and pulled her dress midway up her thigh.

"I just wanna know what I'm gonna get," Harold said, and now his voice was hoarse and parched and he feared he was going to lose it all.

"We tryin to show you!" said Sabrina. "You wanna do it or talk about it, man?"

"Talk about what?" asked Harold Bloomguard who was oh so close to his arrest.

"Ballin! Frenchin! What the fuck you think?" shouted Sabrina.

"Sucky fucky, five bucks, oh thank you," whispered Harold Bloomguard who felt he had his case at last.

"What?"

"Sabrina!" said Tammy as she adroitly unzipped Harold's pants and shoved her hand inside. "He's hung like a hummingbird. He don't wanna ball. He's some kinda freak! Probably wants to beat on us with his shoe or something!"

"No, I don't," said Harold Bloomguard, pulling her hand from his pants and trying to rezip, but getting caught on the shirttail of his white dress shirt which protruded six inches from his fly.

"What's goin on here?" Sabrina demanded.

"Yeah!" said Tammy.

"Nothing," said Harold Bloomguard, struggling with the zipper.

"Feel my pussy if you ain't a freak!" Sabrina ordered and took Harold's hand and dropped it on her thigh.

"Let's get in my car and go to some romantic place," said Harold Bloomguard as his cold wet hand slipped off Sabrina's warm dry flesh.

"Shit," said Sabrina.

"Crapsake," said Tammy.

"You a freak," said Sabrina.

"I'm not!" said Harold.

"You a freak!" Sabrina shouted.

"Like hell!" Harold Bloomguard answered indignantly.

Then he pulled free from Sabrina, reached over Tammy's belly, opened her door and crawled over her lap until he was on the street.

"You a freak!" screamed Sabrina, thinking they had lost the fifty dollar trick.

"I not a freak!" shouted Harold Bloomguard, reaching in his back pocket and exultantly pulling his shield. "I a cop!"

And while the two whores stared dumbstruck, Harold reached inside the car and grabbed both purses and the car keys from the ignition.

"Hey!" Sabrina gathered her wits too late to stop him.

"Now I've got your keys and I've got your purses so you're not going anywhere but with me!" said Harold Bloomguard, ripping off the horned rimmed glasses to show them the real man beneath the disguise. "Just don't try anything funny!"

"Well I'll be gud-damned," said Sabrina to Tammy who was about to cry. "PO-lice Department got to be mighty hard up these days to be hirin little cock-a-roaches like this!"

"Out of the car!" demanded the little cock-a-roach, reaching back for his handcuffs, remembering that Scuz had said that in vice cases you *always* handcuff two suspects and sometimes one if there's any doubt at all.

"We goin with you, man, but you ain't gonna be puttin those things on no pregnant lady, hear me?" Sabrina said as the three were standing on the sidewalk beside the Cadillac.

Harold Bloomguard thought it over, decided not to force the issue now that they were obeying so nicely, and put the handcuffs back in his belt, saying, "All right, but behave yourselves."

As they walked slowly to Harold's car on the dark sidewalk, Harold Bloomguard started to feel a little sad once again.

"You're both so young," said Harold. "Bet you're not over twenty-five, are you?"

When the miserable whores failed to reply, Harold said, "Ever been arrested before?"

"Bout thirty times," said Sabrina.

"Bout forty times," said Tammy.

"Oh," said Harold. And he tried to cheer them up by saying something funny, "I have no altourniquet but to do my job." Then he added, "I'm sorry about you and your baby and all."

"Why?" snapped Tammy, dabbing at her tears. "You didn't put it in my belly. You couldn't even get it up when I was playing with your dick, for chrissake."

"Well, it's not that I find either of you unattractive," Harold explained, "it's just that I'm a vice off . . ."

And then Sabrina started to groan and the groan quickly turned into a wail and then to a deathless shriek.

"RRRRRRRAAAAAAAAAAAAAPE!"

Sabrina grabbed Tammy's hand and then Tammy started to do it:

"RRRRRRRAAAAAAAAAAAAAPE!"

"Don't do that," said Harold Bloomguard but they didn't listen to him. Harold looked around at the darkness and the houses and said, "You're resisting arrest, you know."

"RRRRRRRAAAAAAAAAAAAAPE!" screamed the two whores in unison, and then, Sabrina leading, they started to run north on Oxford, hand in hand. Lights began coming on. Doors opened. A woman put her head out a window.

"I'm a policeman," said Harold Bloomguard. She closed the window.

Then Harold slung his purses over his arm and began jogging after the two whores, finding it easy to keep up at first, not particularly frightened now, just confused and embarrassed, wondering what the next move should be, wishing he had never presumed to catch a two-banger.

A strange thing happened. The two whores began to outdistance him as they turned west on Fourteenth Street and crossed over to the north sidewalk still screaming for help. Now Harold's heart began working a bit hard and he sprinted to catch up. Tammy turned and saw him closing in and dashed for the porch of the nearest house on the north side of the street where the front yards were small and the old houses were bunched together.

"Help! Help!" Tammy screamed as she banged on the door with one hand and held her belly with the other.

It was a sixty-five year old white man who came to the door, pulling his pants up and struggling with a bathrobe.

"What's going on here?" he said, switching on the light and squinting through the darkness.

"Help us!" Sabrina pleaded, standing on the porch next to Tammy, catching her breath.

Harold blocked the steps, holding his badge in his hand. "I'm a police officer!" he panted. "Go to your phone and call for help! Give your address!"

"Don't believe him!" Tammy said, leaning against the porch railing. "Please help me. I'm gonna have a baby!"

"I order you to call the police right now!" said Harold Bloomguard.

"But you say *you're* the police," the old man said, scratching his gray jaw stubble and looking from one to the other.

"I *order* you!" said Harold Bloomguard.

"Now just a minute, young fella, this's my house!" the old man said.

"Fred, you come in here and leave those lunatics be!" said a shrill voice inside.

Then Sabrina grabbed Tammy's hand and both girls pushed past Harold and began running back down the sidewalk the way they had come.

"I order you to get me some help, Fred!" Harold Bloomguard yelled as he turned and pursued the girls.

"Maybe you're a cop and maybe not. I wish you'd all stay for a while so I can find out what's happening!" the disappointed old man answered, but Harold Bloomguard had to concentrate on the prostitutes who had now passed a house where five young black men had been playing cards in the kitchen and were now attracted to the commotion out front.

The young men laughed as the girls ran past and the tallest one blocked the sidewalk and drained a bottle of beer and then tapped the bottle on his hand. Harold Bloomguard stopped.

"What for you chasin those little girls, man?" the youth demanded.

Harold Bloomguard puffed and panted and stood his ground. He reached for his badge and said, "I'm a police officer. Let me pass."

Then the others laughed and the tall one said, "That ain't no real badge. How I know who you be? I think you better jam off, baby. Leave those little girls alone."

Suddenly Harold Bloomguard was gripped by strangely exhilarating rage. "Okay, asshole, I'm *not* a cop," he said, pulling his gun and pointing it at the mouth of the young black man. "I'm a rapist! What the hell you gonna do about it?"

"No, I think maybe you *are* the PO-lice," the youth grinned, dropping the bottle to the sidewalk and stepping back for Harold to pass, as all the young men hooted and whistled while the chase continued.

The girls were plodding down Pico Boulevard now, trying to reach Western Avenue. Harold had to run hard to catch them, his purses still over the left arm, the gun in his right hand, the shirttail still protruding from his fly.

Sabrina ran into the street making a desperate lunge toward a car which had slowed on Pico at the sight of the two frantic women. She jerked the door open and was pleading with the man behind the wheel when Harold came running up behind, grabbed her hair and jerked her flat on her back as he fell, taking her with him.

Two women passing in a green Oldsmobile began to scream hysterically and the car screeched to a stop as Harold fumbled with his gun and purses.

"I'm a policeman!" Harold yelled to them, thinking that all a vice cop ever did was tell people he's a policeman.

As Sabrina limped to her feet, Tammy teetered on the curb, puffing, blowing, staring vacantly into space. Then Sabrina was running toward Tammy and pulling her coat sleeve, and miraculously the pregnant girl began to run.

Harold still pursued, catching misty glimpses of people driving and walking by, shaggy blurs. And he heard disconnected sounds as he wiped the sweat from his eyes and caught the two whores at the busy intersection.

Sabrina spun around and swung desperately at Harold but missed, and her hand slammed into the wooden wall of a vacant newsstand. She cried out and turned, but Harold grabbed her hair again and his neck was burning as Sabrina broke loose and fell into the street, crawling twenty feet into the center of the intersection where she sprawled on her stomach, her dress pulled up over her plump pantyless behind.

Tammy then limped frantically into the street, arms dangling, coat half torn from her back, belly bulging dangerously. She skidded while yet fifteen feet from her partner and toppled over slowly to her knees. Then she leaned forward, almost in slow motion, until her distended belly touched the asphalt. Harold knelt on the pavement and panted and stared for many seconds as she tottered on the enormous mound. Then she rolled over slowly and deliberately and floundered there belly up like a harpooned walrus. Tammy blocked two lanes of traffic and Sabrina one and a half.

The air was still razor sharp when Harold Bloomguard, taking large gulps of it, dragged Sabrina bumping and crying out of the traffic lane across the asphalt until her foot lay next to the hand of Tammy who was all but unconscious, lying there, panting softly, eyes closed, pink tongue protruding.

Harold finally had the chance to put his gun back in his waistband, and he handcuffed Sabrina's ankle to Tammy's wrist with no resistance whatever. Then he sat down in the traffic lane, in the glow of many headlights, as motorists yelled and blew horns and made every guess but the right one as to what the hell was going on.

Finally he heard the siren and instinctively behaved like a policeman trying to clear the intersection. He waved his purses at the motorists who became frightened and ran from their cars, leaving them abandoned and making things worse.

They came from all directions, painting the streets with rubber: radio cars, motorcycles, plainclothes units. Five separate hotshot calls had gone out. Neighbors complained of a man with a gun, a woman screaming, a purse snatch in progress, a man assaulting women and a mental case exposing himself. A code four, that suspects were in custody, was broadcast and still they came. Their emergency lights bathing Pico Boulevard in a crimson glow, lining up on both sides of the street, making the traffic jam more impossible.

Sergeant Yanov specifically put out an order for units to resume patrol. And yet they came. For policemen are by nature and training inquisitive and obtrusive. Twenty-one police units ultimately responded and a huge crowd gathered after Harold, Sabrina and Tammy had been whisked away. Officers and citizens asked many questions of each other which none could answer.

The prostitutes were treated at the emergency hospital for contusions and abrasions prior to being booked and Harold Bloomguard was surprised to discover a seven inch cut that began at his left earlobe, crossed the jawbone and ended on the neck. It was not a deep cut and only required a disinfectant.

"Must've gotten it from Sabrina's fingernails," Harold told Scuz when the girls were booked and they were back at the station composing a complicated arrest report.

"Harold, I thought you was smart," Scuz said. "I told you these're fucking misdemeanors. They ain't worth nothing, these vice cases. Who told you to go out and get hurt?"

"Sorry, Scuz, I just . . . I just wanted to win the game."

"I oughtta kick your ass for gettin hurt."

"I didn't get hurt, just this scratch on my neck."

"You coulda got killed! For what? A game? I ask you don't get hurt. That asking too much?"

"Sorry, Scuz."

"There's lots a vice sergeants in this town that'd pat you on the ass and write you an attaboy for bringing down the whores. But I ain't one a them. Risking your life for a shitty vice pinch! I thought you was smart!"

Then Sergeant Scuzzi paced around the vice office stepping on his shoestrings, and Harold sat quietly with the other two new kids on the block. Sam Niles and Baxter Slate were falling down drunk after having sat in the bar for three hours waiting for Scuz and Harold Bloomguard who were busy with other things. The two choirboys had swilled free drinks all evening.

"You kicking me off the squad?" Harold asked sheepishly.

"I oughtta kick you all off. Christ, you almost get killed and these other two twenty-six year old rummies get swacked sucking up bourbon."

"I was drinking Scotch, Scuz," said Sam Niles who held his head in both hands.

"Shut up, Niles!" Scuz said, relighting his cigar which was so badly chewed there were soppy flakes of tobacco stuck all over his lips and chin.

"Okay, you three just watch it from now on. Bloomguard,

you need a keeper. I'm gonna supervise you personal. Make sure you stay alive the weeks you're here. Slate, you and Niles better keep your boozing under control, hear me?"

"Yes, Sergeant," Baxter Slate said. He was sitting woodenly, trying to convince Sergeant Scuzzi that he was cold sober.

"Fucking kids," Scuz said, shaking his head at the three repentant choirboys. "And another thing, Slate and Niles, I'd like to know how Pete Zoony got that knot on his face tonight. He was working fruits with you two a little earlier, wasn't he?"

"Yes, Sergeant," Baxter Slate said.

"Don't call me sergeant."

"Yes, Scuz," said Baxter Slate, who was trying to keep from vomiting.

"Lotta fucking mysteries around here," said Scuz. "Okay, you three go home and get some sleep. I want you in good shape tomorrow night. Gonna try to take a big poker game. And I'll be along to make sure you don't get killed!"

The three choirboys left then. Baxter vomited in the parking lot and felt much better. Sam said his headache was going away. Harold was buoyant from getting three whores his first night on vice. They wanted to go to choir practice but thought they better heed Scuz's advice. Then they decided to stop at the park just to see if any of the choirboys were still there.

"Drive by Pico and Western on our way," Harold said as Baxter aimed his Volkswagen in an easterly direction, not as sober as he thought he was.

"What for?"

"Wanna show you guys how far we ran," Harold said.

"Who gives a shit?" Sam Niles said, already sorry he had decided to come along to choir practice.

"Come on, lemme just show you," Harold pleaded, and Baxter smiled understandingly and said, "Sure, Harold."

When they got to the intersection, Harold insisted they circle the block and told the interested Baxter Slate and the disinterested Sam Niles how the chase began. He showed them Fred's house and the house where he drew down on the young black man.

"You know it's sad working vice," Harold said. "Those girls were young. All the girls I busted tonight were young."

"Their job demands the hope and vigor of youth," Baxter

Slate said. He was beginning to feel better, reviving in the night air.

"Maybe so," Harold said. "Maybe so."

"Just like our job," Baxter added.

"If we're going to choir practice, let's go," Sam Niles said, sitting in the back seat of the Volkswagen with his long legs turned sideways, not enjoying his cigarette because his body wanted more oxygen than he was giving it.

"Right here is where she swung at me and scratched me," Harold said as Baxter stopped, ready to make a right turn on the red.

Then Harold said, "Wait a minute, Baxter. Pull over, will you?"

"Now what, Harold?" Sam Niles sighed, taking off his steel rims and wiping his eyes.

But Harold had hopped out of the Volkswagen as soon as Baxter parked and he stooped, picking up something from the gutter.

"What the hell're you doing, Harold?" Sam asked.

"Look!" Harold Bloomguard said, stepping over to the car.

It was a springblade knife: four inches of steel with a sequined handle. A woman's knife, feminine, well honed. The point had been broken off and Harold felt his heart make light hollow thuds as he walked to the vacant newsstand. He used the broken blade of the knife to dig the tiny triangle of steel out of the wooden wall. It was throat high and deeply imbedded.

"What're you doing, Harold?" Sam Niles demanded and was surprised when Harold snarled, "Shut up, Sam!"

Then the ugly chip of steel popped out and fell into Harold's palm and he looked at it for a moment. Harold Bloomguard propped the knife against the curb and disposed of it cop style with a sharp blade-snapping heel kick.

Baxter Slate figured it out first. "Any chance of getting a lift off the knife, Harold?"

"Rough fancy surface on the handle," Harold said. "No chance for prints. No chance."

Sam Niles started to ask Harold if he still felt sorry for the whores, but when Harold turned toward Baxter, Sam saw how tired and bitter Harold Bloomguard's mouth looked.

There were still a few dogged choirboys in the park when they arrived at 4:00 A.M., but Carolina Moon had gone home and Ora Lee Tingle had not been able to make it. Harold thought the night air was strangely chilled for the end of July. They adjourned when Francis Tanaguchi said that tonight's choir practice was a bummer.

12

Alexander Blaney

Alexander Blaney was not a choirboy but he had witnessed his share of choir practices. He had even come to know some of the choirboys by name as he sat alone two hundred feet across the grass in the darkness of MacArthur Park and listened to the lusty voices carry over the water.

Alexander Blaney often wished he could meet the choirboys, at least some of them. He knew of course that they were off-duty policemen. He wondered what Father Willie looked like and the one called Dean who cried a lot when he was drunk. And he would have liked to meet Harold Bloomguard who was always protecting the ducks of MacArthur Park. There was one he didn't want to meet, not under any circumstances. He didn't want to meet Roscoe Rules whose talk was full of threats and violence. He didn't know what it meant to do the chicken but he was certain he wouldn't like it if Roscoe Rules made him do the chicken.

Alexander Blaney had grown up less than three blocks from MacArthur Park and was well known by some of the Juvenile officers at nearby Rampart Police Station. He was not known to the choirboys of Wilshire Station. Alexander was a handsome boy, even more handsome than Baxter Slate. He had dark curls and bright blue eyes, and though he was six feet tall, he hardly ate, weighing only 130 pounds.

Alexander Blaney was known by Rampart Juvenile officers because since the age of fourteen he had come to them with complaints about men who allegedly accosted him in MacArthur Park where he had played as long as he could remember. Alexander, an only child, had usually played alone. Since the neighborhood around Alvarado Street was predominantly white with a sprinkling of Cubans and Indians, it was not considered a ghetto. His parents never knew about the halfway houses nearby or of the number of men frequenting MacArthur Park who had spent years behind bars buggering young men who were not half as handsome and vulnerable as Alexander Blaney.

This is not to say that the neighborhood made Alexander Blaney what he was. No one, not even Alexander Blaney, knew what made him what he was. What he was *not* was the golden young conqueror his father had read about in his salad days when he dreamed of being more than a semi-invalid elevator operator. But if the lad had never acquired his namesake's taste for battle and glory, he had developed the sexual preference of the Greek warrior. For Alexander Blaney was, at eighteen and a half, a rubber wristed, lisping, mincing faggot.

While Alexander Blaney began getting accustomed to being gay and could not fool anyone by trying to hide that fact, Harold Bloomguard, nearing the end of his two weeks of vice duty, got drunk and came to the same conclusion.

"You're what?" Sam Niles asked as he and Sam sat alone in a vice car on a nighttime whore stakeout after having drunk six pitchers of beer in a beer bar they failed to operate effectively.

"I'm afraid I'm turning homosexual, Sam," said the beery choirboy. "And I'm terrified. I'm probably going to shoot myself or go to live with my mom in the funny place!"

"Oh please! Why me? Why me?" cried Sam Niles, slumping down in the car seat and pushing up his steel rims, so he could look to a heaven he did not believe in, to a God he knew did not exist. "All right, let's get this over with. When did you discover you were gay?"

"Just this week working the traps. You see, I started to wonder if a guy couldn't begin to identify, what with seeing that all the time, and with identifying comes acceptance and then . . . well, once I wondered if I might get a blue veiner watching that stuff sometime, and if I did it would mean I'm turning. And I'd have to kill myself."

"And did you get a blue veiner?"

"Well no, but maybe it's only my straight inhibitions stopping it. See what I mean?"

"I see," said Sam, lighting a cigarette. "And what's your next move? Gonna shoot yourself over on Duck Island?"

"I don't know," Harold belched. "You know how insanity runs in my family. I'll probably end up with Mom no matter what."

"You know, Harold, I think having you around might be more effective than electroshock. Your mother'll probably cure herself just to get away from you."

"Don't get testy with me, Sam. You're the only real friend I've got. I'm a sick man."

"You've been a sick man since you joined my fire team in Nam! You've been a sick man all your life, I'm sure. But somehow you survive all this by telling *me* all the screwy loony goofy neurotic fears you have THAT I DON'T WANNA HEAR ABOUT! I tell you *I'll* be the one doing the nudie tap dance with your mom in the state hospital!"

"Sam, you can tell your problems to me. I'd love to hear about *your* fears and . . ."

"I don't *want* you to be my confessor. I don't *need* a confessor, Harold."

"Everybody should tell his problems to someone, Sam, and you're my best . . ."

"Don't say it, Harold," Sam interrupted, trying to calm himself. "Please don't say I'm your best anything. We've been together a long time, I know. God, how I know."

"I'm sorry, I'll never burden you again," Harold said boozily.

"Oh yes you will. In a day or two you'll tell me you've discovered you're a sadist and you want me to keep an eye on you in case you start sticking pencils in somebody's eyeballs."

"I'm sorry, Sam. I never meant to be a burden."

They sat quietly for a moment and then Sam said, "Harold, did you ball Carolina Moon Tuesday night at choir practice?"

"Sort of, but only because I was drunk. And first."

"Well anyone who likes pussy enough to screw *that* fat bitch *can't* be a fruit, okay?"

"You know I never thought of that!" said Harold Bloomguard, brightening. "I never thought of that! Thanks, Sam. You always come through for me. If it weren't for you . . ."

"Yeah, yeah, I know," said the bored and disgusted Sam Niles.

Then Harold Bloomguard thought a moment and said, "How do I know I'm not bisexual?"

Harold Bloomguard's fears of being a bisexual were soon displaced by a more pressing fear when he decided he had cancer. Harold's discovery of the cancer came as a result of Scuz giving them the vice complaint against the Gypsy fortune teller, Margarita Palmara, who lived in back of a modest wood frame cottage near Twelfth and Irolo. The tiny building had been painted a garish yellow but was otherwise not unlike other homes in the area. The residence of Margarita Palmara was a garage apartment which had been converted from a chicken coop. The husband of Margarita Palmara literally flew the coop one day and left Mrs. Palmara to fend for her five children which she did in Gypsy fashion by con games, shoplifting and fortune-telling to supplement the welfare check. But then she had the good luck to tell a woman thought to be dying of a radium treated cancer that she would soon get well, and lo, she did. From then on Margarita Palmara was called upon by neighborhood women, who hailed from a dozen Latin countries, to cure everything from acne to leukemia. Just prior to the Wilshire vice detail's receiving a complaint from a disgruntled patient, Mrs. Palmara had quickly earned more than ten thousand dollars from the Spanish speaking women of the neighborhood. Never one to overdo a good thing she was thinking it was time she flew the coop herself before the cops heard about her.

But she waited a bit too long and the cops *did* hear about her. A middle aged Mexican-American policewoman named Nena Santos was ordered to pose as a neighborhood housewife and attempt to operate Margarita Palmara to get a violation of law.

"I see you will soon be cured of that which you believe to be cancer in your breast," the Gypsy said in Spanish to the undercover policewoman. "And this thing which is not a cancer, but an evil visitation, will leave your body. And you will feel twenty years old again and enjoy your man in bed as you have never enjoyed him before. And your luck will change. Your husband will find a better job that will pay as much as twelve thousand dollars a year. All this will happen if you keep the charm I am going to give you and if you faithfully say the words I am going to teach you and if you donate three hundred dollars to me which I shall use to support the orphans of my native land."

But instead of crossing the Gypsy's palm with three hundred scoots, Nena Santos crossed the Gypsy's wrists with sixteen bucks worth of steel, and Margarita Palmara was busted.

Harold Bloomguard and Sam Niles were only two of the vice cops detailed to the stakeout across the street, and after getting the signal from Nena Santos, they went inside to meet the Gypsy and drive her to jail where she would be booked and released on bail that afternoon. Ultimately she was made to come to court and pay a fine of 150 dollars before she moved to El Monte, California, where she was able to make fourteen thousand dollars telling fortunes before being arrested again. It kept her and her children in fine style even after an angry judge then fined her 250 dollars to teach her a lesson.

But before she was taken from the house that day she left a curse or two behind.

Harold Bloomguard, along with Sergeant Scuzzi, Sam Niles and Baxter Slate, was roaming around the Gypsy's chicken coop waiting for the woman to make arrangements with a neighbor to take care of the children until she could bail out. In a little bedroom of the chicken coop the officers found a frightened seven year old Gypsy girl in a communion dress.

She was a husky child, with a broad peasant face and black hair which grew too far down her forehead. Her skin was so dark it made the antique Communion dress look marshmallow white to Harold Bloomguard.

"Cómo se llama?" Harold Bloomguard asked with an atrocious accent which embarrassed Sam Niles and made him snort in disgust.

In fact every time Harold made a good natured attempt to speak Spanish to people it embarrassed Sam Niles who said he knew enough Spanish to keep his mouth shut by not trying to speak it.

Sam argued with Harold Bloomguard later when Harold claimed the homely little girl was beautiful and that her dress was charming, when Sam could see it was a hand-me-down and almost gray from so many washings. Sam said that she was nothing but an ugly little thief who would grow up to be an ugly big thief like her mother.

As they were leaving the house the angry Gypsy turned a sagging chamois face to the gathering of vice cops and said in English, "You believe I not have power? That I cheat people? Very well then. I prove you are wrong. I can cure. I can make sick. You!" And the golden bracelets clanged as she pointed a scrawny finger at Harold Bloomguard. *"You* shall get the sickness!"

It was a terrified and bleary eyed Harold Bloomguard who was in the district attorney's office the next day nervously blowing spit bubbles as he filed a complaint against the Gypsy for grand theft. He was absolutely certain that the prosecution of the Gypsy would seal his fate.

It was actually weeks before Harold stopped asking other choirboys to feel his breasts for suspicious lumps he knew lurked beneath the flesh. He only desisted when one night at choir practice Spermwhale Whalen agreed to feel the left one and got Harold in a headlock and stroked his tiny nipple lasciviously and said, "Harold, this's givin me a blue veiner!" And threw Harold down on the grass, dropping on top of him, making the little choirboy scream for help. After that Harold suffered in silence and never asked anyone to feel his breasts.

Alexander Blaney didn't know he was going to be an admitted homosexual and arrested at age eighteen and a half, when at the age of fourteen he started noticing the cruel looking men with pasty jailhouse complexions who would stare at him in the park rest rooms. But he became aware early on that

MacArthur Park was more than a place for old men to play at lawn bowling or for immigrants to kick a soccer ball or city dwellers to sit on the grass and picnic, throwing crumbs to the ubiquitous ducks in the large pond.

Alexander saw and understood the eye signals, the furtive smiles, the men who met and paired off to disappear in the bushes at night or to meet and join inside the rest room where vice officers often arrested them and sometimes got in bloody fights before the eyes of the boy.

The lad was once reading a book on the grass by a park rest room when he was startled by the noise inside and saw a huge ex-convict they called The Hippo crashing through the door, beaten to a bloody pulp by a cursing, burly vice cop whose lip was split and hanging loose and who was playing catchup on The Hippo with a sixteen ounce sap.

Alexander Blaney saw far more than that in the same park rest room. He once saw a young man masturbating at a urinal and watched in fascination until the young man stepped away and ejaculated against the dirty tile wall between the urinals and toilets only to have a white haired man with flesh like onionskin and arms like pencils get up off the toilet and wipe the semen off the wall with his fingers and put it in his mouth. He smiled at Alexander Blaney and sickened the boy.

And it was about that time that Alexander Blaney became known to Rampart Juvenile officers. The boy would come in at least once a month to report a lurid sex act he had observed in MacArthur Park. Once he claimed to have seen a big man sitting on the toilet with his trousers at his ankles stuffing his penis in his own rectum. And then there was the hermaphrodite who found Alexander Blaney lying on the grass composing madrigals to his music teacher. Alexander was fifteen and the busty hermaphrodite showed the boy her undeveloped penis and said she liked women not men, having been given male hormone shots since birth. And when darkness fell proved it was a lie by attempting to rape Alexander.

And all of the lad's stories were more or less taken with a grain of salt until at sixteen he finally came to the Juvenile sergeant and said that a handsome young man had dragged him away into the bushes and made Alexander Blaney orally copulate him and in turn forcibly performed the same act on Alexander. When he was finished with his account, the Juvenile sergeant said, "Is this the first time, Alexander?"

And Alexander Blaney cried and said yes and he wanted the police to arrest the young man but didn't know his name. The Juvenile sergeant bought the boy an ice cream bar and walked him to the door and told Alexander he wanted to talk to his parents.

When the boy was gone the sergeant said, "Well, Alexander finally turned himself out. We won't be seeing him anymore."

And the sergeant was right. Alexander Blaney came out of the closet at that time and was promptly beaten bloody by a high school friend whom he made the mistake of propositioning and who had hitherto liked and befriended him.

Alexander, who had always been a sensitive, nervous lad, then began getting even thinner than usual and suffered from insomnia as well as weight loss and spent many tearful evenings with his mother and father saying over and over, "But I don't *know* why I'm gay, I just am."

His mother wept and his father pleaded with him not to be what he could not help being. Finally, after many homosexual encounters, most of them in MacArthur Park, which terrified, excited, degraded and confused the boy, he was arrested by a Rampart Division vice officer.

The vice officer was to Alexander Blaney not unlike the first young man whom he had reported to the police for dragging him unwillingly into the bushes. The vice officer was tall and clean, and Alexander, not knowing he was a vice officer, was unable to control the tremble in his voice when their eyes met. They sat not far apart on the grass where Alexander tossed popcorn to the ducks, some of which he actually knew one from the other.

But the vice officer was not anxious to work fruits and wanted Alexander Blaney to get on with an offer so he could bust him and go to a favorite bar to shoot snooker for the remainder of his tour of duty.

Therefore when Alexander said shyly, "I don't meet too many people here," the vice cop replied, "Do you have something in mind or not?"

And Alexander, startled by the young man's boldness, almost decided to say, "No, no I have nothing in mind," but he was afraid to lose the young man who looked so clean and decent.

Alexander said, "Well, I thought we might go to a movie and get to know each other."

The vice cop sighed impatiently and said, "Look, do you suck or not?"

Alexander felt like crying because this one would be no better than most and probably even more cruel than some. Alexander arrogantly replied, "Yes, I'll do that. If that's all you want. I guess I can do that all right."

The vice officer whistled for his partner who was hiding behind the trees and showed his badge to Alexander Blaney and looked disgusted when the boy lowered his head to weep.

The vice cop later wrote in his arrest report: "Defendant stated: 'I'll suck you or do anything you want. I guess I can do that all right.'"

Alexander pled guilty to a lesser misdemeanor after the city attorney dropped the lewd conduct violation in the plea bargaining session, and Alexander Blaney had a police record. But the thing which he could not forget, and which made him burn with humiliation, was that the vice cop didn't seem to care one way or the other what happened to him. If he had hated homosexuals and beaten him up Alexander would have found it more tolerable. It's just that he was *nothing* to the policeman, and even in court the vice officer didn't seem to recognize him and just shrugged when the city attorney asked him if he had any objection to Alexander's lawyer getting the charge reduced and pleading him guilty.

The tour on vice for the three choirboys ended on an unsuccessful note in that a call girl they had been staking out never took the bait which was a phone call from Baxter Slate who was given a duke-in name of Gaylord Bottomley. A snitch said Bottomley was a savings and loan executive who had introduced certain circumspect friends to the exotic call girl.

The snitch was a paid confidential informant who belonged to Pete Zoony and the moustachioed vice cop jealously guarded his informant's identity. Real policemen, unlike movie cops, actually cherish and protect a good informant as they would a sibling. Informants are people to be bribed, threatened, cajoled, but above all protected. It was not uncommon for a policeman to guard the identity of a good snitch even from a partner he rode with nightly.

As Pete Zoony said, "I never gave a snitch's righteous name since I been on the job. Once we ripped off some dopers and some stupid cop calls me on the radio and gives the snitch's name right over the air! But we always used a code name and he didn't get a rat jacket behind it. Nobody knows my snitch's name, not even my lieutenant. Nobody."

Pete's informant told them about Gina Summers who lived in a thousand-a-month apartment near Wilshire Boulevard. Allegedly she was a specialist in applying just the required amount of imaginative punishment to genteel but eager customers who paid from fifty to five hundred dollars for her unique services.

Sam and Baxter had watched one man and sometimes two a night come and go and often saw the voluptuous brunette herself leaving and entering the apartment. None of the vice cops had been able to operate her successfully. The informant had told them that the vivacious girl had a chamber of horrors in her bedroom closet which included ancient thumbscrews, brands, scourges and other collector's items. Actually most were seldom needed. Customers could usually be satisfied by less painful acts of degradation such as a urine shower. And often an ordinary spanking with a leather belt would do them just fine.

Because she was such an extraordinary hooker the vice cops naturally wanted to arrest her badly but the hours of stakeouts were to no avail.

On a sultry August night Baxter Slate watched through binoculars as she undressed before an open window on the sixth floor of her apartment house, and said to Sam, "If that bitch weren't a brunette she'd remind me a lot of a nude dancer I used to know."

"Yeah?" Sam answered, totally bored with the stakeout and his two weeks of vice duty. "The other one that good looking?"

"Oh, I guess they don't exactly look alike. But they're both sisters at heart."

Sam Niles never bothered to ask Baxter to explain the allusion. He was just glad it was their last night on vice and that the choir practice they had planned should be a memorable one.

The choir practice which celebrated the return of the three choirboys from the tour of vice squad duty was *bound* to be a memorable one. After all Roscoe Rules outdid himself when he scrounged fifteen bottles of booze from the liquor stores of Wilshire Division in a single night.

"I tell you the captain's throwing a big *big* party, godamnit," he informed some of the more reluctant proprietors who were offering only one fifth to Roscoe, wearing his black gloves, standing tall and menacing.

And what Roscoe couldn't scrounge with intimidation Spencer Van Moot obtained by his incredible rapport with the merchants on his beat. They said they couldn't wait for his retirement from the police department when he would open a retail store on the Miracle Mile and implement his merchandizing genius for the mutual benefit of all.

Therefore there was enough liquor, wine and beer to kill them all, and trays of foil covered barbecue, salami, pastrami, roast beef and turkey, not to mention German potato salad, bean salad, sourdough rolls and condiments.

Strangely enough, despite the humiliation of his arrest, or perhaps because of it and the overwhelming guilt it engendered, Alexander Blaney was back in MacArthur Park for every homosexual contact from then on. It had never been more enticing now that he was aware of the possibility of vice officers and the courts and the impersonal retribution of the law.

So at eighteen and a half, with a genuine affection for policemen which was a remnant of his numerous trips to Rampart Juvenile Division and which was not vitiated by his single arrest by the Rampart vice officer, Alexander Blaney loved to sit across the water at night in the cool enveloping darkness and feed the ducks and listen to the antics of the choirboys and wonder if Calvin Potts was the only black man among them and if Francis Tanaguchi was as comical to look at as he was to listen to and to hope that Whaddayamean Dean would never become like his partner Roscoe Rules.

He had never let the choirboys see him, but on this night, when gunfire would shatter the sylvan stillness, he revealed himself to the two roommates, Ora Lee Tingle and Carolina Moon. The plump cocktail waitresses trotted across the grass from the yellow Buick which they always left on Park View Street when they got off work.

Alexander had been lying very still listening to the crickets chirp and watching Jupiter, the only star one could see in the Los Angeles summer sky when it was very smoggy. Alexander watched for it ever since he heard the policeman called Baxter telling the others that it was reassuring to at least have one great star pierce the smog and that Baxter would find the sky unbearably lonely without it.

As the laughing, chattering girls approached, Alexander was afraid he might frighten them sitting there in the dark, so when they got within thirty feet the boy called out, "Hi, nice evening isn't it?"

"Real nice," Carolina said, slowing a bit until she saw the slender harmless boy lying in the grass with three ducklings.

"Whatcha doing out here in the dark, honey?" asked Ora Lee Tingle as Alexander looked at her massive bustline and wide hips and sticky upswept blonde hair and thought she looked exactly as he pictured her.

"Just feeding the ducks," said Alexander.

"Watch yourself, honey," Carolina said. "There's rapists around here."

"Yeah," Ora Lee giggled, "and we're gonna go join a bunch of em."

They hurried off across the grass and Alexander heard Carolina say, "Feeding the ducks. Sure."

All ten choirboys were there that night and already half drunk an hour after arriving. They wore their usual summer-time choir practice garb: safari jackets, sweatshirts, tank tops, LAPD baseball or basketball shirts, faded jeans and denim, Nike and Adidas athletic shoes, or Wallabees. They wore nothing which would be ruined if someone fell or was pushed in the duck pond when a choir practice got rough. They were absolutely delighted when Ora Lee Tingle and Carolina Moon surprised them by bouncing across the grass at 1:00 A.M. The girls were still wearing their mesh stockings and short skirts which barely covered their red ruffled panties. They wore peasant blouses with laced midriffs which forced their enormous breasts up and out, guaranteed to drive bar patrons wild and keep them swilling booze at $1.85 a throw.

"Surprise! The boss let us off early!" yelled Carolina as both fat girls literally threw themselves into the festivities by bouncing on the blanket of their favorite, Francis Tanaguchi, burying the little choirboy under a total of three hundred and ten pounds of young willing flesh as he joyfully screamed, "You girls just gotta do a part in my dirty movie! Now part your legs and let's see how you act!"

The choir practice had officially begun. As usual, they first had to ventilate with a gripe session. Spermwhale began it by complaining about Lieutenant Finque who had brought charges of Conduct Unbecoming an Officer against the nightwatch desk officer, Lard Logan, resulting in a five day suspension.

"That eunuch, Finque!" Spermwhale growled. "Snuck around like a spy and nailed Lard for remarks to citizens which he decides are unprofessional. I can't wait til I get my twenty in so I can tell that gelding what I think a him!"

"What happened to old Lard?" Roscoe beamed, thrilled that Spermwhale was actually talking to him.

"First one, this dingaling came in off the street and told Lard she wants to see the captain. Naturally he tries to shine her on. Finally she starts tellin him her problem which is that her sixteen year old girl got knocked up from swimmin in the L.A. High School pool. And her little girl's a virgin and she read that spermatozoa can swim and she wants the crime lab to go make a sperm count in the pool so she can sue the Board of Education. And all Lard did was listen patiently and say, 'Lady, if the water done it it musta been awful hard water.' And boom! The lieutenant writes him up for cue-bow."

"Well that ain't enough to get five days for," Roscoe observed.

"No, but then the lieutenant adds another count when Lard takes this theft report from some rich broad in the Towers who had her two Persian cats ripped off. Just for a gag he writes in the MO box: 'Suspect deals in hot pussy.' "

"I'd say fuck that lieutenant," Roscoe said. "Probably be a good one at that. He's enough of a cunt!"

"Then poor Lard gets shanked in the back by the lieutenant for making his press statement, hear about that, Sam?"

"Haven't heard anything," Sam Niles yawned, bored by all the talk of Lieutenant Finque.

"You remember the slut roamed into Sears and had the baby in the rest room?"

"What about her?"

"She cut the cord with her fingernails and just dumped the little toad in the trash can and left it for the janitor to find next day. And the dicks couldn't prove the baby ever drew breath and she cried all over the courtroom and they couldn't find her guilty of manslaughter or nothin. Anyways, some dude from one a these Right to Life groups comes into the station to interview the detectives on how they felt about it and the dicks kissed him off down to the desk officer who happened to be Lard. And Lard says, 'You want my opinion, the little third-generation welfare pig shoulda been sterilized when she turned fourteen so she wouldn't be runnin around foalin in every shithouse in town. Far as a crime's concerned she did the taxpayers a favor. Only crime she should be found guilty of is litterbug.' "

"So what happened?" Roscoe asked. "I suppose the Catholic bishop reported Lard to the captain?"

"The very same day."

"You gotta learn not to tell the truth in this world. Some guys never learn," Roscoe said. "I got two days off once when I had to make a notification in Watts to this bitch. Her old man got his ass killed in a poolroom knife fight. I knocked on the door and when she answered I said, 'You the widow Brown?' She said, 'No, I ain't a widow.' I said, 'The hell you ain't.' "

"Hey, Spermwhale," said Father Willie, "is it true one time your neighbors complained and the captain got you for cue-bow and gave you two days off for refusing to mow your lawn?"

When Spermwhale muttered something unintelligible, Whaddayamean Dean said, "I heard your lawn was four feet high just before you left your third old lady."

Roscoe Rules, now near the beer cooler, decided it was time

to gripe about the headhunters of Internal Affairs Division whom they all naturally despised.

"Yeah, I remember a few years back when I worked Central they get a rumor me and my partner was rolling drunks," said Roscoe. "You imagine? Rolling drunks in the B-wagon? How many pissy ass winos have more'n a dollar fifty anytime? So one a those headhunters gets himself all dirtied up, thinks he looks like a drunk and lays down on the corner of Fifth and Stanford and pretends he's passed out. With a wallet sticking outta his pocket no less. So we drive up and see the asshole but my partner recognizes the bastard from when he worked Foothill traffic. So he winks at me and gives me a note saying this drunk's a cop and probably working IAD. So we pick the cocksucker up and throw him in the wagon just like any wino and then we go down East Fifth Street and prowl the alleys till we find three old smelly shitters. You know, with the skin rotting off them and the piss and vomit all over them? And just for good measure we scoop up some dog crap and put it in their pockets and we throw them in the wagon with the headhunter. Then we ride around for an hour and a half before we make the Central Jail booking run. And *that's* what I think a headhunters!"

"You know, Roscoe, maybe I been misjudgin you," said Spermwhale. "You're startin to sound like a class guy after all."

And as smoky clouds crossed the moon and shadows deepened and a summer breeze rippled over the duck pond, the choirboys settled back to eat and drink and unwind. Baxter Slate looked skyward, reassured to see that the light from the great star slithered easily through the smog tonight.

Spermwhale's rare praise had put Roscoe in good enough spirits to turn storyteller. He scratched his head and leered at the two fat girls who were still making over Francis Tanaguchi, feeding him beef like a shogun in a geisha house.

Roscoe said, "I just loved working that B-wagon. Only thing I liked about Central in fact. Never forget the night we got the old fag wino in back a the wagon. I turn around and see him through the cage going down on some young drunk that's passed out. So I stop the wagon and me and my partner open the back door and know what? He won't stop. Said later it was the first taste he had in a year and he just wouldn't give it up. I took out my sap and hit him upside the gourd every time he went down on the guy. His head was like a clump a grapes when I finished sapping him. Goddamn it was fun working that wagon!"

Baxter Slate then said, "Tell you what, Roscoe. For our next choir practice we'll go to a hatchery and buy a gross of rabbits. Then we'll get a yard of piano wire and all come to the park and sit around the whole night watching you garroting baby bunnies."

And Roscoe, who was getting very drunk very early, said, "You know, Slate, I *never* liked you."

Spermwhale Whalen said, "Roscoe, you got class all right and it's all low. You got the class of a hyena."

Since Roscoe Rules was scared to death of Spermwhale Whalen he merely pouted and said, "All right. See if I come to choir practice, that's the way you feel. How would you like to start *buying* your booze instead of me bringing it?"

"Now wait a minute," said Calvin Potts, jumping off his blanket, "don't let's get hasty, Roscoe!"

And Spermwhale quickly added, "Right. I was only kiddin, Roscoe."

"You're a hell of a guy, Roscoe," Sam Niles said, patting Roscoe on the cheek as Roscoe smiled and accepted it all magnanimously.

Whaddayamean Dean, whose mind was not yet obliterated from the bourbon, was trying to console Father Willie Wright who had begun to pine for No-Balls Hadley. The chaplain had seen her that night driving by the station on her way to meet a neurosurgeon she was dating.

Father Willie had waved hopefully, but No-Balls Hadley, now working Central daywatch, merely curled her lip and mouthed an obscenity and flipped Father Willie the middle digit.

"God she's so beautiful, Dean!" said Father Willie. "I swear I'd leave my wife for her."

"I know how it is, Padre," said Whaddayamean Dean sadly. "You'd eat the peanuts out of her shit. I know how it is."

"She's *so* beautiful!"

"Confidentially, what'd her poon look like, Father?"

"Dean, it was *all* perfect," said Father Willie who really didn't remember.

"Wow! Even her asshole?"

"It was a pearl," said the choirboy chaplain as he gulped down the Scotch.

"Imagine that!" said Whaddayamean Dean, visibly impressed. "An asshole like a pearl!"

And as the choir practice gained momentum, a slender boy sat across the water quietly feeding the ducks from a sack of breadcrumbs he carried. Alexander Blaney sensed that this was going to be a memorable choir practice since at 2:00 A.M. six choirboys were roaring drunk and four others were not far behind.

Arguments began raging all over the grass there by the duck pond.

"You can't prove it was me who had the Dragon Lady call you up that time," said Francis Tanaguchi who had his head in Carolina's lap and his feet in Ora Lee's.

"I can't prove it but I *know* it was you," said Father Willie Wright who was in an extremely rare mood of belligerence thinking of No-Balls Hadley's upraised finger.

"Well you should have proof before you accuse somebody," Francis said, his little eyes glowing wildly in the moonlight.

"You sound like a hype on the street," Calvin Potts said, turning on his partner. "Prove it. Prove it. Shit!"

"And you sound like Roscoe Rules the time he tried to choke me because the Dragon Lady called him. Fine partner you are!"

"I think you're guilty is what I think. And I'd like to meet the Dragon Lady to prove it," Calvin Potts challenged. And then Calvin lay back on the grass, savoring the Scotch, fantasizing about the Dragon Lady, who in his thoughts greatly resembled that bitch, Martha Twogood Potts.

"That was a filthy thing to say, Spencer! I heard that!" Carolina Moon suddenly yelled to Spencer Van Moot who was drinking with Harold Bloomguard.

"I wasn't talking about you."

"Yes you was. I heard you say fat!"

"My wife's got an ass twice as wide as yours. I wasn't talking about you!"

"What'd he say?" asked Ora Lee who was drinking champagne out of Francis Tanaguchi's tennis shoe.

"He said he'd like to rebush somebody by sticking a picnic ham in her unit and pulling the bone out, is what he said!"

"I swear I wasn't talking about you! It was my wife!" Spencer pleaded, fearing that Carolina might pull that train tonight and leave him off. "Why is everybody so sensitive tonight?"

"Oh stop it," Francis said. "Carolina, want some Japanese food?"

"You cute little shitbird," she giggled, pounding Francis on the head. "Is it like Chinese food?"

"Better," said Francis lasciviously.

"That Chinese food," Ora Lee giggled. "You know a half hour later . . ."

"Way she accuses me," Spencer pouted. "And I like her so much I balled her on the same night my first wife was delivering our last kid."

"You *both* had a baby on the same night!" Harold Bloomguard observed.

"Hey, munchkin!" yelled Roscoe Rules to Harold Bloomguard. "You're the littlest guy around here. Settle this argument. Do you think there's anything immoral about screwing a midget?"

"I didn't say immoral," protested Father Willie. "I just said it seemed a little perverted."

"Well I'm not sorry," said Roscoe, sneering at Carolina Moon. "She was a lot better than some big girls I could name."

"Roscoe'd screw the crack of dawn," said Father Willie who was creeping closer to Carolina Moon who was sick of playing with Francis' bare feet while he sang Spanish songs.

"You're bilingual, ain't you, Francis?" asked Carolina Moon.

"Does that mean he licks girls *and* boys?" asked Spermwhale.

"I'm just afraid my marriage isn't going to work," Father Willie said to Carolina Moon who was suddenly holding *his* head in her lap.

"Why do you say that?" asked Carolina.

"My wife just doesn't like sex. She'd rather hand out Watchtowers than . . ."

"She ever catch you coming home with a slight odor of vagina on your breath, Padre?" Calvin Potts giggled as he tried to decide at what point Carolina Moon would become more exciting than the fifth of Johnnie Walker he was demolishing.

"Gosh no," blushed Father Willie as Carolina Moon groped him good naturedly under his blanket.

"Oughtta be glad she wasn't like that bitch I was married to," grumbled Calvin. "I hadda check to see if the toilet seat was up or down every time I came home."

"Why don't you get a hair transplant, Spermy?" asked Ora Lee Tingle, waddling past the fat policeman who was sprawled back on his elbows. She bumped him on the side of the head with her enormous ass saying, "Make it pubic hair. Stands up when a girl walks past."

Then Ora Lee squealed as he rolled over and made a grab for her. She eluded him and jumped over Whaddayamean Dean and fell on Sam Niles, slapping him on the side of the face with one gigantic tit which knocked his glasses into the bushes.

"Where's my glasses? Where's my glasses?" yelled Sam Niles, crawling around Calvin Potts who decided the Johnnie Walker was preferable to Carolina Moon for the moment.

"Calvin probably stole your glasses," said Spencer Van Moot. "You know you shouldn't leave nothing around these people."

"Your daddy had three dollars stead a two dollars you'd be black too, chump," said Calvin Potts as Sam Niles found the glasses and cleaned them on his shirttail.

"Where'd Roscoe go?" asked Father Willie who staggered around several sprawling choirboys. "Roscoe! Where are you? Roscoe!"

"Hey, Roscoe! Roscoe!" yelled Francis.

"Roscoe!" yelled several choirboys who didn't give a shit where Roscoe was.

"Roscoe, you there?" yelled Spermwhale Whalen, unzipping his fly and looking inside at which time Carolina Moon made a grab for him.

"Ain't time yet, me beauty," said Spermwhale, zipping up and kissing the girl in a quivering fleshy embrace.

"I'll pay you two *anything* to do a dirty movie for me!" screamed Francis Tanaguchi.

"You looked like a blue eyed home boy," said Calvin Potts to Whaddayamean Dean who was leaning against a tree gnawing on spareribs with barbecue sauce all over his face.

"Whaddaya mean? Whaddaya mean?" asked Whaddayamean Dean, and all the choirboys looked knowingly at each other, silently agreeing that Whaddayamean Dean had done it again.

"You gonna slip old Carolina a roll of tarpaper tonight, Calvin?" Francis whispered.

"Not if I ain't first. I ain't drunk enough for that," said Calvin Potts.

"I feel like a construction engineer," Spencer Van Moot said, overhearing the conversation. "Gonna lay some pipe, six inches at a time!"

"Stealing a girl's cherry is cock robbin," said Carolina Moon to Whaddayamean Dean who looked at her blankly.

"Darn it, did you fart?" Father Willie suddenly asked Sam Niles.

"No, was I supposed to?" replied the weary choirboy.

"So I can't take you away from Carolina, huh?" said Ora Lee Tingle to Spermwhale Whalen after she won a two dollar bet by finishing a half bottle of champagne without taking it from her mouth.

"I said you can't get me there right *now,*" Spermwhale corrected her and gave one of her huge thighs a playful pinch, tearing her mesh stocking.

"Well it's easier to . . . let's see. Padre! Father Willie!" Ora Lee yelled. "How's it go? In the Bible about the camel and the eye of a needle?"

"I dunno, something about a humping hype," said Father Willie, reaching the stage of drunkenness wherein he was revolted by his uncontrollable sinfulness, yet not to the point where he goatishly succumbed.

"Mothers, brothers and others, lend me your ears," said Harold Bloomguard, staggering to his feet. "Hear about Calvin and Francis almost blowing up some dude tonight?"

"No, what happened?" asked Baxter Slate as the choirboys quieted down for a cops 'n' robbers story.

"No big thing," Calvin said. "Cat on a family dispute almost draws down on Francis when he tried to lay the iron on his wrists after the dude had went upside Momma's head."

"It was nothing," Francis said. "He was drunk. Makes a grab for what I thought was a gun. Was his wallet. All I did is whack him across the arm with my flashlight."

"I almost blew the sucker away," Calvin said. "Thought it was a piece the way he went to the drawer. Was ready to bust a cap between his fuckin horns."

"Be glad you didn't," said Baxter Slate soberly.

"Could you live with yourself if you blew up a guy by mistake that way?" asked Father Willie Wright.

"I could a blowed him up and lived with his foxy old lady," said Calvin Potts.

"Remember that time you busted your flashlight on the black belt guy, Spermwhale?" Spencer Van Moot asked. "This hamburger they were busting thinks he's Kung Fu and tries to drop Baxter. He says, 'Yaaa!' and kicks Baxter and Spermwhale yells, 'Ever-ready!' and hits him with his flashlight. Then Spermwhale gave him nine from the sky with his stick."

Spencer Van Moot then stumbled over Spermwhale's feet and fell against Calvin Potts.

"What's a matter? Fall off your wallet?" Calvin asked the richest choirboy.

"Must give you a hernia carrying that money belt around," said Sam Niles.

"Careful a your head when you fall," Spermwhale said. "All that fuckin hair spray you use could cause brain damage."

"With your money why don't you hire a coolie to pull you around the park so you won't be tripping all over everybody?" said Harold Bloomguard.

And Spencer Van Moot, the best dressed and richest choirboy, lay back on the grass and laughed uproariously when Carolina Moon fell on him lovingly and smothered him in kisses while she felt his body up and down to see if he really *did* have a money belt.

Roscoe Rules looked at his comrades and now thought they

weren't such bad guys. He was even able to tolerate the Gook and the Spook tonight.

Roscoe had met Francis and Calvin at the first choir practice months before when Francis was going through his vampire period.

When they met, both Calvin and Francis were drunk and sullen and sat together in the shadows examining the new choirboy.

"Are you the two they call the Gook and the Spook?" Roscoe had asked with a big smile that was met with stony silence.

"Yeah," said Calvin Potts finally, glaring at Roscoe since Calvin didn't yet know that Roscoe had brought three fifths of Scotch with him.

"Uh, what do your friends call you?" Roscoe asked, having a hard time seeing their faces in the dark.

"You can call me the Gook," said the Gook.

"You can call me the Spook," said the Spook. "But if you do I'll kick your face off."

And after that Roscoe had sat furious and quiet and wondered why people didn't like him. After all he had been willing to treat them all the same, even niggers and slopeheads. Then he started looking hard at the Gook. And it looked as if his teeth had grown grotesquely. Roscoe was sure it was the drink because there in the darkness of MacArthur Park it looked as if the Gook had fangs! But of course that was silly. Yet five minutes later when Roscoe got up to walk off into the trees to relieve himself, he was bushwhacked by a hissing demon which leaped on his back and bit him on the neck while Roscoe screamed in terror and tried to reach for his gun as he wet all over his shoes.

It had taken Spermwhale Whalen to pry Francis Tanaguchi from Roscoe Rules' throat that first night, and as Roscoe threatened to kill Francis, it was Harold Bloomguard who explained to Calvin and Francis that the new kid on the block had brought *three fifths* of Scotch to choir practice which they could expect at any future choir practice Roscoe might attend.

After hearing that, Francis and Calvin became very tolerant of the insufferable prick and Roscoe Rules was an accepted choirboy. He was able to sit now at this memorable choir practice and not think that nobody liked him. And he could pinch Ora Lee and Carolina just like the other guys.

While Roscoe remembered his first choir practice and felt all cozy and secure because now he belonged, he started talking to Sam Niles who was already mightily pissed off because one of the lenses on his glasses got scratched when Ora Lee slapped him in the face with a tit.

"Niles, we just gotta get the department to give us good ammo," Roscoe began. "You see, high velocity shock waves're like sonic booms and they burst the veins and arteries. But they don't stop like the hollow points and the blunt nose. A copper casing holds the lead together. Centrifugal force breaks up the lead. You only need a pointed projectile for accuracy. Get it?"

"I get it," Sam sighed.

Then Roscoe said, "I ever tell you what I used to do to all the pricks in the juvie gangs when they turned eighteen? I used to send them a Xerox of the page of the LAPD manual which tells about shooting at adults only. With the page I'd enclose a dumdum bullet and a greeting card. On the card I'd write, 'You are now, by law, an adult. Have a nice eighteenth birthday, asshole.'"

"That's about as interesting as a night in the drunk tank," said Sam Niles, who lay back smoking, looking at the great star while the bourbon went to work on his entire body, turning it to rock.

"Looky here, Ora Lee," said Calvin Potts as he was starting to think that the fat girls weren't so repulsive after all. In fact, depending on how you looked at her, Ora Lee was starting to get downright gorgeous.

"Looky here, what?" asked Ora Lee. "You boys aren't interested in us girls tonight. You're all sitting around like that bunch of fruits hangs around the other side of the duck pond."

"Well you know, consenting adults!" said Francis Tanaguchi, kissing his partner Calvin Potts who pushed him away.

". . . and I been thinking about buying this baby falcon," said Roscoe Rules to Harold Bloomguard. "I live out in the country with decent people. Room for an eagle even. I could train him to kill on command. Shit, how many guys own a hunting hawk?"

"Last guy I know of was William the Conqueror," said Baxter Slate.

"Would really be great!" Roscoe mused. "Your own killing bird!"

"You could feed him raw meat right out of your hand," said Baxter.

"Sure!" said Roscoe.

"And to save feed money you could train him to fly over the kindergarten and carry off kids," Baxter Slate said.

"You know, I never liked you, Slate," said Roscoe Rules, turning sullen.

"Roscoe needs his steel plate buffed!" Spencer said gleefully.

"Are you trying to incinerate that Roscoe belongs in the funny place?" asked Harold Bloomguard, taking pleasure in the thought that someone else might be going there with him someday.

"What're you trying to say? What're you trying to say?" Whaddayamean Dean blurted, still propped against the same tree, a pile of rib bones on his lap, a half empty bourbon bottle resting on his chest.

"I don't think it's fair," said Father Willie, arguing a point of law with Spencer Van Moot. "In these unlawful sex cases a boy of thirteen *can* be booked as opposed to the old statutory rape charge where he couldn't. Who enjoys it more, the ear being scratched or the finger scratching?"

"If they're doing it in the ear they deserve to be booked, the perverts!" said Carolina Moon as Spermwhale Whalen threw her down and kissed her again.

"I'd give anything to direct this scene!" cried Francis Tanaguchi.

"You know she wouldn't do nothing in front of everybody. They're just kissing," said Ora Lee Tingle as Spermwhale kneaded and squeezed every inch of Carolina's ample body.

"Why doesn't a Jap have a camera anyway, I'd like to know?" Roscoe remarked suspiciously. "Maybe Francis is really a Chinaman. A Commie, no doubt."

"I'm a Mexican and you can go scratch your ass," said Francis Tanaguchi.

"I'm gonna have you defrocked, Padre," Ora Lee giggled when Father Willie groped her.

"Anybody gets frocked it better be me!" Carolina whooped when Spermwhale let her breathe.

Just then Harold Bloomguard staggered a few paces away and threw up. He was the first. Everybody jeered and hooted and he walked ashamedly down to the duck pond and washed his face in dirty water.

". . . so this guy demands his rights when I arrest him," said Roscoe Rules to Whaddayamean Dean who hadn't the foggiest idea what Roscoe was talking about. "And I say, 'You'll get your rights and a few lefts too, asshole! Bang! Pow! Splat!' "

Whereas Spencer Van Moot only whined to Father Willie Wright when he was sober, he was now whining to as many assembled choirboys as would listen now that he was drunk.

"This dirty scummy rotten bitch that lives next door . . ."

"Watch that fuckin language," said Spermwhale Whalen who was passionately kissing Carolina Moon a few feet away in the shadows while Francis Tanaguchi knelt beside them, grinning.

"Sorry, Spermwhale. Sorry, girls," said Spencer who belched sourly and quickly took a few sips of beer. "Anyway, this bitch always wears these short shorts and comes out by the fence when I'm down on my knees trimming the grass. So finally after three months of this I kneel there and look right at her bird and up it goes!"

"A blue veiner?" asked Father Willie.

"A goddamn diamond cutter!" said Spencer and Ora Lee said, "Oooooooohhhhhhhh, Spencer, that's sexy!" and fell over backward as Francis Tanaguchi pounced on her and smothered her with kisses.

"Why do you wear those sissy faggy mod clothes, Spencer?" asked Roscoe, beginning to turn mean. "And why does a man your age have one of those kiss-me-quick haircuts?"

"Lemme finish my story, goddamnit."

"Spencer's so mod he wears flared jockey shorts," said Harold Bloomguard who was trying to stand with the aid of a broken willow branch.

"Why do we need a motel?" Ora Lee said to Roscoe who

whispered something in her ear. "You can beat off in a nickel toilet, ya cheap little fuck, ya."

"Anyway," Spencer continued, "my neighbor sees my diamond cutter and she runs into her house. Runs. And I mean after she'd done everything but rub my face in it. She runs in and calls my wife and tells her that I'm going around the yard looking at her with a big hard on."

"Probably a libber," said Roscoe Rules. "All these cunts're like that these days. Wanna be truck drivers. I say back em up and give em a load, they wanna be truck drivers."

"You ain't got a load, Roscoe, you dirty mouthed chauvinist pig!" said Carolina Moon, coming up for air, while Spermwhale Whalen looked around, saw double, got dizzy and had to stagger away to relieve himself.

"Who asked you? You a libber or something?" Roscoe challenged.

"I *know* you ain't got a load," said Carolina, taking a drink from Calvin's bottle. "You walk into a wall with your little hard on and you'll break your nose."

To keep Roscoe and Carolina from fighting, Harold Bloomguard began to sing a soothing song he just made up called "She'll not puncture your kidney, Sidney. And he shan't rupture your spleen, Kathleen."

But Spermwhale Whalen hobbled back in their midst and his enormous presence looming over Roscoe quieted down the meanest choirboy. Especially when Spermwhale said, "You look like a ruptured rectum sittin there with your mean little mouth all scrunched up. Why don't you quit pickin on the ladies?"

"Yeah, it makes you ugly, Roscoe," said Ora Lee. "You get drunk you get uglier than usual."

"I don't have to take this," Roscoe Rules said, struggling to his feet and heading toward the duck pond, hoping to find a duck he could kneedrop.

"He gets so ugly he looks like something carved off the back of Quasimodo," Spencer Van Moot observed.

"Hey, stick around, Roscoe!" Carolina yelled. "Every choir practice needs a soprano."

"Don't get nasty now," Spermwhale whispered as he bit the

fat girl on the neck and sent her into paroxysms of passion. They resumed their interminable kiss and rolled around on the ground, making the earth shake under the ear of Francis Tanaguchi, who said, "Dynamite!" and lay next to them hoping the behemoths would couple before his very eyes.

Just then a park homosexual with sandals, long hair and beard walked by the group curiously.

The choirboys looked at this Biblical apparition and Sam Niles said, "Think he'll take us to heaven?"

"I can use *my* ticket validated by somebody," said Father Willie who was furiously trying to think of a way to steal Carolina Moon from Spermwhale Whalen.

"All I can say is I get treated like a dog at home," Spencer Van Moot whined, returning to his favorite subject.

"Anytime they wanna teach you a lesson they just hold back the sex," Father Willie agreed, suddenly having a miserable vision of the chubby Jehovah's Witness seeing him drunk and playing with the thigh of Ora Lee Tingle.

"Well who cares?" said Spencer. "The three most overrated things in the world are: home cooking, home pussy and the FBI."

"You know, Spermy, you got more hair in your nose than on your head," Carolina Moon said from the shadows where she and Spermwhale and Francis Tanaguchi rolled around.

"What dialogue! What dialogue! I could make you a star, girl!" cried Francis. "Say something back to her, Spermwhale! Something romantic!"

"Okay. I adore you, my darling," Spermwhale crooned to the sighing fat girl. "Your ass is springy as a life raft."

"And I love *you*, Ora Lee," Francis Tanaguchi blurted suddenly, running to the other cocktail waitress, dragging his fingers through her upswept hairdo, which was no mean task given the half can of hair spray that was on it.

"That's just whiskey talking, you cute little shit."

"No it ain't! I love! I love you!" Francis proclaimed. "If you had a hysterectomy and took your teeth out and owned a liquor store, I swear I'd marry you!"

"Thanks, Junior," said the disgusted waitress as she pushed Francis away. "You handled that love scene like a real pro— a prophylactic!"

Just then the bearded park fairy with the ascetic face, shoulder-length hair and sandals encountered Roscoe Rules down by the duck pond trying to entice a black duck out of the water so he could hit it with a rock and drown it.

"Hello," said the Jesus fairy.

"Holy Christ!" said Roscoe Rules and the remark was not that inappropriate.

"Are you with those others?" asked the bearded man, stooping to scoop some water in both hands.

"Yeah. Who the fuck're you, John the Baptist?"

Ignoring the remark the man said, "Do you men actually screw those women in the park?"

"No, in the cunt," said Roscoe. "Now take a walk, John, before I bring your fucking head to Salome."

Meanwhile, back at the choir practice Father Willie was going to hell in a hurry. He had stripped off his shirt and shoes and was asking Ora Lee if she dared him to streak through the park as Harold Bloomguard composed a song called "I Left My Heart in Titty City."

"Put your shirt back on, Padre," said his partner Spencer Van Moot. "I gotta quit feeding you all the cherries jubilee. You're getting to look like a basketball."

"How's your *como se llama* these days, Ora Lee?" asked Francis as he tried to squeeze a finger inside the leg of Ora Lee's ruffled pants, causing her to honk him severely, making him cry out in pain.

"How do *you* like being a sex object, huh?" the fat girl grinned.

"See, you're not a *real* Mexican!" yelled shirtless Father Willie who was staggering around looking for trouble. "You're not even a Jap! A real Mexican like General Zapata could take a little hurt without whimpering!"

"How'd you like to get your nuts crushed by this big moose?" said the injured choirboy, holding himself.

"Who's a moose?" demanded Ora Lee Tingle, glowering at Francis. "You call me names I'll hit you so hard and fast you'll think you was in a gang fight!"

"Carolina's putting on a little more weight," Baxter Slate observed as he sat next to Sam Niles and the two quietly tried to drink themselves into unconsciousness.

"Maybe she's pregnant," Sam observed.

"What're you trying to say, what're you trying to say, Sam?" Whaddayamean Dean cried out but quieted down when Baxter handed him a full bottle of bourbon.

"If she's pregnant I'll take her soon as her milk comes in," said Spencer Van Moot. "I can't feed my wife and kids no more on a policeman's pay what with the inflation and all."

"That's cause you spend all your money on faggy clothes! A man your age!" said a voice from the darkness as Roscoe Rules got tired of waiting for someone to coax him back to the flock.

Then Francis Tanaguchi staggered away from the other choirboys and they heard him retching on the grass.

"Booo! Booo! Zapata my rear end!" giggled Father Willie Wright.

And while the party entered its final phase, Alexander Blaney slept on the grass not a hundred feet away beside two friendly ducklings while his mother wept at home and imagined him locked in the cruel embrace of a tattooed merchant seaman in some skid row flophouse.

At the end of that memorable choir practice some ordinary and extraordinary things started to happen.

An ordinary thing was that Whaddayamean Dean broke out in several crying jags and sobbed, "What're you trying to say?" every time a choirboy was foolish enough to send a remark in his direction.

An extraordinary thing was that Spermwhale Whalen lost his diamond cutter and in fact lost the use of all his muscles. He could only sit against an elm tree and snarl at anyone who came near him. Spermwhale, the biggest strongest and bravest choirboy, was so drunk he was as helpless as the baby ducks out of water.

Another ordinary thing was that Roscoe Rules became as mean as a rabid dog, and with Sam Niles drunk and Spermwhale Whalen helpless, it seemed for a time that no one was around who could tame the young policeman. He was going around jealously insulting Ora Lee and Carolina because they didn't feel like pulling that train and in any event wouldn't let anyone as mean as Roscoe have a ride.

"Pig fuckers!" Roscoe Rules sneered. "If you don't oink they won't touch you! Gotta lead you up to a trough first to see if you're worthwhile, huh?"

Sam Niles looked up from where he lay on his stomach groaning, and said, "Roscoe, this just might be the night I get you in a lip lock and shut you up for good."

"Yeah, go ahead and try it, Niles," Roscoe said. "You and your friend Slate together couldn't handle me. Don't think I don't know you dopeheads go over there by Duck Island and smoke grass. You ain't fooling nobody, you two."

"Who's got grass?" piped Harold Bloomguard.

"Better knock off that talk about grass, Harold," Father Willie advised as he tried in vain to slap Spermwhale Whalen alive so he could scare Roscoe Rules and make him quit throwing his weight around.

"I told you about smokin grass, Harold!" the paralyzed Spermwhale growled. "I got nineteen and a half years on the job and that don't ring the bell. You bring any pot here and get me fired and lose my pension with only six months to go and I'll buy a whole kilo a grass. And I'll pound it right up your ass and bury your head in the dirt and let the fuckin ducks get loaded by eatin the seeds outta your shit! YOU GOT ME?"

"I was just kidding, Spermwhale," Harold gulped.

"Well I know Slate and Niles smoke grass, the fucking degenerates," said Roscoe Rules.

Actually Roscoe was partly right. Baxter and Sam *did* go down by the duck pond occasionally for an illicit drug. But it wasn't marijuana. Baxter had been dating a nurse who lived in his apartment building who was an inveterate pill popper and kept Baxter supplied with sedatives and hypnotics. So it was red capsules and yellow ones which Baxter and Sam swallowed with their booze down by the duck pond, both knowing the risks involved when they mixed the drugs with heavy drinking. In fact, Baxter Slate only seemed to want the barbiturates when he *had* been drinking excessively.

Roscoe walked over to Father Willie Wright who was telling Ora Lee Tingle how cute she was as the fat girl's head started to drop on her shoulder.

Roscoe sniffed and said, "Padre, fucking that pig without a

rubber is like playing the Rams without a helmet. Hope you got protection."

"Well I like her!" shouted Father Willie, lurching to his feet combatively. "She's better'n Frank Buck any old day. She really brings em back alive!"

"Siddown, you drunken little prick," Roscoe Rules said, shoving the chaplain to the ground, making Father Willie yell, "Darn you, Roscoe! Gosh darn you, you bully!"

"Hey, Tanaguchi!" the jealous Roscoe yelled as he saw Francis stroking Carolina's quaking buttocks. "I hear when Carolina was living with that Greek bartender he used to butt-fuck her all the time."

"Never on Sunday!" Carolina answered and Francis' giggles made Roscoe angrier.

"Her box is so big she wouldn't even feel your hand unless you wore a wristwatch," Roscoe grumbled.

"You can bet you ain't gonna know, Roscoe!" said Carolina, throwing Francis off her as she sat up and rearranged her clothing. "Cause Father Willie told me you got clap!"

"I didn't say that!" Father Willie protested. "I just told how when we were at Daniel Freeman Hospital that time you talked to the doctor about the strain you were having down there. And he said, 'Do you have a discharge, Officer?' and you said, 'Yes, Honorable.' And then you turned red when the doc and me cracked up. Oh God, that was funny!"

The chaplain rolled up in a little ball and cackled hilariously until Roscoe Rules was standing over him saying dangerously, "Padre, I thought I warned you not to tell anyone that story."

Then Father Willie sobered up and said, "Gosh I forgot, Roscoe. I'm sorry."

"I oughtta punch your lights out," Roscoe said, eyes like a cobra.

"I'm sorry, Roscoe."

"I oughtta kneedrop you right now."

"What a cunt!" Spermwhale Whalen said to Roscoe, stirring around against the tree, trying to get control of his legs so he could come over and throw Roscoe Rules in the duck pond.

Father Willie started sniveling and said, "I'm really sorry, Roscoe."

Spermwhale Whalen got disgusted with the chaplain and glared at him, saying, "What a cunt!"

And Carolina Moon squatted by the liquor case and found the Scotch all gone and thought Roscoe Rules was ruining the choir practice. She started to cry great drunken tears.

Spermwhale Whalen looked at her and said, "What a cunt!"

Carolina sniffed and said, "Thank you, Spermy. At least somebody appreciates me."

Whaddayamean Dean suddenly said, "What's it all about, Roscoe? What's it all about?"

"Oh the hell with all a you," said Roscoe Rules. "You're all a bunch a scrotes!"

The meanest choirboy took a full bottle of bourbon, the last in fact, and stalked off into the darkness to think about what he'd like to do to all of them and drink bourbon and absently pull on his whang while he fantasized.

"Gimme Scotch," said Ora Lee Tingle suddenly as her head stopped lolling.

"Ain't none," said Carolina who stopped crying and got happy again now that Roscoe was gone.

"Gimme beer," said Ora Lee Tingle as Francis Tanaguchi lurched toward the duck pond to soak his head so that he wouldn't miss the rest of the choir practice by passing out like his partner Calvin Potts who dozed next to one of Ora Lee Tingle's big legs.

"I wish we had a stereo," said Spencer Van Moot, mummified on the grass, his blanket wrapped tightly around him until only his face was exposed. "I'm older than you kids. I'd like some old music."

"I'm older than Christ Almighty," groaned Spermwhale Whalen, at last able to wiggle his fingers and toes.

"I'm old," Spencer continued, "so I remember things you kids only saw in movies. Like the big bands. They were still around when I was young. Great times. Christ, I graduated high school in 1952. Imagine that."

"I was killin gooks in 1952," Spermwhale muttered. "No offense, Francis. And that was my *second* war."

"If we had a stereo we could dance on the grass," said Spencer nostalgically.

"God, you can get sweet sometimes, Spencer," croaked Ora Lee Tingle as she crawled over and lay on top of the blanket-wrapped choirboy, making him gasp for air.

"I've got a portable stereo," offered Harold Bloomguard. "But my tweeter and woofer aren't very big."

"Get some hormone shots," offered Father Willie Wright, scrounging desperately through the debris of boxes and packages for some more beer.

"Oh, that's funny!" Carolina Moon screamed suddenly. "Francis just says he told this waitress he wanted to be a counterspy and so he leans over the counter and spies up her dress. Oh, you horny little Nip!" and she honked him so clumsily he fell to his knees groaning in pain.

"Boooo!" cried Father Willie. "Booooo! Mexican my rear end!"

"Knock it off, Padre!" said Calvin Potts. "You jist woke me up."

"Well he oughtta be able to take a little pain, he's Pancho Villa or somebody," said the choirboy chaplain, belching up some beer on his bare chest and making them all boo *him.*

The weight of Ora Lee Tingle on the blanketed Spencer Van Moot caused the choirboy to gag violently and the fat girl leaped off him surprisingly fast.

"My cop runneth over!" whooped Ora Lee Tingle, causing Harold Bloomguard to collapse in hysterical laughter in her great pink arms.

Just then Roscoe Rules, still holding his bourbon bottle which was only two thirds full, came staggering back among them. "Yeah? I'll tell you what *you* are, you big titted scrote. You're just a camp follower! A station house groupie! A cop sucker!"

Then Roscoe wheeled and headed back toward the duck pond where Spencer Van Moot was already washing his vomity blanket. Roscoe paused only for an instant by Baxter Slate's blanket and quickly grabbed a set of car keys and when he was sure no one was watching, threw them into the middle of the pond.

Then Carolina Moon started showing off. The big girl quickly overpowered Francis Tanaguchi and got him in a wristlock Spermwhale had taught her, which came in handy with rowdy customers at the cocktail lounge where she worked. As the other choirboys cheered, Carolina played rough by forcing the groaning choirboy forward until his head was on the ground and his LAPD basketball jersey was falling down over his face. Then she picked him up by the belled bottoms of his faded white jeans and started bouncing him off the grass.

"Yea, Carolina! Yea!" shouted Father Willie Wright who was still shirtless and barefoot, pacing around the wrestlers.

Then while the puffing fat girl was shaking the upside-down choirboy against her plump dimpled belly, some coins, keys, a comb and a package of prophylactics fell out of Francis' pocket causing Carolina Moon to drop him abruptly on his head.

"Rubbers!" exclaimed Carolina in sweaty disbelief, her stiff lacquered hair stuck to her face. "Rubbers! Ora Lee, this chick-enshit is carrying rubbers!"

"Pancho Villa, my rear end!" said Father Willie. "Booooo! Booooo!"

"A cundrum!" cried Carolina Moon. "This is what you think of us! I oughtta pull it over your head, you little prick!"

"Black Jack Pershing woulda whipped faggy Mexicans like Francis!" yelled Roscoe Rules from his exile in the darkness.

"I'll never forget the first time I met Carolina Moon," said Spencer Van Moot romantically as he limped back from the duck pond, smelling of vomit and rancid water, causing Carolina to scurry away from him.

"She was younger then and *so* lovely," Spencer said with a liquid burp that scared everyone. "It was before your time, guys, and I was a younger buck and this gorgeous blonde girl with bazooms like volleyballs walks up to my radio car when we're parked in the drive-in on La Brea, and she looks me right in the eyeball and says, 'Gee, I thought I blew every cop in Wilshire.' I just loved that girl from then on!"

Carolina smiled shyly and said, "Spence, honey, you're a doll. But why don't you think about going home to your wife and kiddies now? You smell awful ripe."

Spencer wrapped his blanket around him like a toga and downed a can of warm beer he found in the grass and belched perilously again. His pinky ring glittered and his little blond toothbrush moustache twitched as he breathed the night air and looked at the smog filled night sky for the great star and yearned for his lost youth.

"Gud-damn, Spencer stinks," Calvin Potts complained. "I think we better call the coroner."

"It's all right, Spencer. You look like Marcus Aurelius," Baxter Slate grinned, raising his head surprisingly well from where he had dozed for over an hour. "You long for those days when we didn't think we would fail. When we didn't think we would die! When we were *young.*"

"I heard you, Slate," a slurred gravel voice shouted from the darkness. "So don't start that faggy talk. And don't think you and Niles can sneak off and smoke pot. I'm watching you!"

"But who guards the guards, Roscoe?" Baxter yelled.

"Who said that?" Roscoe suddenly confused the voices.

"Juvenal," Baxter Slate said.

"Who you calling a juvenile?" snapped Roscoe Rules.

"Now's the time for drinking! Horace said that, Roscoe," Baxter Slate yelled.

"Horace! Horace!" answered Roscoe. "Never catch a cop with a name like that. Some faggy friend a yours, huh?"

And with his bottle of bourbon three quarters gone Roscoe Rules decided to punch Baxter Slate's faggy lights out once and for all. But he found his legs didn't work and he fell heavily on his chest and panted quietly for a moment and went to sleep.

"Yeah I remember the good old days, Spencer," said Carolina Moon who also felt nostalgic. "We was wild young kids then, Ora Lee and me. Remember how we used to say we did more to relieve policemen than the whole Los Angeles Police Relief Association?" she asked her slightly older room-mate who had fallen fast asleep and was snoring noisily.

Carolina shrugged and said, "When they put that slogan 'To Protect and To Serve' on all police cars we had one made for our Pontiac saying, 'To Protect and To Service.' One time Ora Lee and me figured we sucked off more cops than the whole police wives' association."

"Impossible!" cried Harold Bloomguard.

"Well it's true," said Carolina. "We got seven thousand cops in this town, right? And I bet there ain't five hundred whose wives belong to that group. Am I right, Spencer?"

"Right," said Spencer starting to be offended by his own smelly toga.

"Most of em are ladies, ain't they, Spencer? Probably only blew one, two policemen?" Carolina asked.

"No more than that," said Spencer Van Moot.

"My wife never even did one," Father Willie Wright noted. "That's my trouble."

"See," said Carolina to the assembly. "That means they couldn't a did more than eight hundred at most. Christ, Ora Lee and me done more than that *one* summer when we were hanging around Seventy-seventh Station!"

"They *do* have a lot of guys working down there," Spencer had to admit.

And it was finally conceded that the two girls had easily outfaced the entire police wives' association. But just as the girls were thinking about pulling that train for a couple of their favorites Francis Tanaguchi came charging into their midst from the direction of the duck pond.

"Come see what I did!" giggled the choirboy prankster.

"Whaddaya mean? Whaddaya mean?" asked Whad-dayamean Dean.

"Not now, not now," said Spencer Van Moot, leering at Carolina Moon.

"Now! Now!" said Francis Tanaguchi, shaking all the drunken choirboys.

"What's it all about? What's it all about?" cried Whad-dayamean Dean.

"Oh shit, oh shit," said Calvin Potts as Whaddayamean Dean had them all talking double action.

Carolina Moon got up and stumbled after Francis. And all the choirboys, even Spermwhale Whalen, walked or crawled toward the duck pond where Roscoe Rules slept soundly on his back with a large white duck hanging out his fly.

"My word!" said Baxter Slate.

"How'd you manage that, Francis?" asked Sam Niles, impressed out of his ennui.

"Now that's class!" mumbled Spermwhale Whalen gravely as he was finally able to stand up shakily like an enormous toddler.

"I just took some bread and sprinkled it from the water to Roscoe's crotch," giggled Francis Tanaguchi. "Then I un-zipped his pants and dropped some inside!"

"He'd a caught you he'd a said it was a faggy thing to do," Father Willie remarked.

"Boy, that duck's really working out on old Roscoe," Carolina Moon said admiringly as the fat white body worked itself between Roscoe's legs and the greedy head burrowed and ate.

"Roscoe was never one to duck a fuck, but to fuck a duck?" said Spencer Van Moot.

"Wake up, Roscoe, you cunt!" growled Spermwhale, throwing an empty beer can at Roscoe which startled the duck and made it flap and jump around.

"Don't throw things! You might hit the duck!" said Harold Bloomguard.

"Hey!" Calvin Potts said. "That sucker can't get his pecker outta Roscoe's pants!"

"They got bills not peckers," said Francis.

The choirboys watched in fascination as the duck thrashed and flapped and squawked with his head entangled in the fly of Roscoe's jockey shorts. Suddenly the meanest choirboy, who had always hated and feared the loathsome creatures, awak-ened to see one attacking his balls.

"YAAAAAA!" screamed Roscoe Rules, awakening Alexander Blaney who had been sleeping peacefully on the grass across the water.

Then there was pandemonium as the hopelessly drunk Roscoe Rules lurched to his feet and began running in circles, screaming and pulling at the duck who was panicked and quacking in rage and terror.

"Don't hurt the duck!" yelled Harold Bloomguard as several choirboys rushed to aid the creature before Roscoe broke its neck as he ran shrieking and fell headlong into the pond.

"He'll drown it!" Harold Bloomguard cried as Father Willie and Francis plunged into the water to rescue the bird.

Roscoe Rules pitched wildly in the slime and choked on filthy water and shouted for Spencer who didn't want to get his eighty dollar shoes wet.

They grabbed Roscoe and dragged him and the duck onto shore just as the bird got a death grip on the sac containing Roscoe's left testicle. Roscoe shrieked again and broke through the drunken ranks and ran bellowing toward the blankets where he had left his gun, wallet, and keys. He fell over the body of Ora Lee Tingle who woke up to blink sleepily at the dripping man standing six feet away with a fat white object swaying wildly between his legs. She said, "I don't know who *you* are, honey, but welcome to choir practice!"

"He'll break its neck!" yelled Harold Bloomguard who led the charge toward the horror stricken Roscoe Rules who was pitching wildly side to side, the duck swinging like a pendulum.

Harold tackled Roscoe at the ankles and several choirboys pulled off Roscoe's pants and extricated the bird from his shorts. Then there was more pandemonium as Roscoe Rules, naked from the waist down except for wet shoes and socks, made a screaming lunge for the gun. But by then they were crawling all over him. Sam Niles jumped on Roscoe's gun and Father Willie yelled, "Handcuffs! Anybody got some cuffs?"

"I do!" yelled Baxter Slate and ran to his gunbelt which he had wrapped in his blanket.

"Over there! Over there to the tree!" commanded Spermwhale Whalen as they dragged the kicking biting Roscoe Rules to the elm tree where he snapped and snarled like a rabid dog.

"Put his arms around the tree!" Spermwhale ordered, and then Roscoe found himself hugging the elm, his wrists locked together in front.

"I'll kill you for this!" Roscoe screamed. "I'll kill you all!"

"Don't kill me, Roscoe, I'm your pal," Father Willie belched but the half naked policeman kicked out at him with a drippy shoe.

"Did the duck hurt your dick, Roscoe?" asked Carolina Moon solicitously.

"I'll kill you for sure, you scrotes!" Roscoe howled, now kneeling against the tree, the bark rough against his wounded genitals.

"Let's just leave him alone for a few minutes," Spermwhale Whalen said. "Just leave him be."

"I think he's really mad at us this time," said Father Willie as they went back to the blankets to suck the last few drops of booze out of the empty bottles.

"I think we should make a rule, no guns at choir practice," said Harold Bloomguard.

While the handcuffed Roscoe Rules raged and cursed around the elm tree, the choirboys returned to their places because Carolina Moon announced that she was going to take her blanket off into the bushes and pull that train.

"I'm first! I'm the engineer!" cried Harold Bloomguard.

"I'm second! I'm conductor!" cried Spencer Van Moot.

"I know who rides the caboose," Father Willie pouted.

But Carolina Moon put Spermwhale Whalen's big arm around her shoulder and helped the hulking choirboy off to her nest while Calvin Potts yelled grumpily, "You're gonna die in the push-up position, Spermwhale. You oughtta slow down, man your age."

By now it was after 4:00 A.M. Alexander Blaney had gone home and was at this moment trying to explain to his bawling mother that he had been asleep alone in MacArthur Park and hadn't been bedded by a tattooed merchant seaman.

And by now Ora Lee Tingle had decided to pull her own choo choo and made public her choice of engineer.

"I want Whaddayamean Dean," she said.

"Why him? He can't even understand what we're talking about," Spencer Van Moot whined.

"Him first or nobody," said Ora Lee Tingle.

"What're you trying to say? What're you trying to say?" asked Whaddayamean Dean blankly and the choirboys cursed and swore and walked in nervous circles.

"Well I'm taking my blankets and going to the bushes in private," announced Ora Lee Tingle, "and if there's gonna be a choo choo, I better see Whaddayamean Dean first."

So then the choirboys squatted and began lightly slapping Whaddayamean Dean on the cheeks and rubbing his wrists and ankles as he stared vacantly from one to the other with a drunken, sincere, idiotic smile that chilled their hearts.

Especially when Spermwhale Whalen stepped out of the brush and said, "Train jumped the track."

"Whaddayamean? Whaddayamean?" asked Father Willie, not Whaddayamean Dean.

"I mean Carolina passed out. I guess I ain't so old after all, boys. Just wear em out is what I do."

"Well passed out or not, I'm next," whined Spencer Van Moot.

"No you ain't," said the glowering Spermwhale Whalen. "We ain't animals to take advantage of a passed-out girl!"

Then there was wailing and gnashing of teeth in MacArthur Park as several choirboys pleaded in vain with Spermwhale Whalen who of course dominated them all by his age, seniority, courage and ability to kick the living shit out of them.

"What's the matter with Ora Lee? She's conscious, ain't she?" asked Spermwhale.

"Yeah, but she wants Dean first or nobody," Father Willie whined, starting to sound like his partner Spencer Van Moot.

"I see," said Spermwhale, shaking his head sadly as he looked over at the simpering choirboy sitting on the grass, red hair tousled by Harold Bloomguard who still worked frantically massaging his wrists and neck.

Then Francis Tanaguchi sat by Whaddayamean Dean, telling him exaggerated lascivious impossible things that Ora Lee Tingle was going to do to him, and Father Willie shouted, "That's exactly what the Dragon Lady promised to do to *me* the night she phoned and made my wife punch me in the eye! Now I *know* who the Dragon Lady works for, ya dirty Godless heathen little fuck, ya!"

And temporarily everyone forgot Ora Lee and looked at Father Willie in astonishment because he had uttered the second vulgarity of his life.

"I can't help it," Father Willie said sheepishly. "That was the dirtiest trick anyone ever played on me."

"Lemme try," said Calvin Potts. "Since Dean can't understand regular English I think you should talk to him like we talked to the whores in Vietnam. We always managed to communicate and they couldn't talk no English."

Several choirboys agreed that it was worth a try, so Calvin knelt in front of the placid redhead whose face from eyebrows to chin was caked with dried barbecue sauce and tried pidgin.

"Ora Lee like bang bang. Her plenty good. All time bang bang. Plenty good. You sabby?"

And Whaddayamean Dean clapped his hands happily and chuckled.

"Jesus, you're just entertaining him," said Spencer Van Moot. "That ain't getting us nowhere. He ain't a gook. That rice paddy talk ain't the answer."

"You got a better idea?" Calvin asked.

"Yeah I do," said Spencer. "I been analyzing this. He's sitting there now with the mind of a three year old, right?"

"Approximately," nodded Harold Bloomguard.

"Okay," said Spencer. "We couldn't tell a three year old to go screw in the bushes, could we? You have to talk to a three year old *like* a three year old."

Spencer Van Moot elbowed Calvin out of the way and squatted in front of Whaddayamean Dean. "Spencer has secret for Deanie," Spencer said desperately. "Ora Lee loves Deanie. Ora Lee take Deanie and blow up like biiiiiig balloon!" And Spencer Van Moot drew a biiiiiig sausage-shaped balloon in the air before the watery eyes of Whaddayamean Dean who sat cross legged in his barbecue-stained Bugs Bunny sweatshirt and clapped his hands like an infant. And squealed.

"My God, he's regressing," said Harold Bloomguard grimly.

"He'll be spitting up in a minute," Father Willie observed.

"We'll have to burp him, for chrissake," said Francis Tanaguchi.

"All right, all right, outta the way!" said Spermwhale Whalen, staggering forward and sitting on the grass next to the simpering redhead who now had his hands folded uselessly in his lap, his brain marinated.

"Gimme a can a beer," Spermwhale said and Baxter Slate flipped him one.

While the other choirboys watched, Spermwhale popped it open and soaked a paper napkin in beer and sat in front of Dean and washed all the barbecue from his face and plastered down the tangle of hair as Whaddayamean Dean sat unprotesting.

When the young man was cleaned up Spermwhale said, "Listen, Dean. Listen, son. It's me, your da da. It's Spermwhale. You know me, don't ya?"

And Whaddayamean Dean licked his chops happily and cried, "Beer! Beer!"

"No no," said Spermwhale Whalen. "First you listen. Then beer beer. Get it?"

Whaddayamean Dean eyed them all craftily and chuckled at some private joke.

"Now, Dean, my boy, we been pals awhile and I know you trust old Spermwhale. So listen careful. This thing that booze does to you, turnin you into a carrot, this ain't a good thing for you. You gotta master the effect a that booze. I been doin it for years. Remember when I flew us on that Palm Springs raid, dead drunk?"

And Whaddayamean Dean filled their hearts with hope, for he nodded at all of them.

"That's right!" Spermwhale said. "You *do* remember! See, I *know* you understand. Just concentrate. Okay, so here's what's happened tonight. Old Spermwhale's just too much man and screwed old Carolina Moon till she went fast asleep. Now that means there's only Ora Lee Tingle to pull that train for a few a the boys. And guess what? She picked *you* first. And *that* means you gotta go over there behind those bushes and show Ora Lee what a sport you are. And then maybe a couple a other fellas can get on the track. Get it?"

But Whaddayamean Dean cocked his head and wrinkled his brow in confusion and filled their hearts with dread.

"I'll make it simpler, son," said Spermwhale. "You just gotta go over there and do a number on Ora Lee, that's all you gotta do. So I want you to stand up now and show these fellas that my boy ain't no radish. Now you just listen to old Spermwhale and go over there and fuck old Ora Lee's socks off. Get it?"

The eager ring of faces shone sweatily in the moonlight and no one breathed as the grinning simpering redhead struggled valiantly with the words. They came and went from his consciousness and at times almost hung together coherently.

Finally he looked Spermwhale Whalen dead in the eye and raised a hand to the oldest choirboy's pink jowls and said sincerely, "Whaddayamean, Spermwhale? Just tell me what you *mean.*"

And then eight choirboys—minus Roscoe Rules who was handcuffed to a tree and Whaddayamean Dean who sat and flashed a bewildered smile—beat their own heads with their fists or strangled phantoms in the air or showed white eyeballs and groaned pitifully.

Suddenly Spermwhale Whalen roared to his feet and grabbed Dean by the belt and the back of the shirt and lifted him four feet in the air as Harold Bloomguard yelled, "Don't hurt him, Spermwhale!"

And Baxter Slate shouted, "He can't help it, Spermwhale!"

And Spencer Van Moot yelled, "Kill the fucking idiot!"

And Whaddayamean Dean broke into tears and bawled, "Why's everyone picking on me? I don't get it! I don't get it!"

Spermwhale Whalen carried the weeping choirboy toward the bushes, toward Ora Lee Tingle and threw the redhead on top of the snoozing fat girl. "There!" Spermwhale bellowed. "You stupid goofy simple minded idiotic fuckin moron! Is exactly WHAT I MEAN!"

"Oh hi, Dean honey," said Ora Lee Tingle, waking up and pulling him down on her bulk.

The whimpering choirboy wiped his eyes on his sweatshirt and sniffled and looked back at Spermwhale and the others and then down to the fat girl he was sitting on as she licked her lips seductively.

"Oh!" said Whaddayamean Dean. "Oh! Why didn't you say so? Now I get it! Now I get it!"

And the choirboys sighed in unison and staggered back to their blankets and fell to the ground in relief.

Meanwhile, a fifty-one year old insomniac hairdresser who lived in an Alvarado Street hotel had come for a very early morning stroll through the cool invigorating darkness of MacArthur Park and found a man nude from the waist down sitting beside an elm tree with his arms enveloping the trunk. The hairdresser's name was Luther Quigly and it was the most carnal erotic sight he had ever seen. It was his wildest libidinous fantasy come true.

"My God! My God!" Luther Quigly whispered.

"Who's there?" Roscoe exclaimed.

"Oh!" said Luther Quigly. "Oh!" And the tiny balding hairdresser leaned back against a eucalyptus and tried to calm his pounding heart.

"Who're you?" Roscoe demanded, suffering terrible pain in

his shoulders and back from having been totally forgotten by the drunken choirboys.

"Anyone you want me to be," answered Luther Quigly.

"Listen, goddamnit, go over by the duck pond. There's some drunks there. Go get one of em!"

"Who needs anyone else?" gasped Luther Quigly. "Three's a crowd!"

"I do! I'm chained to this tree!"

"Chained!" cried Luther Quigly. It was truly a mad salacious fantasy! It just couldn't be! A man naked except for his shirt and shoes! *Chained* to a tree!

"Oh, my lord!" cried Luther Quigly, getting faint.

Roscoe scurried around the elm, keeping it between himself and Luther Quigly, saying, "Stay away from me! I'll kill you you touch me, you faggy son of a bitch! I'll kneedrop you, so help me! I'll puncture your kidneys! I'll rupture your spleen! SPERMWHALE!"

Then Luther Quigly heard running footsteps across the grass. He jumped up and fled toward Seventh Street and ran all the way home to sit shakily in his room and wonder if it had all been a fantasy after all. He decided it had and called his psychiatrist later that morning.

The choirboys were full of apologies when they took the handcuffs off Roscoe Rules and brought him his wet underwear and pants.

"We forgot, Roscoe," said Harold Bloomguard.

"Real sorry, fella," said Spermwhale Whalen.

"Forgive us, Roscoe, forgive us," said Father Willie.

"It was that goddamn Dean," said Spencer. "We got preoccupied and forgot."

"You okay, man? How's your wrists?" said Calvin Potts.

Roscoe betrayed nothing in his manner as he put on his underwear and wrung out his pants, stepping into each soppy leg, and walked slowly and deliberately back toward his blanket.

"Roscoe, wait up a minute, will ya?" Spermwhale said, the first to get suspicious. He tried to trot past Roscoe who was heading directly toward his belongings.

But he was too late. Roscoe broke into a mad thirty yard sprint as Spermwhale screamed, "THE GUN!"

Seconds later Roscoe Rules was running back toward the ducking diving fleeing choirboys with his four inch magnum in his hand. Sphincter muscles and bladders were loosening all around and Francis Tanaguchi thought he was dead for sure as three explosions deafened the closest choirboys.

Harold Bloomguard was the first to look up and see Roscoe Rules insanely wading into the duck pond blasting away at the birds whose bills had been tucked securely under their wings but now squawked and flapped and swam for their lives from the orange fireballs and the terrifying explosions. Then when he clicked three times on empty cylinders Roscoe caught a hapless duck by the throat and tried to pistol-whip it and punch its lights out and drag it to shore where he could knee-drop it, rupturing its spleen.

"Stop him!" screamed Francis Tanaguchi.

"Get the gun!" yelled Spermwhale Whalen.

"Save the duck!" yelled Harold Bloomguard while five frightened choirboys jumped on Roscoe and took away his gun and held his head under water for twenty seconds.

Then they dragged him and the duck onto the shore as Roscoe bellowed, "Lemme go! Lemme go! I'll strangle that cocksucker! I'll make that fuckin duck do the chicken!"

And as they pried the duck's neck from Roscoe's fist he swung a left and a right, the first of which socked the hissing bird on the bill, the second of which caught Spermwhale Whalen in the eye. There was yet a third punch thrown, this by Spermwhale, and it knocked the rabies right out of Roscoe.

The choir practice ended in a hurry with everyone running to his car to get away in case someone heard the shots and was calling the police. Unfortunately Roscoe could not leave, not after he discovered it was his own set of keys he had thrown into the middle of the pond. He waded in the buttery mud and dove in the mucky water until daybreak.

The quietus was uttered by Ora Lee Tingle as she and Carolina Moon were bouncing half dressed across the grass toward Park View Street at 5:00 A.M.

She turned and yelled, "It was a swell choir practice, fellas! And don't worry, Roscoe, we ain't gonna start calling you a duck socker!"

13

Catullus

It was two weeks after that memorable choir practice before there was talk of going to MacArthur Park. Roscoe's shootout with the ducks had unnerved everyone and had caused ten choirboys and two cocktail waitresses to study the newspapers the next day for any mention of persons hit with stray bullets in the vicinity of the park. There was none. They were ready to try again. It was scheduled for a Thursday night near the end of August. Harold Bloomguard intended to make sure all the choirboys left their guns in their cars.

"We can't have any more shooting at ducks," Harold had informed the others.

"How about shooting at fags?" Roscoe Rules had remarked.

"Believe it or not it's kind of nice to get back in a radio car after two weeks on vice," said Sam Niles to Harold Bloomguard the Tuesday night before.

"I was getting tired of those smelly rest rooms," Harold agreed as he blew a spit bubble against the steering wheel.

Sam slouched in the black and white and glanced languidly at the traffic which was light at this time of night. He didn't mind when Harold drove toward the Miracle Mile for a change of scenery.

"Remember the whore who lived there?" asked Sam as they passed a freshly painted lemon and white townhouse apartment building.

"Yeah, sometimes vice was fun," said Harold.

Then Sam Niles said something he would profoundly regret: "Just for kicks, drive by Gina Summers' apartment, right off Wilshire."

"Who?"

"That sadist whore, the one who takes those special tricks and does a number on them in her little torture chamber."

"Oh yeah," Harold said. "I never did see her. I remember you and Baxter talking about her."

"Wanna see if she's undressing up by her window tonight?" Sam asked. "Then you can see her. Tits like avocados."

"All *right!*" Harold said.

When Harold pulled to the curb beside Gina Summers' apartment and turned the lights out, Sam Niles said, "Yeah, she's home. See the light up there in the sixth floor corner apartment? Just sit for a minute, see if she parades in front of the window naked."

"Got lots of time." Harold had his eyes glued to the light.

But after they sat for five minutes Harold got antsy and said, "Well?"

"No action tonight. Let's split," said Sam.

Just then Gina Summers walked in front of the window, a long piece of leather draped around her neck. She unbuttoned her blouse and stood naked to the waist, the leather resting on one breast as she lowered the shade.

"Outta sight!" Harold Bloomguard exclaimed.

"Harold, that was a man's belt, wasn't it?" Sam Niles asked.

"It was a long fat leather belt. Mighta been a whip!"

"Goddamn. She's got a trick up there."

"So what?"

"So what? Do you know that Scuz had Baxter and I stake out four nights straight trying to close the vice complaint on this bitch? We never got close. Now she's got a trick up there. And she's got her whip!"

"So? We're not working vice anymore."

"It's police work, isn't it? Besides, Scuz'd get his rocks off if a couple of bluesuits brought in Gina Summers on a vice pinch when his squad's been working on her so long."

"Come on, Sam," Harold said. "It's only a lousy misdemeanor like Scuz always said. Besides we can't sneak and peek in full uniform."

"Let's try. You might get to see her bare ass, Harold."

"That's different. Let's go," Harold Bloomguard said, and the partners gathered up their hats and flashlights and locked the radio car.

"But how the hell we gonna get a violation?" Harold asked.

They crossed the street, looking up at the lighted window, entered the unlocked apartment building, took the carpeted stairs two at a time, clear to the fourth floor.

"We have to be able to hear the offer and the action," Sam said.

"That's impossible," Harold answered, puffing up the stairs.

"I've got good ears."

"Scuz said never to perjure yourself for a chickenshit vice arrest, remember?"

"Don't worry. Did you see the fire escape by her window? Baxter and I always had it planned if we saw a trick inside we'd go out on the fire escape. It's only three feet from her bedroom. I'm positive I could hear anything that was happening from there."

"Well," Harold shrugged and then they stopped and rested on the fifth landing.

Harold longed for the elevator. But he knew why Sam disliked the confinement.

At last they reached the sixth floor, and while Harold Bloomguard had second and third thoughts about doing vice work in uniform, Sam Niles climbed out on the fire escape and was squatting in the darkness catching his breath. Then Sam heard female laughter and a muffled male voice in Gina Summers' bedroom.

He took off his hat and glasses and wiped his forehead on his blue woolen shirtsleeve and cleaned his glasses with his handkerchief, catching a breeze near the rooftops.

He listened. The voices were low but after three minutes he heard a woman's voice say, "Is *this* what you want?"

And then the crack of leather and a man's gasp of pain.

"I can do better, honey. This isn't much," said the woman's voice again, followed by another crack and a man's cry and then another crack and a groan.

Then the woman's voice got more husky and guttural. She said, "You feel like you belong to me now, don't you, baby? Well you do, you bastard! You worthless son of a bitch! Right now Gina *owns* you! You're not a man. You're an animal! Gina's animal!"

Then there were three cracks of leather and unbroken groaning. Sam Niles was chilled from the rib cage to the top of his head and furiously beckoned for Harold to climb out on the fire escape.

"But I can do better." The woman's laugh was like a bark. "I can *really* hurt, baby, you give me a chance. There's no extra charge. Same price."

And the man whimpered and moaned. Then there were three quick sharp cracks. And silence.

Harold Bloomguard crawled through the window and huddled next to his partner during the quiet moments.

"We've got it," Sam whispered. "Goddamnit, we've got it. I heard it. The money offer. The act."

Sam crawled back through the window into the hallway and Harold followed him down the hall where they ducked into an alcove.

"I heard her saying something about no extra charge," Sam said. "I heard the act. It's a good legal pinch!"

"What act? Screwing?"

"No. She's whipping some guy!"

"Far out!" whistled Harold Bloomguard. "I sure never made a bust like this. Sex, money. We got her for prostitution. And him. Wait, is whipping considered a sex act?"

"I think so," Sam Niles said, putting his hat on and pushing his glasses up on his nose. "Isn't it?"

"You got me. I haven't had that fantasy yet," said Harold Bloomguard who thought he probably would by the time he got in bed tonight.

"Let's go. I say we've got her," Sam said. "We'll just wait until he comes out . . ."

"Can't we knock? I don't wanna waste the whole night here. I haven't eaten all day."

"Okay, let's go. They're probably through by now. Unless he's gonna let her beat him to death."

While Harold stood back against the wall Sam Niles knocked at the door. There was no response so he knocked again, saying, "Miss Summers!"

Then they heard frantic footsteps and a woman's voice, soft and sultry now. "Who is it?"

"Assistant manager, Miss Summers. There's a gas leak on this floor, ma'am. We're evacuating the building."

The door opened a few inches, but before she could slam it, Sam Niles shouldered it wide open and the naked girl was thrown back against the wall saying, "Hey, what's the big idea?" as both policemen rushed into the apartment past the naked brunette.

"Just go in the room there with my partner while I have a talk with your friend," Sam Niles said as he rushed down the hall to arrest the other party to the prostitution.

Then he was in the bedroom face to face with the customer who was putting on his pants. Shivering. Sweat soaked. Face like alabaster.

"Baxter!" Sam Niles gasped. Freezing in his tracks. Face to face with Baxter Slate who was naked to the waist, his body wet and gleaming.

Then Sam heard Gina Summers threatening Harold Bloomguard with false arrest while Harold nodded placatingly and leered at her naked breasts.

Sam Niles closed the bedroom door and Baxter Slate went to the window and looked out and choked off a sob. Sam Niles stared at the ugly raw welts and stripes on Baxter's body which already were swelling and said, "Why, Baxter?"

Then Sam went to a chair and sat. And disbelieved. He removed his hat and ran his hand through his hair and looked at his friend who wiped his pale sweating face with a shirt but never turned from the window.

"Why?" groaned Sam Niles who couldn't take his eyes from Baxter's welted flesh.

"What's happening, Sam?" called Harold Bloomguard from

the hall outside where Gina Summers was demanding to call her lawyer.

Yet she made no move to the phone nor to the closet where her robes hung with the whips and boots and exotic underwear. Harold Bloomguard went on explaining the arrest to her while she stood nude, hands on her hips.

"I thought we didn't work vice anymore, Sam," Baxter said finally with a quivering smile which was nothing, *nothing* like a Baxter Slate smile. He went to the bed and sat, his wounded back still turned to his friend.

"Why?" Sam Niles asked. "Why?"

"I don't know for sure, Sam."

"Does she know you're a cop?"

"No, of course not."

Sam Niles lit a cigarette and sighed and turned from the sight of Baxter's tortured flesh and said, "I'll tell her it was a mistake. She'll be damn glad not to be hitting the slammer so she won't ask any questions of me."

"And Harold?"

"I'll tell Harold the guy in the room was a deputy from the sheriff's department and I decided to give him a break. I can take care of Harold. You tell that fucking whore you bought me off for fifty bucks. Then everybody's happy."

When Sam stood and turned to go out the door, Baxter Slate called desperately, "Sam!"

"What is it, Baxter?" Sam answered without looking at his friend.

"It's . . . it's just that I was afraid to park my own car near here. I took a cab from Pico and La Brea. And I gave her every dime. Well . . . ," and then he tried another twisted smile which was so unlike Baxter Slate's easy grin it made Sam Niles want to turn and run. "Could you maybe drop Harold at the station and think of some excuse to come back? I could use the ride. I'm too weak to walk, Sam."

Then Sam dug in his pockets and found seven dollars and some change. "Here!" he said, throwing the money on the bed. "Catch a cab!"

"You . . . you couldn't . . . I wouldn't mind waiting if you could drive me, Sam. I could wait out front. . . . I'd really appreciate . . . I could maybe meet you after you get off work and talk . . . explain . . ."

"Goddamnit, I gave you my last dollar for a cab! What the fuck do you want from me?"

"Nothing, Sam. Nothing. Thanks for the money," said Baxter Slate.

And as Sam Niles jerked the bedroom door open he heard Baxter Slate say, "It's not evil, Sam. I haven't enough dignity to be evil."

Then Sam was stalking down the hall to the living room where Gina Summers was sidling up to Harold Bloomguard and trying to convince him that his partner could not possibly have heard what he thought he heard and why doesn't everyone just forget the whole thing?

"Come on, let's go, Harold," Sam said.

"Go?"

"Yeah, go. We made a mistake."

"A mistake?"

"Goddamnit, let's go! We made a mistake!"

As Sam started for the front door with his bewildered partner trailing behind, Gina Summers then made the mistake of saying, "Well I coulda told you that. You'll be lucky if I don't sue over this. You'll be lucky . . ."

She was astonished by how quickly Sam Niles moved as he whirled and grabbed her by the throat and pinched off the carotid artery with his powerful right hand. Gina Summers came up off the floor, naked, clinging to his wrist with both hands, fighting for breath, gaping at Sam Niles' unblinking iron gray eyes, slightly magnified by his steel rimmed glasses.

"If I *ever* hear you complain about *anything,*" he whispered, "I'll be back here. And if you're not here I'll be where you are, baby. You groove on handing out pain? Well maybe you don't know what it is to *feel* pain. I'll show you. Can you dig it?"

And as Gina Summers nodded and gripped his wrist and gurgled, Sam Niles released her throat and she fell to her knees, gasping. The two policemen burst out the door quicker than they had come in.

Sam Niles literally hurtled down those six flights, leaving Harold half a landing behind. He hated Harold Bloomguard like he never had before. As he hated Baxter Slate. They were weaklings. They were bleeders. They were sick, wretched, disgusting.

Sam Niles got dizzy as he flew down those stairs and swung past the landings holding the handrails. Hating them. They bleed. They need. Like the Moaning Man as he lay there bleeding and needing past the grave. Hands reaching out. They never let you alone. Reaching past death. Until someone touched them. He despised them all. He hated them as he had hated his weak sick disgusting parents. Sam Niles had never needed anyone. Except for one minute, sixty seconds in his life.

He stopped on the last landing and waited for the puffing little man who had seen him need that one time. And he feared that if Harold had *ever* mentioned that moment in the suffocating blackness of that cave, he would now, at this moment, draw his revolver and shoot him dead on the staircase. But Harold had never talked about it. Not even to Sam. Sam hoped that Harold had somehow forgotten it in his own terrible fear. Sometimes Sam Niles even believed that it never had happened.

"What's the hurry, Sam?" Harold stammered, trying to catch his breath before the last flight of steps. Never once suggesting they use the elevator because he understood his partner better than his partner dreamed. "What's the rush?"

"Nothing," Sam said viciously. "There's no rush. None at all."

Five minutes later in the car Sam Niles shouted, "Goddamnit, he was a deputy sheriff I know from court! You don't know him. Never mind his fucking name. I wanted to give him a break. He told me he had a wife and kids and was going to a psychiatrist. I made a decision and I DON'T WANT TO EVER TALK ABOUT IT AGAIN!"

And though they never did, Harold Bloomguard scratched his neck with a penknife and blew spit bubbles not only that night but the next afternoon when Baxter Slate suddenly called off sick, saying he had the flu. Harold heard Sam Niles question Baxter's partner Spermwhale Whalen as to whether he had heard from Baxter. Harold saw that Sam seemed troubled that Spermwhale had not.

When Baxter Slate did not come to work the Thursday of choir practice and Sam Niles was jumpy as a cat while putting on his uniform, Harold Bloomguard developed a brand new rash all over his neck and began to suspect that Gina Summers' trick was not a deputy sheriff after all.

The choirboys were happy that Thursday afternoon in the assembly room because Sergeant Nick Yanov was conducting the rollcall alone. But Nick Yanov entered the room grimly and didn't seem to hear a few jokes directed his way from men in the front row. Though his jaws were as dark and fierce as always from his incredibly thick whiskers which he had shaved only three hours earlier, his forehead and Baltic cheekbones were white. He was white around the eyes. His hands were unsteady when he lit a cigarette. The men quieted down. Something was very wrong with Nick Yanov.

He took a deep puff on the cigarette, sucked it into his lungs and said, "Baxter Slate's dead. They just found him in his apartment. Shot himself. Spermwhale, you'll be working a report car tonight. Seven-U-One is your unit. Would you like to go down now and get your car?"

The rollcall room was deathly still for a moment. No one moved or spoke as Nick Yanov waited for Spermwhale. One could hear the hum of the wall clock. Spermwhale Whalen finally said to the sergeant, "Are you *sure?*"

"Go on down and get your car, Spermwhale," said Nick Yanov quietly. But as shaky as Spermwhale looked when he gathered his things and walked through the door, Harold Bloomguard looked even shakier when he looked at Sam Niles who had broken out in a violent sweat and had ripped open his collar and was having trouble getting enough air.

Then Sam jumped up and burst through the door behind Spermwhale Whalen. Harold Bloomguard started up, thought better of it and sat back down.

Nick Yanov called the roll and dismissed the watch without another word.

There was speculation and many rumors in the parking lot about Baxter Slate's suicide, and several members of the Wilshire nightwatch spent a lingering fearful evening handling calls, cruising, smoking silently, trying to avoid thinking of that most terminal of all policemen's diseases. Wondering how one catches it and how one avoids it.

None of the choirboys took the initiative to do police work that night. It was as though a monotonous routine would be somehow comforting, reassuring. The only thing out of the ordinary done by a nightwatch radio car was that 7-A-29 drove to West Los Angeles Police Station, the area in which Baxter Slate had resided because he loved Westwood Village and the cultural activities at UCLA and the theater which showed foreign films and a small unpretentious French restaurant with wonderful wines.

"I'd like to see the homicide team. Whoever's handling Officer Slate's suicide," Sam Niles said to the lone detective in the squad room.

"All gone home, Officer. Can you come back tomorrow?"

The detective wasn't much older than Sam and like Sam he had a moustache. His suit coat was thrown over a chair. He wore an uncomfortable looking shoulder holster.

"I'd like to see the death report on Baxter Slate," Sam Niles said.

"I can't go into homicide's cases. Come back tomorrow. You can talk to . . ."

"Please," said Sam Niles. "I only want to see the report. Please."

And the detective was about to refuse, but he looked at Harold Bloomguard who turned and walked out of the office, and he looked at Sam Niles who did not walk away. He looked at Sam's face and asked, "Was he a friend?"

"Please let me see the report. I have to see it. I don't know why."

"Have a seat," the detective said and walked to a filing cabinet drawer marked "Suicides—1974" and pulled out a manila folder, removed the pictures in the file which Sam Niles definitely did not want to see and gave the file to the choirboy.

Sam read the perfunctory death report which listed the landlady as the person discovering the body. The person hearing the shot was a neighbor, Mrs. Flynn. He saw that Baxter's mother who was in Hawaii had not been contacted as yet. His married sister in San Diego was the nearest relative notified.

The speckled pup which Baxter had been caring for since he found her on the street outside Wilshire Station was taken to the animal shelter where she would soon be as dead as her master. The narrative told him nothing except that Baxter had fired one shot into his mouth at 11:00 A.M. that morning on a sunny smogless delightful day.

In the file was a note to the milkman which Baxter had written asking that two quarts of skim milk be left. The hand-writing was scratchy, halting, not the sure flowing stroke of Baxter Slate. No more than that horrible grimace of consummate humiliation in Gina Summers' apartment had been a Baxter Slate grin.

The report said that several books were scattered around the table where the body was found. Baxter Slate had gone to his classics at the end. Disjointedly. Desperately. The detective had torn several pages from the clothbound texts. He had thought the pages marked by that same spidery scrawl might prove enlightening.

One marked passage from Socrates read: "No evil can happen to a good man, either in life or after death."

Another from Euripides said: "When good men die their goodness does not perish, but lives though they are gone. As for the bad, all that was theirs dies and is buried with them."

Baxter had marked a passage from Cicero, the only one not specifically mentioning good and evil and death. It made Sam Niles moan aloud which startled the nightwatch detective. It said: "He removes the greatest ornament of friendship who takes away from it respect."

Sam removed his glasses and cleaned them before reading the last page. The page was powdery from dried blood. Sam's hands were shaking so badly the nightwatch detective was alarmed. Sam read it and left the squad room without thanking the detective for his help. The passage was underlined. It simply said: "What is it, Catullus? Why do you not make haste to die?"

14

The Moaning Man

At the end of that tour of duty on the day Baxter Slate died, the choirboys were more anxious for a choir practice than they had ever been. When Father Willie asked quietly, "Are we still going to have choir practice?" Spencer Van Moot said angrily, "Of *course* we're having choir practice. What the fuck's wrong with you?"

Never had the choirboys drunk so obsessively in MacArthur Park. They were snarling at each other and guzzling sullenly, all except Roscoe who had gotten a station call to transfer an overflow of five drunks from Wilshire to Central Jail and had not yet shown up at choir practice by 1:00 A.M.

Before they could be too thankful for the absence of Roscoe a blue panel truck appeared from nowhere, grinding and rumbling across the grass in MacArthur Park with its lights out, clanking to a stop under the trees in the darkest shadows.

"I was hopin I could get drunk painlessly," Calvin Potts said as Roscoe Rules, still in uniform, jumped out of the drunk wagon and came trotting across the grass.

"Hey!" yelled Roscoe *cheerfully*, which was enough to make everyone mad to begin with, "I was on my way back to the station but I couldn't wait to tell you!"

"Tell us what, Roscoe?" Spermwhale grumbled. He was lying on his blanket, a can of beer on his huge stomach, looking up at the moonless, smog-filled summer sky which even hid Baxter Slate's great star.

"Down at Central Jail after I transported the drunks I ran into a guy I know. Works homicide downtown. Guess what they found when the coroner posted Baxter Slate's body? Whip marks! All over his back! Whip marks! They think he musta been a pervert. I always said he was weird, but whip marks!"

"What? What did you say?" Sam Niles said as he sat in the darkness on the cool grass and cut his hands when he suddenly tore an empty beer can in half.

"Well I liked him as much as the next guy," said Roscoe, "but kee-rist, whip marks on his back! The dicks think he was some kind a freak or pervert. You know how faggy he always talked . . ."

Then Roscoe Rules was even more astonished than Gina Summers had been at how quickly Sam Niles could move. Roscoe was hit twice with each of Sam's fists before he fell heavily on his back. Sam lifted him by the front of his uniform and hit him so hard the third time that Sam's glasses flew farther than the chip from Roscoe's tooth.

Spermwhale Whalen overpowered Sam and several others restrained Roscoe who tried to kneedrop Sam as he lay pinned to the ground by Spermwhale, and the park was alive with shouting choirboys and quacking ducks, and four park fairies came running to the sounds of fighting.

Father Willie Wright staggered drunkenly over to examine the body of Roscoe Rules who fell in the bushes just as a park fairy said, "A policeman! What happened to him?"

"Stand back, give him room to breathe," commanded Father Willie. "Lemme work on him."

"Are you a doctor?" asked the second park fairy.

"I'm a priest," answered Father Willie as Spermwhale roared the fairies away.

"People like you killed him!" Sam Niles yelled as Spermwhale Whalen enveloped him in his enormous arms and pinned him to the ground saying, "Calm down, kid. Calm down."

"I'll kill *you,* you scrote!" screamed the revived Roscoe Rules as three choirboys held him and took away his gun.

"Shut up, Roscoe!" Spermwhale barked as Sam Niles began to weep for the first time since the spider holes. But only Spermwhale saw and he said softly, "Listen, son, Roscoe's an asshole but he didn't kill Baxter."

"I'll puncture your kidneys and rupture your spleen, Niles!" screamed the thrashing Roscoe Rules.

Now that Spermwhale was sure he could release his grip on Sam Niles he did so. Spermwhale then stood up and walked across the grass to the pile of bodies on the ground and said, "Roscoe, if you don't get your mind together and relax, I'm gonna relax you."

And he held up a big red fist which Roscoe Rules remembered.

After that it was only a matter of everyone dusting Roscoe's uniform off and apologies all around except from Sam Niles who stalked off to the duck pond to sit and drink and try not to think of Baxter Slate.

Roscoe Rules rubbed his lumpy jaw and touched the broken tooth with his tongue and became appeased by everyone apologizing for Sam Niles and patting him on the shoulder and being nice which he was totally unused to. And Roscoe said, "I'm already long past end-of-watch. I'll just have a beer before I drive the wagon back in."

With the police drunk wagon parked on the grass in MacArthur Park under the trees, Roscoe sat there in uniform and had a beer which led to three while Sam Niles drank Scotch without mercy to his flaming throat and stomach. He relentlessly sought the intellectual oblivion which alcohol brought to Whaddayamean Dean Pratt.

At 2:00 A.M. Harold Bloomguard walked quietly up behind his brooding partner and startled him by saying, "Sam, let's talk."

"I've got nothing to talk about, Harold. Leave me alone."

"We have to talk."

"Look, goddamn you. You got problems? A new neurosis that's bothering you? Eat your fucking gun. Like Baxter. But leave me alone."

"I don't wanna talk, Sam. I wanna listen. Please talk to me. About Baxter. About anything you want."

But Sam Niles cursed and struggled to his knees and pushed up his drooping glasses and held up a fist bloodied by Roscoe's teeth and said: "I don't need you. I've *never* needed you. Or anybody. Now you get away from me. YOU LEAVE ME ALONE!"

Harold Bloomguard nodded and trudged back to his blanket, back to the others, and drank silently.

At 2:30 A.M. Spencer Van Moot said, "Hey, Roscoe, don't start on the hard stuff. You're sitting here in uniform, case you didn't know. And that funny blue wagon over there is a police vehicle."

"So bust me for drunk driving," Roscoe giggled, the pain in his jaw almost anesthetized by now. "Besides, Ora Lee and Carolina might be here soon and they ain't never seen how good looking I am in uniform."

"I wish he'd just walk toward Duck Island till his hat floats," said Calvin Potts.

The choirboys drank quietly and speculated about Baxter Slate and felt the closeness of death and stole glances at Roscoe's gun and thought how near and familiar the instrument always was to men who somehow contract this policeman's disease. They wondered if the closeness and familiarity of the instrument had something to do with it or was it the nature of the work which Baxter always called emotionally perilous? Or was it a clutch of other things? And since they didn't know they drank. And drank.

It was a miserable choir practice. All attempts at jokes fell flat. Harold often looked toward the duck pond where Sam was drinking himself into paralysis but did not go to him. Whaddayamean Dean got on a usual crying jag but this time he cried without respite. Spermwhale took him away from the others and put him down on his blanket and gave him a pint of bourbon.

"Spermwhale! Spermwhale!" Dean cried. "Baxter's dead! Baxter's dead!"

"I know, son. I know," said Spermwhale Whalen, leaving Dean to drink alone on the grass on a gloomy night under a very black sky.

They were grateful that Ora Lee and Carolina didn't show up that night. Finally as the moon misted over, Spermwhale looked at the glowing Roscoe Rules and said, "Roscoe, you better get that fuckin wagon back to the station. You're gettin swacked."

"You guys gonna be here when I come back?"

"I'm going home," said the miserable Francis Tanaguchi.

"Gimme that fuckin Scotch," said Calvin Potts as he raised himself up on an elbow.

"I'm going home too," said Father Willie Wright who was sitting quietly by the trees.

Then Spencer Van Moot stood and tried to walk toward the pond but fell flat on his face.

"Jesus!" said Spermwhale as three choirboys struggled to their feet dizzily and tried to pick up their groaning comrade.

"He can't drive home," Father Willie said.

"Somebody drive him home," said Spermwhale. "Padre, why don't you drive his car to the station parking lot and one of us'll take him home?"

But then the body of Spencer Van Moot reacted logically to the abuse being done to it. Spencer sat up and retched and vomited all over himself in enormous bilious waves as the choirboys cursed and scattered.

And that normal physical reaction sealed the fate of a human being in that park.

"Oh shit, he's *covered* with puke!" Francis Tanaguchi said.

"Oh gross!" said Harold Bloomguard.

"I ain't taking him in *my* car," said Calvin Potts who strangely enough could not get drunk while thinking of the suicide of Baxter Slate.

"Okay, okay," said Spermwhale. "Put him in the back of the wagon. Roscoe, you drive him to the station parking lot. Padre, you drive his car there and put him in it and let him sleep it off for a few hours. I'll get up at six o'clock or so and go down to the station and wake him up so he can get cleaned up before anybody notices him."

"Can't he sleep in the wagon all night?" offered Roscoe.

"Fuck no, stupid!" said Spermwhale. "A sergeant finds him there tomorrow he'll get racked. Do like I say."

"Well who's gonna put him in the wagon now? I don't wanna touch him!"

"Goddamnit, get outta the way," Spermwhale said. He grabbed the semiconscious Spencer by the feet and dragged him across the grass and rolled him over on his stomach and back to wipe off some of the vomit. Then he and Calvin Potts took his wrists and ankles and flipped him up to the floor of the wagon and got inside and lifted him up on the bench.

"Better put him on the floor," Father Willie said. "He'll fall off the way Roscoe drives."

As Spencer Van Moot was being ministered to and as Sam Niles was finding himself too drunk to get to his feet and was searching in vain for Baxter Slate's great star Jupiter, an eighteen year old boy was strolling toward Sam on the other side of the pond, tossing bread crumbs to the ducks, making hopeful plans about his life, how he would make a career for himself and care for his parents.

When Alexander Blaney approached the staggering figure by the pond he stopped in the shadows. He saw that it was a drunken man and he heard the voices off by the trees and saw a blue panel truck parked between the drunken man on the grass and the others. He knew it was the group of policemen again and he debated about whether to try to help the drunken one or to mind his own business. For all he knew the drunken policeman might be the one called Roscoe who raged about fags and might kneedrop him, whatever that meant.

Then Sam Niles, who did not see Alexander Blaney, managed to get to his feet and swayed toward the subdued choir practice. But he made it only as far as the panel truck where he found the doors open and saw a pair of feet and a body on the floor.

"That you, Harold?" mumbled Sam as he leaned into the foul and shadowy truck and tugged on the sleeve of the snoring figure.

"That you, Dean?" asked Sam Niles who crawled into the truck and collapsed on the floor next to Spencer Van Moot.

"That you, Padre?" he asked, and tried to help the sleeping figure up to the bench in the truck but got dizzy and sat down on the opposite bench. Then Sam Niles became nauseated and violently light-headed and he had to lie down on the bench while the earth spun madly. Within seconds he was dozing.

Alexander Blaney watched all this and saw that the policeman was safely inside the blue truck and he sat down on the grass closer to the choir practice than he had every been before and listened to the voices which were not loud and funny tonight. But quiet and bitter.

Then Alexander backed into the shadow of the trees when he saw a uniformed policeman and another man walking toward the truck.

"Hey, look at this, Padre," Roscoe Rules said when he got to the back of the wagon.

"Sam!" said Father Willie.

"Spencer's got another drunk for company. Fuckin scrote, probably been smoking pot and passed out. Just like that dopehead friend of his, Baxter Slate."

"Baxter's dead," Father Willie reminded, thinking Roscoe didn't look sober enough to drive.

"I liked him as much as the next guy," Roscoe said. "I just didn't like his pervert ways."

"What'll we do about Sam?"

"Take him with Spencer, I guess," said Roscoe.

"So somebody's gonna have to drive two cars to the station."

"Let's get it over with before we have the whole fucking bunch back here," Roscoe Rules said, pushing Spencer's feet inside and slamming the door to the wagon.

After the wagon was closed Roscoe urinated on the grass and Alexander Blaney heard him laughing as he rejoined the dying choir practice.

Then when they were out of sight Alexander Blaney heard a muffled scream from inside the wagon.

It was less the clanging wagon door and the snapping of the lock than it was the feel of the body on the floor beside him, but Sam Niles' eyes popped open. It was black. There was no light. He didn't know where he was. For a brief instant he didn't know *who* he was. Then he felt the body. He leaped to his feet in the darkness and slammed his head against the metal roof. He screamed and turned to his right, smashing his glasses on the wall of the wagon. He clawed at those unyielding walls.

He walked on the body and his alcohol weakened legs slipped and his ankle turned and he fell on the body. He screamed again.

"Harold! Harold!" Sam screamed. And he smelled fish sauce and garlic and pressed his face to the slimy wall and awaited the molten horror from the flame thrower.

Then he wept and screamed, "Harold! Harold!" But instead of saying, "Now now now. Hush now, I'm with you. You're not alone," the body said nothing. Because it was dead. It was Baxter Slate!

While Roscoe was laughingly reporting to Spermwhale Whalen that he found Sam Niles asleep in the wagon, Sam Niles was pleading, "Baxter! Baxter! Baxter!"

But the body beside him did not answer. Not in a human tongue. It only said, "Mmmmmmmmmm. Uuuuuuuuhh."

The top of Baxter's head was gone and crackled under Sam Niles shoes as he backed against the doors of the wagon, his head bent from the low roof, his face bleeding from the broken glasses. He screamed. He couldn't breathe. He was hyperventilating.

But the only one who could hear those dreadful cries was a boy named Alexander Blaney who summoned enough courage and came out of the shadows and hurried to the back of the truck to open the doors for the screaming policeman.

Back at the blankets Harold Bloomguard said, "You what!"

"We left him in the back of the wagon," said Roscoe.

"Did you close the door?"

"Yeah, why?"

"Sam doesn't like to be closed in. I better go have a look!"

But before he could get there Alexander Blaney was standing at the back door of the wagon trying to get the rusty bolt slid to the right as Sam Niles was hiding his bloody face in his hands, screaming like a woman, trying hopelessly to escape the body that was Baxter Slate. And the Moaning Man. Trying to breathe.

Then Sam reached for the M-14 which wasn't there. He instinctively went for his waistband for his off-duty Smith and Wesson .38 caliber two-inch revolver which *was* there. The thundering explosions commenced just as the right door flew open. The first two fireballs missed Alexander Blaney by a foot.

The third splattered into his throat, throwing out a pocket of blood. The fourth and fifth would have hit him except that he dropped and lay on the grass grabbing his throat, gasping for the oxygen that was always there for Sam. Spencer Van Moot scrambled through the door, covering his ears and screaming louder than Sam Niles.

Then Sam found himself being pulled from the wagon by Harold Bloomguard who sat him on the ground holding him in his arms. Roscoe Rules stood over the convulsive body of Alexander Blaney saying, "It's a park fairy! He shot a park fairy!"

Then Roscoe was on his ass so fast it didn't even surprise him anymore. Spermwhale Whalen, who had hurled him aside, was on the ground reaching inside Alexander Blaney's mouth, pulling the swallowed tongue free.

Then Spermwhale was sitting on the grass holding the boy like a baby, blowing his hot lusty lion's breath into the lad's mouth, pausing every so often to hammer on the thin chest and say, "Come on, boy! Come on, son! Breathe!"

Alexander Blaney had given up very easily. When death offered, the lonely boy accepted, and his life leaked away. Still Spermwhale stubbornly tried to force his brawny vigorous life into Alexander. Most of it bellowed into the chest of the boy, some foamed out the hole in his throat.

It was a full five minutes before Spermwhale Whalen looked up, his face and arms and hands smeared with blood, his balding head wet and shining, his white eyes glimmering in the moonlight. Had that indolent moon appeared when Sam Niles was clawing at the blackness, it might have shined in the window of the truck and reassured the drunk and panic stricken choirboy, bringing him to his senses.

As Spermwhale got to his feet, leaving the sprawling body, several choirboys started walking in circles babbling incoherently. A dozen plans were made while Spermwhale Whalen wiped the blood of Alexander Blaney, shining black in the moonlight, from his own face and hands.

But finally it was a strange and stern and determined Harold Bloomguard standing next to Sam Niles whose face was bleeding and lowered. Sam shivered and smoked silently and was content to let others think and do for him.

"I'm taking Sam to Wilshire dicks," Harold said evenly. "I'm telling them that we bought some booze and were on our way to my pad to have a few drinks when we decided to stop in the park and have a beer. While we were here we both got a little drunk. Sam dropped his gun. When he picked it up he fell on his face and broke his glasses."

"I'll sweep the broken glass outta the truck!" Roscoe jabbered frantically, "in case they . . ."

"Shut up!" Spermwhale said. "Go on, Harold."

"That's it. He fell and must've pulled the trigger and this boy was walking by and . . . that's it."

"That fucking gun was fired five times!" Calvin Potts said.

"I'm replacing four of the rounds," Harold said. "It's a dirty gun. It's been fired several times between cleaning."

"I dunno, Harold," Spencer said.

"The rest of you can go home," Harold said. "Only Sam and I are involved. Sam's career is finished. And I'm not staying on the job without him so I've got nothing to lose anyway."

"I don't know, Harold," Father Willie said. "Maybe we should . . ."

"No sense anybody else riding this beef," Harold said stubbornly. "Spermwhale, you've got *almost* twenty years to protect. It's too late for you to be involved in something like this."

Spermwhale Whalen sighed and the others waited for him. He walked over to Sam Niles and put his hand on Sam's shoulder without looking at him. He patted Sam's shoulder and walked wearily to his blanket to gather up his belongings. Choir practice was over.

Within ten minutes Roscoe was pushing the blue truck for all it was worth down Venice Boulevard.

Within fifteen minutes hasty plans were made after several violent arguments as to whether they should lie, but finally Harold Bloomguard replaced four of the empty shells in Sam's gun with four live rounds.

Within thirty minutes Sam Niles and Harold Bloomguard were sitting in the detective bureau at Wilshire Station and a homicide team was on the way, as was Captain Drobeck, as was a team of officers from Internal Affairs Division.

Since the killing was officer-involved, the homicide team that showed up at Wilshire Station that night were strangers.

There was an old one with bifocals who was even more near-sighted than Sam Niles. There was a young one with a hair style longer than was permitted at Wilshire Station.

Harold Bloomguard had swabbed most of the blood from around the eyes of Sam Niles before they were separated. When the detectives entered the interrogation room Sam's right eye was puffy and cut at the corner. He squinted myopically at the detectives until they sat down in front of him.

"Lost your glasses, huh, Sam?" the older detective asked.

"Yes."

"Wanna talk about it now? Tell us how it happened."

"Yes. We went to the park just like Harold said. We drank some b-b-b-b-beer. W-w-w-we . . ."

"Wanna smoke, Sam?"

"Th-th-th-thank you," Sam Niles said, accepting the cigarette from the detective.

"Internal Affairs will be here real soon," the younger detective said. "Let's get the story now before you have to tell the headhunters."

"Sure," said Sam Niles, looking blankly at both detectives. "W-w-w-well, I d-d-d-dropped my gun and p-p-p-p . . ."

"You picked it up?"

"Sure," Sam nodded, looking from one face to the other.

He sat perfectly still, did not sweat, did not tremble, looked normal, except more earnest than laconic. It was only the stutter which was different.

"Did the gun go off, Sam?" the younger detective asked impatiently as the older detective sat back and studied the choirboy.

"Y-y-y-y . . ."

"All right, that's enough for the moment," the older detective said.

As the two detectives started out the door Sam Niles made his last statement on the subject of the shooting at MacArthur Park. He said, "The h-h-h-head was all shot off. The b-b-b-blood was everywhere!"

"Whose?" the young detective asked as they turned in the doorway.

"Th-th-th-the Moaning Man!" cried Sam Niles. "He said, 'Mmmmmmmmmm. Uuuuuuuuuuh.'"

"Who?" the younger detective asked.

"Baxter! He said, 'Mmmmmmmmmm. Uuuuuuuuhhhhhh! I couldn't touch him! He was too . . . revolting! How could I take his hand? How *could* I?"

"Who?" the younger detective asked.

"Baxter Slate!" Sam Niles sobbed.

"Holy mother," said the younger detective.

"Okay, Sam," the older detective said. "You just relax and finish your smoke. We're gonna let you go to bed soon."

The older detective came out of the interrogation room and walked straight to Sergeant Nick Yanov and said, "I want a radio car to take this boy to the Hospital Detail for immediate commitment to the psycho ward at General Hospital."

"But the headhunters're on the way," said Nick Yanov.

"It's *my* case and I'll take the responsibility," the old detective answered. "This boy isn't fit to be interrogated by *anyone*, especially not the headhunters."

"They won't be able to get to him in the hospital," Nick Yanov said with a grim smile. "They're not gonna like it."

"Too goddamn bad," the old detective said, making a decision which would cost him a suspension and ten days' pay.

By the time the black and white arrived at Unit Three, Psychiatric Admitting, Sam Niles was described by a young intern as catatonic.

15

Dr. Emil Moody

"Niles and Bloomguard!" said Lieutenant Elliott "Hardass" Grimsley, formerly of Wilshire nightwatch, now of Internal Affairs Division, when he was telephoned at home that morning by his investigators who could not break Harold Bloomguard's spurious story. Nor could they gain admission to General Hospital Psychiatric Ward to talk to Sam Niles, who by now could not even have told them his name.

"I remember them," Lieutenant Grimsley said. "Troublemakers. Friends of that slob, Spermwhale Whalen. Listen, I heard rumors they used to go to choir practice with several other officers from the nightwatch. MacArthur Park? Maybe that's where they go. Get to Whalen's house. Roust the fat pig outta bed and bring him down to IAD. Let's sweat him."

At 9:00 A.M. the two headhunters sat with Spermwhale Whalen in an interrogation room on the fifth floor of the police building. They looked at his bristling red jowls and huge stomach and fierce little eyes filled with contempt and rebellion.

"You don't expect us to believe that you know *nothing* about this shooting?" the unsmiling investigator said. "We have reliable information that you were there."

Spermwhale Whalen looked at both young plainclothes sergeants and said, "You know so much, what're you fuckin with me for?"

"Listen, Whalen." The other plainclothes sergeant leaned over the table. "We found empty booze bottles not far from the body. You boys didn't clean up everything well enough. And we found tire tracks and casts've been made. One of you had a car parked there."

"I told you I went home after work last night. I don't know what this's all about and I resent the shit outta you two bringin me here."

The investigator who played bad guy stood up disgustedly and stormed out of the door so his partner could play good guy which of course Spermwhale wasn't buying.

"He say anything?" asked Lieutenant Grimsley who was waiting in the corridor outside with Commander Hector Moss and Deputy Chief Adrian Lynch who had spent the night in a motel with his passionate secretary, Theda Gunther, and predictably had his toupee twisted.

"Whalen's a good actor, Lieutenant," the investigator said. "Unless it's the truth. Maybe Bloomguard isn't lying. He's sticking to the original story right down the line."

"Bullshit!" Lieutenant Grimsley interrupted. "I know Bloomguard's lying. Those beer cans and bottles . . ."

"We can't prove they put them there," the investigator said.

"How about that bra you found?" Lieutenant Grimsley asked.

"Looked like it'd been there several days. Covered with leaves and debris."

"What size was it?"

"Enormous. Forty-four, D cup."

"Any station groupies with tits that big?" pondered Lieutenant Grimsley, unconsciously glancing at the amorous deputy chief.

"What're you looking at me for, Lieutenant?"

"Oh. Sorry, sir," Hardass Grimsley blanched.

"Why don't you have a try at him, Lieutenant?" asked Commander Moss, and Lieutenant Grimsley smiled nervously as he visualized a scene with Spermwhale Whalen telling about the black woman from Philadelphia he had caught

Grimsley going down on when he was the Wilshire watch commander.

"I don't like to interfere with my men's investigations," Lieutenant Grimsley said, hoping that Spermwhale Whalen wouldn't see him and wink and muss up his hair.

"Well I took the liberty of going through his personnel package in your office, Lieutenant," Chief Lynch said. "Do you mind if I have a try?"

"Not at all, sir," Lieutenant Grimsley said, enormously relieved. "After all, you're an old IAD man."

And it was true that Chief Lynch was an old IAD man, it being pretty much agreed upon that Internal Affairs Division experience was the best springboard for promotion. Headhunters made rank consistently better than other investigators, the regular detective bureau being a dead end for the ambitious.

His three years as a headhunter were the most pleasurable in Chief Lynch's entire career. He understood certain things about policemen. He knew the polygraph worked extremely well on them because of their job-induced guilt feelings, whereas it was almost useless on guiltless sociopathic criminals. Also he knew that all men fear something and he guessed what a fifty-two year old patrol cop like Spermwhale Whalen probably feared most.

Five minutes later Deputy Chief Lynch was sitting across from Spermwhale, drinking coffee, offering Spermwhale none. Chief Lynch was smiling. "I'm not going to waste time on you, Whalen."

"That's good, Chief, because I got nothin to say and I don't know what this is all about."

"You're a goddamn liar!" Chief Lynch suddenly said and Spermwhale's little eyes narrowed. The furry eyebrows dipped dangerously and the Z-shaped scar showed very white through the eyebrow and across his red nose. Chief Lynch, despite himself, glanced anxiously toward the door and wished he'd have let one of the investigators sit with him here in the stark room, with the table and wooden chairs and tape machine hissing.

"I'm not going to try to fool an old veteran like you,

Whalen," Chief Lynch said, continuing more amiably. "Of course we're going to tape your statement. I'm not going to try to fool you about anything."

"That's good," said Spermwhale, "because I got nothin . . ."

"Quite a record you have," Chief Lynch interrupted. "You have quite a history of being insubordinate. I see why you've remained in uniform patrol for twenty years."

"I *like* uniform patrol," Spermwhale said, sitting motionless, his big hands on his knees, wishing for a cup of coffee, his mouth dry as ashes.

"Did I say twenty years? Well not quite. You only have nineteen and a half years, don't you? Less some bad time you have to make up. My, my, you were so close to that twenty year pension. Now you'll get nothing."

"Listen, Chief . . ."

"*You* listen, Whalen," Chief Lynch snapped. "You listen good. Maybe Niles wasted that fruit practicing a quick draw. Or shooting at beer bottles. I don't know how he did it and I don't really care. But I'm going to get the truth from every man who was there. You can cooperate or I'll push for at least involuntary manslaughter against Niles and I guarantee you'll find your ass on trial as an accessory after the fact. Ever hear of the crime of harboring and concealing after a felony's been committed?"

"Listen, Chief . . ."

"*You* listen, Whalen," said Chief Lynch, warming up, leaning across the table, his breath smelling lemony from Theda Gunther's douche powder. "You're fifty-two years old. Fifty-two. Think of that. Look at you. You're a crude, fat, aging man. You going to go out and get a job? Doing what? Flying airplanes? No chance. You aren't going to be able to get a job cleaning out shithouses after you're *fired* from the police department. How're you going to live? I'll bet after you serve your six months in *jail*, and after your whole career's down the drain, without a *dime* of pension money, that you end up on skidrow with the other bums. I'll bet you're begging for nickels or selling your blood for a few bucks. Know some of the other things the old winos do to make a few bucks, Whalen? Want me to tell you? Think it could never happen to you?"

And then Chief Lynch tried the inquisitor's device of lie and half lie to get truth and half truth. "We found a very interesting fingerprint on a bourbon bottle there in the park. You have five minutes to make up your mind. I'm walking out this door right now. You either give us the full story on this killing or you're on your way to a trial board and criminal prosecution. Then it'll be too late to make a deal. Nineteen and a half years, huh? You almost made the pension, baby."

Spermwhale Whalen found himself staring at a vacant chair. He didn't move for three minutes. He had never felt more alone. He listened to the muffled voices outside. He listened to his heart and to the hissing tape machine. Sweat studded his upper lip. He heard it patting to the floor. Then the bravest and strongest choirboy, the veteran of three wars, the only Los Angeles policeman to fly combat missions while an active member of the department, the winner of a Silver Star, six Air Medals and two Purple Hearts, who feared no man, nor even death from any hand but his own, the bravest and strongest and *oldest* choirboy, found that he feared life. The horrifying life described by Chief Lynch. He feared it dreadfully. He felt the fear sweep over him. His throat constricted and his scalp tingled from fear. The tape recorder was unbearable. Hissing. His big red hand almost slipped off the doorknob when he rushed to open the door. He stepped tentatively into the hallway where five men waited.

Deputy Chief Lynch looked into Spermwhale's little eyes. Chief Lynch smoothed his toupee, his own scraggly hair curling behind his ears. He stepped back into the room smiling confidently. Spermwhale held the door for him.

By 11:00 A.M. that day eight choirboys were separately sitting in various offices on the fifth floor of Parker Center. By 4:00 P.M. that day Sergeant Nick Yanov, who by now knew the story from Captain Drobeck, who had gotten it from Commander Moss, was on the phone calling Lieutenant Rudy Ortiz who often defended accused officers at department trial boards.

Nick Yanov was raging into the telephone, hurting the ears of the defender. "The stupid goddamn idiots cooked up a story and stuck to it except Whalen who informed on himself and the others!"

"Christ!" Lieutenant Ortiz said. "All they had the others for was maybe cue-bow for getting drunk in the park. They just should've called the dicks and told the whole story at the scene. Niles was the only one in *serious* trouble, except for the dummy who was in uniform."

"I know. I know. The idiots!" said Nick Yanov. "Now they've got them *all* for withholding evidence and lying to the investigators and insubordination."

"They can fire their young asses behind this caper," Lieutenant Ortiz said. "They could even prosecute them in criminal court."

"I know. Can't you help them?" Nick Yanov pleaded.

By 5:00 P.M., Deputy Chief Lynch was on the phone, chatting good naturedly with Assistant Chief Buster Llewellyn.

"Right, Buster, I wish we could fire them too. And throw them in the slammer. But that would attract attention. As it is we've got it under control."

"Thank God the victim was just some fag. Imagine if it'd been someone decent," said Assistant Chief Buster Llewellyn, sipping on his coffee, wondering for the hundredth time about the mysterious stain on his hand tooled blotter.

"Nobody decent would be in MacArthur Park at that time of night. Nobody *except* fruits. And this group of policemen."

"Talk to the victim's mother, Adrian?"

"Personally," smiled Chief Lynch. "She took it pretty hard. But you know, I think his old man was actually kind of relieved."

"Better off," Chief Llewellyn nodded. "Woulda got his throat cut in some fruit hustle sooner or later anyway. If he didn't die of syphilis."

"So we came out all right. Mr. and Mrs. Blaney know there were some policemen in the park and that one of them dropped his gun and it went off and that the perpetrator went nuts after the accident and is now in the squirrel tank getting his head shocked. The newspapers know basically the same information except I had to level with them that the officers had a beer or two. And that nine were involved and that there was some withholding of all the facts at first but that it was an accident pure and simple."

"Thank God that officer went crazy afterward."

"Well actually he went nuts before, Buster. When they locked him in the wagon."

"No one know about that?"

"Not necessary to tell all the details. Doesn't change the facts. We've got it effectively stonewalled."

"Blast it, Adrian, don't use that word!"

"Sorry, Buster."

"What're we going to give them?"

"The maximum, short of firing, which we can't very well do if we don't want too many rumors about choir practice to come out. Of course I'd be happy if we could scare all of them into voluntarily resigning under the threat of criminal prosecution."

"Think they will?"

"Maybe. One of them already has: Bloomguard. Of course, Niles is really batty they tell me and if he doesn't come around that's two down right away. Not to mention that Officer Slate who killed himself the other night. He was one of the gang, I'm told. But he had the good grace to blow his brains out before this shooting in the park."

"It's these young policemen we're getting these days," said Assistant Chief Llewellyn. "No morality in the country anymore. The young policemen reflect it. Imagine them trying to withhold the facts and cover up something like that!"

"Yes, sir, it's pathetic. Honesty is a rare commodity nowadays."

"Well you did a fine job, Adrian. You should be commended. There was hardly a mention in the papers and nothing on television."

"Thank you, Buster," said Deputy Chief Lynch, hoping this would be only the start of his praise and recognition for the coverup.

Dr. Emil Moody, the police department psychologist, was sick and tired of being nothing but a marriage counselor. And he was sick and tired of writing his monthly column in the police magazine. He rarely had the opportunity to examine psychotic officers like Sam Niles. The department and the city got great public relations mileage from the infrequent knifing, slugging and shooting of policemen but hated to admit that something as unglamorous and *expensive* as mental illness should be added to heart disease, tuberculosis, hernia and whiplash, the more common job-induced police cripplers.

Lacking the information for a psychological workup, he did a brief profile on the MacArthur Park choirboys for his own education. He found that unlike policemen from other generations these were not of the working class and not of foreign born parents. Bloomguard, Slate, Pratt, Potts, Wright, Tanaguchi and Van Moot had solid middle class upbringing. Whalen and Rules were of working class families and only one, Sam Niles, had a childhood history of poverty and parental neglect.

Only three were married: Van Moot, Wright and Rules. Three had been divorced: Potts, Whalen, and Niles, Whalen having been thrice divorced, Van Moot divorced and remarried.

Van Moot was a veteran of the Korean War. Niles, Bloomguard, Rules and Potts were Vietnam vets. Tanaguchi had seen service but not combat. Slate, Wright and Pratt had not been in the military. Whalen had, incredibly enough, seen combat in World War II, Korea and even in Vietnam on weekend flights from March Air Force Base.

Nine had college training and most were still making efforts to obtain a degree. Three had bachelor's degrees: Bloomguard in business administration, Niles in political science, Slate in classical literature. Most were pursuing degrees in police science or prelaw. Whalen had never gone to college.

With the exception of fifty-two year old Herbert Whalen and forty year old Spencer Van Moot, they were all young men in their twenties, all apparently in good physical health.

In short the brief profile proved exactly nothing. Dr. Moody wrote it, read it and threw it in the wastebasket. He had hoped to promote a thesis that policemen are entitled to effective preventive medicine for job-induced mental illness.

He wanted very much to contact Officer Niles' best friend, Officer Bloomguard, who had resigned on the morning of the shooting. He wanted to consult with psychiatrists at General Hospital where Niles was committed. He wanted most to visit Niles himself. He suspected there was more to the incident than the administration knew. He suspected that the suicide of Officer Baxter Slate contributed to the deadly episode in the park.

But Dr. Moody went back to his innocuous writing of an innocuous column for the innocuous police magazine. The police department liked people who could get along. He had a nice steady job and wanted to keep it.

Just as Chief Lynch thought everything was going to work out smoothly Spencer Van Moot got stubborn. Since he was unconscious during the shooting he didn't think he deserved a six month suspension. He pleaded not guilty at his trial board. Father Willie Wright, hearing Spencer plead not guilty and thinking what six months loss of pay would do to him did the same thing.

Some said theirs were the quickest trial boards anyone ever had for a firing offense. The witnesses were heard in two hours. Spermwhale Whalen was the chief witness for the department advocate. He was gray and trembling when he testified against his fellow choirboys. He had lost twenty pounds since the shooting. His fat had lost its ferocious tone. He looked soft. And old.

Theoretically the trial boards are unbiased hearings before superior officers of the rank of captain or higher. But like any hierarchy, particularly a hierarchy of quasi-military persuasion, the captains knew exactly the wishes of Assistant Chief Buster Llewellyn who answered only to the big chief and to God. And they also knew the wishes of Deputy Chief Adrian Lynch who answered only to Assistant Chief Llewellyn and to Theda Gunther, who was so impressed and thrilled with Chief Lynch's masterful subjugation of Spermwhale Whalen and the subsequent uncovery of the disgusting orgy that she banged him in his office one afternoon, putting a stain on *his* blotter and tearing his toupee to shreds. His hair piece looked motheaten. It lay on his head like a dead squirrel. When it was time to go home to his wife he had to leave the police building in a golf cap.

Spencer was found guilty of insubordination, lying to investigators and withholding evidence. His defender, Lieutenant

Rudy Ortiz, pleaded for leniency. Sergeant Nick Yanov testified to Spencer's good character and work performance. But there were examples to be made. The custom of choir practice was to be discouraged. He was fired in record time. Sixteen years went up in smoke.

Lieutenant Rudy Ortiz angrily accused the trial board, Internal Affairs Division and the department brass of being ruthless and cavalier. He admitted that for some time he had been in favor of civilian review boards. Not to protect citizens from overzealous street cops since there were legal remedies for that. But to protect street cops from overzealous disciplinarians within the ranks. He denounced forced polygraphs and their admission as evidence, the acceptance of hearsay, investigator's opinion as to truth and lie, the arbitrary searches of person and locker, private cars and officers' homes under threat of insubordination, a firing offense.

Lieutenant Rudy Ortiz finally had his say about internal investigations and the constitutional rights of policemen all right. And so did Assistant Chief Adrian Lynch. He said privately that the only way that dumpy little greaseball Ortiz would ever make captain was by joining the Mexican Army.

Father Willie Wright's trial board was even quicker. Unlike Spencer, who went out shakily but defiant, Father Willie openly wept at the penalty.

When Spencer and Father Willie were fired the other choirboys stopped complaining. They all freely admitted their guilt at their own trial boards. They gladly accepted the six months' suspension. Spermwhale Whalen was given only a thirty day suspension as a reward for helping Internal Affairs crack the case by informing on all of them.

Sam Niles was still hospitalized and was quietly released by the police department. Since he had less than five years' service, the city did not have to pay him a pension for the incapacitating illness which the city said did not happen as a result of police service. Sam Niles was confined for a time at the Veterans Hospital and was later transferred to Camarillo State Hospital.

Harold Bloomguard was asked to stop visiting him because his visits seemed to upset the patient.

Epilogue

It was somehow eerie to be standing there in MacArthur Park on a cold and damp and shadowy winter night in February. Sergeant Nick Yanov was looking at a place he had never cared to visit, satisfying the curiosity of his new boss, Lieutenant Willard Woodcock, a recently promoted thirty-one year old whiz kid who they said was going places in the department. They said he had lots of top spin.

"So this is where it happened?" Lieutenant Woodcock observed, his brand new hat with the gold lieutenant's badge a bit too large. It slid down to his ears over the fresh haircut.

"Yes, right here from what they tell me," Sergeant Nick Yanov said, his hands in the pockets of his blue jacket, a cigarette dangling from his lips, white against his glowering jaw. Since he had only shaved once today his lower jaws were dark and fierce.

"Been about six months now, hasn't it?"

"Just about."

"They'll be back to work very soon then. I think we should make plans."

"Plans."

"We can't let them bunch up again."

"Aren't many in the bunch anymore," Nick Yanov said,

pushing his hands deeper into the pockets and pulling up the collar of the old wool jacket with the frayed sergeant's chevrons ripping from one sleeve.

"There're enough to cause trouble."

"Slate's dead. Niles is mutilating himself from time to time in the state hospital. Bloomguard resigned . . ."

"Where's the big one now? The one who became a witness for the department?"

"Whalen, he's retired. Took his pension last month. I hear they're sending his checks to some remote little town in Utah. Wright's fired. Van Moot's fired. That only leaves four, Lieutenant: Rules, Dean Pratt, Tanaguchi and Potts. After six months without pay I'll just bet they're pretty well pacified."

"I still think it was a bad idea to leave them in Wilshire Division. They should've been scattered to hell and gone after their six months' suspension."

"But this way the department can show that discipline works on troublemakers. They'll be tame ex-troublemakers, isn't that it."

"Yes, I suppose that's the theory," said Lieutenant Woodcock.

"Except that they *weren't* troublemakers."

"What do you mean by that?" the lieutenant said, trying to examine the face of the sergeant who had his cigarette half smoked, not touching it with his hands.

Nick Yanov stared at the sleeping ducks in the peaceful pond and said, "They were just policemen. Rather ordinary young guys, I thought. Maybe a little lonelier than some. Maybe they banded together when they were especially lonely. Or scared."

"Ordinary! How can you say that, Yanov? I've heard they were animals. They brought sluts here for orgies. One of them was possibly a pillhead and a pervert. The one that killed himself. What was his name?"

"Baxter Slate. I liked him."

"Christ, Yanov, there's a lesson to be learned here for policemen everywhere!"

"What lesson have *you* learned, Lieutenant."

Lieutenant Woodcock glared at the big chested sergeant who never took his eyes off the shimmering water. The lieutenant made a mental note to keep tabs on this field sergeant and mention the incident to Captain Drobeck and perhaps cancel the special day off which Nick Yanov had requested. Finally the lieutenant said, "Suicidal degenerates. Drunken killers. Whore-mongers. Probably dopeheads. Sergeant, these guys would try to seduce an eighty year old nun. Or break her arm."

"Maybe," Nick Yanov said, blowing a cloud of smoke through his nose, the cigarette glowing in the darkness. "But they wouldn't steal her purse."

"Is that the test of a policeman, Yanov? Is that all there is to making a good policeman?"

"I don't know, Lieutenant. I truly don't know what makes a good policeman. Or a good anything."

"Let's go back to the station," said the disgusted watch commander. "It's cold out here."

But for a moment Sergeant Nick Yanov stood there alone on the wet grass, his weight pressing footprints in the black spongy earth. The grass smelled washed and fresh and the rows of trees crouched like huge quail. The duck pond was silver and black sapphire. The treetops shivered and rustled in the cold wind and loosened the white blossoms of a flowering pear.

Nick Yanov looked up at the brooding darkness, at the tarnished misty moon. There were no stars. Not even the great star could pierce that black sky. Nick Yanov stood where they had put their blankets down, close enough to the water to pretend they were with nature, here in the bowels of the violent city. He felt some light mocking rain, yet longed to stay in the solitude, while dead leaves scraped at his feet like perishing brown parchment.

Then he flipped the cigarette into the pond and heard the hiss and watched it float. He was immediately sorry he did it. Yet there was other debris on the still water and in the bushes if one used the moonlight to look closely.

He didn't want to look closely. He preferred to think it was lovely and clean and pastoral here by the silent lagoon and the slumbering ducks in the icy water. Where the choirboys frolicked in the duck shit.